A Fate Found In Clues

Kelli Cooke

First Edition March 2026

Copy Edit: Sarah Taig

Proof Edit: Cassandra Moll

Cover Design: Sam Palencia (Ink & Laurel)

www.kellicooke.com

Author's Note

Dear Reader,

Can you believe we are on my third—actually, fourth if we count the one I co-wrote—book? Yeah, me neither! The funny thing about writing books is that as much as I plan, strategize, and attempt to predict (not very well, might I add) what the future will bring, being an author is unpredictable.

With *Coincidentally Kismet*, we saw ex-lovers become friends who went on a heart-wrenching, nineties romcom adventure to find love. And in *A Heart On A Sleeve* (the first in the Mage Hollow Magic series) we witnessed Olive learn to love herself again while falling for the guy that decorated her porch with all the pumpkins. Both books were wrought with emotion—featuring FMCs that faced self-confidence issues and challenging relationships with their mothers.

This is where you start asking questions: "And? Why are you telling me this, Kelli?"

Answer: Because this book is different. A Fate Found In Clues was hands down the hardest book I've ever written, and that's for one reason only—it's *low drama*. Think beach reads, margaritas, or a night under the stars with nowhere to be. While I pride myself on reflecting 'real' love in each of my stories... sometimes it really is simple. Sometimes our main characters don't have to struggle with communication or childhood trauma—sometimes they can just fall in love.

Question: "Why was it so hard if you had an obvious goal in mind?"

Answer: I don't know! Maybe I'm a masochist who likes the pain of self-exploration. Or maybe I asked myself a million times if it could really just be that simple. The bottom line is... this book is fluff. It's meant to be easy, light, and laugh-out-loud funny to the point that tears run down your face and you maybe even pee a little. It's meant to warm your heart, make you believe in the power of a good family, and ache for a fun summer adventure.

Max and Sadie made me work for every laugh, every moment that makes you smile, and every time you ask yourself if a love so perfect could exist (did you think I'd really let you get away without at least one existential crisis?). But I love them for it, and I hope you will too. Kick back, soak it in, and pay careful attention to the magic in this one... we're going on a spellbinding journey, babe. And you never know when something happening here might be important down the road.

As always, your mental health matters to me most. Below you'll find a list of potential triggers. If these could be difficult, please opt out.

- On Page Sexually Explicit Material

- Magic/ Witchcraft

- Hospitalization of the FMC (non-life threatening)

- Near-drowning of the FMC

Love Always,

KC

Note: This is book 2 in the Mage Hollow Magic series. It is an interconnected standalone, therefore it can be read on its own. However, reading A Heart On A Sleeve first could help with character recognition and some of the magical themes experienced in the book.

Dedication

To the Workaholics—

That email will still be waiting for you tomorrow, and that meeting could have been a Slack. Take your PTO and live a little, would ya!

Prologue

Beth

Mage Hollow, 1793

They say there's only one surefire way to hide your true identity—do it in plain sight.

"Watch it!" a man with a round belly and rosy cheeks bellows at me as I brush past him.

Nodding my apology as water sloshes over the bucket I'm carrying, I offer him a soft smile. It's been a long night, one of many in the endless stream that have poured in since we opened, since our sister went away.

A pang of guilt worms its way through me as I think of her, of what she did for me. The look on her face haunts me. Her gift and her sacrifice are weights that grow ever heavier on my shoulders. I remember it all as if it had happened yesterday.

"Papers, get your papers."

"Fresh fruits and vegetables . . ."

"Candy, try our new candy."

A woman with a grim expression and cheeks flushed from carrying a basket full of vegetables, stomps on my toes as she makes her way around me. Instead of yelping in pain like I want to, I grunt quietly and smile, tucking myself closer to Irina's side.

The market is bustling more than usual, every member of the town desperate to get a glimpse of the famous Mrs. Peabody. Every person, including me.

I'm curious about her story, about how she survived such a treacherous journey. Josephine wouldn't allow me to come alone. She insisted Irina escort me, as if that would quell my curiosity. Her job is to make sure we grab what we need and get home unscathed.

My sisters claim our quiet way of life is necessary, that we mustn't let anyone know what we are. They try their best to appease my need for something more. And while maybe that is safest, I long for the time when I didn't need to hide or be placated. The memories made when it was only us and magic.

"Excuse me. Are you in line?" a soft-spoken voice rings out.

To my left, I notice a handsome individual wearing a frock coat paired with trousers. There's a woman with beautiful blonde hair and cerulean eyes hanging on his arm, awaiting our answer.

"No, we don't see what all the fuss is about," Irina says. It's practiced, poised, exactly what she should say. But hypocritical at best, a bald-faced lie in reality.

Irina thinks I'm not onto her, that I haven't noticed her sneaking out, or the way couples somehow keep finding true love in unexpected places. She's as guilty as I am of wanting more, just better at hiding it.

"Can you tell me why she's here, more about her stor—"

"Move aside," the man commands.

Instead of answering my question, the couple does what people always do. They dismiss our existence, stepping around us with their noses in the air.

"Stop it, Beth. You're drawing attention by asking trivial questions." Irina grabs my arm, pulling me away from the crowd as the woman from before snickers at us.

"You stop it. You're the one who's lying about who you are."

Irina is matchmaking, forcing people together that likely wouldn't have found each other without her help into the kind of love she believes she missed out on. It's her entertainment, while the dismissal I was just dealt is my nightmare.

My sisters never listen. They care for me only because it's what's expected of them. And that couple isn't actually curious about how Mrs. Peabody survived, or what she learned from her ordeal. Fate and what the future holds are meaningless notions to them, with their predetermined and seemingly insignificant lives. The lives that will be lucky to last over thirty years.

We are not the same. They haven't seen what I've seen. They don't know what it was like when we first arrived here, and they can't imagine what it'll be like a hundred years from now. I shouldn't fault them, but I do anyway. The luxury they have in their contentment seizes hold of me, turning me green with envy. I don't have a choice. I have to know what's next because it's the only thing I have to hold on to. My future, my understanding of the world around me, and what my role is are the only things that ensure my survival.

"You're finding fault where there is none. You're going to be the one to seal our fate, to get us strung up on the cliff's edge like our family." *Irina stomps her foot as her face reddens in anger. She's not wrong to call back to our history. But the witch hunt in Salem has been over for a century... is it wrong to hope people have moved on?*

"It's cruel—the way they treat us, the way they look beyond us as if we don't exist. I want more. No, I need more... I need to know my future isn't simply more of this." I swing my arms out wide, symbolizing the vast nothingness that has become our existence.

"*Hey, I know you. What have you done to my daughter?*" *A brutish man yells from behind me, charging toward my sister.*

Irina's eyes widen, but in the blink of an eye she grasps my hand and sweeps me into the air with her. Guilt is etched on her features.

"*Stop! Put her down, witch!*" *The man yells at her as we rise higher. My heart races wildly, and my limbs flail with the lack of stability. It's been a long time since I've practiced magic—and doing it in public is forbidden. We soar through the air, descending only once we've cleared the trees.*

"*I know what you need, Bethy.*" *My sister pulls me close once our feet are settled on the ground. She's jubilant, high on adrenaline, like we didn't almost just get caught.*

I hesitate. This is the exact thing Josephine was afraid of—the one thing we promised we'd never do after escaping in the middle of the night.

Exposure equals certain death.

"*Take this, Bethy.*" *She shoves a series of parchment papers into my hand. They're scribbled with words and empty boxes.* "*Find your fate, sister.*"

Irina steps away, releasing me as she heads deeper into the trees.

"*Wait! What is this?*"

"*Everything you've been seeking—trust me.*"

"*Why are you leaving? When will I see you again?*" *Tears trace paths down my cheeks. I was so angry with her, but now that she's walking away, I'm gutted.*

"*You know I must go now... your future depends on it. I'll return when it's safe... when there's no soul left to bear witness.*" *A single tear and a halfhearted smile appear on her face, and then she's gone.*

"*I see that look. She's fine, Beth. This is what you were meant to do... it's what you wanted. Don't waste the effort she went to,*" *Jo grits out between clenched teeth.* "*Take this ale to the table over there and smile.*"

I set down the bucket, exchanging it for the metal pitcher my sister placed on the bar top. While I know the puzzle Irina gave me six moons ago led me here, I can't help feeling that Jo holds resentment in her heart, and why wouldn't she? *My* fate was found in clues, but it came at a cost—Irina.

I carry that guilt, the knowledge that while Jo and I get to hide in plain sight, our sister is forced to live in the shadows. Sometimes the grief feels like walking carefully across coals, never knowing which step will bring a mild tinge and which will feel like a thousand hornet stings that ache so deep you can feel them in your soul.

Approaching the table, the group of gentlemen continue in their deep conversation. "More ale?" I ask, awaiting any form of response.

One of them raises his cup, and I carefully top it off. Another follows suit, and so on it goes, a never-ending cycle.

This is what I wanted—to live amongst the locals, to see them, to know them, to be them. I hope one day it pays off, that one day I'm able to help someone else play my sister's game.

One

Sadie

Unexpected Gifts

There's a defining moment in every person's life, one where the path you thought you had charted out changes in an instant. And with that change, you either learn to adapt, or you get swallowed whole by life itself. For me, Sadie Marie Wells, that moment started three days ago when my boss witnessed me having a full-blown panic attack brought on by none other than my own delusions of grandeur. It was in that moment, with clammy hands, sweat-soaked hair, and rapid yet shockingly hard-to-come-by breaths, that he looked me dead in the eyes—with pity on his face—and told me to leave.

"Sadie, I know this feels like the last thing on earth you want to do right now... but for both our sakes, you're taking a leave of absence."

Gravel crunches under my tires as I park between a row of arborvitae and a peeling white picket fence that's almost invisible with the bushes spilling over it. I squeeze my eyes shut and take three deep breaths.

It was like he thought the whole thing was so obvious—the workaholic hit a wall, and he was doing me a solid by forcing me out. Or maybe this was just the easiest way for him to avoid an HR shitstorm. He's the most beloved coach in the NHL, and it probably wouldn't look great to have his biggest charitable program run by a ball of stress on two legs that can't keep her shit together—even if I'm the one that keeps things interesting.

Squeals and laughter erupt from the direction of my mother's backyard, drifting in through my half-lowered window while silencing my reflection. My sister must be over.

I guess I can't wait here forever.

I push out of my car, heaving two overstuffed suitcases out of the trunk and dragging them with me to the sidewalk. Stopping, I take in the familiar sight of my hometown. It's been a while since I've visited. I'd almost forgotten how much I appreciate its whimsical nature. Limelight hydrangeas line the street, lavender sprouts cheerily from the bases of mailboxes, the scent of freshly cut grass wafts in the sticky breeze, and gardens spill over the edges of their cedar walls. It's picturesque, homey, welcoming to all—like Martha Stewart herself became a fairy godmother and bibidi bopped a splash of pastels onto the historically witchy town.

"Sadie? What are you doing here?"

My sister, Mallory, floats through the screen door and down the front steps of my mom's small, sage-green cottage. It looks exactly as I remember, just a little worse for wear. Years of snow-piled winters have finally taken their toll. The painted cedar siding has peeled, and the wooden porch has splinters in places.

"Surprise." I hold my arms out and force my lips into a smile so fake I'm sure she can see right through it. I'm happy to be home, but I wish it was under different circumstances.

In typical Mal fashion, she skips down the stone pathway and wraps her arms around me. I lean into her embrace and tamp down the urge to immediately spill everything that's happened over the past week. It's been too long since my family has come to visit me in the city, too long since we've had a wine night filled with gossip and what my mother likes to call, *twinkle moments*—her version of taking a metaphorical photo. I want to catch up before dumping bad news on them.

"Let's go. Mom's out back filling up the baby pool so the kids can splash around." She loops her arm through mine and uses her free hand to grab the handle on one of my suitcases. "Are you going to tell me why you're here?"

"It's compli—"

A loud buzzing sound blares in Mal's pocket, and she holds a hand up to me while thrusting it toward her ear. Instead of eavesdropping on what is probably her husband, Sebastian, calling to check in, I shuffle forward in silence and lean on my mother's picket fence. From this side of it, I can see the jumbo periwinkle blue hydrangeas bounding over it, and a hummingbird flitting around in search of nectar. The sweet floral scent tickles my nose, and I can't stop myself from leaning into the petals to inhale deeper. There's comfort in these flowers, memories of days spent cutting stems for Mom to display in the kitchen. Or the time we ran out and our neighbor Helen didn't appreciate that I snipped hers instead.

"Sorry, Bash just wanted to tell me he's going out on a call and not to wait for him to eat." Mal hip checks me before continuing, "I can tell by the look on your face that you don't want to answer my question. But you will... after the kids are in bed and you've had a few glasses of red."

I smile softly at my sister. She has it all: four rowdy kids, a husband she can't seem to keep her hands off of, and a dream job. I don't know how she always keeps it together, but I send a silent wish toward the sky that maybe one day I'll be able to juggle more than one ball at a time too.

Following Mal up the steps and into the house, the scent of warm honey and peaches wraps around me like a familiar hug. My sister rolls my bags into my old bedroom, not waiting for me to toe off my shoes.

"Aunt Sadie? Why are you here?" Lily, my eldest niece, skips into the entryway, nearly knocking me over. The eight-year-old never minces words, but I can't fault her for the question. She's got a toothy grin, missing a couple in the front, making her awkwardly adorable.

I lean down so that I'm at her height. "I just wanted to make sure your mom was being a good girl and not breaking any of Grannie's rules."

That makes her laugh and run right back the way she came, toward the backyard. Her voice rings out, not-so-faintly yelling to anyone that'll listen that I'm here. I finish slipping my shoes off, lay my purse that doubles as a laptop bag on the first chair I see, and follow my niece, wishing I had her ability to celebrate arbitrary moments like this one.

Walking the long hallway that serves as the center of our rectangle-shaped home, it's clear that not much has changed in the way of decor. Mom still has a collection of our childhood photos on the wall nearest the kitchen, except now there are photos of my nieces added in. The pine floors are scuffed in that comforting way that can only come with years of memories being beaten into them. And the screen door that leads to the fenced backyard is still propped with the same coffee-can lantern that Dee Dee, my mom, filled with cement after Mal got her second and third fingers smashed when we were kids.

Peeking my head out the door, my eyes immediately connect with Mom's. She's sitting in a wicker rocking chair, holding my youngest niece, Marigold.

"Sadie girl? What are you doing here?" She smiles her brightest smile at me, but there's a question set in her brows when she looks to her right, connecting eyes with our close family friend, Beth. She looks fantastic. I swear Beth hasn't aged beyond fifty in the entire time I've known her.

"That's three in a row. Can't a girl just come home to see her family?" I shrug, stepping out onto the porch and sliding into the loveseat beside her. There's a charcuterie board sitting on the glass-top table between us, and I help myself to a cracker with cream cheese and pepper jelly.

"A girl could, ye—"

"Aunt Adie, come dance me." Poppy, the three-year-old, tugs my hand, pulling me to follow her.

"Sorry, Mom. Looks like I'm needed elsewhere."

She shakes her head at me and then shoos me off with a wave of her hand as my sister chuckles from the edge of the screen door. It's nice that I can slip back into my family as if I never left. You'd think the kids would barely know me, or at the very least be tentative. But Mal made a point when I moved away to make sure we did a video chat every week, and despite my hectic schedule, it's the one thing I never allow myself to miss.

"I get a turn next, Pop. You can't hog her." Magnolia stomps her feet in the baby pool, splashing water over the edge.

"Hi Mags, how's the water?" I shift my attention to the five-year-old, who's ready to throw down her little sister for a moment of my time.

"*So* cold. Come try it." Her lips are almost as blue as the royal bathing suit she has on. Despite the warm summer temperatures, water from the hose in New England is never above a chilly sixty-five degrees. Letting the sun warm it isn't something my niece was willing to wait for, apparently, but kids are funny that way—never afraid to jump into fun headfirst.

I walk over, slipping one bare foot into the icy-water, while balancing on the other and holding Poppy's hand.

"You weren't kidding. That *is* cold. Why don't you get out and come sit on the hammock with us? I'll tell you a story while we wait for dinner." At that, she jumps out of the eight-inch pool, grabs a towel from her mom, and still beats me to the canvas that's stretched between two trees.

I settle in, pulling the two girls tight to my side before leaning back. "Okay, what kind of story would you like to hear?"

"A printhess stowy," Poppy exclaims.

"No, a story about a butterfly," Magnolia shouts.

"Hmm. How about a story about a butterfly that was actually a princess?"

"Yes!" they shout in unison.

"Once upon a time, a princess got summoned for a meeting with her boss..."

I slump into a cushioned patio chair, shifting to get comfortable before pulling my feet up underneath me. "I feel like I probably need to sleep for three days after that, and I *never* run out of energy."

My sister laughs at my statement, turning to grab two bottles of red from her husband's outstretched hands.

"I feel like I should say thank you, since they'll be easy to put down to bed. But you also kinda stole my wife on my first night off in three days." Sebastian winks at me, leaning to kiss Mal on the cheek.

"Honestly, you're welcome for both." I grin back at my brother-in-law. "If you've been on shift that long fighting fires or saving cats from trees, I'm sure you could use the rest instead of whatever else you'd be doing."

My sister and her husband both laugh. We all know what they'd be doing—four kids under eight only happen one way.

"Don't worry, Seb. She might have snuck into town without telling anyone, but I already texted Howie." My sister winks at me, then turns to walk him out. Howie, my cousin, has always been my best friend. But I haven't seen him in a long time, so telling him before I had the chance was a dirty move, and she *knows* it.

As Mal sends Sebastian off, my mom sinks down into her rocking chair, and Beth takes the seat next to her. "I'm glad you're home, my girl." She reaches for one of the bottles, sticks a wine key in, and removes the cork. "But now that it's just us, you're going to explain yourself."

I follow her lead and snag the bottle, filling my glass higher than what would be considered an average pour. My family won't be upset with me—it's not that. I just don't like admitting I need help. I left home and created my career through nothing other than *my* blood, sweat, and tears. It's all mine, but that also means that I have to own the meltdown, too.

As the first hit of tangy red wine bursts on my tongue and warmth floods my veins, Beth releases a breath that comes out sounding like she's been holding onto it for too long.

"Sadie, why did you sneak into town without letting us know you were coming?" Beth asks, with a hint of curiosity and something else I can't pinpoint in her voice. My sister slides into her chair, crossing her arms like she means business.

Beth is a family friend. Her relationship started with my mom back when Mal was just a baby, but she and I have been close since the minute I was born. I wouldn't call her an aunt per se, but more of a best friend to each of us in our own way. For Mom, she helped her navigate having two young kids and then the journey to being a single mother when our dad walked out. Mal and Beth talked a lot when she was in high school, as

Beth became her guide for dating, dealing with mean girls, and choosing an alternative education path that didn't include college. Yet, for me, Beth has been more of a lifelong confidante. From the time I was little, she was always there to wipe my tears or kiss a skinned knee. When I got older, she gave me a job at her diner waiting tables and became the keeper of all my secrets.

"Sorry Bethy. I just, well... it wasn't really planned." I tap my fingers lightly on the edge of my chair.

"Sade, just tell us already. I can't take the suspense," Mal whines. She's got an eyebrow raised and her legs crossed, challenging me to get on with it.

I take another sip of my wine, leaning forward to place it on the glass table that sits between us. "Okay, fine. I'm on leave from work."

"Like PTO?" my mom asks, confusion etched on her face. She tucks a chunk of hair behind her ear and sips her wine.

Beth rolls her eyes. "No, it's not PTO, Dee Dee. She's in trouble." I rear back, shocked that she somehow knows what's going on and at the audacity she has to call me out so boldly. "Go on, Sadie Marie, tell them what happened."

I look at her, staring into her eyes like that will help me figure out how she already knows. But this is typical of her. She's always had a weird way of knowing things, and telling them what happened *is* inevitable. "I sorta had a tiny panic attack from all the stress of adding on two more kids to the program, and my boss found me soaked in sweat in my office." The pressure eases in my chest as the words release from my body.

"Jesus, with all the build-up, I wasn't sure if you were going to admit to murdering one of the NHL players," Mal finally chimes in after tamping down a burst of laughter. "Panic attacks are totally normal. I get them all the time."

"You do?" My mother turns her attention to my sister with even more concern on her face.

"Oh please, Mom. It's not like you don't. It's part of our allure." Mal waves her hand in the air. "Our neurospicy blend of ADHD and anxiety makes for quite the party."

"There's nothing wrong with being a little spicy, if you ask me. That's what makes you three of my favorite people." Beth raises a wine bottle in the air while popping a cracker from the still-lingering charcuterie board into her mouth.

"Yeah, the problem is... you know how hard I've worked to build this program. Levi told me I had to take a leave of absence. It wasn't a choice." I look at each of them, trying to convey how nervous I am that he won't let me come back from this. "What if he—"

"Stop!" My mom shifts forward in her chair. "There is no way he's not bringing you back after this leave. You've worked *too* hard for *too* long."

While I appreciate the support and sentiment from my mother, it isn't really that simple. Yes, I helped create the program—our annual gala was essentially my idea. But his fiancée is on staff and could absolutely take over running it in my absence—nepotism has its perks.

"When was the last time you went out with friends? Or on a date?" Beth's question throws me a bit. My social life has nothing to do with being on leave from work.

"It's been a while." I cover my face with my hands briefly, releasing a strangled breath when I make eye contact once again. "If I'm being honest, my boss has been nagging at me for the last year or more about my work-life balance. Levi's always going on about how only having a career and nothing else doesn't make a full life."

"I mean, you told my kids a story about a corporate princess whose boss was pressuring her to become a butterfly to close a deal." My sister smirks into her glass, finding amusement in my lack of a life outside of work.

Beth's eyes are sympathetic when she looks at me, and it makes me feel worse. I don't want or need anyone's pity. I only need to get back to work, organize everything so the pile isn't too heavy to carry, and continue to put one foot in front of the other. I'll re-evaluate after next season.

Our conversation continues, switching from my situation to what the rest of them have been up to recently. My mom tells a story about how my niece, Poppy, doesn't like to wear clothes and apparently stripped mid-grocery. I can't help but admire her free spirit. Poppy's always doing whatever she feels like with no consideration of what the world might think.

"—and there she was, throwing a fit because I told her it wasn't appropriate to show our lady bits in the potato chip aisle," my mom finishes while Mal covers her face, and I bite my cheek trying not to laugh too hard.

Beth has grown quiet, not piping in to add color to the story as she usually does, and just as I'm ready to comment—to ask what's wrong—she stands.

"Sadie, will you walk me out?" Beth moves closer, reaching for my hand.

"Oh, uh, sure." I scramble out of my chair, the wine buzzing a little harder than I'd realized when my feet hit the patio. I follow her out after she bids my mom and sister farewell.

We amble down the hallway, stopping near the front door where she bends down to put her shoes on. Practical white sneakers, her standard.

"I hate to say it, but Levi's not wrong, my dear." Beth moves closer to me and grasps my hand. "Not all hope is lost... I have just the thing to help you." She reaches into the large olive green satchel she's been carrying around for the better part of five years and pulls out an aged, leather-bound book. "I can sense that you want to sit around and stew about this job, but I think you should do this instead."

I take the book from her outstretched hand, running my fingers over the embossed title: A Fate Found In Clues. Sliding my fingers under the twine tying it closed, I slowly unknot it. When I flip to the first page, I see a crossword puzzle that's filled out except for the last clue. I know Beth shares my affinity for solving puzzles, as we often exchange our favorite ones or discuss unique words we've discovered. Yet, I can't quite piece together why or how this is going to help me—who would give someone a puzzle that is all but almost solved?

"It's basically complete." I lift the book toward her. "This is yours. You should be the one to finish it."

I'm no stranger to getting odd gifts from my mother's friends. It's one of those things that just seems to happen, like when you accidentally comment that you need to buy a new set of Tupperware and the next thing you know you're walking out of Sally Jo's house with a full set, well worn in with spaghetti sauce stains that will never come out. The kinds of things that probably belong in the trash but you have to seem grateful to receive—thankful for the gesture.

"Sadie, I wasn't really asking." Beth pushes my hand and the book back toward me. "Your life, as you know it, isn't the one you've been seeking. All the answers you need are here." She glides a hand over her heart.

"Thanks? I'm not really seeking anything other than a few extra hours in the day to get everything done." Her brows furrow, a look daring me to refuse the gift. "But I guess this will give me something to do," I course-correct. For a woman who's not a mother—she's got the guilt thing down.

Beth doesn't respond. Instead, she simply walks out the front door. I watch her retreat, expecting her to turn back or to say something else.

I guess the conversation is over?

Returning to the patio, my sister raises an eyebrow. "What was that about?"

"Honestly, I have no idea. But she gave me this." I hold up the book. "She said it would help with my situation?"

"Well, that's bizarre as fuck. Can you put it down and pass me the wine? My glass has been empty since you left."

"Mallory!" my mother scolds.

"What? It is."

I can't help agreeing with her. I appreciate that Beth was trying to help, but this is just another weird gift to discard with all the others so I can focus on what's really important—getting my job back.

Two

Max

Help Wanted

Sweat drips down my forehead, blurring my vision as I dig my skates into the ice. I've been floating across this frozen glass for most of my life, but even Coach Perkins' post-game sprints weren't enough to prepare me for my current challenge.

"Bro, I'm going next," Miles shouts.

"It's my turn. I already called it," Brady whines.

It doesn't take long before the mites are brawling for the chance to race me, and while I'm a little proud, I'm also fucking tired. I spent my morning in the gym, then met some guys here for a skate, and now I'm racing kids for no other reason than their enjoyment.

"Listen up, if you don't quit fighting, I'll make you race each other until someone gives up." My ultimatum straightens them out instantly, but it also means I have to go again. "Miles, you had a turn already. Get outta here." I wiggle my eyebrows up and down, trying to keep a stern face. "Alright, Brady... think you can take me?"

Brady just turned eight, and while the kid has potential, he also looks like a flailing duck on a frozen pond when he gets going too fast.

"Eat my dust, Skibidi," he spits out before taking a head start toward the opposite end of the rink. I let him get almost to center ice when I take off after him—he's a funny kid and by far my favorite, sue me for giving him a little bigger advantage than the rest.

I chase after him, handing him a clear victory, before fist-bumping his tiny gloved hand and nodding toward the exit. His mom waves at me with a shy smile as her husband stands with his phone plastered to his ear on what I can assume is another work call. I've noticed he's usually preoccupied, which is fine, but I've spent enough time around Brady to know it affects them both.

I toss her a wink, smirking. Every woman deserves a little harmless flirting to make them feel good. The same way my very devoted mother used to love getting hit on at the gas station. It's a reminder that despite what she may get at home, she's not invisible—someone still notices. No different from the boy beaming up at me being the real reason I help coach this team. I love kids and hockey—volunteering here is the only thing that's keeping me sane after everything I've lost.

Brady glides to the boards and steps out of the rink, and I move around the circle picking up the cones from practice. Finishing my cleanup, I follow not far behind the mini version of myself, stepping out and taking a seat on the bench to undo my skates.

"Max, a word?" I look up to see Brady's dad, Thomas, standing behind the bench.

"What's up?" *I'm probably about to pay for the kind gesture I showed his wife.*

"I was thinking if you put Brady at goalie, he'd have a better shot at making a college team." *What? The kid is eight, and we are thinking about college?*

"Uh, yeah... maybe. But at this age, we like them to learn all the positions." Thomas looks at his too-expensive watch and raises an eyebrow at me, so I continue, "I wouldn't lock him into a specific position just yet. He's got potential, but it's a little early to tell what his sweet spot will be."

Thomas huffs and crosses his arms. "Do you *know* how much I'm paying for this?"

"I do." I stand at my full height, skates still on, putting me at least a foot taller than this jerk. Backing down from an overzealous parent isn't my style. If he's not above trying to pull strings, maybe our size difference will make him back off. "And frankly, that's cheaper than it'd be in Golden City, Tommy"—I pat his shoulder—"you aren't gonna get very far making demands in this sport."

His cheeks turn pink, but he glares at me anyway. "You'd know, since *you* never made it out of this rink." With that, he walks away, and I squeeze my hands into fists so hard that my nails bite into the skin on my palms. *Fuckin Asshole!*

I sit back down and finish removing my skates, skin still vibrating with rage from the reminder that I did not, in fact, fulfill my dreams. I've spent most of my life working to be the best hockey player I could be, but like most professional sports, it's not that easy to break in. You have to be either incredibly lucky, know someone, or just be so talented that there's no denying your ability. For me, I'm good, some would say great, but it never panned out. On top of that, hockey isn't a gentle sport. When I suffered my last concussion, one of many over the years, my doctor gave me an ultimatum: quit or risk serious brain damage. I chose to keep what's left of my functioning brain cells intact.

It hasn't been easy. I still find time to pass the puck around with my former teammates, and I coach the little kids, but nothing will ever give me the high that came with stepping out onto the ice prepared for battle. And finding a job that makes a decent wage beyond the private lessons I teach is even harder. Unlike my older brother, Sam—he left the sport to open his own tattoo shop—I never considered anything outside of the rink, so looking now just feels like settling.

"Hey, Max. Good to see you back out there." Coach Perkins smiles at me as he walks toward his office, clipboard in hand.

I hurry to follow, wondering if maybe he knows what I should try next. He was in a similar situation back in the day, and let's be honest, I promised my mother I would ask. Mabel hasn't stopped worrying about me since the MRI results came in.

"Coach, wait up. Do you have a second?"

He spins on his heel, checking the time on his phone before nodding. "Sure, but only five before I have to meet with the league affiliates to discuss the schedule for next season."

We duck into his office, where he takes the worn rolling chair behind his grey desk, and I slump into the single metal folding one opposite.

"I was wondering if—"

"Max, I can't pay you." His face twists, mirroring the way my stomach feels.

"No, I know. I was just wondering if you knew of any openings. Something that would keep me close to the sport but also put me somewhere above my mom's leftovers and ramen."

He scans his computer, likely prepping for his next call. "Maybe... let me do some digging and see what I can find." Perkins turns his lips in, pausing as if he doesn't know how to tell me what's coming next. "But you'd probably have to move. And I don't know if I want to be on Mabel O'Reilly's shit list."

"I'll handle Mabel when the time comes. Just let me know if you find something. I can't lose hockey altogether, Coach." He nods at me in understanding while pity forms on his face. Over the years, we've spent so much time together that I know he gets what this means to me.

Walking out of his office, a knot forms in my throat. I don't want to leave Mage Hollow, but it was always the plan. If I had made it to the NHL, the closest I would have been able to stay was Golden City—and the chances of that were slim. Coach Montgomery only recruits the best—not twenty-eight-year-olds with more concussions than years left playing.

That's life, though. If being an athlete has taught me anything, it's how to pick yourself up and set a new goal. Now, I just have to figure out exactly what that is.

Waltzing through the back door of Union Tavern, it's immediately apparent that the lunch rush is over. There are a couple of locals lingering at the dark wood bar, but most of the place is empty. I enjoy coming here on a summer afternoon. It's peaceful in this lull—one we rarely get during the fall tourist season, with people pouring in from all over to learn about Mage Hollow's witchy past. It's an opportunity to catch up with my friend without having to fake a smile.

Howie and I have become pretty close over the last several months, and he's helped me through some of my darkest days. Most of them when I was four beers deep and stuck in my head. On top of that, last fall he helped my future sister-in-law, Olive, when she was unexpectedly cursed by a witch named Irina—that witchy past isn't as far back in history as most believe. Between knowing our secrets and always showing up for me, he's practically family.

"Max, how's it going?" Instead of standing across from me, Howie grabs two beers from the cooler, pops the tops, and rounds the bar to slide onto a stool next to me.

"Pissed off a dad at practice, and asked Coach Perkins if he knows of any job openings, so... an average day. You?" I shrug and take the first sip of my lager.

"I had to host the town meeting, and a few of the elders hung out after lunch. I also got a weird text from my cousin saying her sister's back in town." He chugs down half his beer, and it takes everything I have to stifle my laugh. I know for a fact that Howie hates hosting the town meeting. All the shop owners flood his space, make him race around for food, and then forget that tipping still applies at a private event.

"Do I know this cousin?" I rack my shitty memory to figure out who it could be. There's one that works here. I'm basically a regular in her section on Saturdays for lunch. But I didn't think I knew there were more actually living in Mage Hollow.

He runs a hand through his red hair, releasing a long breath. "Remind me exactly how many times you've been hit in the head with a skate." Howie shakes his head before continuing. "She tutored you in high school."

I don't correct him on his assessment of how I got my concussions. A skate to the dome would have been more scarring, but he doesn't need to know that.

"Does she have red hair?" His mouth gapes at my question, but to be fair, I had a redhead phase and at the time a handful of girls would have called themselves my tutor—even if studying wasn't typically the prior- ity. I remember having an *actual* tutor junior year, but it was only for a few weeks to prepare for exams. She was incredibly smart, so intelligent that I was nervous to be around her. She was witty too, and would work on crossword puzzles while I was finishing whatever assignment she gave me. But she was nothing like Howie. I would be surprised if they were related.

Howie drains the rest of his beer, stands and moves to the POS machine behind the bar and punches something in. Once he's done, he spins on his back heel, pulls another beer for me out of the cooler and uses the gun to fill a plastic cup with Diet Coke.

"No, Max. She does not have red hair, and she definitely *was* your tutor. Does the name Sadie ring any bells?" He shifts on his feet, staring at his shoelaces. "I'm worried about why she's here."

"Smart Sadie? I can't believe I forgot her name." I wouldn't have been eligible to play if she hadn't helped me pass that test. She changed my life in just a few short weeks, and I went on to have a record-breaking season. "Why? Isn't it a good thing when family comes to town?"

Howie glances around the room after rolling his eyes at me. "It's just Sadie, and she doesn't visit. She hasn't bothered to make the short drive home in three years. I think it's a little out of character for her to show up out of the blue, and Mal seemed concerned when she messaged me."

I take a drink and wonder what could be so bad about coming to Mage Hollow. I can't imagine that I'd stop visiting regularly if I took a job elsewhere. Especially one that is close. But maybe that's what everyone thinks before they leave.

"Maybe you should just talk to her... check in. If there's something going on, you already know we will all do whatever we can to fix it. It's the least we could do for you."

"I know"—Howie smiles at me and reaches over the bar to pat my shoulder—"you're a good friend, Max. Sadie isn't really the type you check in on, though. She's independent, doesn't like to ask for help, ya know?"

"Okay, but back up a second." I point to my temple, my usual sign for saying *Hey, I have a shit memory, explain it to me.* "Who's Mal?"

"My cousin, Sadie's sister." He shakes his head and chuckles under his breath.

"And she lives in Mage?"

"Yes, Max." Howie glances around the bar, likely checking to make sure no one needs his attention.

"Could you talk to her sister again? See if she knows more?" I run a hand through my hair. I would help because it's the right thing to do, but also this might be the first interesting thing to happen around here in months. The busybody in me can't miss an opportunity to be a part of what I'm sure will headline Mage's rumor mill soon.

Howie laughs. "Mal is supposed to send me an update, but maybe it's better if I wait for Sadie to come to me. It worked last time. Ariella and Olive reached out first when they were dealing with the Irina stuff."

"But this is family. According to Mabel, it's okay to be a little extra when it comes to your genetic line." I smirk, thinking about how very much my mother would be up my ass if I forgot to tell her that I was coming home. "How is Ari anyway? Haven't seen her in a while."

The door jingles with more guests filtering in for happy hour, and Howie shifts on the balls of his feet. He's clearly eager to get on with his shift. Or he's avoiding talking about the crush he has on my sister-in-law's best friend—a crush he can't seem to let go of.

"She's noncommittal—"

"Can I get a little help over here?" A patron seated at the other end of the bar calls out.

"It's about to get busy here. I'll just text you if I need anything, and don't tell Ollie I said that about *her* friend." His face contorts as a nervous laugh rolls out of him. I nod my head, stand from my chair, and make my exit when he hollers out to me. "Give Benny a hug from his uncle Howie!"

"Will do, How. Will do."

Three

Sadie

A Beguiling Book

Fl@mes1234!

Your password is incorrect. Please try again.

The computer screen taunts me on what feels like my hundredth try. Each time I type in a potential option, I'm met with a denial. I've tried everything from Alex's (my boss's fiancée) middle name to keeping it simpler with things like TheFlames, Hockey123, and SparkThe-Flame25. Levi is not *that* creative. It has to be something obvious, yet nothing I've punched in has resulted in what I desperately want: access.

I know I'm on leave, but it's temporary, supposedly. And with the program I lead expanding from featuring just one kid last year to multiple this year—I can't afford to let inquiries pile up or emails go unanswered. Most bosses would champion this kind of dedication, or at the very least, not deliberately lock you out.

Giving up, I sit my laptop on the hardwood floor and tuck my feet underneath me as I lean back in my mother's rose velvet wingback chair. Grabbing my coffee from the end table beside me, I sip it gingerly, letting the warmth soothe my nerves.

I get why he did it, but also I don't. Over the past few days, my mind hasn't quit analyzing what happened. I had a meltdown, a panic-induced moment that I created entirely on my own through a series of complicated choices. Yet, if I had to do it all over again, I wouldn't change a thing.

Six years ago, I was fresh out of college and searching for any position that would allow me to use my human services degree, while also not stepping foot in a counseling center. When the position opened to work with youth in sports, connecting them with opportunities they wouldn't have otherwise, I knew it would be a great fit. I wasn't qualified in the slightest—my only previous athletic experience being the one time I tried track in high school—I lasted less than a week. Yet, something about it spoke to me—to my *need* to always be moving, and to have a chance at a life I wouldn't otherwise afford on *my* own.

So, I hustled—like I always do—and made sure that the staff conducting my interview knew that they wouldn't find another candidate who would work harder. I came to my interview prepared with detailed plans for the programs that would make the biggest difference, research to back up my claims, and the hope that they'd take a chance.

Over the years, I've not only grown the program to something revered in professional sports, but I've also made it fun. I've connected with families and truly impacted lives. Hell, what I didn't tell my family last night is that I've neglected any semblance of a social life because a night out could never be as important as making a difference for these kids. But all of that has led to a near-debilitating pressure that is so heavy it's almost crushing me under its weight. Keyword, almost.

My phone buzzes against my leg from deep inside the pocket of my robe. I pull it out only to find a message from the one man I wasn't expecting to hear from.

Levi

Sadie, are you kidding?

Why is he texting me at 6:30 in the morning?

Huh? Going to need a few more details, Coach Montgomery.

Levi

I've told you no less than a hundred times to call me Levi.

Text bubbles appear again before I can respond and remind him I'll never be able to do that. He's my boss, and as much as he wants me to... my sense of respect won't allow it.

Levi

Stop trying to get into your work email. It's called a leave of absence for a reason. Alex reset the password, and she won't tell me what it is.

Alex knows her future hubby is a softy, even if everyone else doesn't. I could probably beg or bother him enough to get it out of him *if* he knew it.

Fine. But can I make you a list? Because there's a lot going on, and three weeks is too long for an email to go unanswered.

I close my eyes tightly, willing him to give in. I need this. I need to be able to do this one thing right. My job is all I have, and while my family thinks this is all a good lesson for me, I've worked too hard to let it all slip away in exchange for a Mai Tai on a beach somewhere or completing the puzzle book that's all but finished.

Sadie, we never agreed on a timeline, and there's more to life than working. I had to learn that the hard way. But if a list will help you feel better, call me Monday at 9 to walk me through it.

I choose to ignore the timeframe comment and instead send back a quick thank you, paired with a thumbs up emoji. It's not the same as doing the job myself, but at least I won't return to a horde of angry pee-wee coaches and players. That is assuming he lets me come back.

Trudging down the hall, my mind makes a list of all the things I need to do today: a shower, food, planning. My stomach bellows, practically begging for pancakes from 1793—Beth's diner. I need to plan for what I can accomplish while I'm on leave, and what Levi can do in the meantime, but I could do that over a stack with extra syrup.

I feel better already. What's that saying? Failing to plan is like hoping in one hand, and—nope, that's not it.

With one foot on the threshold of my room, I stop moving.

How?

The book I shoved in my dresser last night is laid out on my patchwork comforter, but I could swear I didn't put it there.

"Mom, did you move the book Beth gave me?" I holler down the hall toward her bedroom.

"No, hunny."

How did it get there? Did I pull it out and not remember, or is this thing like my car keys that always seem to be somewhere different than I recall placing them? *Could be either, honestly.*

Reaching across my bed, I clutch the book, pull open the small drawer on my nightstand, and shove it inside. It takes some effort—there're all sorts of random stuff lingering from my teenage years—hoarder could be my middle name when it comes to anything with sentimental value.

Maybe I should add cleaning out my room and closet to the list.

I head into the bathroom, undress, turn the shower on as hot as it will go, and step into the spray. As the water skates down my body, thoughts of last night flood my mind.

Mom, Mal, and I spent the evening catching up. Mom confessed to continuing her biweekly frozen food delivery from Schwann's solely to stare at her delivery driver's ass in his navy blue shorts. I'm fairly confident she's been harboring a secret crush on Bill for the better part of a decade. Then Mal filled us in on the judgmental PTA moms at Lily's school. She apparently isn't "good enough" because she has a full-time job and can't volunteer daily, not to mention three other small children—they would hate to see me coming.

Finishing my shower, I turn off the water and step onto the plush green floor mat, grabbing my towel. My stomach grumbles audibly, but I take my time drying off. Massachusetts is humid in the summer—all but winter, actually—and while my long hair is pretty manageable, blow-drying it is the only way to ensure it stays frizz-free. Breakfast, and the rest of my agenda, will need to wait despite my body's protest.

Roughly an hour, and a full episode of the lady boss podcast I've been listening to pass by the time I'm making my way out of the bathroom. Years of practice still haven't made me more efficient at the effort it takes to look presentable. I'm convinced curling irons were made specifically to torture women. My delayed path to pancakes couldn't have been stalled by the thirty minutes I sat on the floor punching notes into an app on my phone with ideas for new event marketing. Or the time I spent looking at all the junk under the sink.

On cue, my phone buzzes with a reminder to take my medication. I frown at the device while feeling both grateful and a bit like it's trolling me after the very unnecessary exploration of body sprays I've had since seventh grade that I just completed. Choosing to listen instead of being annoyed, I dig the prescription bottle out of my makeup bag, pop one in my mouth, and steal a sip of water from the sink.

Stepping into my room and tossing my towel on the foot of the bed, once again the book catches my eye. This time it's lying open to the first clue, near my pillow as if I had been reading it.

"What in the actual hell?" I shout loud enough the neighbors probably heard me.

"Sadie, are you—" Mom rushes in, halting when she finds me in nothing but my birthday suit staring at my bed.

I snatch the towel and cover myself. It's not like she hasn't seen it all before, but I'm twenty-eight. I don't really need my mother to be the first person in *way* too long to see me naked.

"I'm good. Just thought I saw a spider." The lie sounds as forced as it feels slipping out.

"Good Lord, Sadie." Dee Dee shakes her head at me. "You nearly gave me a heart attack." She shuffles out of my room, and I promptly lock the door behind her.

This is unacceptable. I mean I can't be losing it enough to have misremembered stuffing it in the bedside table. And frankly, I don't have time for whatever game this is becoming. Beth must think this is funny—toying with me—but all it's doing is pissing me off.

Dropping to the floor, I inspect under my bed—nothing but dust bunnies. I move to the closet with quiet steps, although if someone is hiding, they would have heard my freak-out. Whipping it open, it's empty too. Giving up on the notion that she's physically here, I slip into a pair of panties and a sundress. The entire time I'm getting dressed, my eyes remain trained on the book.

I grab my crossbody, checking to make sure my wallet and anything else I might need is inside. There's a moment where I contemplate bringing my laptop, but the book seems to wobble in its place like the creepy game in that movie with Robin Williams where all the animals appear. I half expect it to beat with the sounds of an elephant stampede.

I leap toward the bed and grab the book. The leather is buttery yet rough on my fingertips, and a weird sensation travels down my spine. It has to be fear. I'm making this whole thing up in my head, catastrophizing for no reason. Shaking myself, I shove the book into my bag.

Heading for the front door, my mom narrows her eyes at me from her spot on the couch. "Are you okay?"

I nod. "Yeah, I'll be back soon." My words are rushed as my feet slide into my sandals and I push out the front door. Bounding down the steps, I start my trek on the sidewalk. But when I spot our neighbor's trash can—a plan clicks into place.

Peering around to make sure Mr. Bradley isn't outside, I quickly extract the book from my bag and shove it inside the bin.

That'll show her!

It's silly, but I keep looking around as if someone will have spotted me doing something illegal, or Beth will pop out and know I ditched it. I made the mistake of putting one bag of trash in my neighbor's bin across the hall two years ago—the rage on his face when he found out still haunts my dreams—and this feels similar.

Continuing toward 1793 Diner, the warm summer breeze coasts across my skin. I should feel guilty for throwing out the book when Beth gave it to me, but all I feel is relief. And honestly, what she doesn't know won't hurt her.

Stepping up to the glass door, I push on the metal handle and slide inside.

"Well, now... how long has it been since I've seen that sweet face?" Josephine, Beth's sister, smiles at me before continuing to refill napkin holders.

Not a single thing has changed since I last visited. Red jewel-toned booths line each of the three exterior walls that don't contain the kitchen, below clear glass windows. The same chrome bar with an off-white top that's aged from years of patrons eating on it sits off to one side of the room. Small stools that match the aesthetic dot the bar to provide the old-school feel this place has always had. It's like a fifties soda shop or something you'd see in an old-timey movie. There's even a jukebox that I'm not convinced ever worked sitting angled in the far corner, leading to the bathrooms.

I smile softly at Josephine, noticing her long hair that's tied into a neat bun. I worked here for years in high school and summers during college, and the entire time I've known her, like Beth, she never shows signs of aging. There's not a single streak of grey amongst her golden strands. It's a bit bizarre, but then again some celebrities look the same no matter their age. Making a mental note to ask her what vitamins she takes, I walk further into the diner.

"I couldn't come back to town and not stop in." I shrug, taking a seat in the booth furthest from the door. It's my booth, the one I spent hours doing homework in—hours preparing to leave this place.

Jo nods before hitting the button on top of the Bunn burner to start a fresh pot of coffee. I watch from afar as she works through setting up everything needed for a normal weekend brunch rush, and I'm surprised when a wistful feeling in my chest takes over. I've never missed working here, at least not doing the actual job. Yet something about knowing what she's going to do next, even after all these years, has me ready to grab an apron to assist.

Taking a deep breath to remind myself of the agenda I planned, I sink further into the springy booth and look through the menu I could practically recite word for word.

After a few minutes, Jo slides up to my table. She places a coffee mug down and fills it with 1793's specialty blend of rich hazelnut java.

"You dropped this on your way in the door." She places her free hand on my shoulder, squeezing lightly, before sliding the freaking puzzle book across the table.

My mind is racing. *How the hell? What in the? There's literally no way.*

I glance up at her, trying to decipher whether this is some sort of joke. "Beth gave me that." I slide my hand over the leather binding, and chills run up my arm. "I need to return it. Is she here? There's something—"

"No, she's on vacation." Jo sets the coffeepot on the table behind mine. "You need to do it, Sadie. She gave it to you for a reason." There's a hint of disdain in her voice that gives me pause.

What reason? To drive me crazy? I've never been a fan of busy work and that's exactly what this is. A ruse, a hoax, a freaking trick meant to make me see that there's more to life. But guess what? I don't need it or want it, especially with the weird way it keeps showing up in places. It's not quieting my mind—it's making me lose it.

I shake my head. "No, I literally just saw her last night." I'm not saying her sister doesn't know where she is, but it's only been like twelve hours and she never mentioned leaving. "I need to see her now," I demand.

Jo smiles at me once more. "Early flight, she went to visit our other sister on the French Riviera. Are you ready to order?" Jo digs into her apron pocket and pulls out her notepad.

I ignore her subject change. "Okay. When is she coming back?"

Instead of answering me, she grumbles, then simply turns and walks away. Apparently, she is done with my questions.

Fine, two can play that game.

I stand from the booth, darting behind the counter to grab a to-go cup—I'm not a monster, the coffee is coming with me. Once I've poured my hazelnut drink into it and secured the lid, I grab my bag and march toward the exit, leaving the book sitting right where Jo set it. She can return the damn thing or burn it for all I care.

I pick up the pace when she glares at me and our eyes lock, but I don't back down. I've faced off with NHL coaches, kids' parents, the media—I will not lose whatever staring contest she's trying to have. I hear the door jingle faintly, but before I can turn my head, my face collides with something solid and my bag flies to the ground. I stumble backward, catching myself on... Mr. Wallingham?

The portly man in his late seventies frowns as his coffee flings to the left. The edge of the ceramic mug hits the edge of his wife's plate, catapulting scrambled eggs in the air, and a baby somewhere I can't see cries out—probably in the same horror I feel.

"Sorry, I didn't—"

"I wasn't looking, I—"

"Smart Sadie?"

My shoulders tense at the nickname coming out of his mouth, and my head spins, meeting his gaze for the first time in years.

"Max?"

The boy whom I tutored for a whole three weeks during junior year of high school has transformed into a man—a man that's staring at me. My skin heats in embarrassment.

He drops down, grabbing my bag and shoving the contents that spilled out all over the floor back into it. I scan the items, hoping and praying that a super tampon isn't lying out for all to witness, but even worse, his fingers are wrapped around the brown leather book. *This honestly isn't funny anymore!* Max stands and slips the bag onto my shoulder.

"Thanks."

"Yeah. How've you been?" He smirks at me, and while it's kind of adorable, it also reminds me of every player in the locker room that's at one point or another tried to get my attention. If I didn't have time for Brett Burns, the Flames' resident flirt, I for sure don't have time for this golden retriever to be smiling at me.

After what just happened, I don't have time for anything other than getting the hell out of dodge.

"Max, it was good to see you, but I need to go." I turn slightly, whispering an apology to the couple whose breakfast was ruined, then shove past him, pulling the door open and making my way toward Mom's. I'm halfway across the parking lot when he calls out to me.

"Sadie, I think you dropped this." Max jogs over to where I stopped, sliding a letter into my hand.

Without saying another word, he turns and goes back toward the diner. I look down at the crinkled envelope that's only marked with my name on the front in Beth's handwriting. Knowing I have no other choice than to let this thing wreak havoc on my life or take control of it, I move to a bench across the street, sit down, and slide my fingers under the edge to open it.

Sadie-

I know that you're probably wondering why I didn't tell you I was leaving. And the truth is twofold. I didn't want to put a damper on our only day together, or for you to think you could get away with not completing the puzzles I gave you.

Was it that obvious that I found the whole thing kind of bizarre? I mean, I love crosswords. I swear by them for many reasons, such as memory control, fun, stress relief, and even how they've helped me broaden my vocabulary. But I don't really see how filling out a book of them is going to do anything in the way of getting my job back or helping me discover my future. That's a little too presumptuous, even for me.

When I was younger, I was lost. I felt trapped in a life that wasn't authentic, and I acted out often because of it. While that may not be the same thing as the stress you're feeling from work, it has the same root cause. Happiness, true fulfillment in life, is only found when we embrace the things that are uniquely designed for us. And you, my girl, are not doing that. I've watched with bated breath as you've strung yourself out to build the career you sought. But I cannot sit idly by and watch it any longer.

I don't understand why she never said anything. Beth and I have always had a very honest relationship, the kind where we can call each other on our bullshit as soon as it happens. This makes it seem like she hasn't agreed with my choices for a long time, and while I wouldn't change any of them, I can't believe she said nothing.

There are things you don't know about me, things that have been kept secret for far longer than you could ever imagine. I need you to trust me and take this seriously, Sadie. Seize the moment and complete these puzzles before my return—your fate quite literally depends on it.

Here are a couple of clues that will help along the way:

- *Two is always better than one.*

- *What's over three but less than five is a number in time.*

- *A whisper in the wind is where the fun begins.*

- *When something is right, it's like a golden light.*

With all my love,
Beth

I sit staring in disbelief at the letter. This is all so ridiculous. Yet, there's a weird knot in my stomach and an itchiness in my brain telling me to actually do this. I'm not one to back down from a challenge typically, but this can't really be more than a simple distraction that she cooked up to keep me from spiraling out about work.

I grab my coffee cup, pulling the top off to make sure it's cooled enough to drink. As I raise it toward my lips, my eyes catch on words floating right on top. It's elaborate, like the fancy latte art that you'd get in a boutique coffee shop, except I never put cream in my coffee. I blink my eyes three times, convinced that I'm seeing things. But when I open them once more, the words are still there: **Trust Me. — B.**

Four

Max

Hot For Teacher

Pushing open the door to 1793 for the second time, I move to grab a broom from one of the servers and promptly clean up the mess Sadie and I just made. It only takes a minute with Mr. Wallingham assisting. Handing it back to the woman, I spot Sam and Xavier in a booth toward the back corner—laughing at me. Or maybe with me?

We are meeting up for breakfast before my brother forces me to get poked and prodded for two hours by a tailor who thinks my hockey thighs stand a chance of fitting nicely into dress pants. I'm annoyed about the fitting, less so about the pancakes I'm planning to consume, and still a little in shock from seeing Sadie.

I knew she was in town since Howie told me as much. It's just been a long time since I've seen her. Yesterday I barely remembered who she even was. But now, I'm not sure how I ever forgot. She's pretty and certainly knows how to make an entrance?—exit?—but that's not the thing that's so memorable. It's the way she carries herself—confident, a little quirky, and in a very specific way that screams she always has her shit together. Sadie Wells is the kind of girl that's so far out of everyone's league she has her own category—or at least she used to be. I don't really know her now.

Sliding up to the table, I scooch in next to my brother while ignoring the amused look on his face.

"Morning. Remind me again why we needed to do this so early?"

"Ten is basically brunch, Max. And you know Olive has that book thing later. I promised we'd be done in time." Sam shakes his head before sipping his coffee. "Who was the girl?" he asks as he picks a clump of scrambled eggs from my hair.

"I know... but Benny doesn't really let me sleep all night." I pull the coffee from his hands and take a drink. "Ah, shit. That's hot. Howie's cousin, Sadie."

Xavier's eyes get as wide as saucers. "You think Benny's bad, try a baby," he mumbles.

I scoff. "Benny is a baby. He's only three months old."

"Benny is a dog, Max." My brother's best friend deadpans.

So he might not be walking around on two legs, but he still needs me. He's my baby, and I treat him as such. But Xavier and Cami have been through it, from what Sam has told me. Their daughter—the one they named after my brother, in a weird show of respect—Sammy, still doesn't sleep more than two hours at a time. "Fine, whatever. What's the plan for today again?"

Sam grabs a menu and places it in front of me. "Did you hit your head when you ran into Sadie? I just told you we are eating, then the tux fitting, followed by Black Kettle's adult book fair." He sips his drink again.

I take a minute to look, although I'm not sure why. My order hasn't changed in roughly five years—pancakes, two eggs sunny-side up, a side of bacon and sausage, hash browns, and a coffee, black. When I shut the menu and place it back on the stack in front of my brother, a server approaches.

"Do you gentlemen know what you'd like to eat?" She sets a coffee mug in front of me and fills it up. I've seen this one here before, but she's normally behind the counter or in the kitchen. Beth, the owner, is usually the one handling the tables. We order quickly, and she's off once more.

Sam and Xavier drift into a conversation about wedding planning, which, to be honest, sounds super stressful but fun at the same time. I'm a little jealous, not that my brother is getting married, but that he's getting to do cool things like tasting ten different kinds of cake at once. I've always had a healthy appetite, and that sounds like my personal Super Bowl. When I tried to convince Ollie to let me come, she said it was going to be hard enough to choose without me moaning over how good each one was.

As they continue talking about babies and weddings, my eyes wander around the diner. There's a family a few tables away with a couple of rowdy kids that remind me of Sam and me when we were younger. Mr. Holland and his wife Cathy are seated at the bar just down from the Wallinghams, and then there's the waitress—she's staring at me with a look similar to the one my mom gets when she's up to no good.

"Earth to Max, I asked you a question."

"Sorry, what?"

"Did you ask Perkins about a job?" My brother fiddles with his napkin.

I sip my drink slowly so I don't burn myself again. "Yeah. He said he's going to ask around, find some openings." I reach behind my head, scratching my neck lightly. "But they probably won't be local."

Xav sucks his teeth, and Sam blows out a whirring breath. "How are you planning to break that one to Momma O?" Xavier asks.

"I'm not sure yet. But this was always a possibility, right? If I got picked up, it probably would have meant moving." My thoughts drift back to my conversation with Howie. He mentioned Sadie rarely visits Mage, so I have to assume that's because of work. I'd be different—my whole life is here.

Sam chuckles. "Max, there's a big difference between a million-dollar hockey deal and whatever salary you'd make as an assistant coach in juniors."

I know what he's implying—that I'd be giving up a lot here, and without an NHL salary maybe it's not worth it. But I also know that he never considered leaving home. He always had a backup plan. Hell, he started tattooing before he was even done playing.

"I get that, I do. But you never know what opportunities might come up. It could be bigger than you think. And nothing says I have to do it. Maybe something else will come up here that will change my mind." It's a vague response, but the only one I feel I can give in this moment—the moment when zero jobs have presented themselves.

Xav has a shit-eating grin on his face when I look across the table. "Opportunities like the girl you nearly knocked out on your way in here?"

Now I'm the one sucking my teeth and rearing back. "No." I look around the room to make sure there aren't gossipy ears listening. "Howie said something's up with her. That she never comes home and something is wrong. I vaguely know her from high school. It's not like that..."

"Sure didn't seem like he wasn't interested, did it, Sam?" Xavier chuckles.

"Not with the way he was checking her out and so quick to help," my brother adds while he fist-bumps Xav across the table. "I guess we'll see how helpful you get with figuring out her problems."

They erupt with laughter, and at the same time the server delivers our breakfast. I'm not saying I don't think I could go there with Sadie—she's beautiful and smart as hell. But I'm probably leaving, and it sounds like she's got her own shit to deal with.

"Turn to the right." The tailor, a gentleman who can't be younger than eighty, stretches his measuring tape up my inner thigh. "Okay, I have what I need."

Giving him a curt nod, I step down off a round platform in the center of the room and shuffle toward the changing area. The last twenty minutes of my life were spent being measured, poked, pinned—twice his shaky hands literally jammed a needle into my ankle. Yet, none of that was as bad as the shit that my brother and Xav have been giving me since breakfast.

It started with the conversation about what could keep me in town and spiraled from there. They don't really understand the upheaval that my life has had in the past six months. I put on a brave face, only really showing my emotions for the first few weeks, and only in certain settings. I'm not exactly walking around sharing my lack of direction or concern over finding something outside of odd jobs and teaching private lessons to earn money.

"Why does he look like that?" My sister Bridget's voice carries across the room. My whole family is meeting us here to walk over to the event at Black Kettle.

Sam outright laughs. "He literally ran into a girl today, knocked her bag off her shoulder, eggs went flying... It was a real shit show. But also adorable."

"Who's running into girls?" My mother, the legendary Mable O'Reilly, best known for her meddling, barrels into the store.

Spinning on my heel to face them instead of the gold velvet curtain that separates the changing room, I give them all my best glare. "It was an accident. She ran into me." I run my hand through my hair. "It's Howie's cousin actually, remember Sadie, the one that tutored me."

My mom grins at me. "Oh yes, Sadie... the one that really was a tutor and not a fling. What a sweet girl. She was so focused, wasn't she always doing puzzles or something?"

"It was crosswords, Mom. But today was nothing, over in two seconds, probably less."

Xavier exits his changing room.

"Yeah, maybe that's all true. But what he's not telling you, Momma O, is that the once nerdy girl grew up. She's like the girl next door mixed with a business Barbie." Xav tosses his tux onto a cart next to the register. "Oh, and did we forget to mention that when she tutored him in high school, our boy was hot for the teacher?"

God, why did they always have to snoop through my journal when I was younger? They fucking knew everything, and they still lord it over my head.

Bridget claps her hands and bounces up and down. "Does this mean I get to watch you fall all over yourself trying to impress her like this one did?" She tosses a thumb in Sam's direction, and I'm thankful that he's the one getting barbed.

"No, you knuckleheads. Howie told me that his cousin had returned to town unexpectedly." I run a hand through my already messy hair. "I think she's in trouble or something."

My mom walks over to me and pats my arm. "Tell me more about what seemed to be wrong."

"I honestly don't know. But something was off, and Howie said—"

"Speaking of Howie, where the hell is he?" Sam checks his watch, suddenly bored with the details surrounding Sadie.

The door slams open, and we all shift our focus. "I'm here... is it too late? Beatrice Bushnell was in early, giving me a lecture I didn't need." Howie bends over, sucking air into his lungs. "What did I miss?"

"Max ran into your cousin, like physically." My sister tosses out from her spot in a green high-back chair.

"Which one?" He looks at me, curiosity on his face.

"Sadie. It was an accident. But she's fine. I'm fine. Everything's fine."

"Okay? How do I get measured?" Howie spots the tailor and follows him toward a dressing room, while I duck into mine and hope they all let whatever drama they're trying to stir up go. I don't remember my family being this nosy or gossipy, but maybe I've just always been the one dishing it out or fucking with them for the fun of it.

Five

Sadie

A Ruined Sweater

Seeing Max O'Reilly wasn't on my bingo card. Not that it really makes that big of a difference, I didn't really know him then, and I'm indifferent to knowing him now. He's changed physically since the last time I saw him. Where he used to be tall and a little lanky, he's now solid muscle—my face *still* feels like it hit a brick wall. One thing that hasn't changed is that panty-dropper grin, he's had that forever, and I'm sure he still knows how to use it. Luckily for me, I'm immune to that sort of thing after years spent near a locker room.

I'm not, however, immune to whatever juju Beth put into that letter. I mean, it's completely unhinged. I couldn't have actually seen anything in my coffee, and a few puzzles won't solve anything. When I got home, I shoved it and the book into the bottom of my suitcase, zipped that baby up, and stuffed it into the back of my closet. It can stay there until Beth returns, and she'll just have to get over me not completing it. I have important things to do, like finding a way to work without getting caught.

That's something I can thank Max for, actually. I internet stalked him—like any normal person—and it turns out that he was still playing hockey until about six months ago. I found an article from the Mage Hollow Gazette that noted him doing some coaching, and a picture on his social media confirmed it. The deep dive made me wonder if the team here in Mage Hollow would be interested in having a spotlight player.

My phone buzzes with a text on the yellow-painted nightstand my mom made for me in sixth grade. One leg is a little shorter than the others, but with a stack of magazines under it, you can hardly tell. Dee Dee might not be the strongest craftswoman, but she tried.

Mal

Are you guys coming to the farmer's market?

I hadn't planned on doing much other than relaxing at Mom's or maybe the beach, but I guess I could go. I'm not very good at sitting around mindlessly with nothing to do.

I roll out of bed and slip my feet into my slides before making my way downstairs. The scent of freshly brewed coffee and cinnamon rolls beckons me, and my stomach growls.

When I turn the corner and peek into the small, square kitchen, Mom's head whips around. "There's my girl." Her face blooms into a genuine smile as the curlers holding up her blonde hair shake lightly. "Your sister has invited us to the farmer's market."

"I know. She texted me too." I move closer to the mismatched collection of mugs that hang on the wall above a coffee cart and next to an etched wood sign she had made that reads: Dee Dee's Coffee Delights. "Should we go?"

My mom steps up beside me, moving me out of the way with her hip as she prepares a latte just the way I like it. "Well," she starts. "That depends—"

"On?" I cross my arms and lean back against the faux marble-topped island.

"Are you going to tell me where you went yesterday?" She spins to hand me the drink she made, throwing in a raised eyebrow that's laced with guilt. When I got home yesterday, I was pretty freaked out and, honestly, annoyed. I'm an adult. I'll be thirty in two years. The last thing I need is for someone else to think they can step in and control my life. So, I holed up in my bedroom like I'm fifteen again—isolating myself.

I groan internally, snatching my drink and sitting down on the wooden stool closest to the pan of warm breakfast pastries. Quickly dishing one onto a plate, I make a big show of humming over the taste. It's not really faking. Dee Dee is a great cook, and these are my favorite. But I can't exactly tell her about the coffee situation or what the letter said—she'd think I'd lost my mind.

Maybe I have?

"You can ignore me, but you're not leaving this room until we talk." She moves to the opposite side of the island, so I'm forced to either look directly at her or very obviously avoid eye contact. "I've known you for twenty-eight years, three months, and five days. You can hardly keep a secret from me, and when you walked in the door yesterday, it was clear something was bothering you."

I sip my latte, washing down the bite I just swallowed. "Mom, it's not a big deal. I'm fine. I just went to see Beth."

"I'm sorry. I'm just a mom, and worrying is my job." She picks up my fork and stabs a piece of cinnamon roll, pulling it to her mouth. "Did you go for guilty pleasure pancakes? Shame on you and Beth for not inviting me."

"She wasn't there."

"Beth?" my mother questions, mouth full of cinnamon goodness.

"Yeah. Josephine said she went to visit their sister."

"Irina? I thought she was still around here." My mom tosses her fork in the sink and spins toward the hallway. "You should shower and change. I told Mal we would meet her in about thirty minutes."

My mouth gapes open. "I didn't even know she had a sister?"

"You've always been a little too focused on your goals to notice the world around you. But her sisters keep to themselves. It's not a big mystery, darling." She runs a hand over mine, squeezing gently, and then walks out of the kitchen.

I continue chewing on the cinnamon sugar perfection in front of me, while thanking all the powers that be that I had the foresight to shower last night. I only need ten minutes to get changed.

Do I really not notice things?

My mom's words stick in my brain and churn my stomach. I never thought that being so committed to my goals was a bad thing. I work twice as hard because I *have* to. Yet here I am, the last to know one of my closest friends has not one but two sisters.

We strolled through the farmer's market for about an hour until Lily saw a flyer for berry picking and conned my mom and sister into taking the kids. I drove us uptown, intending to pick up a couple of books from Black Kettle Bindery, not wanting to schlep them plus whatever produce Mom picked out back six blocks. That turned out to be the perfect excuse not to go on the *berry fun adventure*, as Magnolia called it—taking two cars would have been impractical when it costs money to park, and Mal only had one seat empty.

Instead of going into the bookstore, there was a local author from Salem, Jules Cohen, selling her books at the farmer's market. She was adorable and funny. We talked for a few minutes, and I decided to support her instead by buying both of her books—The Art of Us and The Flavor of You. They sounded fun, with small-town vibes and a coffee shop—exactly what I need to fill my free time.

I cross the street, waving once again at my new author friend, and step up onto the sidewalk. I could go back to Mom's, but I know if I do, I'll only stress over making a list of things for Levi so that I can make sure all my bases are covered. Diving into a new book by the coast feels like the perfect way to sort of take his request for balance seriously, and at least I'll be able to say I'm trying when I talk to him.

The breeze blows stronger with each step I take, and it's refreshing with the temperatures rising. The wind curls around me, wicking the sweat from my skin as the soothing, salty scent drifts in with each breath I take. That's one thing I miss about being here. In the city, the air doesn't feel as crisp or clean.

I trudge through the shifting terrain where a cobblestone walkway turns to rock and sand. The sea oats sway back and forth as if they're dancing to their own unique beat. There's a lighthouse up ahead, towering above the horizon, its beacon circling to signal sailboats. And just before a new path veers off for guests to approach, there's a soft spot of grass with a bench—the exact spot I was hoping would still be here.

I slip my bag off my shoulder, pulling out the green cardigan I stuffed inside this morning and the first of Jules' books. Wadding the sweater up, I place it at the end of the bench, hang my bag on the corner, and lie down. I might look a little funny, but this feels like the perfect spot to read and the perfect position to do it in. Stretching my legs out in front of me, I cross my ankles so that passersby don't get an unsolicited look up my linen shorts.

Holding the book in front of my face, I flip to the acknowledgments. It might seem backward to most, but I appreciate how much time it takes to write a novel and the dedication that the author must have had. Reading the acknowledgments first feels like a way of honoring that effort.

I lose track of how much time has passed, engrossed in the story, but the lyrical sound of an ice cream truck blaring *The Entertainer* by Scott Joplin as it passes pulls me back to the present. I need silence when I read. I'm not one of those people who can listen to music while they do it. Reaching into my pocket, I pull my phone out to pass the time—zero missed calls, zero texts, but worst of all, zero emails.

I lay the book open over my face and groan. "What the hell is wrong with me? And how did my life go from completely on track to off the rails in less than a week?"

"Do you make a habit of asking questions directly into the pages? Or how does this work?" Max's gravelly voice comes out of nowhere, scaring the shit out of me. I shoot straight up—not realizing he's hovering above me—and when the book falls to my lap, my forehead smacks him square in the nose.

"Did I say that out lou—"

He yelps, stepping back as blood begins to pour from his face, dripping onto his blue t-shirt and khaki shorts.

"Oh my god. I'm so sorry. Let me help." Jumping up, I grab my cardigan and press it on top of his hand, covering his face. But Max lightly pushes my hand away.

"Jesus fuck." He sucks air through his mouth. "Are you trying to kill me?"

"What?"

"You hit me in the face and then tried to smother me with your cardigan." He laughs now, shaking his head lightly while still pinching his nose. "It'll stop in a second... it's just touchy after the, uh, nevermind."

"Oh blow? Or is it called something else now?" I run my hand across my chest, a little shocked that he'd do drugs, but then again, he wouldn't be the first athlete to try to enhance their performance.

"What?" Now it's Max's turn to look confused.

"Does it bleed a lot because you know"—I make a sniffing noise and plug one side of my nose in demonstration—"you do blow, or whatever?" I clarify.

Max lets go of his nose, the dripping now seemingly stopped. "You're twisted as fuck, you know that, right?"

I take a step back, chewing my lip. It was a legitimate question. I don't see how that makes *me* the one with the problem. The ice cream truck passes again, blaring the song that started this catastrophe once more, and making it even harder for me to concentrate.

"Okay, so no drugs? And no, I was not trying to kill you." My mind races with how I can fix this mess. "Sit." I wave my finger, directing him. "On the bench. I'll be right back."

I grab my bag and run, following a pack of kids coming up from the beach toward the current bane of my existence. When I finally make it to the front of the offensively long line, I order two strawberry shortcake popsicles and a bag of ice.

Smiling, I hand the cashier a twenty. "Keep the change, please. And thanks for the ice."

"Hey, Martin, can you change the song?" Beth's voice rings out from behind me, and I spin, searching for her in the crowd.

My heart rate increases, and my chest tightens. Goosebumps trail down my arms, and chills race up my spine. *Where the hell is she?*

"Here you go." I hear the man speaking to me, but I keep scanning the horde of people waiting. "Ma'am, take your stuff. There's a line!" He shouts.

I turn back around, smiling politely as I grab my items, but when I walk away, the lyrics from *A Whisper in the Wind* blast from the truck's speakers.

A whisper in the wind is where the fun begins.
You've got to be kidding me!

Six

Max

Hard Headed Woman

Sitting on the bench, I'm still not entirely sure what just happened. I spent my morning helping Beau with restock after yesterday's event and decided to take the long way back to Mom's to pick up Benny. He can't be left home alone because he refuses to go to the bathroom anywhere except on the right back leg of my couch, or a pee pad that I have to place exactly two and a half feet in front of the back door.

It's infuriating.

Strolling along the water has become one of my favorite things to do since everything imploded. Listening to the waves crashing on the rocks has healed something in me, and I find myself ending up here more and more.

When I rounded the corner that cuts back to the sidewalk by the lighthouse, I didn't expect to see Sadie sprawled across the only nearby bench. She looked peaceful, in a pale purple top, her hair blowing in the light breeze. I shouldn't have approached her, but I haven't been able to get her out of my head. I'm curious what it's like to leave Mage, to start over somewhere different. And to be honest, I want to know what her deal is.

Howie and I talked a little more at the book fair, but he didn't seem to know much about what was going on, just that Mal said she wouldn't spill what is her sister's story to tell. He shared how close they used to be, though, and I could tell that he's not just worried—he misses her.

My intention was to come over and make small talk, see if she's the type who'd word vomit her problems to almost strangers. Instead, I'm pretty sure she broke my nose, or at least bruised it pretty good. When Howie told me she's independent, I assumed hardheaded—but I had no idea just how accurate that would be.

Sliding my phone out of my pocket, I check a missed text from my mom.

Mabel

> Taking my grand-dog to the park. Don't worry about coming to get him. I'll bring him home when I'm done spoiling him.

Shaking my head, I can't help but laugh. She's been begging for a grandchild since the minute Sam put a ring on Olive's finger. I guess Benny is filling that void for her. If she doesn't mind dealing with his unique potty demands, it's fine by me.

"Okay, so I brought you ice and ice cream." Sadie moves toward me at a rapid pace, with something close to terror on her face.

"I'm okay. It's not even bleeding now." I point my index finger toward my nose. "See?"

She rolls her eyes and hands me both the ice and a strawberry shortcake popsicle. I lean back, draping the bag over the bridge of my nose, and scan the ingredients on the package.

"Oh my God, you really are trying to kill me."

"What?"

"Strawberries—it's listed right here."

I watch her process, her eyes scanning the ingredients and then my face. "Are you allergic?" She rips the ice cream from my hand. "I swear I didn't know."

A laugh rips out of me. As much as I find myself enjoying giving her a hard time, I can't contain it, and it worsens when her eyes bug out of her head. She crosses her arms over her chest, cocking a hip out. "Just kidding. But you should really see your face."

Sadie drops to the ground, dramatically clutching her chest and both of our ice creams. She folds her legs into a pretzel and closes her eyes. "I swear to God, I might actually consider killing you now."

I laugh again, and she joins in before throwing the still-wrapped treat at me. Her laugh is bright and melodic. The kind that's contagious without being forced.

We fall into an amicable silence as we eat. It's a little harder for me with the bag of ice covering most of my face, but I manage. When there's nothing left but the stick it came on, I drop the ice onto the bench beside me and lean forward.

"So, smart Sadie, do you make it a habit?"

She shoves her stick into the wrapper, does some weird maneuver to stand that my brain can't stop from registering as, *Jesus, she's flexible*, and holds her hand out to me.

"Make what a habit? Give me your trash."

I slide it into her awaiting palm. "Hanging out with people who do drugs." A hint of pink creeps up her neck and onto her cheeks, and frankly, it's adorable. I want to make it happen again. Something tells me she doesn't laugh or let loose—just a feeling, nothing concrete—and that's a fucking shame.

"No." She walks away, depositing our trash in a nearby bin, then returns. "I just... you said nevermind, so I assumed it was something bad. Like something you wouldn't want to admit, which equals drugs, I guess... or murder...or—"

"Or I used to play hockey but can't anymore because I have had too many head injuries, many of which resulted from fighting... i.e., a nose that bleeds easier than others." I raise an eyebrow at her, smirking because I can't help it. "But see... I knew murder was on your mind. Thanks for confirming."

She scoffs, flipping her hair over her shoulder. "You're still infuriating, you know that, right?"

"Still? Me? You're the one that's accosted me twice in two days." I place a hand on my chest as if she's wounded me. "You're lucky I'm such a selfless guy."

That makes her snort, and her hand flies up to cover her mouth as if that will make me forget it happened. "What's it gonna take, Max?" I raise an eyebrow at her. "Name it. What's the price for never telling anyone about what happened here today?"

She used to say the exact same thing when attempting to teach me algebra—there was always a bribe involved, and it was never a fun one. I make a show of acting like I'm thinking, resting my hand on my chin and tapping a finger to my cheek. "Trying to buy my silence? That's murderess behavior, Sade."

"Seriously? I'm not trying to kill you, but if I wanted to, I'd prob—"

I hold up my hands in surrender. "Jesus, okay, let's maybe not continue that sentence." She smirks, a quiet laugh rolling out of her. "Tell me why you came home."

Sadie looks surprised, like maybe she thought I'd throw her an easy question—I probably should have.

She sits down on the bench facing me, tucking one leg underneath her. "It's not a great story." Sadie releases a long, steady breath. "I'm on break from work, and I didn't really have anywhere else to go."

That's not exactly the dramatic answer I was expecting.

"Oh, hmm." I run a hand through my hair, lightly scratching the skin at the base of my neck. "I'm not gonna lie, I really thought it was going to be more exciting than that. Howie made it seem—"

Sadie holds up a hand to stop me. "You know Howard?"

"Who doesn't? The man is a legend in this town." Sadie's mouth gapes, and I smirk at her reaction. "We're practically besties."

Her eyes widen as the sun reflects off the normally chocolate circles, highlighting tiny flecks of amber. That shock quickly slips into something more cautious as she chews her lip. "What did Howie tell you?"

"Not much." I hesitate. While I'd normally take pleasure in being a shit stirrer, I can't this time. "Just that you don't come home often. Did you say you plan events, or I'm sorry? My memory is kinda shitty. What do you do?"

Sadie blows a raspberry, and I can't help but watch. Xav was right. She's the girl next door, but also sort of uptight and a little quirky. It's endearing as hell.

"I manage a youth outreach program that gives kids opportunities and access they wouldn't otherwise have."

That felt practiced.

"Access to what?"

"Max, what do you do now that hockey isn't on the table?"

Sadie's attempt at changing the subject is shaky at best. "Nope. You owe me, remember." She stands, reaching around me to grab her bag and bloodstained sweater. As her fingers wrap around the plush green material, she stares at the stains for a minute. "You really know how to ruin a sweater," she mumbles—hopefully to herself since that's her fault—walking over to the trash can and throwing it away. I expect her to turn back, but she starts down the path back toward the square.

I should probably let her go. It's obvious that she doesn't want to get into it. But the fact that she's willing to walk away mid-conversation only fuels my intrigue. I stand, following quickly behind her until we're in lockstep. I'm hyper-aware of how close our pinkies are from touching, so I know there's zero chance she hasn't noticed me.

At the crosswalk, I step in front of her, reaching out to press the walk button. A small harrumph coasts out of her, making me smirk in her direction.

"What do you think you're doing?" Sadie crosses her arms and glares at me.

"Oh, hello ma'am. Nice to meet you. What's your name?" I hold out my hand to her, and Sadie furrows her eyebrows.

"Max—"

"Wow, that's so weird. My name is Max, too." I keep holding my hand out toward her as the walk sign illuminates and people shuffle around us. "But people usually call me Mr. Altruistic."

Sadie rolls her eyes again, but there's a small smile threatening to break free on her lips. Instead of saying anything, she darts across the street, opens the door to a sleek black sedan, and slips inside.

When she fires it up, she rolls down the window and pushes her hand out in a wave.

"Until next time, Max!"

Seven

Sadie

The Pothole

"Okay, so you need to make sure that you don't agree to anything just yet." I twirl a piece of my hair as I pace my childhood bedroom.

Levi crunches on whatever he's eating, not responding to my statement.

"Are you listening?" This is clearly more important to me than it is to him.

"Oh, sorry, yeah. Just trying to get some breakfast in at the same time." He goes silent once again, and I hope it's because he's washing down whatever it was with a drink. "What would agreeing to something look like?"

I shake my head, trying to stuff down the groan that's dying to escape. "Who did you promise?"

I love the guy, and he's a great boss. But also, he's a sucker for kids, always showing up with jerseys or promising things I will need to find a way to deliver. You'd think for someone that puts grown men in their place for a living, he'd be a little better at negotiating.

"I wouldn't say I promised anyone specifically. But the coach from Coop's team hinted around about having another player get the spotlight, and well—"

"That would be a no, Coach Montgomery. I know that it's the easiest and goes a long way for your kid, but we have to spread it out. Make it fair for other teams." I plop down on my bed, the springs bellowing from age and a bed frame that's worn far past the point of squeaking. I wince, hoping he didn't hear it.

Levi sighs. "I know. And look, I only said I would see what I could do." He must be leaving, likely headed to the arena, as a door shuts in the background. "We'll cross that bridge when the time comes."

"When *is* the time going to come?" I shouldn't pester him about coming back, it's not even been a full week. But this is exactly the reason I should be there instead of staring at the poster of a young Chad Michael Murray plastered to my ceiling. "I need to work, and you need me to work. It seems pretty simple to me."

"About that..." Levi's voice deepens to a more serious tone, and I imagine him glowering at the phone. Despite only being a stepdad for a few months, he's got the dad-voice nailed down. "What have you been doing to learn to live a little?"

Giving a guy I used to tutor bloody noses? Or should I go with trying to ditch a book that's following me around?

Straightening my shoulders, as if he can see me, I take a deep breath. "I bought a couple of books yesterday and got ice cream from a truck."

"Wow, riveting," he chuckles. "You need to embrace this whole thing, Sadie. I'm not going to get into why it's so important, I think we both already know what happened."

"A panic attack."

"Yeah, but you need to understand why it happened. And don't give me some lame-ass excuse like you took on too much. I've seen you balance a hundred different tasks without breaking a sweat. Sometimes we get so focused on the goal, the achievement, the fucking trophy—that we miss the whole point of why we wanted it so badly in the first place."

I don't disagree with him that *he* may have struggled with determining why he set the goals he did and what he sacrificed to achieve them. Yet, I don't feel that way about myself. I've always been so clear on where I saw my life going—never without a solid five-year life plan. There's never been a moment that I've regretted missing a night out, a dinner with friends, or losing a relationship over my work schedule.

"What do I need to do to convince you that I'm ready to come back?" *Please, just give me a checklist.*

I can almost hear him thinking, the gears grinding in his head. "Give up control. Get out of your comfort zone. Go do something that scares you."

I close my eyes, willing myself to be respectful. This whole thing feels like it's way outside of what my boss can legally require of me. At the same time, it's exactly what I should've expected from him. He's a coach, on the ice, off the ice—I doubt he ever stops thinking like one.

"Fine, but you'll let me know if you need me, like for work stuff?" Opening my eyes, my gaze immediately lands on the freaking book that Beth gave me. It was stuffed in my suitcase, and I thought I'd won. But now, it's propped open at the foot of my bed like it's just waiting for me.

"Sure, talk to you in a few weeks."

"Like two? Three?"

"Sadie, I'm hanging up now. Take the month." The call goes dead, and I toss my phone onto the bed next to me.

A month, fuck my life.

I pick up the pillow opposite mine, push it over my face, and scream. I've never felt so out of control in my life.

"Sadie, everything okay in there?" my mom shouts.

I guess the pillow didn't muffle my frustration as much as I'd hoped. "Yeah, I'm good."

Throwing the offending feather sack to the side, I sit up and grab the book. Beth's letter falls out on my lap, and the first words I notice are: **What's over three but less than five is a number in time**. Levi said a month, what's between three and five—four weeks.

A rush of adrenaline courses through me. I don't want to do this, but maybe if I do it on my own terms, if I choose it, then it won't feel like such a burden. I don't know if completing a crossword qualifies as something scary, and it's definitely well inside my comfort zone. But submitting to it—that's the very definition of giving up control.

"Mae, I promise I'll be back in a few weeks. And I'm good for the rent, so don't get any ideas about subletting my—"

A rabbit leaps and bounds across the road in front of me, stealing my train of thought and causing me to swerve. My car jerks as I barrel into the same pothole that's lingered on this road for the last decade—a spot the town should have fixed where loose bricks gave way to nothing but gravel. A loud pop follows with a whistle of air that sounds like it's rapidly escaping a too-small hole. The whizzing drifts through my rolled-down window. I hesitate for a moment, wondering if I'm actually hearing it, or if by chance I'm assuming the worst when everything is fine.

"Your room?" My roommate chirps at me, bringing me back to the conversation. "You think I'd rent it for three or four weeks, Sadie? Do you not remember that I have trouble taking the trash out, let alone posting an ad online?"

Realistically, her confusion is valid. Why would she rent my room for what I explained would be a long vacay? But then again, what if it isn't—what if Levi tells me I can't come back from what happened, that I've become too much of a liability and failed to find the balance he thinks I need?

My car thumps, and the puzzle book flips open to the first clue taunting me from the passenger seat. I stifle a groan as I take stock of my location and remind myself that none of this is Mae's problem to deal with.

"Mae... I have to go. Don't rent my room. I'll be back soon!" I say, smashing the end call button as quickly as I can.

At least I hope I will.

The clunking intensifies as I push my black sedan further, tightening my grip until my knuckles are white, as if it will help. The sound of what's surely a flat tire, and a likely ruined rim, screeches and grinds against the cobblestone street, and my heart rate picks up further. Sparks bounce off the bricks, and smoke begins to plume.

"You've got to be kidding me, universe!" I shout into the void, relenting as I ease onto the curb in defeat. I'm supposed to meet Howie for lunch, and now I'm absolutely going to be late.

I push out of my car to assess the damage. "Stupid, useless piece of rubber"—I mutter to myself while I kick at my deflated and all but shredded tire—"it wasn't enough to be bad for the planet, you had to ruin *my* day too?"

The street is empty, aside from Mr. Holland and his vastly overweight dachshund, who I know from many run-ins is named Spencer Lee. Both the dog and the man are hard of seeing, hearing, practically everything. They're not going to be any help.

Opening my phone, I search for my cousin's name and call him.

"Sade? Is everything okay?" He answers after a half a ring, the noise of the lunch rush at Union Tavern bellowing in the background.

"No." I release a frustrated breath. "I have a flat."

"Sade, I can't hear you. Did you say no?"

I yell into the phone, "I'm stranded on the side of the road." Mr. Holland looks in my direction, cocking his head to the side, but continues walking.

"Why are you whispering?"

"Howard! I'm not, turn the volume up on your freaking phone!" I shout, shaking my head, annoyed that this is a regular occurrence.

"Shit, sorry. I didn't realize it was on low. I'm leaving work now. Where are you?"

"I'm on Crow, just down from Mrs. Sullivan's." I lean against the side of my car, banging my head softly on the window.

"I'll be right there."

Younger than me by a couple of years, Howie and I have always been close. He was my awkward sidekick, and I was his overly anxious leader. Inseparable. I was looking forward to catching up over sushi, not dealing with more shit.

I swallow down the thick emotion that forms in my throat and decide now's as good a time as any to start playing Beth's little game—it's not like I have much else to lose. I slide into the driver's seat and grab the book.

Across

1. Acting without regard for one's self: Benevolent

There are ten empty boxes. I grab a pencil from my purse, quickly writing in selfless. Nope, not enough letters. I erase it. Unselfish also isn't enough, and it can't be benevolent. Charitable or thoughtful could work, but they don't feel right.

The loud rumble of Howie's Bronco roars as he makes his way down the street, saving me from the question. I snap the small, tattered book closed and peer out the window. He could have chosen a quieter, less conspicuous vehicle, but apparently Howie *is* the King of Mage these days.

His door slams, the sound echoing through the car, followed by a soft knock.

"Sade, are you ready? Let's go."

Holding up a finger, I fumble around, grabbing my purse and laptop, before giving the interior a once-over to make sure I'm not forgetting anything. I hop out of the car and stare at the deflated tire.

"Come on, Sadie. Toss the keys onto the tire so the mechanic can move it later."

Instead of continuing to sulk over the repair I'm going to have to pay for, I straighten my shoulders, do as instructed, and slide into my cousin's front seat. "Thanks for the rescue."

"Don't mention it. Glad you called and didn't just stand me up." Howie side-eyes me before pushing the gearshift into drive and peeling away. "What's it been... like three days and you couldn't stop by to see me?"

There's hurt in his eyes. I should've called, or gone to see him right away. But something about admitting what's going on to Howie hits a little harder than it does with Mal and Mom. I've always cared what he thought, wanted him to be proud of me. We had big plans to make it out of Mage together, to make all our dreams come true as kids. But life had other plans for him, and I feel like a jerk for leaving him behind.

It was never about the town—we both love it here. Our goals were just bigger, grander, wrapped in a big-city bow where we could be ourselves and not the quirky kids we were back then.

Shaking myself out of yet another trip down the gloom staircase, I roll my shoulders back and take a deep breath.

"I'm sorry." It's not enough, and I know it. I'd be pissed off if he came to the city and didn't tell me. "There's been a lot going on, a lot that's not ideal. It didn't feel like a conversation we should have over the phone."

"Okay, but a text or something would've been nice. I'm worried about you." My cousin flips on his blinker to head toward the seafood spot our uncle owns, while smartly keeping his focus trained on the road.

I peer out the window, searching for any topic other than the one he so badly wants to discuss. The streets pass by, each one more inviting than the next. Everyone makes a big deal over Mage Hollow in the fall, but summer here has always been my favorite. There's something enchanting about it—the way the willow trees dance in the breeze as if they're finally shaking off the bitterness of winter.

Howie turns onto one of the side streets we used to ride bikes on, bringing a gaudy black and gold for-sale sign into view.

"The Caldwells are moving? Since when?" My voice shakes with the obvious signs of one trying to change the subject to literally anything else. But it's a legitimate enough question. Brian and Amy Caldwell lived around the corner from us our entire lives. I can't picture her watering flowers anywhere else. Or him hanging Christmas wreaths on anything other than the eight rectangular windows that mark the front of their classic 18th-century home.

"Three years ago. Their renters had been staying long-term, but I guess they finally decided that Florida is home now. It's better for Amy's joints with the arthritis." Howie's eyes widen at me, as if to call attention to my sudden need to know about neighbors I clearly haven't seen in years. "Would you like to tell me what's going on? Or should we talk about you giving Max O'Reilly two black eyes?"

Shit! I hoped that was going to stay between us.

"That was an accident, I swear." I hold both hands up in front of me, and Howie laughs. "I can't believe he ratted me out."

"It's kind of hard to hide something like that. What were you guys doing anyway?" Howie turns onto the highway, taking us toward the beach.

Now I'm the one that laughs. "*I* was reading peacefully, and he scared me." Picking at my nails, I can't hold back a smile. Max is different than I expected, or at least has changed from when we were in high school. Back then, he didn't seem to know I even existed outside of study hall. Yesterday, he treated me like a friend, as if he didn't mind my company even if Mr. Altruistic—as he calls himself—gave me shit the entire time.

"Holy Shit. That's it!" I grab the book and a pencil from my bag, flipping open the first page to scribble the letters into the boxes.

Altruistic

"What?" Howie glances over at me briefly.

"Beth gave me this book. She said it would help me figure out my future or something like that. Obviously, that's a load of crap. Each puzzle has only one clue left unsolved. It's clearly just her version of busywork." I open the book, flipping to the first page, to show Howie the clue.

"What kind of pencil is that?"

I look at him sideways, turning the wooden stick over in my fingers. "A number two, I think."

"Then how does the lead show up in gold?"

What is he talking about?

Howie maneuvers his Bronco into an open parking spot and turns off the ignition as I move the book back to my lap. Scanning the page, staring back at me are the exact letters I just wrote, but instead of being dark gray like they should be, swirly gold script settles into the parchment.

"I honestly have no idea." I shudder. "Did you know Beth has another sister?"

Howie's face shifts in confusion. "What? Who?" He spent as much time with Beth as I did growing up. Take that, Mom, I'm not the only one who didn't pay attention.

"Her name's Irene, or maybe Ariana." I toss the book back into my bag, my stomach swirling over the change in color.

"Irina?" Howie asks, his face turning pale.

"That's the one." I snap my fingers and point at him.

As I'm pulling the handle on the door to get out, I hear Howie mumble to himself, "Not again."

Eight

Max

A Carjacking

I wake to the sound of Benny whining. Pulling the comforter over me, I sink deeper into my pillow. As the warmth and softness of my sheets envelop me, the alarm clock on my bedside table blares like a foghorn on a silent night.

"No, need more sleep." I swing my arm over to the offending device and attempt to hit the snooze button, but a wet, rough tongue streaks down the side of my face as tiny fur-covered paws pad my chest.

"Ugh... fine. I'm up, Benny." My three-month-old beagle sits back on his haunches as I give up and sling the covers off of me. "But you aren't going on the pee pad this time. It's time to be a man, Benny."

It was a late night, with too many beers and too many jokes about my face looking worse after a run-in with Sadie than it did after a gnarly fight on the ice. Walking to the back door of the cottage I rent, I twist the knob and sling it open to let Benny do his business. Instead, he looks at me with his big puppy eyes and sits down.

"Benny, we talked about this." I wave my arm toward the small back-yard, but he doubles down by curling up at my feet. "The grass is soft. I even lay in it sometimes, I promise."

Benny cowers, a look of disgust on his little wrinkly face, and I release a frustrated breath. "Okay, fine. You win." I close the door, locking it, before turning to grab a pee pad from the small closet tucked behind the door. As soon as he sees it, he leaps to his feet and spins in a circle. Laying it out, I make my way to the kitchen and give him some privacy.

Checking my phone, I see there's a missed text.

Coach Perkins

When you wake your ass up, come to the rink. I have some job news.

Benny waddles into the kitchen, pulling my focus. The little guy is adorable in every way except that he is apparently the only dog who has an aversion to grass. It's not just when it's raining—which I'd actually understand, but he insists on using the bathroom indoors *every* time.

I scoop him up, cradling him in one arm while I pour myself some coffee. *Thank God for auto-brewing.*

"What do you think, Ben? Am I getting a job today?" He looks at me with confused eyes and then puts a paw over his face in what I can assume is embarrassment—for me and my hopeful nature. "Don't give me that. You're supposed to be my wing-dog. Encouraging, ever heard of it? This is the exact reason Grandma Mabel got you for me."

I'm sure my mom didn't actually rescue Benny with the intent of him giving me a pep-talk. But she did explicitly say that he would make a good companion and keep me out of trouble. Come to think of it, maybe my mom somehow bribed my dog into his terrible potty habits with the sole purpose of making sure I don't spend my suddenly abundant free time wasting away at the bar. Somehow, it wouldn't surprise me if she had that kind of talent—Mabel's ability to get her way knows no bounds—and there's nothing she wants more than for me to be settled.

"What do you say, Ben? You gonna help your dad today?" He licks my bicep, and I take that as a yes. "Alright, let's get ready and see if we can con someone into hiring us."

After a much-needed shower, I grab my bag, toss my skates and a couple of pee-pads inside, and wrap my hands around my keys while heading for the door. Coach is always happy when I bring Benny with me. The kids love him, and I think the man secretly does too. I figure I might as well let him get his fix while I get in a workout—after we talk.

I secure Benny's leash, lock the door behind us, and we hop in my truck. The drive to the rink is quick, but when I'm about a block away, my phone dings with another text.

Howie

Any chance you're free today?

I pull into the parking lot, coasting into a free space near the door before responding.

Just headed to the rink to talk to Perkins. What's up?

Howie

Sadie got a flat. We're at lunch now, but I was hoping you could fix it. I have to go back to work after this, or I'd do it myself.

I glance at Benny, waiting patiently in his safety harness on the seat next to me. "Should we fix the girl's car, Ben?" He turns his head to the side and stares at me. "She did this to my face, might be a good way of showing her I'm one of the nice guys so she'll stop beating me up."

What happened yesterday was an accident, but a part of me isn't mad about the time I spent hanging out with Sadie. She's funny and too easy to get riled up. It was nice to talk to someone new, to joke and laugh with a person outside my usual circle. And something about her puts me at ease. Like maybe she also has something going on that everyone else seems to want to talk about—except her.

> Yeah, where's it at?

Howie

> On Crow, by the rink. She called Sid already, but with the conversation we just had, she needs a win. I don't want her to pay for it. Also, we need to talk later...

> Got it.

My stomach lurches. Now I really want to know what's going on with her. If Howie thinks she needs a win, she isn't just on vacation. Stepping out of my truck, my focus immediately goes a couple of blocks down where Sid's tow truck is lifting the same black sedan she got into yesterday onto his flatbed.

I quickly unhook Benny, grab his leash, and we run toward the scene. I'm huffing right outside Sid's window in a matter of minutes. He smirks at me as he idly pushes the button to bring the flatbed forward.

"Max, funny seeing you here."

I smother a small, ironic laugh. "Yeah? This one is mine."

"Not today, Max. You and your brother can't just go around stealing *my* business for damsels in distress. Looks like it's just a flat, but it'll probably need a new rim—that's good money for me."

Over the last few months, we've had an unfortunate number of car problems. Olive got a brand new one and immediately hit a fire hydrant to avoid a squirrel. Nora backed over a parking pylon at the grocery store. And Ariella... let's just say she spends more time driving on the sidewalk than the road lately.

"Take it off the truck."

He looks at me sideways, like I've officially lost my mind, and maybe I have.

"Max, I—"

I hold a hand up, stopping him from telling me he can't.

"You can, and you will." I run a hand through my hair. "Take it off the truck."

Sid shakes his head back and forth but pushes the button that will bring it back where I need it. "You fucking owe me, Max. And I'm pretty sure Sadie won't be happy about this either. She called *me* for a reason."

I smirk at him, then round the back of the tow truck to assist with unhooking the straps securing it. "As long as I'm the one she's mad at, why do you care?"

"Fine... but I'm not breaking the news."

"Never said you had to. Just don't mention it to her." I shrug and finish unwrapping the neon green tow strap from around her wheel well. "I'll have it returned to her tonight."

After Sid does his last checks to make sure everything is disconnected, he hops into his truck and pulls away, only to stop a second later. "Hey, Max. You're gonna need these," he calls before tossing her keys in my direction.

I catch them with a nod and a smile that lingers until I look at the bundle in my palm—a Golden City Flames keychain stares back at me. I never took her for a hockey fan. The endless studying in high school and now just her vibe doesn't really scream sports fan, but maybe she's multifaceted. I turn it over in my hand, engraved on the back, one word catches my eye: **Staff**. I thought she worked with kids? Why wouldn't she tell me, of all people, that she works in *my* sport?

Union Tavern doesn't really have a parking lot. There're spaces out front, on the street, and a few in the back alley for staff. But those are strictly monitored, and Howie's uncle Lonnie doesn't play nice with anyone who dares to snag one. So when he told me to pull Sadie's car around back when we talked earlier, I was a little nervous. Now that I'm actually doing it, I feel like I'm breaking all sorts of rules. It's exhilarating in a way, or maybe that's just the anticipation of seeing her face when she realizes I'm her mechanic.

I slide out of the front seat, bending so I don't hit my forehead on the way out. It's a sedan, but it feels like it was made for people much smaller than I am. I round the vehicle, locking the car with the button on the fob, and head toward the back door. It swings open when I'm only a few feet away, and Howie marches out.

"Everything turn out okay?"

I hold the keys up. "I drove here just fine, so I'd say so."

Howie runs a hand through his red hair and paces. "So, two things." His face twists before turning pale. "She doesn't know you fixed the car. I sorta thought you'd enjoy delivering that message after... well, after your face. Oh, and I think she's been cursed."

I lean against the brick wall next to the door, confused and a little thankful. I don't know what about Sadie is so interesting to me, but I'm looking forward to sparring with her again.

"Cursed? Like because she has bad luck?"

Howie's eyes nearly double in size. "No, Max. Like how Olive was cursed."

That makes me laugh. There's no way. I saw both of her arms just yesterday, and she was completely tattoo-free. Olive had a changing tattoo that displayed her emotions. I wouldn't have missed that. Also, I know Irina left after everything went down. Sam personally searched every inch of this town looking for her after he and Olive reconnected. He was on a mission to make sure nothing like that ever happened again—even if it helped him find his future wife.

"I'm serious, Max." He crosses his arms, tension radiating off him. "She has this book, and when she wrote in the answer to one of the clues earlier, the pencil lead turned gold. Like magically."

"Yeah, okay. But that might just be one of those color-changing papers. You know, like we used to get invisible ink pens at the book fair."

"I never did." Howie's voice is low, a grumble mixed with a whisper.

"You know what I mean. There's an explanation."

"Did you know she has sisters?"

"The Mal girl, yeah?"

"No, Irina." Howie starts to pace again. "Beth and Josephine, from 1793."

The diner I've been going to my entire life is run by a witch's sisters? I find that hard to believe, yet it's shockingly not the craziest thing I've heard this year. I feel like there would have been signs. Wouldn't we have seen her there?

"Let's say that's true. Is the color-changing ink the thing that's wrong with Sadie? The reason she came home?"

He hangs his head. "No. But she should be the one to decide if she wants to share what's going on. Sadie is private. I can't cross that line."

"But you will tell me she's been cursed by a witch?" I raise an eyebrow at him. That seems a bit backward.

"She doesn't really believe in magic. I mean, she knows it's weird, and the things that have happened are unexplainable. She's not as closed off to it as your brother was, but she's in denial. I had to tell someone who's lived it, or at least knows it's real." Howie blows out a deep breath. "I helped keep a secret the last time. I can't do it by myself, especially when I work so much these days. Lonnie barely lets me out of here. She might need help."

I walk up to him and pat him on the shoulder. "I got you, bud. If she needs help, I'm available. But I think we need to let her decide if she wants *my* help. I've already committed a carjacking... I can't exactly run in there and start talking about her being hexed."

I push past Howie, jingling the keys so he understands where I'm headed, and pull open the back door. As I walk inside, I can tell it's busy, especially for a Monday night. There's a Gators game on, and from the T.V. screen it appears that Liam Montgomery, their star shortstop, just threw someone out from deep in the hole. Scanning the bar, I spot Sadie sitting with a bubbly blonde in one of the back booths.

Babs, one of the regular bartenders, pushes past me with a tray full of drinks. "Hey, Max. Snagged this for ya when you walked in." She slides a bottle of lager into my palm before continuing to a rowdy table near the front. I tip the beer to my lips, letting the smooth and tangy taste coat my throat while I continue my trek.

"Hey, ladies." I halt near the edge of Sadie's booth. "Girls' night on a Monday?"

"Max..." My name rolls off Sadie's tongue as the other woman smirks. "I'm so sorry about your fa—"

"What's wrong with my face? Did I cut myself shaving or something?"

The blonde one laughs, but Sadie rolls her eyes. "Jesus, Sadie. You told me you head-butted him, but it looks like you beat the shit out of him." The other woman's face gives away everything she's thinking—her eyes bulge and her cheeks turn pink.

"I'm tough, and I hear the ladies love a man with battle scars." I can't help myself. A smile tips my lips up. "But that's not really why I'm here." I hold the keys up, dangling them above the table.

"How did you get those?" Sadie's eyes are now the ones doubled in size.

I glance between the two women, debating how long I should keep the mystery going. "Found them. I'm Max, by the way, since Sadie here hasn't bothered to introduce me." I set my beer on their table, reaching my hand out to the blonde.

"Mallory Hayes." Her dainty one pushes into my palm, giving me a firmer than expected handshake. "But my friends call me Mal. I'm Sadie's sister—older and funnier."

I laugh. She is witty. I'll give her that. "Hayes? Like Seb Hayes?"

"Guilty." She holds up her left hand, flashing a diamond ring toward me. "That's why we're out on a Monday. He goes back on shift tomorrow."

I've known Sebastian Hayes since I was a kid. He was in Sam's class and is an all-around good guy. He works at the fire department and has helped rescue Mr. Pickles from a tree at least three times that I know of.

"Nice, you'll have to tell him I said hello—"

"Alright, Mr. Small Talk... my keys? Where did you supposedly find them? Tell me what's going on." Sadie crosses her arms, huffing a little.

I smirk at her, motioning for her to scoot over in the booth. When she does, I slide in right next to her, my fist still clutching the thing she covets.

"Tell me, Mal, is your sister always this bossy?"

Nine

Sadie

Stolen Property

Max O'Reilly has my keys. That was a turn of events I didn't see coming. The man of the hour slides into the booth next to me, taking up nearly all the legroom while saying something cheeky to my sister. I've never quite understood why men feel the need to spread their legs so far—obviously a little is needed, but I could fit a stuffed full Ikea bag between his knees, and there's not a man alive packing that much heat.

"Can you..." I wave my hand toward his lap, trying to get him to give me some space. But Max... he could *never* make this easy on me. I'm starting to think he takes pleasure in making me squirm. He scooches even closer, pinning me between the wall and his muscular thigh—the one I don't want to admire but physically can't help from noticing.

"I guess you could say that yes, she's always been a little bossy, but we prefer the term confident in our house." My sister winks back at Max after rightfully putting him in his place, and I want to shout in glee. Mal may give me more grief than anyone else in the world, but she's also the first to defend me.

"Touché. Tough crowd." Max takes a swig from his beer, and in this close proximity I try not to stare at the way his throat works when he swallows. Actually, it's hard not to notice every little detail about him with only inches between us. He smells of linen laundry soap and something more manly. His eyes are crystal blue from this angle—the bluish-purple shiners he's sporting highlighting their color—and his hair curls up a little over his ears in all its unruly glory. Objectively, he's hot. I've always known it, everyone in town knows it, and worst of all—he knows it.

Reaching for my wine, my elbow bumps into his bicep. "Sorry," I mutter as my eyes meet his. "Actually, no. I'm not sorry. You're here, invading my space after stealing my car."

"I didn't steal it, not really anyway." Max finishes his beer, still twirling my keys around with his fingers, while I'm momentarily transfixed by the motion.

Of course, he just has to have attractive hands. While some women love a man with a nice ass or perfectly straight teeth, I have always had an obsession with hands. Too many men have either short, stubby sausage fingers, or too long, oddly gangly ones. But Max's are the perfect size, proportionate with veins weaving their way across the back of his hand, calloused palms, and neatly trimmed nails. They are working hands, ones that you know could get you out of a jam but would also feel good jammed into you.

Jesus, I need to slow down on the red.

"You okay, Sade? Looking a little flushed." My sister, the asshole, takes this moment to call attention to my staring. She knows about my little obsession, so naturally she has to exploit it, it's some sort of older sibling law.

"Yeah. I'm great. Just wondering when, if ever, you're going to answer my questions." My eyes lift, connecting across the tavern to my cousin. Howie ducks his head and pretends he didn't see me. "Actually... I think I just got all the answers I needed."

Max lifts his hand in the air toward the server, then points at his drink. She nods her head, smiling shyly at him—because of course she would. "Is that so, slugger?"

"Hilarious." I purse my lips into a tight, sarcastic smile. "Howie asked you to get my car and fix it. Now you're here to return it because if you had brought it to my house like a normal person, there wouldn't have been an audience to see what a selfless guy you are."

"Sadie!" Mallory scolds.

Max puts a hand on his chest and acts like I've stabbed him. "And here I thought your head was the most dangerous thing about you." He takes a deep breath. "That mouth—that shit cuts deep."

I cross my arms over my chest, bumping into him yet again from the lack of space. "Tell me I'm wrong then? Did you steal my car from Sid for some other reason I'm not aware of?"

Max drops the keys on the table between us, slides out of the booth, and begins to walk away. Mal stares at me, eyes wide, horror present on her face. When he's three or four steps away, Max turns back.

"Sadie, I know it's been a while since you've lived in Mage Hollow, but people around here try to help each other out. Your cousin is one of my best friends, so when he called in a favor, I jumped at the opportunity to assist *you*." He turns back toward the bar and really walks away this time, pushing out the front door of the tavern.

"You should be ashamed of yourself." My sister's words echo in my mind, but I almost can't hear it over my now guilty conscience shouting at me. *I was rude, shit.* I hate being a jerk to people, most of all when they don't deserve it. The whole thing is just too much, though. I've had too many boxes checked in the loss column lately, and his taking control of my auto repair without telling me—the very definition of too much.

I know I have to make it right. He did a nice thing, and no one deserves to be treated that way. I look at my sister, realization dawning on her face that I'm going after him. "Pay the bill and meet me around back."

I slide out of the booth, hightailing it toward the front door. My hand collides with the handle at the same time my shoulder slams into it, and the door flies open. I look left, no Max. I look right, no Max. Finally, I spot him across the street, sitting on a bench near the center of the square. I jog, as much as one can in slide sandals, until I'm standing right in front of him. Max doesn't look up from his phone, and I'm suddenly tongue-tied.

After a few moments pass, he lifts his chin. "Did you come over here to give me the evil eye, or what are we doing?"

My mouth opens and closes a few times before I motion with my hand for him to scoot over. I sit down next to him, turning my body sideways so he can see my face. "I'm sorry." I don't know if it's a good idea, but I reach out and grab his hand from where it's resting on his thigh and give it a light squeeze. Electricity runs up my arm, not like the little shock that you get when folding towels fresh from the dryer, but the kind you feel in your bones. "There's no excuse for my being rude. I really appreciate your helping me out. But I feel like I should explain."

Max pulls his hand out of mine, shifting so he's also somewhat sideways and staring right at me. "Okay."

"I have sort of an important job, maybe not to most, but to me and the families I work with." I fidget, tucking my hair behind my ears and blowing out a breath. "I worked really hard to get where I am, but I've been trying to expand the program, and it's been a lot. Last week, I sorta had um..."

"Had what?" He urges me to continue.

"I had a panic attack." It was hard to admit it to Howie because I was embarrassed. Yet saying it out loud to Max, I don't feel the same shame. It's odd, maybe because we aren't really friends, or he doesn't know me that well. "My boss made me take a leave of absence. He said I need to find balance in my life, learn to live, you know. It's whatever, but I feel like I'm sort of spiraling out of control, and when you came in with the keys, having my car without my knowing. I guess it felt like one more thing that was happening *to* me."

This time, Max is the one grabbing my hand. When his fingers trace my palm, goosebumps erupt on my skin.

"I actually understand that more than you know. And I'm sorry too. I really meant it to be a nice gesture, one that meant we could be friends. But I see how it made you feel, and I apologize." There's such sincerity in his voice. His words don't seem calculated or manipulative—he seems genuinely good, and that in itself is foreign to me.

My dad abandoned us soon after I was born, and since then, trusting people hasn't come easy. Couple that with being in the professional sports world where anyone and everyone wants to use you for something—I don't make it a habit of letting people in.

"Can we call a truce?"

Max grins, still running his thumb over my palm. "Only if we can make a secret handshake while we do it."

"Nope. Nice knowing ya, Max." I push to stand, pulling my hands to my sides.

He follows suit, chuckling to himself. "Sadie, wait. Let me give you my number, just in case you need anything while you're in town. You never know when you might need a friend."

"Ugh, fine. But are you always this... this—" I swirl my arm in the air toward him.

"Lovable? Hilarious? Devastatingly handsome?" He slides the screen open on his phone and opens a blank text message, then holds it out to me. "The answer is yes to all of the above. Now, please send yourself a message so you can store my number."

I take the phone, type out a quick hello, input my number, and hit send. My phone buzzes in my pocket as I hand his back to him.

"See ya around, Max."

I cross the street and head down the sidewalk toward the back of the bar.

"Did you kiss and make up?" Mal coos as I turn the corner and walk into the alley behind Union Tavern. She must have been spying as she's pinned up against the edge of the brick.

"Has anyone ever told you that you're insufferable?" I smile at her and roll my eyes.

"So I shouldn't tell Seb that you chased after Max O'Reilly tonight?" My sister asks as if she's forgotten all about the reason I followed him, that I had to apologize.

I scoff at her lightly. "Yeah, actually, did I forget to tell you we're best friends now? Practically connected at the hip."

She looks at me out of the corner of her eye. "You know, I heard something about him recently." She pulls me close, slinging an arm around my shoulders. "He quit playing hockey."

"I know. There's a thing called the Internet, have you heard of it?"

She points her finger at me. "You like him."

"I do not. He's my friend, sorta."

She shakes her head and bounces on the balls of her feet, releasing me. "Nope, you think he's cute. And don't even act like you weren't fantasizing about those hands. I saw you." She twirls on one foot, spinning in a circle toward my car, the same way Magnolia does when she's excited.

"You should ask him to hang out."

"I'm not asking him a thing." I hold my hands up in surrender. "I'm just here to spend time with you, those sweet girls you have, and Mom." I hit the unlock button on my key fob.

Mal laughs. "Mmmk, we'll see how long that lasts," she says, pulling the handle on my car door open and sliding in. When I settle into the driver's seat, the car smells like him—I wish I hated it. "He's Mage Hollow royalty, you know? You could do a lot worse than spending your summer with Max O'Reilly. That family practically runs this town."

I put the key in the ignition and turn it. "Yeah, well, I'm busy. I've got Beth's puzzle book, remember."

"Oh please, you'll have that shit done in no time." She reaches across the center console and grabs my hand, but I shake her off. "What? You don't want to hold my hand? You didn't seem to have any problem holding Max's."

A groan slips between my lips as I ease my car out of the alley and onto the street. We walked over, so this is a convenient surprise being able to drive back the six blocks. "It wasn't like that, Mal. Drop it, please."

"No can do, sis. I have a photo of it and everything. Mom's gonna lose her mind, and Seb... maybe I should make a bet with him over this."

I roll my eyes. "If you've ever asked yourself why I don't visit more often—this is the reason."

"Sure. Did he give you his number?"

"He did. Not that I intend to use it."

Mal claps from the passenger seat, and I don't know why, but it makes me giggle. She's ridiculous, like an overjoyed mom whose daughter just got asked on a date with the prom king.

The truth is, I don't plan to text him. The only exception would be if I need something and there's literally no one else to call. He's nice, too funny for his own good, and charming as hell. But I don't have time for any of that. I only have time for solving Beth's clues and finding a way to get back to work.

Unless... maybe he could help me solve the next one like he unknowingly did the first time.

Max

Role Play

"Hunny, I'm home!" I push through the front door of Sam and Olive's house, kicking my shoes off.

"Back here!" Sam's voice floats through the open-concept home.

Making my way toward the back screen door, I notice all the little touches Olive has made. When Sam bought her this house, Bridget did the decor. Since then, it's become a little more lived in, with books scattered on the coffee table, wedding signs leaning against the wall near the fireplace, and about a million pairs of shoes scattered around. Olive is a clean freak, unless it comes to footwear.

I press my hand to the wood frame, slipping out onto the covered deck. Olive is perched on an iron chair, surrounded by what look to be lists—or maybe schedules—while Sam is sprawled out on a wicker loveseat with a beer in his hand.

"Should I have brought a Franklin Covey?" My brother laughs at my comment, knowing full well I've never owned a planner.

Olive huffs, grabbing a stack of the papers and tapping them on their glass tabletop. "Laugh it up, boys." She lays the same stack down on top of another pile. "You'll both be thanking me when this wedding goes off without a hitch."

Sam sits up, pursing his lips to stifle his laugh. "Babe, everything is going to be perfect." He motions for me to sit while widening his eyes at me. "Isn't that right, Max?"

I slide into a chair opposite my clearly stressed-out and soon to be sister-in-law. "Of course it is." I reach across the table and pat her hand. My eyes catch sight of her tattoo, one that she now cherishes, and my thoughts immediately go to Sadie. Could she really be cursed?

"Hey Ollie, I have a few questions about the wedding... and one that's completely unrelated."

Olive settles back further into her chair and grabs a wine glass that's full of sparkling water to take a sip. The girl has developed a serious addiction to Pellegrino recently—she's not pregnant, just fancy.

"Wedding first... so then I can stop thinking about it for the rest of the night."

I grin at Sam, wiggling my eyebrows. This may or may not be payback for all his heckling yesterday—or, my whole life. "Okay. So I was thinking about my role, and I'm wondering how Richard is going to take the news."

Her face twists in confusion. "What news?"

"Well, I mean, Sam said I could walk you down the aisle. I'm just wondering what your dad's going to do during that part."

My brother practically spits out his beer. "I did not say that, and you know it."

"Max, no. You're not—"

"Ollie, it's my dream. If I don't get to do that, then what will I do?" I put on my best impression of Benny, widening my eyes to the point that they water.

"You're the best man, Max. You'll be front and center with Sam the whole time." She looks between the two of us like she can't believe she's explaining this.

I bite the inside of my cheek, trying not to laugh. "Okay, so I get to make a speech then. Should it be at the rehearsal or during the reception?" I snap my fingers and point one at her. "Or actually, I could do both."

"No shot." Sam stands and moves to the table we're sitting at as he cuts off my request. It's brave honestly, the daggers she's throwing him could make the toughest guy cower. "Xav is making the speech since he doesn't get to be my best man."

I motion toward my chest, as if I'm pulling a dagger out of it—gutted twice in one night. "Say it with a little more disdain for your bloodline, would ya." I shake my shoulders out. "So no walking you down the aisle, no speeches... What is the point of my role again? I think we all know this day is about me. I need to be a star, Ollie."

A laugh rips out of my brother's fiancée. It's almost maniacal as she straightens her papers once more. Sam glares at me, not finding any of this funny.

"Oh, actually. I have something I need someone to do. It'll be the perfect job for you." Olive picks through her stacks, stopping once she finds a list titled: **Wedding Party**. "Do you want the most important job of all?"

"Ollie!" I slam my hand on my heart. "I can't marry you, sweetheart. But thanks for asking." I place my hand by my mouth, blocking Sam's view of my lips. "Remember the time we almost kissed? Spoiler alert... I do too!" I whisper shout.

"Shut up, idiot." Sam's face goes from a glare to downright murderous, while Olive rolls her eyes.

"Very funny, and that's exactly why you don't get to make a speech." She sips her drink once more. "I was serious, though. I have a very important question to ask you." Olive places her hand on top of mine. "Will you be one of my flower girls?"

"Do I get the biggest basket of petals?" I ask with zero hesitation.

Olive giggles, chancing a look at Sam, who's still not finding any of this funny. "Well, Sammy is the other one, and I'm pretty sure she can't even carry a rattle, so how about you get to carry her and throw all the petals."

"Sold!" I stand, pushing away from the table. "I'm going to grab a drink to celebrate. Does anyone need anything?"

My brother finally laughs but shakes his head no, and Olive points to her mostly full beverage. "Okay, cool. Be right back." I exit the porch, heading directly to the fridge inside, where I know I'll find a Diet Coke waiting just for me—and maybe a snack.

My fingers wrap around the stainless steel bar as I pull the French-door refrigerator wide open. These two have been shredding for the wedding, or so they say, but I'm pleasantly surprised by the leftover Chinese that greets me.

"Hey, Ollie!" I shout toward the back door, hoping she can hear me.

"Yes, Maxwell?" There's an edge of amusement in her tone. I'm sure she was expecting me to ask for something to eat once I was given a drink—like that mouse in the storybook my mom used to read to me, I always need something more.

My eyes scan the fridge again. "Is this lo mein old?"

My brother's heavy hand lands on my shoulder, causing me to jump. "Shit! Give a guy a heart attack, why don't you." I shake my head. "Not a good look to kill the best man and flower girl before the ceremony."

Sam chuckles, swatting my back a little too hard. "She bought that shit the second I told her you were coming over." He reaches around me, pulling out another beer. "I've had nothing but chicken and steamed broccoli for weeks. Can you get a girlfriend so my wife stops taking care of you?"

I grab the carton from the fridge and a fork from the drawer next to it. "No can do. I have everything I need right here."

Sam mumbles something under his breath, but I don't stick around to listen. Instead, I make my way to the safety that comes with being near Olive, and plop back down at the table outside.

"Ew, you're not even going to heat it up?" She sucks her teeth, her face turning mildly green. "What took you so long to get over here, anyway? I ordered it at six when I *thought* you were coming."

"Ewand," I attempt with a mouth full of noodles.

Sam walks past me, taking a spot next to Olive after sliding my drink in front of me. I forgot to grab it, but big brother knows what I like. I pop the tab on the crisp Diet Coke, using it to wash down the noodles.

"I sorta stole Sadie's car and had to return it."

"You did what?" My brother barks.

"I mean, it wasn't technically stealing. Howie asked me to take it from Sid and fix her flat tire, so I did." I wave my hand as if to say it's no big deal.

A smile forms on Olive's face, and now she's the one wiggling her eyebrows. "Who's Sadie?"

"Nope." I stop my fork halfway to my mouth. "Don't look at me like that."

"It's the cousin. Remember, I told you he ran into her at 1793 and then she beat him up." Sam laughs into his beer.

Olive follows suit, laughing to herself while widening her eyes at me. "Fixing her car seems like a *friendly* thing to do, and while I know you two"—she points between me and Sam—"have a history of saving stranded women. Why would she think you stole it?"

My mouth is full of lo mein, but I mumble my response at her anyway. "Sha din know."

"Stop!" Olive's hands fly to her face, covering her eyes. "She didn't ask for help... you just did it? You're a stranger, Max. You can't just take people's cars without telling them. Oh my God, Ari is going to die when I tell her."

Sam blows out a whirring breath. "Max, don't stick your nose where it doesn't belong." My big brother assumes I just inserted myself—normally, I would. But in this case I was asked.

Holding my hands up in surrender, I pause before delivering my rebuttal. "I didn't. I already told you that Howie asked me to. Did you really want me to deny him help? After all he's done for you two?"

"Well, no. Of course not." Olive sips her fancy water. "How did she take it? Is that why you're late?"

I push the empty lo mein container away from me, leaning back in my chair a little further. "Not great at first. But we talked it out. I think we're friends now, which is good considering—"

"Considering what?" Sam places both hands on the table, his interest finally piqued.

I roll my lips in, deciding the best way to break the news to them. Obviously, everyone survived what happened last year—Olive's probably better for it, to be honest. But that doesn't mean that either of them likes to discuss Irina or her whereabouts. It's sort of become one of those unspoken topics, and we all pretend it didn't happen most of the time.

"How told me he thinks she's cursed... like you were." I look at Olive, gauging her reaction before I continue. "Not by Irina, and not with a tattoo. But I guess she has sisters, the ones that own 1793."

Olive's face twists, and she wipes her forehead with the back of her hand. "Did he say how she's cursed? Did she ask for something, or what happened exactly?"

I shrug. "No, he didn't have any hard evidence. Said something about a book she has, and when she wrote something, the color of the ink changed." I take the final glug of my drink. "I can't really tell if he's just being cautious, but she opened up to me tonight about some other stuff. I'm going to keep an eye on it, but it's nothing either of you need to worry about."

I stand, grab my trash, and push my chair in. "I'm going to head out. But please keep that between us until I know more."

Olive nods, her face a mixture of confused and amused—like maybe she's as curious as I am.

"Yeah, bro. We will. Be careful though, we don't need you getting mixed up in anything like that." Sam's declaration makes me laugh. He didn't shy away from Olive when she had something similar going on. And we don't even know if there's anything real to this. Howie could just be being Howie. He's naïve in a lot of ways—it's not that far-fetched to think he'd jump to conclusions.

I toss my brother a nod, then leave. As I step up to my truck, my phone dings in my pocket.

Unknown

Hey, Friend...

It has to be from Sadie as she's the only person whose number isn't stored in my phone. Oh, and the message above it is the formal *Hello* she sent herself earlier.

> New phone, who dis?

I quickly store her number before she responds, adding all the descriptors I can think of.

Sadie/Smart/Witty/Maybe Cursed?

> Max!

> Weird, that's my name too.

Sadie/Smart/Witty/Maybe Cursed?

> That joke is old. You used it yesterday.

> Fair. What's up? Miss me already?

Sadie/Smart/Witty/Maybe Cursed?

> No… but I need help, and if I'm really trying this friend thing out… figured I'd give you a shot. ONE SHOT, to be clear.

> Alright, bet… I'm a lot of things, Sade, but a loser ain't one of them. Do your worst.

Sadie/Smart/Witty/Maybe Cursed?

Solve this clue, give me one word.

A very useful toolbox: Like a good neighbor.

I don't hesitate.

Statefarm

Sadie/Smart/Witty/Maybe Cursed?

That's two words, even if you smash them together and pretend it's not. Try again.

Thought I only got one chance?

While I wait for her response, I rack my brain for what the answer could be. I really thought I had it the first time, but overconfidence is a personality trait. It's probably something simple, like helpful. But wouldn't she have gotten that? I quickly Google synonyms for the word, but then decide to just go with my first instinct. I mean, that's what I'm doing here—being helpful to her.

Sadie/Smart/Witty/Maybe Cursed?

I'm feeling generous.

Helpful

Sadie/Smart/Witty/Maybe Cursed?

Thank you!

Eleven

Sadie

A Knight in Shining Armor

"Okay, ladies." I hitch the diaper bag higher onto my shoulder, trying not to squish Marigold's tiny hand where it rests on my side. She's strapped to my front, like a baby kangaroo hanging in its mother's pouch, sound asleep. "Let's grab our trash and head back to the car."

Lily collects the ice cream-soiled napkins from our table, while Poppy and Magnolia look at me like I'm speaking a foreign language.

"You can't expect others to clean up your mess... move it." I wave my hand at the girls and attempt a stern face. Instead of being intimidated, they fall into a fit of giggles, and Lily rolls her eyes.

Mallory started a candle company a few years ago—one that specializes in custom scents and branding for businesses. She called to say a new mercantile is considering placing a large order today, but only if she comes to their store, so I knew I needed to help. Sebastian is working, and Mom has a doctor's appointment—I'm the only viable option, but I didn't know what I was signing up for. What was supposed to be a quiet morning of reading followed by lunch and naps at home, turned into a bit of a shitshow.

Ten minutes after walking into the library, Marigold had a blowout, which resulted in the other girls running amuck while I changed her. Mrs. Rawlings, the head librarian, attempted to settle them for me, but when Poppy decided she no longer felt the need to wear clothes, we were asked to leave. Ice cream wasn't really a reward for them—it was more for me—a sugar cone with caramel pecan to save the day.

I swipe the lone napkin left in the holder and finish wiping the table before grabbing the two remaining bowls and depositing them in the trash. Turning to the three girls, I put my hands on my hips.

"Okay, we need to make it to the van with no issues or it's straight to bed at Grannie's." I blow out a breath, knowing that wrangling four kids while weaving through the event setup in Mage Square will not be ideal. Lobster Fest starts this coming weekend, and navigating the square was precarious the first go-round. That was two hours and three forklifts ago.

The girls stand from their seats, nodding that they understand. "Magnolia and Poppy, you need to hold hands the whole way. Lily will be our line leader, and Marigold and I will be the caboose." This makes them giggle uncontrollably.

"Aunt Sadie said caboose!" Magnolia shouts, shaking her booty around.

I glance around the parlor, only to be met with sympathetic eyes from worn mothers and a few frowns from the Red-Hat ladies. I nod at Lily, and she starts toward the door.

When we make it onto the sidewalk, the girls do as I instructed, and we head toward my sister's van. It's parked about two blocks down, and we don't need to cross the street—I've got this. Everything will be fine.

Lily leads the way, and my phone dings with an incoming email. I shouldn't look at it, but when the name in the sender box says *Levi*

Montgomery, my priorities shift. It's the first email from my boss in days, and I refuse to miss it.

"Poppy, no!" Magnolia shouts. "Aunt Sadie!" My gaze lands on Magnolia, her eyes wide with urgency, her hand dangling...empty. I turn my head, scanning the sidewalk for Poppy as my heart lurches into my throat. At the edge of the sidewalk, her bouncing blonde curls come into view between a truck and a car, and I dart after her.

"Stay put. Do not move a muscle!" I shout at the other two, who stand stock-still on the sidewalk.

Leaping across and slipping between the vehicles, I chase Poppy. A metallic purple balloon floats in front of her, drifting down the street with the breeze. I'm within five or six feet of her—out of breath from a lack of consistent exercise routine and the extra twenty-five pounds strapped to my chest—but she picks up her pace. For a girl with legs only a foot long, she's shockingly fast.

The balloon drifts further, rising in the air with each sweep of the wind. A motorcycle barrels toward Poppy, and I do what anyone would—I scream. "Poppy!"

Tires screech, and I squeeze my eyes shut tight, like I'm the one bracing for impact. The thrumming of the engine creates a steady cadence in my ears, but there's no crunch or crash. Snapping out of my hesitation, I open my eyes at the same time a familiar voice rings out.

"I got her, Sadie. She's all good."

Max.

My heart rate slows slightly, and my feet move. Max is carrying my niece and the stupid balloon that caused this mess toward the sidewalk. His muscular body shifts effortlessly with each step. When I reach them, I look to my other nieces and motion for them to join us—it's only twenty feet, but it feels like I'm watching them walk a mile.

"Oh my God, thank you." I glare at Poppy, but she curls her sweet little face into Max's neck, nuzzling the collar of his grey t-shirt. *Traitor*. "Poppy Ann. You scared me."

She looks up at me, tears glistening as they streak down her face. "I sowy, Aunt Adie." Reaching a hand out, I rub her back lightly before leaning entirely too close to Max to press a kiss to her forehead. His linen scent surrounds me—it's delightfully infuriating.

"Let's just get to the car and go home. Can we do that?" My tone is softer, knowing she's probably just as freaked out as I am. She's practically a baby still. I should have known better than to take my eyes off her for even a second.

Max nods, then motions with his arm for me to lead the way. Poppy's still snug against him, clutching his bicep with one hand and the balloon with the other.

Our group walks in silence, making it to the van in a matter of minutes. I unlock it, and the sliding door opens for the girls to pile in. Lily hops in first, helping Magnolia get into her seat. Carefully, so I don't knock Marigold into anything, I lean in and secure Mag's five-point harness the way Mal demonstrated. Lily buckles her own seat belt across her booster, leaving only two.

Max places Poppy into her seat, carefully holding the balloon string between his teeth while he works the buckle closed and tightens it. He hands her the balloon, tucking it inside so it doesn't blow away. "You'd better be a good girl for your aunt, Pop."

Poppy's cheeks turn pink, and her eyes sparkle. I get it—that charming little smirk he's giving her is deadly. I'm glad it's not trained on me, because while I haven't been looking at him in that way, adrenaline *is* coursing through me, making it hard to think straight. Max, with a small child in his arms, does weird things to my hormones—it would to anyone.

Taking a step back from the van, I reach behind my head to undo the carrier like Mal showed me. It should be simple, but these things always look easier than they are. My fingers can't seem to grab the buckle, despite having done the same thing earlier when I changed her.

"Do you need help?" Max steps around me, standing at my back.

"Yes, please." I release a shaky breath. "I buckled it myself, so I don't know why I can't reach it now."

His hands gently move my hair over my shoulder, and his fingertips dance lightly across the back of my neck as he works to unfasten it. Goosebumps pebble on my skin from the contact, but in a matter of seconds the carrier loosens, and nothing but the sticky summer breeze replaces his hands.

I work quickly, softly setting Marigold in her car seat and buckling it tight. She sleeps through the entire transfer, small puffs of air blowing from her pouty lips. There's a second where her mouth moves in a sucking motion, so I quickly tuck her pacifier in and close the door quietly.

When I turn to round the car, Max is still waiting on the sidewalk.

"Thank you for saving me today."

"You mean Poppy?" He smirks.

I roll my lips in. "No, I mean me. My sister would have killed me if something had happened to her, and I would've deserved it for not paying close enough attention."

Max steps closer, his feet inches from mine. "Don't mention it." His jaw tightens slightly. "You can't be perfect all the time."

I roll my eyes. "I can try to be."

He shrugs. "Sure, I guess. But that's going to make for a pretty big letdown one day."

"I'll survive." I turn, taking one step toward the front of the vehicle when Max grabs my arm.

Whipping my head back, I realize just how close we are, and my breath stutters. "What—"

"Just figured if you're aiming for perfection, I shouldn't let you walk around with caramel on your face." He pulls his thumb between his lips, wetting the pad, then quickly runs it along the corner of my mouth.

My body short-circuits, tingles race in every direction, and breathing becomes difficult. Max smirks, a dimple popping in his cheek unfairly.

"See you around, Sade."

This time he walks away, and I stand next to my sister's van dumbstruck as he goes. Texting him for help was a bad idea—just as bad as continuing to have these little interactions. Max O'Reilly is a distraction... one I'm starting to look forward to a little more than I should.

"Any plans today?" Mom asks, sliding into the rocking chair next to me.

I slip my bookmark into my latest read and look over at her. I've stayed close to home since the incident with Poppy, not sure what else to do with my time and not wanting to run into a specific someone. I wouldn't say I'm avoiding him altogether, but I just can't stop replaying our latest encounter.

There was something a little different about Max—a quieter confidence. Each time I've talked to him, there's been an air of flirting—that's his M.O. But the last time, he seemed to take up more space.

Maybe it was just the situation, but between that and the book that has continued to follow me around, I can't seem to shake the feeling that I'm safest not straying too far outside my comfort zone.

"Nope. Just reading, and thinking I'll do some research for work later." Opening my book, I scan the page, attempting to find my spot.

Mom makes a clicking sound with her tongue. It's not a tsk really, but there's a shame-filled undertone to the noise. "You're not supposed to be working."

"And?" I bite the inside of my cheek.

"And have you considered attempting what Levi suggested?" Her face puckers as if the words tasted sour coming out.

I grab my water, taking a long drink before responding. "How would you suggest I do that? The puzzles? Some late-night partying with people I barely know?" My tone is snarky—not all that respectful. But like everyone else, my mom has latched onto the idea that there's something wrong with me, something broken.

"Sadie, come on." She's obviously perturbed by my lack of effort. "Can't you just give something a try? Beth generously gave you that... maybe it would be a good distraction."

"I've solved two clues." The words are out before I can stuff them back in. I've been avoiding talking about it because there's so much I can't explain—it follows me, weird signs appear in unexpected places, like my coffee, and the ink changes color when I get an answer correct.

Mom's face illuminates, a sprinkle of hope evident. "What were the answers?"

I set my book down on the table, spinning so my body faces hers. "Altruistic and helpful."

"That's interesting."

I raise an eyebrow and stare at her. "Is it?"

"I think so. Traits maybe? About you, probably." Her assessment isn't all that convincing as the clues aren't about me. Beth said they would lead me to something—if anything, they're things I need to become.

"Doubtful." I push myself to stand, grabbing my water bottle and book. "I'll be in my room."

"Some things never change," Mom grumbles, and I roll my eyes.

She's not wrong—I've always enjoyed the solace of my quiet spaces. This time though, I simply need to escape a conversation that's bound for nowhere. I told myself that I'd take control of the book, solve the clues on my own terms. And for the most part, I have. *With Max's unknowing assistance.*

I step slowly through the house, depositing my glass in the kitchen sink. Out of the corner of my eye, I can see the leftover mess from when Mom babysat the girls earlier. Paper plates with sandwich crusts lingering, strawberries half eaten, and that damn balloon that caused all my problems the other day. Grabbing the trash from the counter, I begin cleaning up. It's a small gesture—look at me, being helpful already. With the majority of the garbage in hand, I press my foot to the pedal at the bottom of the wastebasket and toss the pile inside. Spinning to collect the rest, I come face to face with Poppy's balloon.

The metallic purple has cracked at the seams, and the helium has started to lose its strength. But the most notable thing is that where minutes ago it had a giant number 2 in the middle with the words *too cool to be one* beneath it, it now says: *always better than one* under the number.

For the love of all that's holy!

Snatching a pair of scissors out of the junk drawer, I slice into the Mylar, and the balloon deflates to a shriveled-up sack. Collecting the remains, I toss them in the trash and head straight to my bedroom.

Walking in, the only thing waiting for me is the puzzle book opened to the third page.

Twelve

Max

Go Touch Grass

Sadie/Smart/Witty/Maybe Cursed?

Hey, are you busy?

Why? Someone wander into the street again? Or are you trapped in the baby carrier?

Sadie/Smart/Witty/Maybe Cursed?

Neither, actually. But I wanted to run something by you.

I'm headed to the dog park.

Sadie/Smart/Witty/Maybe Cursed?

Max O'Reilly… Do you have a dog?

> Nah. I'm just one of those creepy dudes who hang out at the park to play with other people's pets.

I laugh as I scroll through my photo album, looking for the perfect picture of Benny and me to send her. My phone buzzes in my hand.

Sadie/Smart/Witty/Maybe Cursed?

> That feels shockingly believable, actually.

I find the one I was searching for. It's a photo of Benny and me cuddled up on the couch. Do I need to be in the picture to get the point across—no. But do I sort of want her to see me with him—yes. I send it, not stopping to assess the weight of the decision.

Sadie/Smart/Witty/Maybe Cursed?

> SHUT UP! I'm in love.

> Feels a little fast to be making those kinds of declarations, Sade. But I really like you too.

Sadie/Smart/Witty/Maybe Cursed?

> Max! I meant the dog.

> Okay, rip my heart out then. Benny is great, though. Very lovable. Are you coming to meet him?

I push open the gate, sliding my thumb down the lock as we make our way into the park. Mage Hollow has always been pet-friendly, but in the past few years they've made several upgrades to this area—Benny loves them all except for the grass-covered ones. Reaching down, I disconnect the leash from his collar, and my buddy takes off, tearing down the paved sidewalk until he finds a series of tunnels to race through.

"Hi Max!" Cindy, a bleach blonde dog park regular, waves from a few yards away where she's perched on the bench of a picnic table.

I lift my hand, returning the gesture. Instead of walking over and chatting with her like I do every Friday afternoon, I wait by the gate for Sadie. A few minutes pass, and I watch Benny as he races around the paved areas. He pushes a ball toward Cindy's pug. Buster just looks at him and walks away. Benny follows him, but when Buster trots into the grass, I swear he turns around and smirks at Benny. Can a dog be an asshole? Because if they can, then Buster definitely is—he was smug, prancing away knowing Benny won't follow.

"Still not touching grass?" Cindy's saccharine voice sneaks up beside me.

"What?" I bark out, glaring at her jerk dog and my sweet one still pacing the edge like he's contemplating trying it out.

I get that it's a weird thing for a dog not to like, and it even frustrates me most of the time. Benny is an angel, though, and he deserves a better friend. *Jesus, I'm acting like he actually is my baby.* Maybe Xav was right, and I need to get a grip.

"I asked if he was still refusing to touch the grass," Cindy repeats, judgement in her tone.

I grumble quietly. "Yeah. We're working on i—"

The gate behind me unlatches, bringing a sweet peach scent with it, and Benny takes off, racing toward me. He veers left, steering around Cindy and me, plowing through the grass like it's never been an issue. As I spin, a woman with long chocolate hair and a flowy green dress is bent over, picking him up.

Sadie.

"Oh my gosh, you're such a sweet boy." Sadie's voice is melodic, and something about the way she's cuddling my puppy makes me feel... things. Her eyes lift, searching for mine. "Max, how could you keep him from me?"

I hear Cindy scoff as her feet slap the pavement walking away.

I run a hand through my hair, smiling at Sadie. "How did you just do that?"

She's back to staring at Benny, running her hand along the back of his head and nuzzling her face into his. "Do what?"

"He doesn't like grass. He's never touched it. Why did he run to you like that?" I shift on my feet. I'm happy it happened, but did she wave a dog bone around or something? I've been bribing him for weeks, and nothing has helped.

"I just waved at him." She kisses his wrinkly face again, and I feel oddly jealous for the first time in a long time. "What do you mean he doesn't like it? Is this one of those insults like, *hey you need to go touch grass*?"

Her sarcasm makes me laugh. "No, like he literally won't walk in it." A couple with three dogs enters through the gate, so I reach for Sadie's elbow, steering her out of the walkway. "I've tried to get him to go in my yard a million times, but he refuses... or I should say *did*—until you came along."

"That's interesting." A shiver runs through her, and I notice goosebumps pebbling on her skin near my fingers, still wrapped around her arm. I squeeze gently, and the subtle shake of her shoulders happens again. *Maybe I'm not the only one affected here.*

The last week has been different for me. I'm not a stranger to dating, or even a random hookup. But since Sadie blew into town, I haven't been able to get her off my mind. I've been chalking that up to my curious nature and the mystery surrounding her. But whenever I spend time with her, I leave feeling lighter, dare I say happier than I have in a long time. She's sassy—the mouth on this one is brutal—but she's also pragmatic, funny as hell, and there's something just so attractive about her. It's an effortless beauty, not overstated or glaring. She's pretty, poised, as if she thinks through every piece of her aesthetic but does it so quickly no one notices.

"Do you want to sit down?" The question comes out gravelly.

"Oh, sure." I take Benny from her arms, whispering in his ear about how proud I am. "Should we go to a table so he can play with his friends?" she asks, and my heart triples in size. Sadie cares about Benny spending time with his friends, and I think I might have just tumbled off the edge of a cliff that I shouldn't have been anywhere near.

We walk to a table on the other side of the park, one far enough away from Cindy that our conversation will remain only ours. I sit Benny down, his tiny fur-covered paws landing on a fluffy patch of green. Waiting for the yelp that usually comes, I remove my hands slowly, backing away.

Benny picks up one foot, angling his head to the side as if he's unsure. Instead of glancing in my direction for approval, he looks to Sadie. She smiles at him, all straight white teeth and rosy cheeks—it's a stunning sight. My dog practically leaps through the air, more confident from one look from her than he's ever been, and charges toward Buster, who's playing happily with a ball.

I slide onto the picnic table bench, sitting next to her so that we can watch him together. There's space between us, but the pull to scooch closer is strong. "I still can't believe this is happening."

Sadie laughs. "I mean, I never thought I had a gift with animals, and this seems like normal dog behavior..."

My gaze shifts to the side of her face. I can't help noticing her hair as it whirls in the breeze, and a stray piece that's slightly curled sticks to her cheek. There's a smattering of freckles along the bridge of her nose, and a small gold stud in her ear—simple, understated.

"Take the win." My voice is barely above a whisper, so I clear my throat and shake my shoulders. "What did you, uh... want to talk about?"

"Is that one his friend or no?" Sadie nods her head toward Benny and Buster. They're fighting over a ball, and it looks like Buster's back on his bullshit.

"That one is an asshole"—I point at Buster—"he's always taking stuff from him. And before today, pulling it into the places that Benny wouldn't go."

Sadie cracks up, laughing so hard she's clutching her chest. I raise an eyebrow, not sure what's hilarious about it. "*She's* a bitch. Probably not unlike her owner."

"Wait, what?"

"Buster is a girl, Max. Not very difficult to see that... and that means she's, you know, a bitch." Her eyes widen meaningfully.

"Who the fuck names a girl dog, Buster?" I chuckle to myself, not believing that I never noticed.

Sadie shrugs, twirling a piece of hair between two fingers absentmindedly. "Glad I could clear more than one thing up for you today." She turns her attention toward me, smiling at me the same way she did to Benny earlier—it's breathtaking.

"What did you need help with today?" I ask again, reaching to brush the stray hair off her cheek without thinking. My fingers tingle when they touch her skin, and her mouth opens slightly when she inhales.

There's a moment of silence that passes between us, eyes locked like we both feel something we haven't allowed ourselves to consider—until now.

"So you know how I told you about my job..."

"Yeah, do you need a reference or something?" I blurt, too eager to help.

Sadie smirks. "Um, no. But thank you." She fiddles with her hands, staring at her fingers as they roll over themselves. "Some strange things have been happening, and I just... I need to work them out before my leave is over."

"Strange how?" I lean my elbow onto the picnic table and inch my upper body toward her.

Her cheeks warm to a light pink, and she chances a glance at me. "Do you believe in magic? Like the paranormal kind, where things can't be explained."

A wave of awareness settles into my bones. Maybe Howie wasn't lying. "If you'd asked me that question six months ago, I would have said no." I spin my hat backward. "But now... I do."

Sadie visibly shifts through a range of emotions: shock, followed by fear, then something close to relief in her features.

"Can I ask what changed? Like, why now?" She chews her bottom lip, her eyes trained on me.

"My sister-in-law was cursed last fall." I scan the park, making sure Benny is still good before continuing. "She went to a tarot shop uptown—"

"When did we get one of those?"

I laugh at her interruption. "We didn't. Irina sought Olive out at the Hollow Hearts Festival. She asked to wear her heart on her sleeve, or so I'm told. I wasn't there." Sadie leans in closer, enraptured by the story. "She ended up with a tattoo on her arm that changed with her thoughts and feelings. It was pretty crazy and definitely threw Sam for a loop."

Sadie gasps, covering her pouty lips with her hand. "Is she... how is she now?"

"Ollie is fine. She found the Irina lady on Halloween and asked her to undo it."

"Irina... like Beth's sister?"

I shrug. "Guess so... although I didn't know she had any."

"That's what I'm saying!" Sadie shouts, standing abruptly to pace in front of me. Her emerald dress whips with each step she takes, and her chest heaves above the cinched top. "Sorry, continue." She waves her hand at me.

"There's not really much else. She reconnected with my brother. It was a whole weird breakup thing... and the tattoo came back, but it's a permanent picture of their love story."

Sadie takes her seat next to me once more, this time close enough that our thighs touch. "But like, she's fine... so if someone was in a similar situation, she would probably tell them to roll with it? Hypothetically, of course."

I narrow my eyes at her. "Olive is fine, but I think she'd tell you she only got through it because she has great friends like Howie... and me."

I reach out and wrap my hand around hers. "If you need help, Sade, all you need to do is ask."

Thirteen

Sadie

Let's Make A Deal

How can I ask for help when I'm not sure exactly what I'm dealing with? The puzzles themselves aren't the problem. It's all the other complications that feel impossible to explain. He said he has experience, though, and that in itself gives me hope.

Max squeezes my hand gently, his gaze encouraging me to spill all my secrets. My skin itches under the intensity, as this isn't what I do. I don't ask for help. I'm more of a figure it out myself or die trying kind of girl. Not to mention the way my heart flutters each time he looks at me... like I'm someone he's starting to adore.

"It's Beth—"

Max inhales deeply.

"She's my friend."

"Okay? Didn't see that coming..." he spins his hat so it's facing forward again, and I wish he didn't. Max in a backward hat is a sight to behold.

"Like a best friend, she's been in my life forever. And when I came home, she gave me this." I reach into my bag, pulling out the leather-bound book.

Max holds his hands out, and I drop it into them. His fingers trace the embossed title before he unties the knot holding it closed. I watch as he flips to the first page, and his eyes widen when he sees the word altruistic in gold lettering. Max flips through a couple more silently. When he reaches the back, his hand runs along the letter tucked there—the one *he* gave me in the parking lot.

He sucks his teeth. "Is this? Did I give you—"

"Yes, that's just one of the bizarre things. She gave me the book, but there wasn't a letter until you handed it to me. I mean, to be honest, the book wasn't even in my bag until you ran into me."

"I didn't run into you," Max challenges.

"Whatever, you know what I mean. It wasn't with me, Max." I chew my lip, waiting for him to grasp what I'm saying. "I think it's hexed. It keeps showing up in places, the words change color when I solve the clues, and some other strange things. Beth said if I solve these, I'll find my fate. I'm not sure I believe that... but it won't stop taunting me. I figure I either take control, or it controls me, you know?"

Max's lips tip up into his signature flirty smirk. "Are you into that? Giving up control, Sade?"

"Max," I warn, trying to tamp down the sudden heat that's racing through me. Is he trying to suggest? He'd be surprised to learn *I've had nothing better than vanilla if so.*

"I'm kidding"—his face suggests otherwise, and I don't hate the idea—"so what do you need me to do? Or did you just want someone else to know?"

I look out across the park, spotting Benny as he leaps from the top of one of the doggie tunnels, a look of pure joy on his face, pure freedom. It may sound bizarre to compare myself to a dog, but if I'm taking anything from Levi's endless nagging and Beth's meddling, it's that I don't ever just take the leap. Maybe it's time I do, even if it's small.

Taking a deep inhale for courage, I settle my gaze back on Max. "The first two clues were solved by you. One was because I thought of our conversation at the lighthouse, and the second was when I texted you." I flip the pages and show him both clues before pulling the letter out of the back. Unfolding it, I use my finger to point at the hint that reads: two is always better than one. "I had already figured out the word helpful, but it wouldn't change color until you texted me. I think this means I'm supposed to have help, that maybe I can't do it alone."

Benny rushes over to us, panting until Max takes out a collapsible bowl from his pocket and pours some water into it. "So you need me. I'm honored, Sade, truly." He leans forward, petting Benny's head. "It's gonna cost you though."

"What?" *He can't be serious.*

Max laughs, scooping Benny up into his lap. The adorable pup crawls over to me, working his way up my chest to nuzzle my neck. "I have my own opinion about what you need..."

A scoff slips out of me. "And that would be what, exactly?"

"Fun, experiences, memories." His arms swing out wide like he's showing me the world in front of me. "I'll make you a deal. One clue solved for every fun thing we do together."

"I don't know. I mean, what if you aren't even the person I need for this? It could have been a coincidence the first two times..." It's not that I don't want to work with him, as I'm the one asking. But I didn't expect it to come with stipulations, and I'm not sure spending more time with Max O'Reilly is a good idea. If the constant buzzing under my skin and flutter in my chest are any indication—spending time with him has the potential to hurt when I inevitably leave.

"I'll give you a freebie then. You got Benny boy to do something I haven't been able to. Seems like a fair trade—"

"And a way to prove my theory wrong." I laugh, sarcasm dripping from my tongue.

"Potatoh, Potahto. You scared?"

I flip the book open to the third puzzle, not willing to back down from a challenge, and together we look at the clue.

12. Down

When pinched: A descriptor for someone who powers through.

"Okay, so it's eight letters, maybe credible or unfailing." I close my eyes, trying to think. It would be a lot easier if he weren't staring at the side of my face. "No, those have too many letters. It could be—"

"Reliable."

"What, how did you..." I shake my head, pulling a pencil from my purse. He was always smart. It was the most frustrating thing about tutoring him—I always wanted him to simply apply himself, but hockey came first. "I was getting there, must be beginner's luck," I say under my breath.

Max points at his chest. "Nah. I'm just that good, Sade. Looks like you need me after all." He stands abruptly, clipping Benny's leash to his collar and grabbing him to place him on the ground. "I've got to get going, but let me know when you decide you're willing to take my deal. I promise it'll be fun."

Max winks before walking away, and I scribble in the letters, waiting to see if the lead changes color. When gold melts onto the page, I can't deny I need his help. He has experience where I don't. He's not completely freaked out by the notion that magic is real... that some things really aren't in our control. I just have to reconcile how much I want it, how much these quick exits we keep making from each other affect me, and how I can work with him without my heart thinking it means more than it does.

"Mal!" I call, walking into my sister's home.

It smells like too many candles are burning, a mixture of vanilla, patchouli, and man? The smell is pungent, not a blend I'd buy—even from her.

"Back here," my sister's voice cracks as it drifts from her workroom.

Tossing my bag on the couch, I don't bother slipping out of my shoes as something is clearly wrong. Stepping quickly down the hallway, the scent intensifies, making my eyes water. I push the swinging door open and take in the sight laid out before me.

This room is supposed to be a pantry, or maybe a laundry room, but right now the ten by ten space is littered with several broken jars, melted wax dripping from a few surfaces sporadically, and Mal—crumpled on the floor.

"Oh my God. What happened? Are you okay?"

Her tear-stained face rises, splotches of red mixed with black streaks from her mascara running down it.

She groans, shaking her head from left to right. I carefully step around the broken glass, finding a bare spot next to her to kneel.

I grab her hand, gently squeezing. "Mal, what's going on?"

"I lost the job." She sniffs into her free hand. "The store I met with chose another vendor."

"Okay?"

"I know this seems like an overreaction... it's just that I try so hard to balance it all. Sales are in the trash, and apparently my dreams are too." Mal pulls her hand from my grip and wipes her face. "They said that they needed to bet on someone whose sole focus was their business... they didn't choose me because I'm 'stretched too thin'... because I'm a mom."

I push back to standing. This is unlike my sister. She never backs down from a fight, never cowers. But if there's anything I understand, it's fighting for what you want, what you deserve.

"Wow, okay. So Mallory Hayes is a quitter. Good to know, because Mallory Wells would never give up and trash her workspace because some hipster jerkoff underestimated her." I should probably be more understanding, as it wasn't long ago that I was the one having a meltdown, but this is bullshit, and sometimes tough love is exactly what we need.

"Fuck off, Sade." My sister joins me and stands. "You have no idea what it's like juggling all of this."

A laugh bubbles out of me, and it's as half-hearted as her excuse. "Yep. You're right, no clue what it takes to give up everything to chase my dreams just to have it all ripped away. Those eighty-hour weeks worked themselves," I spit back sarcastically.

"That's not the same!"

"Isn't it? I have a career that's my whole life, and I love it. You have kids to care for, a husband who loves you, your family, and your business. Just because one leg of that four-legged stool cracked doesn't mean it's falling over." I begin picking up broken glass and laying it on her worktable. "What would you tell the girls if this were happening to them? Hell, what did you tell me just a few days ago?"

Mal grabs a broom from the corner of the room, sweeping chunks of glass into a dustpan. I scooch behind her, grabbing the wax remover to wipe the counters. We work in silence, gathering the mess and disposing of it as if nothing ever happened. It's funny, really. A part of me wishes that cleaning up all of life's messes was this simple—that I could toss a book I don't need in the trash and it would stay there, or that I could explain to Levi, wipe my eyes, and move forward.

When twenty minutes have passed and the just-trashed space is sparkling clean, Mal dips down to grab two waters from her mini fridge. She slips onto a stool and pushes one of the cold, clear bottles toward me with a nod. Following her lead, I slip onto the round chair beside her and crack the drink open.

"I guess you're right. I'm sorry you had to see this. Sorry that you had to help me clean up." She takes a long pull of her water, clearing her throat after downing the cold liquid. "The weight of carrying it all... it's crushing me. And I think I'm about two days away from my luteal phase. I just needed to smash something, cry a little, and maybe buy some chocolate chip cookies."

I get where she's coming from. I've felt that way too. Like, no matter what steps you take, you're stuck in quicksand with no way forward. It's paralyzing, and in those moments, the ones where the walls are closing in and oxygen feels scarce—we panic.

"Mal, I'm always going to be here. I want to help you. I know—"

"What it feels like? I'm worried about you, Sade." She stops peeling the wrapper on the bottle she's holding and grabs both of my hands. "Like you said, my stool has four legs, but yours only has one."

Damn. I didn't expect her to reverse that on me, but she's right. Maybe they're all right. Maybe I need to find some other legs for my stool. Maybe learning to have fun again would be a start.

"Ugh, fine!" I throw my hands in the air. "I'm doing the stupid puzzle book. And I-sorta-asked-Max-to-help-me-do-it," I rush out.

Mal laughs, bouncing up and down in glee. I swear to God, her emotions give me whiplash sometimes. "Shut up! You did not!"

I nod. "I did, and do you know what he said?" My eyes drift to my shoes as thoughts of Max make my heart flutter. "He said he'd only help me if I agreed to do one fun thing with him for every clue we solve."

"Stop, that's so cute." Mal returns to sweeping, getting the last of the broken pieces from the floor. "You're doing it right? Letting loose and having some fun with the prince of Mage Hollow?"

"I am now. I hope I don't regret it."

Fourteen

Max

Tossing Salads

The day has come—my favorite one of the entire year, aside from my birthday—Mage Hollow's Annual Lobster Festival. It's really more of a weekend-long thing, but Saturday is the main event, and I fully intend to stuff myself with every type of seafood available as soon as I'm done helping my mother.

Mabel always has a booth. I guess years of being named *Queen of the Claw* have earned her all of Mage's respect—that and the secret sauce she makes for her lobster rolls. While my mom is famous in the fall for her pumpkin tortellini, nothing tops what she's serving today.

"Max, watch where you're going." Mabel crosses her arms and taps her foot as I maneuver the booth with a fifty-pound tub of what I call lobster salad. It's really just the meat, celery, and scallions, but the way we toss it in the sauce right before serving is what I imagine they do with my leafy greens at Union Tavern before dishing it out—a perfect coating on each piece.

"I got it, Ma." I place it down in the cooler, right alongside the five others I've carried in. "Thanks for the help, bro," I say to Sam through gritted teeth. He's apparently made himself the king of opening and closing the cooler while I do all the heavy lifting.

"Can someone take this?" Nora, my sister, calls, her small arms wrapped around a jar of Mom's sauce that's so big it covers most of her slight frame.

My dad grabs it, stepping away from his designated job of placing red and white checkered tablecloths on each of the ten picnic tables in front of our booth.

This is the largest setup we've ever had. We have multiple coolers, four tables for serving, and plenty of seating for our guests, all arranged underneath a jumbo white tent. But it's not that different from every other setup. Every vendor here takes this event seriously, and *each* one believes this could be the year they steal the crown—they're obviously delusional.

Unlike Hollow Hearts, we don't get to ditch the booth immediately after setup is finished. Mabel makes most of us stick around until the lunch rush has dwindled—this year even Ari and Howie got roped into helping. Mom convinced Howie with the promise of a freshly baked pie all to himself, but Ari, I assume, is here with Olive. They've been best friends since college, and with the recent distance between her and my red-headed friend... I can't imagine he asked her.

"Okay, all that's left is to put the flowers on the tables. Ma, are you okay if we take a coffee break?" Bridget asks, carefully carrying a box full of yellow vases brimming with pink, orange, and purple zinnias.

Mom wrinkles her nose, looks around the booth, then to her checklist. "I suppose. But you all better be back here with hairnets on in..." She glances at her watch. "Forty-three minutes."

I smother the smirk that's trying to sneak onto my face, and instead turn to my brother, tossing him a nod toward the Brewhouse. The group of us make our way down the cobbled sidewalk, steps quickening as the scent of freshly brewed beans wafts in the air. Sam's the first one to the door, pulling it open as our hoard trails in.

Howie snags a round oak table near the back, grabbing a few chairs to make sure we can all fit. In what feels like minutes, a smooth iced black coffee is sliding down my throat, the caffeine buzzing in my veins. I'm surrounded by my family, all four O'Reilly kids accounted for, along with Olive, Howie, and Ari, who's noticeably a little closer to my friend than she needs to be.

"So, Max, any more run-ins with Howard's cousin that beat you up?" Bridget points at my face, where my black eyes have turned to more of a greenish-yellow.

I sip my drink, not sure how much I should share. "Yeah, she met Benny and me at the dog park yesterday." I shrug, making eye contact with Howie across the table.

Howie nods, his eyes widening. He can't seriously want *me* to spill the beans. "Did she tell you anything?"

"Uh," I hesitate.

"Max, she must have told you something," Howie doubles down, running a hand along his stubbled jaw.

"Something about what, Howard? Stop being so suspicious." Ari swats his arm, and his cheeks turn pink from the contact.

"Ari!" Olive whines. "Let Max answer."

All eyes turn toward me like I'm the one with all the information when at least three people at this table already have a hunch about what's going on.

"Yeah, she did." I run a hand through my hair. "She showed it to me."

Howie looks shocked. "She did?"

"Why do you seem surprised? You literally just forced me into saying it."

"I guess I just thought it would take longer for her to—"

Ari huffs, nearly slamming her coffee cup on the table. "To what? Does the girl have a secret or something? We're all on the edge of our seats here."

Bridget and Nora fall into easy laughter, bystanders in this entire conversation. They know what happened to Olive last fall because Sam and I sort of fell into telling them one night over beers at the cabin. I thought at the time they'd be shocked, but both of my sisters seemed completely unfazed.

"Okay, okay. But keep your voices down. This isn't something that can leave this group." I take a long pull of my drink and lean forward, my elbows digging into the table. "Sadie has this book. It's filled with puzzles that are almost all completed—"

Bridget claps. "Let me guess, you volunteered to let her use your special pencil to solve them." Her eyebrows wiggle up and down with innuendo.

"No, Jesus, Bridg." I let out a steadying breath. "She thinks it's cursed or something. Every time she solves a clue, the word changes to gold script on the page. Oh and Beth, the owner of 1793, is the one who gave it to her. She said something about learning her fate."

Nora pushes away from the table. "At least it's not her arm this time." She walks toward the restroom in the back hallway.

"Wait a minute"—Ari crosses her arms over her chest—"I know I'm not finding out for the second time in this coffee shop that someone we know is cursed." Her gaze darts to Olive in a pointed stare.

Howie brushes his hand down her arm, and she visibly relaxes. "Ari, you are." He smiles at her softly. "Sorry to break it to you."

"No fucking way. Isn't it possible this is just like some weird color-changing ink?"

I can't stop laughing. "Nope, I suggested that too. The weirdest part is that Beth is Irina's sister." Ari hisses at the name. Last year wasn't just hard on Olive, Ari was in it with her from the very beginning.

"How can that even be possible? We've been going to that diner for years." Bridget sips her drink, skeptical as ever.

Sam remains stoic, and Olive picks her fingernails.

"I did always think it was weird how the woman never aged. I mean, give me your skincare routine, lady." Ari makes herself laugh.

"None of that matters." I run a hand through my hair and check my phone for the time. "We need to get back, and you *all* need to remember this is a secret. If you see her today, don't say anything. I'm handling it."

Nora returns, and our group begins clearing the table. When we exit the coffee shop to head back to Mom's tent, my sisters slide up next to me, one on each side.

"Maxie-pad," Bridget coos, using the nickname I've learned to love but obviously hate.

"You like this girl, huh?" Nora elbows me gently.

I keep walking, not answering them. I'm starting to, but they don't need to know that before she does.

"Max, I need three rolls for Mr. House. Extra sauce," my mom calls from the other end of the line.

We've been working non-stop for about an hour, I'm sweating in a way that feels unsanitary, and the line of people waiting doesn't seem to be getting any shorter. Mabel has received all sorts of comments, some begging for the recipe, and some wondering when she'll step aside and let someone new win the title. The answer is never—she lives for this shit.

I haven't spotted Sadie or her sister Mal, but that's not saying much since I've barely moved two feet from this assembly line.

Sam hands me a basket and holds the buttered top-split rolls open for me. Carefully spooning the lobster mixture into each, I grab it and hand it off to the gentleman who ordered it at the same time that Beau, Olive's boss and the owner of Black Kettle Bindery, approaches with a... stroller?

My sister-in-law's voice rings out from a few feet down. "Hi Mr. Pickles. I can't believe your dad is finally using the Christmas gift I bought him."

Beau's cheeks turn rosy, but his eyes narrow at his employee. "He has a very busy schedule, Olivia. We've been over this."

She laughs, taking his order and leaning over the table to pet the unamused black cat. Sam and I quickly prepare a roll for Beau and a side of plain lobster meat for Mr. Pickles—my brother rolling his eyes the entire time.

As I go to hand him their meals, he smiles at me mischievously. "Hello, Maxim." I shake my head. He knows that's not my name. "Are you free this week? I have several boxes being delivered on Tuesday."

"It's Max... Maxwell if we're being official." I smile at him. "And yes, I should be free. I'm planning a beach day at some point, but nothing is set in stone."

He nods. "Be there Tuesday at seven. Not a minute later." He walks away, not waiting for a response, and my mother's suddenly high-pitched voice coasts across the space.

"Oh, hello, Sadie. Is this your family?" She knows her family already, but leave it to Mabel to make a big show of things.

My eyes dart to the other end of the line where my mom, sisters, and Olive are gathered around, practically vibrating with excitement.

They're so embarrassing.

Even so, I listen for her response.

"Yes, good to see you, Mrs. O'Reilly. You probably remember my mom Dee Dee, and this is Mal, my sister. Can we please have eight lobster rolls, four juice boxes, and four sodas?"

Bridget scribbles down the order, passing the slip to Sam as Olive and Nora grab the drinks.

"Wow, where are the kids? I bet they've grown since the last time I saw them. How long's it been?"

Mallory chimes in, "a few months, I think. Poppy isn't keen on wearing clothing, so we don't make it out of the house very often."

That makes my mom double over in laughter, while I don't miss the dirty look Sadie gives her sister. *I wonder what that's about?*

"Well, we'll bring them a special treat to go with their meals. Max, why don't you help Sadie carry the food over to their table so these ladies can go sit down?"

I nod, continuing to work on preparing the eight lobster rolls. My mom motions for Sam to grab the secret stash of cookies she made for us—a thank you that seems to be more for her favorite customers than the help. He grabs them, abandoning his post to take them to the girls.

"The hairnet is a good look, Max." Sadie smirks. "Really accentuates how hard it's working to contain your mop."

A snort slips out of me. "Don't hate on the hair, Sade. Some men would kill for these luscious locks."

"Yeah, okay. Are you going to hurry on these rolls or do I need to toss them myself?" Sadie glances behind her at the table with her family. "The girls will start rioting soon."

She's breathtaking as she spins back around to face me—casually dressed in denim shorts, a black tank top, sandals, and sunglasses that frustratingly cover her freckles. Her hair blows slightly in the breeze, gracing me with her peach scent—a sweet relief over the crustaceans that have surrounded me all day.

"Yeah, I'm working on tossing the last two."

"Extra sauce, don't forget." She points at the bowl I'm currently working on.

I narrow my eyes at her, then flash my brightest smile. "I don't need instructions on how to toss your salad, Sade." Winking at her, she opens and closes her mouth a few times as patches of red crawl up her neck.

"I, uh. Wow—"

"Cat got your tongue?"

She shakes her head. "No, I was going to tell you I agree. To the deal, I mean. But now..."

"Now you're even more intrigued? Look, I get it. I'm a catch." I hold my hands up, pushing the baskets of food toward Sadie. "I'm glad you finally realized it."

"Okay, Casanova. Let's not get carried away. I'm agreeing to your help because I have no choice."

I round the table, tossing my gloves in the trash as I do. "Who's Casanova?"

Sadie grabs two of the baskets, while I pull the other two toward me. "Casanova... you know, like the—"

A chuckle bubbles out of me. "I know. Just wanted to hear you say it again."

Sadie rolls her eyes as we walk side by side to where her family is seated. They greet me with friendly smiles as Poppy blushes and waves. Sliding my phone from my pocket, I check the schedule of today's events, and Sadie slides onto the picnic bench next to her mom.

"Hey, Sade. Meet me at the Oyster tent in an hour?"

"For?" she asks, chewing nervously on her bottom lip.

"Your first fun thing."

Fifteen

Sadie

Awe, Shucks!

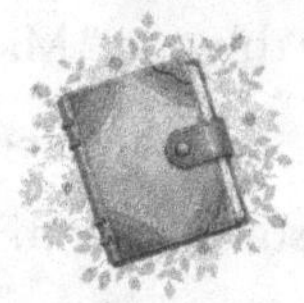

"I can't believe he actually said that!" Mal roars, laughing hysterically as I recount my conversation to her and Sebastian.

"What have I done? I should've never asked him for help." I groan, placing my head in my hands dramatically.

Seb pats my shoulder. "Sade, he's actually harmless. Always been a softy, even when we were kids."

"Speak for yourself. There's nothing soft about that man." My sister fans her face. "Three words, Sadie. Rock. Hard—"

"That's enough." Seb tickles my sister's side. "Do I need to remind you how hard I get?"

"I was going to say muscle, hunny." Mal presses a kiss to his cheek. "But yes, please."

My mom left with all four of the girls once we finished lunch. They were overdue for naps, and she's babysitting so the adults can enjoy the festivities—her words, not ours. It's nice, though. I rarely get time with my sister, and this event is one of my all-time favorites.

The Mage Hollow Lobster Festival is a one of a kind experience. All the stores in the square close for the weekend while vendors line the streets with big-top tents, so many tables we could never fill them all, and enough seafood to make you forget anything else exists. It's one big clam bake, with steamer stations, more red and white checkered tablecloths covered in corn and crustaceans than one could imagine, and my personal favorite—the oyster tent.

Well, that might be second to all the wine tasting stops.

"Oh, Sadie. You have to try this one," Mal says, holding up a sample of a rosé—probably our fifth or sixth sample-size pour at this station.

Taking the small, clear plastic cup from my sister, I tip the sweet and tangy liquid to my lips. It has hints of strawberry and something a little herbal, with a delightfully smooth finish.

"That is amazing. Should we get one to share?" Wrapping my fingers around the stem of the bottle, the blush liquid inside swirls slightly. It has a beautiful, vintage-looking label—something you'd expect to see in Gatsby, very chic.

"I'll grab you a few for girls' nights while you're in town." Sebastian winks at me, pulling his wallet out and stepping toward the cashier.

Mal links her arm through mine, and I drain the rest of the wine from the tasting cup. "Five minutes, little lady," she whispers in my ear. "Do you remember how to shuck an oyster?"

I slip out of her hold, crossing my arms. "Yes, Mallory. I've been doing it since before I could tie my shoes."

She nods with a wickedly devious smile on her face. "Okay, so you don't need me to stick around then? To chaperone?" Mal pulls me close to her once more. "Because I think I'm going to take my baby daddy home. And you're going to go have fun with that hottie that's clearly into you."

"We're just friends." I tighten my grasp on my crossbody, reminding more than my sister where we stand—reminding myself.

"Yeah, okay. Seb's my best friend too, no offense."

"Ugh, fine." I squeeze my sister, releasing her into Seb's awaiting arms. "Don't be a fool, wrap your—"

He salutes me. "Got it, Sade. Same goes for you."

Walking away before I change my mind about this whole adventure, I replay my sister's words in my mind. Max is flirty, but *into me*? I'm not sure. It's difficult to tell if this is just how he is in general or if it's specific to me. I'd be lying if I said I wasn't attracted to him. He's probably the most beautiful man I've ever seen, and that's saying something—I work with professional athletes.

Sleeping with him, heck even just kissing him, is a bad idea, though. I'm leaving, even if Levi won't have me back. The jobs I'm qualified for aren't in Mage Hollow. And yeah, summer flings are something my roommate boasts about when she spends time at the Cape, but I've never had one.

Dodging a group of teenagers near the edge of the oyster tent, I step inside, scanning the space for Max.

"Boo." Max's hands wrap around my shoulders, and his breath coasts across my neck as he whispers into my ear. "You looking for me, Sade?"

My skin tingles from the proximity, heat pooling low in my belly. If my body could get the memo regarding summer flings, it would be great.

"Yeah." I turn so I'm facing my new friend—old friend—I don't know anymore. "You smell... fishy."

Max chuckles. "Worse things than lobster cologne. Mabel didn't give me time to go home and change."

He shrugs as I take in his appearance. Max's style is effortless—comfortable. He looks relaxed, from his boat shoes and flat-front navy chino shorts to the soft grey t-shirt that hugs his impossibly large biceps. Not at all like he just worked all day serving food in a hot tent. His hair curls around the ends, as if he intentionally styled it, when somehow I know he didn't.

"Are you checking me out, Sade?" Max's eyes roam my face.

"Definitely not." I smile. "Just wondering why you wanted me to meet you here."

Max places his hand at the small of my back, leading me to one of the round, linen covered high top tables. There's a laminated menu in the center next to a blue vase with a single pink rose.

"Do you like oysters?" Max plucks the menu off the table, leaning closer so we can both see it. "I was thinking we could do the tasting, but if this isn't your vibe, we can find something else."

I beam at him. Logically, I know he has no idea how perfect this is. But part of me wants to pretend he planned it just for me. "I love them. My favorite food of all time."

"Really?"

"Yeah. I mean, you can't really live in Mage Hollow and not like them, right?" I flip the menu over, my shoulder bumping Max's arm slightly.

"Um, yeah," he hesitates.

I push down on the menu, bringing it back to the table, and spin toward him. "Max O'Reilly, do you not like oysters?"

He shakes his head. "No, I've just never had one."

My mouth pops open. How could that be possible? We have the best oysters in the world right in our backyard. One of Mal's friends, Lynelle, literally ships her catches to restaurants all around the world—they're so popular they're global.

As I'm letting my brain catch up to what he said, a server approaches our table. She has long blonde hair tied back in a ponytail, a baby-blue shirt that's cut way too low in the front, and a smile that says *Notice me*.

"Can I help you pick something from the menu?" She directs her question to Max, as if I'm not standing here. *Rude!*

"Sure. We'd like to do the sampler. Please don't shuck them ahead of time. I can do it." The woman's green eyes meet mine. "I'll take crackers, lemon, and hot sauce too, please."

Her gaze tracks Max's, probably waiting to see if he agrees. But when he dips his chin slightly, she scurries away.

While we wait, Max steals a couple of stools from a group that's leaving, and I walk to the next tent over to grab some drinks. Returning with a glass of white wine for me and a beer for Max, I'm not surprised to find the server leaning a little too close to him while she places a tray filled with ice and six oysters in the center of the table.

"That was quick," he says, grabbing my wine and placing it on the table before linking our fingers. Goosebumps race up my arm at the feel of his calloused hand in mine—at the way they look together, his strong and mine dainty. "Celeste was just asking if we need help, babe." His eyes widen, a plea for me to go along with it.

"Oh, how kind, Celeste? We don't need help, but thank you." I slide onto the stool next to him, forcing my face into a smile, and *Celeste* saunters away. "Babe? Really, Max?" I whisper.

He runs a hand through his thick hair, scratching his neck slightly. "Sorry, she was making it weird. But that's what friends do, right?"

"Friends pretend to be your date to hold off the treasure trove of women that throw themselves at you?" I smother the amused laugh threatening to break free. "Do you and Howie hold hands often? To chase off unwanted advances?"

"Nah. We usually just do it because we want to." Max smirks, and a laugh bubbles out of me. "The guy has shockingly soft hands."

"Wait! He really does. I don't know how he does it." And now I'm sort of jealous of my cousin holding hands with Max. *What is happening to me?*

Max takes the lager I forgot I was still holding from my hand and gulps down a big glug. "God, that hits so hard after the day I've had." He sips it again, less ravenously this time. "So, how do we do this?"

I follow suit, sipping my wine. "Well, you've really never done this?"

He shakes his head no.

"Okay, I'll walk you through it." I reach out, wrapping my fingers around the wooden-handled shucking knife. "There are a couple of ways to do this, but I prefer to use the lollipop method."

"Why's it called that?" Max carefully examines everything on our table.

"You'll see. Okay, first, this is called a shucking knife." I hold it up so he can get a good look. "I'm going to insert it here at the shell hinge."

Max picks up an oyster and points to the spot that I'm pushing the knife into.

"You want to make sure it's really in, even if you have to wiggle it, just keep going."

Max laughs. "That's what she said."

"What? Who said?"

He shakes his head, laughter still rolling through him. "Never-mind."

I get my knife into the shell deep enough and hold it up in front of us. "See... lollipop method, because it looks like one. Now, we hold it here—typically with gloves on for safety—and wiggle it back and forth until the shells separate at the hinge." I follow my own instructions:

popping the top shell off and running the knife under the muscle to detach it.

"Wait, what did you just do?" Max points at the oyster.

"It's attached, and if you don't run the knife through there, you can't slurp it down." Reaching across the table, I grab the toppings. "Do you think you're a hot sauce guy or a lemon juice guy?"

"Hot sauce? I like things spicy." Max winks, and I feel my cheeks heat.

"Oh boy, okay." I add a few dashes to the shell and hand it over to him. "Down the hatch."

His face twists, apprehension clearly etched on his features. "Do I chew it? Or—"

Placing my hand on his forearm, I squeeze lightly. "You can if you want. You've got this. It's good, I promise."

Max gives me one more small smile, then he opens his mouth and slurps it down. I can't tell from the look on his face whether he liked it or if he wants to vomit. He simply stares at the shell, as if he's confused by it.

I squeeze his arm again. "Thoughts?"

"Amazing!" His grin takes over his entire face now, that adorable dimple popping. His eyes are bright, fascinated. "Why have I never done this?"

Holding my hands up, I respond, "I actually have no idea." That makes him chuckle and pull my stool closer to his.

"You're up. Let's go." He nods toward the five remaining shells. "But that knife is gnarly, so you have to open them."

"I'll do mine, but you, my *friend*, are doing your next one."

Working through the steps, I pop the shells on three of the oysters and hand him the knife. Taking my time, I prepare mine the way I like best, with a squeeze of lemon juice and one dash of hot sauce. As I bring the first to my lips, Max stops wrestling with his second and stares at me with his mouth open as if this is the best thing he's ever witnessed.

The salty brine coats my tongue as I swallow it down, followed by the tang of the lemon and the zip of the hot sauce. A subtle moan slips out of me as I close my eyes and savor the moment.

"Damn," Max whispers, releasing an over-exaggerated breath.

Rather than addressing his comment, my eyes pop open, and I narrow them at his oyster. "Come on, mister. Don't let the shell beat you." I nod toward the knife.

"I think I'm doing it wrong... it doesn't fit," he says.

I sip my wine and smirk at him. "Sounds personal. Tell me more."

Max's mouth drops open. "Did you just make a pun, Sade? Like a sexual one?" He wiggles his eyebrows.

"Definitely not." I'm the one winking this time—and I never wink. I didn't even think I knew how.

What is in this wine?

"Let me help you." I place my hands on top of his, pressing so he knows how hard to push. The knife doesn't budge.

"Maybe if you let me—"

"Maybe I should pull—"

Our voices ring out at the same time. But I press harder, and Max pulls. It's a tangle of fingers, the oyster, and the knife.

"Mother fucker!" I hiss as the edge of the blade burrows into the meat of my hand beneath my thumb. "Shit, it's my... I might pass—"

"Nope, I've got you, just lean into me." His sturdy arm wraps around me. "Celeste! I need a towel or a first aid kit," he shouts, as blood continues to drip down my arm and onto my lap.

A few people rush over as Celeste takes her sweet time with a med kit.

"Why didn't you have gloves on?" An older gentleman with grey hair, round glasses, and judgmental eyes asks.

"We weren't given any. And that question isn't helpful," Max spits back, venom in his words.

A woman, maybe the guy's wife, with silver hair examines my hand, pressing a wad of gauze against it. I hiss in pain—it needs pressure, but it still hurts like hell. *I'm probably getting tetanus.*

"We are so sorry. Please take her to the hospital right away. We will cover the bill." She smiles at me, and I can feel the sincerity in her apology.

I turn to look at Max, but he's already sliding off his stool, and before I know it, hoisting me into his arms.

"Max! Put me down. My legs are fine."

"No way, Sade. I promised fun, and stitches aren't that." He grimaces, but quickly fixes his face into a smile. "At least this way you can look back on today and remember being carried through the streets of Mage like a princess."

I groan. "How embarras—"

"It's not. It's magical, swoon-worthy even. Live a little, Sade... while I save your life."

I doubt I'm dying, but a small part of me feels that if I were, this wouldn't be a bad way to go. He hoists me up a little further, one arm beneath my knees and the other behind my shoulder blades. He really does smell like the ocean, and not in a sea salt skin sort of way—but I nuzzle into his chest and inhale, anyway.

Sixteen

Max

Creative Distractions

Carrying Sadie into the Mage Hollow hospital wasn't something I imagined this morning when I had hoped to see her. It definitely wasn't in the plan I had for our "one fun thing" of the day. But sometimes life's like that, throwing curveballs or oyster knives when you least expect it.

Approaching the desk, Sadie swats at my arm. "Max, can you put me down now? People are staring at us."

"Excuse me, my friend here cut herself, and I think she needs stitches." A nurse who's probably my mom's age looks from me to Sadie over the rim of her purple glasses.

"Does she need a wheelchair?" She purses her lips, searching Sadie's bottom half for the cut.

Sadie holds her hand up. "No, I can walk. He just insists on being a storybook character right now."

The lady rolls her eyes but waves us back as a round of grumbles comes from the waiting room full of people. I guess blood wins out over seasonal allergies today.

"I'm Vera. I'll get you checked in and pull some vitals. Gretchen will be in to do the rest before Dr. Toccio sees you," the same lady from the desk explains while stepping through double doors and into a small patient room.

I settle Sadie onto the bed, sliding a large maroon chair over toward the side of it and plopping down. Vera takes her blood pressure, checks to see if she has a fever—she doesn't—and removes the gauze to take a closer look.

I'm not a doctor, but I've had enough injuries to assume she needs stitches. The wound is still seeping, but not as badly as it was before.

"Can you tell me your full name?"

"Sadie Marie Wells."

"How did this happen?"

Sadie looks at me and quietly laughs. "He doesn't know how to shuck an oyster." She points her finger at me, wincing slightly from the movement. "I was trying to teach him."

Vera gives me a once-over, frowning. "And your face? What happened? Do I need to be concerned about the two of you?"

Now, it's my turn to chuckle. We look like quite the pair: two black eyes and a fresh cut in need of sutures.

"Just an accident, unrelated," I say, waving her off. Vera huffs, turning back to the computer she's clacking away on.

"Any medical history that I need to be aware of?"

"No, I don't think so."

"Insurance?"

"Yes, I have it. My card isn't in this wallet, but I work for the Golden City Flames. I can bring it by this week or call in the number."

"That's fine. Congratulations on winning the cup."

"Oh, um, thanks. It was great." Sadie glances at me from the corner of her eye. We've never discussed where she works, not really outside of the one conversation about her leave of absence. I'm curious what it's like, how it feels to be a part of something I've always dreamed of.

"Are you pregnant?" Vera shifts gears.

Sadie's cheeks turn red at the question. "No?"

"Is that a question? I'll need to give you some medication. We need to know if you could be."

The room feels hotter, like maybe I shouldn't be the one in here for this. But at the same time, my stomach protests the thought of leaving her. I'd rather not think about her sex life, at least not outside of my own fantasies.

"No, I'm not. I'm positive."

Relief floods my senses, and I'm overwhelmed by it. I've dated, had hookups, but something about Sadie hits differently. We're friends, of course, but there's more to it—a mutual attraction that's becoming harder to deny. Even when I actively try to stop thinking about her, I can't.

Vera nods, swings around, and looks us over once again before pushing out of the room.

"So, the Flames?" I attempt to make small talk. Sadie twists the cotton hospital blanket with her good hand. "What's it like?"

"It's like any other job, I think." She peeks at me from under her lashes. "Just with people who make millions of dollars. Monte is great when he's not forcing me to take time off. And the kids I work with are awesome."

Her face lights up as she speaks, and it steals my breath. I have a vague understanding of why she's on leave, but it feels like a disservice to more than just Sadie. If she's this happy talking about it, I can only imagine what she feels being there.

"You love it," I say—a statement, not a question.

She beams, the kind of smile that covers her entire face. "I really do. And look, I know it's kind of pathetic because it's my one-legged stool, but it's what I was meant to do—where I'm supposed to be."

"I'm not sure I know what a one-legged stool has to do with it, but I agree. Why did you need to take a leave again?" I reach out, squeezing Sadie's hand. "You don't have to explain it all if you don't want to. I'm just trying to figure out why he'd send you away."

She squeezes my hand back, intertwining our fingers. "It's complicated. Maybe we could talk—"

"Hello, how's our patient doing?" A nurse wearing black scrubs asks as she enters alongside the physician.

"I've been better, but it's fine." Sadie holds her hand up, and the doctor's eyes grow comically big.

"Well, you definitely need stitches." The woman in the white coat with sandy brown hair begins rolling up her sleeves. "Gretchen, please get anesthetic to numb it, a suture kit, and a tetanus shot." She turns to Sadie, a sympathetic smile gracing her face. "We're going to make sure it's as pain-free as possible before I place a few stitches. You will need a shot just to be safe. Do you remember when your last one was?"

"No, I'm sorry I don't. Is that okay? Is it safe to have another one?" Sadie's grip on my hand tightens, and her chest rises and falls faster than it did before.

Doctor Toccio smiles, and Gretchen scoots a tray filled with supplies over to the bed. "Of course, it's completely safe."

"Is that the needle? I can't..." Sadie's face goes pale, and beads of sweat dot her brow.

"Hey, Sade. Look at me. Talk to me." My heart aches for her. She clearly isn't a fan of what's happening here, not that anyone would be.

But I can tell her anxiety has reached a boiling point, that she wants to refuse what has to happen.

"I just don't like needles. How do people get tattoos? Or donate blood for fun? I could never—it makes no sense. I tried once, getting a tattoo. I only made it through ten minutes and I begged the guy to stop, and there was one time I donated blood... passed out before they finished my intake forms." Her rambling is adorable, and my chest flutters with the wings of what feels like a thousand butterflies.

Turning my head toward the doctor, I whisper, "Hey, Doc. How long will it take you to do everything?"

"Ten seconds for the shot to numb it, then maybe three minutes. Are you planning to time me?" Her eyes narrow.

"Nah, just going to try some unconventional methods for distracting her." I wink and give her a small thumbs-up before turning my attention back to my girl. "Sade, can I ask you something?"

She groans but nods anyway. "Do you have a boyfriend?"

"No. What does that have to do with needles?" She searches my face for an answer, and I can hear the medical staff working behind me.

"Nothing, but I watched an episode of *Brown's Bodies* with my mom once, and they said that affection can mimic the same endorphins that you hear about moms using to lift cars and shit."

"The anesthetic is in. Should be numb in just a minute and then we'll continue," Doctor Toccio declares. I guess my talking is working, as she didn't even flinch.

"Max! What does that have to do with this situation?"

I turn slightly, glancing at the doctor. She gives me a nod and a wink, which makes me chuckle. I stand from the chair, inch onto the sliver of bed beside her, and run my index finger from her forehead down to her chin.

Leaning in until I'm only a centimeter away, I whisper, "Please don't punch me in the nose for this."

Sadie tips her chin up, her eyes searching mine for answers. Instead of giving any, I press my lips to hers, firm compared to her pillow-soft. She's stunned, struck so still I'm not sure she's breathing. Inching backward, I scan her face for some sort of reaction until Sadie leans forward, wraps her non-injured hand around my neck, and kisses me.

My hand slides to the side of her face, angling her the way I need her, while my brain is misfiring from the unexpected perfection of this kiss—the one I didn't steal, but she chose.

Chancing it, I slide my tongue along the seam of her lips, and she opens for me. The combination of the brine from the oyster and the wine she was drinking makes the perfect combination of salty and sweet. A groan releases from my throat at the same time she breathes out a soft moan. Kissing her is addicting, like our bodies somehow know the steps to a dance that's just for us.

"Excuse me." The nurse, who I forgot was even in the room, clears her throat. Pressing one more chaste kiss to Sadie's mouth—and one to her forehead—I pull back and turn to face her.

"We're basically done. We just need to give her a shot, so you should probably wait outside." She hands me a stack of papers. "I preprinted the paperwork. Care instructions are in there. She'll be out in a minute."

Looking back at my girl, I see her fingers are pressed to her lips and her cheeks are flushed. She's gorgeous, hair mussed a little from our kiss.

"Sade, I'll be right outside." She nods, still dazed. I hope that means she was as affected by that as I was.

Pushing into the hallway, I lean against the opposite wall and pull out my phone. I'm not sure how long we've been here, and I need to check on Benny. Nora was supposed to let him out for me, so hopefully I'm not returning to a disaster tonight.

When I slide open my phone, there's a text message waiting from Coach Perkins.

Perkins: Paperwork's official. Pack your bags, O'Reilly.

My heart plummets, and my ears ring like a record's just been scratched. I knew this was coming, but a part of me still didn't believe it would happen. My mind races through all the people I need to tell, the arrangements that will have to be made, and to the woman I just shared the best kiss of my life with—she was always going to leave, but now I'm the one moving a half a world away.

The door to Sadie's room opens, so I tuck the phone back into my pocket.

"Hey, gorgeous. Do you come here often?"

Sadie rolls her eyes but smiles. "Sure do. I've been told I'm potentially deadly to be around. Want to walk me home and take your chances?"

Taking a few steps to close the distance between us, I interlock our hands. "I think you might just be worth it."

Seventeen

Sadie

One-Legged Stool

"Order for Sadie," an adorable barista calls, placing my iced black coffee on the counter at the Brewhouse while I scroll through my painfully empty inbox.

Grabbing it and heading out the front entrance, I squeeze past a couple that seem to be on their first date. There's a pang in my chest at the sight of them, an emptiness I think has been there for a while, one that I've been effectively stuffing down in order to prioritize more important things. I haven't had time for a relationship for longer than I can remember, and honestly, I haven't wanted one. Not a real one anyway, not one that requires effort and time.

A companion might be nice. Someone to share things with, someone who doesn't come with expectations. But that's precisely the problem—the chasm between what most people want and what I can offer is too wide. Wanting someone who gets it has always felt too far away, too impossible to find.

And then there's Max. The tension between us has been mounting, so I wouldn't say I'm surprised that we kissed last night. But I rarely make a habit of making out with people willy-nilly, and that kiss was the kind that altered my brain chemistry. It's the soul-bending way our bodies knew exactly what to do, as if we'd kissed a thousand times before, the way he initiated it simply because he'd known I needed a distraction. He wanted to ease my pain, my fears, and that alone is foreign—that alone is cause for trouble.

Past relationships, heck even past hookups, haven't felt that way. They've always felt forced or awkward—all teeth, no tongue. But that's the beauty of them because they're also easy to leave behind. I don't lose sleep wondering if I made the right choice or if I could see playing the balancing act that is juggling a full-time career with another person's wants and needs. There's a sneaking suspicion in me that Max wouldn't be easy to leave behind, that walking away would hurt if our friendship continued to grow.

There's only one way to ensure that doesn't happen—avoid him like my life depends on it.

As I stroll down the cobbled sidewalk that outlines Mage Square, a light flickers on from inside Black Kettle Bindery. The door flies open, and a beautiful woman with long strawberry-blonde hair that I recognize from yesterday pushes a sidewalk sign directly into my path. I'm forced to sidestep her, narrowly avoiding a collision.

"Sorry, I couldn't see around this monstrosity." The woman straightens, smoothing out a pale yellow dress that brushes the tops of her knees. It looks like something a fifties housewife would wear, fashionable in a way that I admire—it's a risky move, a quirky choice.

"Oh, it's okay." I stop, sipping my coffee. "You're Olive, right?"

"Yep." She bumps her hip into the sign, scooching it a little further toward the center of the walk. "And you're... oh, my gosh—"

Her hand flies to her mouth, and I can't tell if she's shocked to see me or trying to smother a grin. "You're Sadie. Max's friend."

My skin prickles. *Max's friend?* Howie's cousin would be more accurate. It puzzles me that she'd tie me to her brother-in-law instead of my literal family.

"I thought you were closed today. With all this going on, I thought every store was." I swing my hand behind me to the tents that are still set up and the vendors carting fresh food in for the last day of Lobster Fest, attempting to change the subject of who I am or whom I belong to.

She smiles brightly. It's genuine and full of life. "Well, we were supposed to be." The woman looks to the sky, rolling her eyes so subtly you'd almost miss it. "But I sorta gave the owner a hard time yesterday, and this is my penance."

"Wait, really? Beau has always been so kind to me. He still owns it, right?"

She laughs, nodding. "Yes, Beau still owns Black Kettle. And no, I was just kidding. I came in to work on some restorations that needed finishing. I have a few people coming in to pick up orders, and I just figured why not open for a few hours before the rush begins." She takes a step toward the entrance. "Do you want to come in and look around?"

Following her through the door, I remember why this was my top hangout spot growing up, aside from the library. It smells like old books, vanilla candles, and something I can't quite put my finger on. Not much has changed in terms of decor. It still has the sliding ladder along the wall for books stored on the top shelves, the tables that line the center of the room—and a personal favorite—the large bay window that's cushioned for in-store reading.

"Do you need me to help you find anything?" Olive asks, pulling off a cream cardigan to reveal the most magnificent tattoo I've ever seen. It's so vibrant with pumpkin vines twisting and toiling amongst little pictures. Max explained it briefly, but seeing it in person is on another level.

I shift slightly, edging toward the stacks. "No, I think I'll just take a look, see if anything jumps out at me." Olive nods, then proceeds toward the back, presumably to the restoration desk that's been there as long as this place has been open.

Running my finger along the edge of the spines, I search for the romance section. Since finishing Jules' books, I'm thinking something else a little steamy but light-hearted, might serve as a needed distraction from the man I'm trying not to like. A loud thud sounds from somewhere behind me, but I ignore it, pulling a classic Cassandra Moll off the shelf. I think this might be her first series, a mechanic and teacher romance—the perfect fictional world to fall into.

"Did you drop this?" Olive's voice rings out from over my shoulder. Spinning, I glance at the book she's holding.

"No?"

"Hmm, weird. Must have just gotten knocked loose." She places it back on the shelf and walks away.

Tucking the book I selected under my arm, I continue perusing the selection. There's everything from dark romance to historical tales featuring men in petticoats and trousers on the covers. I prefer contemporary, but maybe there's something to a swoony read about a man who's an estate owner in nineteenth-century Europe.

Another loud thud sounds, this time near the back of the store. It's quite a commotion, with several huffs coming from Olive's direction. "Are you okay?" I call out after a beat of silence.

Olive rounds the corner, walking toward me with annoyance in every step. "Why did you throw this at me?" She taps her foot and places a hand on her hip. "I thought you said you didn't drop it."

"I didn't. What are you even—"

She shoves the book toward me. It's as thick as a dictionary, bound in black leather that's worn from age. The front reads: **A Guide to the World's Most Difficult Crosswords** in thick gold lettering.

My mouth pops open as my face twists. "You have to be kidding me," is all I can manage.

Olive huffs, tapping her foot more aggressively. "I'm not kidding, and I don't find it funny. I let you in here to be nice."

Holding my hands up as much as I can with a book wedged under my arm and a coffee in the other, I attempt an apologetic smile. "I'm so sorry. I know this sounds wild, unbelievable even, but I didn't. I wasn't anywhere near the shelf you just placed that on."

"So I'm supposed to believe there's a ghost or—"

I see the moment realization blooms on her face. The knowledge that she and I both share, but haven't discussed—some things in Mage Hollow are truly inexplicable.

"I promise, you can ask Beau about me. I've never been one to disrespect books, and I can't even really hold one right now." I nod toward my bandaged hand. "I swear."

Olive releases a breath, and her shoulders slouch. "You're Howie's cousin?"

"The very one." I motion toward my chest. "And you're Max's sister-in-law?"

Her bright smile returns as his name drifts out of my mouth. "Yes. Sam's fiancée." Her face contorts into something a smidge sympathetic. "We should talk sometime. Get to know each other."

"I won't be in town long, but maybe..." How do I say that I really appreciate her kindness but am just looking to get out of here and back to work without being rude. She's offering to help, even if she's not explicitly saying it, and it makes me wonder if Max told her about what's going on, or if this is just some weird cursed kindred spirit vibe she's caught onto. I smile at her. "That'd be—"

The bells on the door chime, and none other than Max's voice rings out. "Yo, Ollie. Does Beau know you turned on the open sign?"

My stomach leaps into my throat. *Perfect!* I was successful at avoiding him for less than twelve hours, most of which I was asleep. I can't face him right now, can't discuss what happened when I haven't had enough time to process how I feel about it.

Olive turns, heading toward the front of the store, presumably to greet Max. I need to find a way to get out of here without him noticing me. I inch as quietly as I can to the end of the row I'm in, peering beyond the end cap for a back entrance. Shoot, it's on the opposite wall but too far into the opening.

Olive and Max continue talking about the store and the festival, their voices growing louder with each step they take. Channeling my inner cat burglar, I back up, but even at a slow pace the clack of my sandals is too loud, too echoey. Glancing side to side, I drop to my knees, abandoning the book and coffee I was holding, and crawl toward my escape.

Is this mature? No. Do I care right now? Based on my pounding heart, also no.

When I reach the end of the aisle, I mourn the loss of the items left behind for a quick second before maneuvering into a crouch. If I time it right, and if he's facing the back of the store, I can dart out the door and down the street without being spotted.

"Who are we hiding from?" Max whispers conspiratorially from behind me, and I scream, falling backward onto my ass like the lunatic I clearly am.

"Jesus, you scared the shit out of me." I shove his arm lightly.

I can't believe I didn't hear him.

"Me? At least I'm not on my knees trying to literally crawl away from you." His eyes narrow, and he crosses his arms. "What was your plan here? Ghost me? You remember how small this town is, right?"

He's hurt, genuinely upset by my antics. "No!" I push to standing, extending my good hand to a still crouched-down Max. "I just, I don't know. Yes. I guess I was hiding after—"

"Not here." Max grabs my hand, standing to his full height. "Grab your stuff and let's go talk... please." His eyes are pleading.

I nod, turning to make my way back toward my abandoned book and coffee with my head hung in shame. It seemed logical this morning to avoid him, to pretend nothing happened—but now, I feel like an asshole.

Once I've gathered my things and paid for the book I selected, with an all too knowing grin plastered on Olive's face as she rang me up, we head out the door and away from the crowd that's beginning to pour into the square. Our walk is silent, so quiet it almost hurts.

"Look, Max, I—"

"Sadie, I—"

A laugh bubbles out of me, and Max follows suit. I'm not sure how our timing is so in sync, but then again, am I sure about anything anymore?

Max spots an open bench on a grassy patch of land surrounded by houses. It's not uncommon in Mage Hollow, as most of the blocks have some sort of park or natural area in the center of them. It's the town's way of preserving its charm instead of throwing up tons of little box houses that fit in perfect rows. I appreciate it. There is room to breathe here, room to sprawl out and read a book, or talk to the guy you kissed while getting stitches for the first time.

We cross the street, sliding onto the bench sideways, facing each other. A willow tree waves over our heads, and the scent of flowers tickles my nose.

"Can I go first?" I ask, reaching out to grab Max's hand. He nods. "Okay, so this is going to be a lot, but I think I just need to get it out. My boss, Levi, made me take a leave for a whole host of reasons, including the panic attack I told you about, but the biggest one was that I have zero work-life balance."

Max squeezes my hand and nods in understanding.

"I've always been this way: study hard, work hard, play later... except the last part rarely happens. It's not that I don't want to have a life outside of work, it's just that there isn't enough time with everything else I need to accomplish, and with ADHD I have to work harder than everyone else to complete even the smallest of tasks... to stay focused."

"Your one-legged stool?" Max smirks, echoing my words from last night, seemingly unfazed by my confession.

"Exactly. Everyone else has multiple legs. Take my sister, for example. She has a family, a career, us... multiple legs. So, if one breaks, she's still standing. But me, I only have one priority in my life, one thing to keep me afloat."

"That makes sense, but what does that have to do with me?" Max runs his hand through his hair. "Why were you planning to avoid me?"

There isn't a good way to explain this to him without making myself sound like a coward. But the genuine interest in his expression makes me feel like I can be honest, even if it's embarrassing. He puts me at ease without even trying.

I release a slow breath, relaxing my shoulders. "I was avoiding you because of this"—I wave my hand between us—"this is fun. Spending time around you, laughing with you, heck, even getting stitches with you is more fun than I've had in years—and that's scary. I have so many goals I want to accomplish, so many kids that I want to help. I'm worried that if I slip, even slightly, my priorities won't ever be the same. And that's not meant to be a big declaration. It's just that giving in to what everyone else says I need feels like I'm doing it for all the wrong reasons."

Releasing Max's hand, I cover my face. "It feels like they're setting me up to fail."

Max tugs on my arms gently, settling my hands on his thigh as he traces my bandage lightly. "Why would anyone want you to fail? Have you considered that maybe they just want you to be happy? Fulfilled?"

"I am happy. I love my job."

"Right, I know. But when's the last time you did something that was only for you?" Max strokes my arm, a light touch of his fingertips running from my elbow to my wrist. "Because the job makes you happy, but couldn't you be happier if you had that plus a few more legs on your stool?"

"I honestly don't know. I've tried dating, and every time it doesn't work out... I'm relieved more than anything else." Slumping back against the bench, I hang my head over the back as I peer at the sky.

"Sounds like you've been dating the wrong guys, Sade."

That's an understatement.

"Are you saying it would be different if I dated you? That you'd understand every time that I had to stay late to do media with a spark the flame kid, or every time that someone called me at eleven at night with a planning question for the gala?"

"No, not exactly." Max stifles a chuckle. "I mean, it would be, but only because I understand hockey and the schedule that comes with it."

"Yeah, about that. What are you doing now that it's over?"

Max slides his thumb and forefinger onto my chin, pulling my face toward him. "Nope, we will get into my bullshit in a second. I have to tell you how to fix this first."

"Wow... you're so cocky sometimes it's astounding," I say, smiling at him. The truth is that's all I want to do when I look at Max. Not only because he's easy on the eyes, but because he's beautiful on the inside, caring and kind. He might be the first genuine friend I've made in years.

"At least I own it." He winks, because of course he does. "Sadie, please don't take this the wrong way... but you need to stop trying to control the uncontrollable. What I hear you saying is that you're afraid if you give away a tiny piece of yourself, there won't be enough left to give to your career. But I think the real problem is that you've decided the outcome without ever starting the race." He brushes my cheek tenderly. "Have you ever played pickup basketball?"

"Do I look like I play pickup basketball?" A whoosh of air leaves me. He can't be serious.

"That's exactly my point. Maybe you don't because basketball isn't your sport. Or maybe you've never considered it because you can't plan it. You'd have to show up, not knowing who your partner's going to be, if there'll even be a game going on, and if someone will pick you. You're opting out of having other things in your life because it's safe, and the alternative is scary."

My throat gets dry, and tears prick my eyes. I've never felt more seen, understood. Refusing to get emotional, I take a deep, steadying breath. "Okay, but the answer can't be as simple as just letting go. You can't expect a leopard to change its spots overnight."

"You're right. It's never easy to face your fears. But you have the perfect opportunity here, and Levi has practically handed it to you. For the rest of the time you're in town, try focusing on two things—solving the puzzle book like it's your job, and having fun—with me."

Eighteen

Max

Public Indecency

"That's not really a novel idea, Max. I already agreed to do those things." Sadie fiddles with the strap on her black tank top, twisting it between two fingers.

"Did you? Because I seem to recall you hiding from me in Black Kettle twenty minutes ago, all because you had a little too much fun last night." I wiggle my eyebrows, and Sadie scoffs. "Are you afraid you're going to fall in love with me?" I try not to grin, but fighting it only makes it worse.

The reality is I like her. I want to enjoy the remaining time I have in Mage Hollow, and hanging out with Sadie will be a welcome distraction from my own fear of change. Kissing her again wouldn't hurt either. I've only replayed what happened last night on repeat since the moment I dropped her at her mom's house.

Sadie scoffs. "No. But you know I'm leaving. Probably sooner rather than later."

"So am I."

"What? Where are you going?" Sadie looks confused, and maybe a tad shocked.

Pushing to stand, I pace in front of the bench. "Well, to answer your earlier question, I still love the sport, and I've been trying to find a way to stay connected to it now that I'm done playing."

Sadie nods. "What team are you going to?" she asks, somehow already knowing where this is headed.

"Washington."

"The Badgers or the Titans?" Washington, D.C. differs vastly from Seattle, but it's still impressive that she knows the teams. It shouldn't be. She works in the industry, but most people don't.

"The Titans."

Sadie blows a raspberry, a whoosh of air releasing from her. "Holy shit, Max. That's amazing. Coach Nash is a legend. Assisting or EM?"

A sense of calm washes over me. I'd be lying if I said it'll be easy to walk away from her after a few weeks—she's constantly on my mind after only a week—but this is one of the reasons I can't allow myself to miss out on the opportunity even if it's quick. This woman knows my sport, understands the industry, *and* she's stunning. Spending time around her is like spotting a unicorn in real life—it just doesn't come along every day—or ever.

"Equipment Manager. I hope eventually I'll move up, but it's a good gig, and you're right... he's a legend." I slide back onto the bench beside her, and Sadie huffs a laugh.

"He is tough, Max. I've seen him in action and the program he runs... a tight ship isn't a strong enough description. It's also very far away. Have you talked to your family about it?" Her tone isn't one of judgment, simply curiosity.

Running a hand through my hair, I scoot a smidge closer to her. "I know, but I think that's what I need. Someone to push me, someone to learn from. And no, but I plan to. Mabel is going to lose her mind."

"She won't." Sadie reaches for my hand, drumming her fingers on my palm. "She will be sad, but she's so proud of you. Mabel O'Reilly is a legend for how fiercely she loves you all, so there's no chance she wouldn't want this for you."

"Maybe." I smile at her. "But enough about my mother. I asked you the other day if you wanted to make a deal, and you only sort of agreed. So, I'll ask you again. Are we doing this? Are we solving some clues and having the best summer of our lives?"

"Max," Sadie admonishes. "Why do you want to volunteer for this? I appreciate your wanting to help me and all, but I don't really see what you're getting out of it."

"The same thing you are—a distraction." Reaching over, I pull her face toward mine, cupping her cheeks. "It's been great hanging out with you, and it's made me feel like myself again after everything that's happened. And don't deny it, Sadie, you know we have chemistry. I know the timing is all wrong, that nothing long-term can come out of this logistically. But if you had the chance to dance on a cloud, wouldn't you take it?"

She squeezes her eyes shut, taking a beat.

"On second thought, don't answer that. We established you wouldn't."

Sadie's lips tip up at the corners, and when she opens her eyes, she kisses me. It's not tentative—it's relenting. As if she can no longer fight it, deny it. Leaning into her, I tilt her head at the angle I need it and deepen the kiss. We take our time exploring each other, savoring every taste, every stroke of her tongue against mine.

Sadie's hands slide up my back, her nails scratching lightly, while I reposition us so that she's straddling my lap. Her fingers dive into my hair, dragging along my scalp each time I pull her bottom lip into my mouth and bite it gently. My hands massage her ass through her cotton shorts, each movement of her hips making me even more turned on.

Breaking apart, we both inhale deeply, attempting to catch our breath.

"Damn, Sadie. What was that for?" I smirk, running the back of my hand down her cheek. "I didn't realize public makeouts were your thing."

"This town deserves a little show, don't you think? And I was just checking to make sure that last night wasn't a fluke." She kisses my forehead. "I didn't want to commit to something without doing my research. How terrible would it be if I agreed to this and then the next month was spent trying to avoid you?"

Chuckling, I narrow my eyes at her. "And what did you learn with said research?"

Sadie smacks my chest lightly. "You already know the answer to that. Fishing for compliments isn't your style, Max." With that, she slips off my lap, checks the time on her phone, and kisses my cheek. "You better get going. No one wears a hairnet quite like you. Wouldn't want to deny the ladies of Mage that particular view."

After a long day slinging lobster rolls, I decided Sadie is right. I have to tell my family I'm leaving, and sooner rather than later. Nerves riot in my stomach as I make the drive over to my parents, replaying how it all went down with Perkins—how I secured a major role for an NHL team and all it took was a brief phone call.

Knocking on Perkins' office door, I wait patiently in the hall. After demanding Sadie's car be pulled from the tow truck and turned over to me, I'm hoping this is an easy meeting—that maybe he finally has a good lead for me after I've looked myself for months.

"Come in," Coach calls.

"You wanted to see me?" I step inside, planting myself in the chair opposite his desk. "Got something good with Washington?"

Perkins smiles, nodding a little too enthusiastically for his normal no-bullshit demeanor. "Do you remember my having sent those videos of you to them a few years back?" I tip my chin in acknowledgement. "Well, I spoke to Coach Nash yesterday, and it sounds like he's looking for an equipment manager. He said he specifically wants someone with coaching potential, someone that knows the sport inside and out."

"Don't all EMs know the sport inside and out? What makes you think I'm the guy?" My heart is racing. I'd love the opportunity, but it sounds like a long shot. There's a million other candidates that fit that description.

Perkins raises his eyebrow and frowns. "You're the guy because he specifically asked about you. Said he wanted someone with swagger, that would look good on video switching sticks out with the players, not an old washed-up man like me." He grins at me. "Pays to be pretty, Max. And looks like your mug—which I'll add isn't that great—is getting you the chance of a lifetime."

"But he knows I'm qualified too, right? That I want more than just my five minutes of fame on social media when some basic-ass thing like switching out blades goes viral with the book girlies?"

My ego doesn't mind the compliment, but this is serious for me. I don't want to move across the country for a position that only values me for my looks. I love this sport, and I believe I have a lot to offer a team.

Perkins narrows his eyes, and his face puckers like he's tasted something sour. "I don't know what a book girlie is, but of course he fucking knows, O'Reilly. He's seen the tapes, and he values my opinion. Like I said, you're not that pretty." He stands, moving around his desk to lean against it with a small piece of paper in his hand. "This is his number. He said to call him if you're interested—you can work out the rest of the details directly."

Taking the paper from his hand, I stand and move to the door. "Thanks, Coach." He nods, and I exit, slinking back down the hall, wondering if this could really be so simple.

Opting to let Benny continue playing with the kids at the rink, I slip into a small utility closet and dial the number. It rings a few times, but just when I think I'm going to have to leave a message, he answers.

"Nash."

"Hello, sir." I run a hand across my forehead, wiping the sweat that's beaded above my brows. "This is Max O'Reilly. Coach Perkins advised me to call you."

"Max, it's great to hear from you. Perkins told me you're looking for a new opportunity. I need a new EM, and based on your recruitment videos, I think you'd be a great addition to my team."

"Thank you, sir. I'm definitely interested, but what are you looking for specifically?"

It sounds like he's in the middle of something as papers shuffle in the background and a door opens and closes loudly.

"Listen, Max. I need someone coachable, someone I can depend on to look great on camera during the games, but that also does solid work. The media manager here is up my ass to keep up with Golden City and a few of the other teams that not only have their players doing fancy ass-shit but that keep winning."

"Okay."

"And apparently there was a video of an EM that went viral, whatever the fuck that means, for passing a stick to a player mid-skate," he grumbles. "I will not lie to you, son. I've never been big on flair—it's all about hard

work and keeping our heads down in Seattle. But apparently, that doesn't play well with the fans. If you can do both, be here no later than the second Monday in July. I'm having my assistant reach out with the paperwork right now. I hope to see you in a few weeks, Max. I have to go now."

The phone cuts off before I can reply, but it buzzes in my hand with an incoming email. My heart beats so loudly I can hear it as I scan the contents of the message. The salary is insane, and the details seem to be in order. It's crazy and fast—but if I've learned anything about this sport, it's that you don't turn down an opportunity when it comes because they're few and far between.

Despite feeling like I might vomit from the unknown and the speed with which this is happening, I type out a reply accepting the position, tuck my phone back into my pocket, and head out to grab Benny.

Holy shit, I'm going pro—sort of.

"Ma, where are you?"

Pushing through the front door of my parents' home, I'm greeted with the scent of apple pie and the sound of music drifting in from the back porch. I put Benny down, unclipping his leash, and he jumps and shimmies his hindquarters in excitement. He either loves my parents' house, or he's just associated it with one too many dog treats.

"Out here," she returns.

After my walk with Sadie, I spent most of the day helping at the booth. Mom won *Queen of the Claw*, a surprise to no one, so we're all coming over to celebrate. It's a tradition that's been running for at least ten years now, and it always involves pie. There's no way I could turn it down.

Walking down the long hallway and out onto the back porch, I'm a mix of nerves. I wanted to tell my family about the job all day. But mid-lobster dressing didn't feel like the most appropriate timing. Benny pushes on the screen door with his nose, and it pops open effortlessly.

"Oh, let me see my grand-dog." Mom springs out of her chair, kneeling to the ground so Benny can attack her with kisses. "What are you doing here so early?" She looks up at me, a knowing furrow on her brow.

"There's something I wanted to talk to you about." I reach down, scooping Benny up so I can hold on to him for this. Sliding onto the loveseat, I settle in. "I received a job offer."

"Oh? I didn't realize you had interviewed." She glances around, likely looking for my dad. When she spots him fiddling with the fire pit, she calls out, "Patrick, come here for a minute, please."

My dad, the ever-obedient husband, saunters over and slips onto a chair next to my mom.

"As I was saying, I got a job offer. Coach Perkins connected me a few days ago, and it all happened really quickly."

"That's great news, Max. I'm proud of you, son." Dad reaches over, patting my arm.

Mabel crosses her arms, worry etched on her expression. "How far away are you moving?"

My mouth gapes. How does she always know what's really going on?

"You wouldn't have come over so early to break the news if it was local, just rip the band-aid off, Max. I can take it."

My dad clutches the arm of the chair he's sitting in like he's bracing for whatever I'm going to say—or maybe for her reaction. My heart beats so hard I can hear it in my ears, and a lump forms in my throat.

"Seattle."

"What!" Mom shrieks so loudly that Benny covers his eyes with his paw and shakes. "Coach Nash is an icon. I'm so happy for you." She jumps from her seat, clapping and bouncing like I just told her I got picked up for the NHL—as a player.

"To be clear, you're not mad right now?" I ask as Benny leaps from his spot, following my mom as she dances around the porch.

"Mad? Why would she be mad, Maxwell?" My dad smiles as he watches my mom, only stopping for a second to frown in my direction.

I pick at Benny's fur that's stuck to my t-shirt, avoiding his gaze. "It's really far away. I've never left home. None of us have." My words almost get stuck in my throat, and the emotion bubbling inside of me is thick enough to choke on.

Dad grabs my hand, and Mom stops her dance, doing the same with the other. "Max, we only want you to be happy. Of course, it would have been great if you had stayed close, but we didn't raise you kids to settle for less than you deserve. This is a great opportunity, and even though we are going to miss you like crazy, we are astonished by your talent and your kind heart," Mom says, squeezing my hand.

I wipe a tear that's fallen down my face. I'm relieved that they are supportive. I hoped they would be. But I'm also terrified of being out there on my own. It sounds ridiculous for a twenty-eight-year-old man to be nervous, but I guess change is hard no matter your age and no matter how exciting it is.

The front door of the house opens with a thud, signaling that my siblings are starting to arrive. Mom takes Benny inside with her to get the pie and champagne ready, and Dad returns to the fire pit. Pulling out my phone, I text the only person I want to talk to right now.

> You were right.

> I usually am... but about what?

> I told my parents. They were excited.

Sadie/Smart/Witty/Definitely Cursed

> Is it bad if I gloat and tell you I told you so?

I laugh right as my brother and Olive step onto the porch.

"What's happening here? Why are we smiling like that?" My sister-in-law slides onto the loveseat beside me, trying to peek at my phone.

"None of your business." I pull the phone away, hiding it in the crook of my arm and typing with one hand.

> Gloat away, just know it'll cost you.

Sadie/Smart/Witty/Definitely Cursed

> Ask me how scared I am… the answer is NOT AT ALL.

> Okay, Ms. Wells. We'll see. Are you up for a beach day on Wednesday?

I can see her text bubbles appear and disappear a few times.

"Is it the girl from the store? Sadie?" Olive asks, trying to stretch her torso so she can peek over my shoulder.

I raise an eyebrow at her, tucking the phone into my pocket. "Wouldn't you like to know?"

"That didn't sound like a no," Bridget coos, joining us on the porch.

Nora follows her. "Oh, what game are we playing? Guess who Max is texting? That one's my favorite." She claps her hands, takes a chair directly across from me, and taps her chin with her finger like she's deep in thought.

My phone dings, and everyone stares at me. "Okay, fine, assholes. Yes, it's Sadie. And yes, we are sorta hanging out?"

Olive elbows me in the ribs. "Sorta hanging out? What the heck does that mean?"

"It means I need a plus one for your wedding. And also maybe don't tell her when it is so I can make it a whole thing." I wiggle my brows at Olive, and she laughs, shaking her head.

"Fine." She holds up a finger. "But no drama. You're only bringing her if things are good because it's going to be perfect."

"I'll see what I can do," I say, pulling my phone out to check Sadie's response.

Sadie/Smart/Witty/Definitely Cursed

I'm in. Let me know what time.

I'll pick you up at 11:00.

Mom pushes through the screen door, carrying a tray of champagne. "Did Max tell you the good news?"

"Jesus, Ma. No one poured bubbly when Olive agreed to a date with me. Max is just sorta hanging out with her, and we're toasting?" Sam grumbles.

"Well, that would've been weird since I crashed that family dinner." Olive smiles at him sweetly, reaching out to stroke his arm.

Mabel places the tray of drinks onto a small coffee table between us. "Hanging out with whom? I was talking about his new job that's half-way across the world."

My siblings all look at me with a mixture of amusement and disbelief.

Facing the peanut gallery, I fill them in. "I'm taking an equipment manager position with the Titans. Moving to Seattle in a little less than a month."

"And you thought now would be a good time to start dating someone? Long distance never works," Bridget chimes in, grabbing a glass of champagne and downing it.

"We're not dating... we're just hanging out, like I said. Everything will be fine." I follow her lead, grabbing my drink and taking a hefty glug.

Mom laughs, Dad shakes his head, and I'm pretty sure Sam grumbles something about me being an idiot. But their opinions don't matter when it comes to Sadie and me. We have an understanding, and they will see why I can't resist the chance to make memories with her as soon as they spend more than five minutes around her.

Nineteen

Sadie

It's a Party

"Sadie," Mom calls down the hallway. "I think your boyfriend is here."

Racing out of my bedroom with my beach bag slung over my shoulder, I practically bowl her over as she stands with her face plastered to the window of our front door.

"He's not my boyfriend, Mom." I slip my toes into my brown leather flip-flops. "He's just a friend."

"With benefits? There better be benefits, or I have officially failed as a mother." She wiggles her eyebrows at me, and I groan.

Max is hot—it's undeniable. And over the last couple of days, I decided to lean into this whole idea of having fun—to give it one-hundred-and-ten percent. But the last thing I need is my mother thinking too hard about what we are doing. My cheeks flush, and my heart races—the very same reaction I had when Bradley Bushnell took me to prom, and Dee Dee took it upon herself to hand him a box of condoms on the way out the door. She's always been great at discussing our sexuality—great at embarrassing us.

"I'm going now."

I use my hand to push her aside gently and open the door. I'm too late. Max is standing with his fist raised, prepared to knock. He's dressed in low-slung black board shorts, a blue t-shirt with the sleeves cut off displaying a variety of tattoos, and a backward hat. He looks like a sexy surfer, or one of those guys that makes thirst traps on the internet.

"Hey, Sade." He smirks at me, the adorable dimple in his cheek proudly on display. Max makes a big show of peering around me and waves at my mom. "Hi, Mrs. Wells. How are you doing today?"

Turning to look over my shoulder at her, the first thing that's apparent is how rosy her cheeks are. I swear, women fall all over themselves when he speaks.

"Please call me Dee Dee." She smiles back at him, pushing her hair over one shoulder. "Do you have a minute to come in? I could make you two a coffee for the road."

She's shameless as hell, trying to swindle him into our home so she can talk to him (translation: make this awkward). "We're in a hurry, Mom. I'll see you later, though." Stepping out onto the porch quickly and closing the door behind me, I grab Max's hand and pull him toward his truck. His shoulders are shaking with the laugh he's trying to hold in, and I can practically feel his body vibrating with each step we take.

Glad someone finds this hilarious.

We round the hydrangea bushes and approach Max's truck. It's a big, black monstrosity, with tires so tall the tops of them are level with my boobs. I'm short, but this is insane. I tighten my grip on my canvas beach bag, wondering how I'll ever be able to make it into the car, let alone to the beach.

Max slips in front of me and pulls the handle on the passenger door. "You think you can get in, or do you need a boost?"

I scan the running board, trying to estimate how high I'd need to jump to reach it, and if I'm even coordinated enough to do so. "Can you maybe just give me directions? How do people usually get into vehicles made for giant people?" Max laughs. It's full and bright.

"It's really not that high off the ground, Sade. You just happen to be fun-sized." Max lifts his foot and sets it on the long piece of metal that stretches the length of the doors. "Just put your foot here and hoist yourself up."

Moving in front of him, I attempt what he said. But my legs are practically in a full split when I do. Thank God I wore shorts. This would be awkward in nothing more than a cover-up and swimsuit. A laugh bubbles out of me, and Max joins in.

"Okay, well maybe it is higher than I thought. How about I just lift you in?" He moves closer behind me, running his fingers under the strap of my bag, removing it and tossing it in the truck. "If you turn and face me, I can lift you straight up so all you have to do is sit back onto the seat."

"Yeah, let's do that. And then we can talk about why anyone needs this type of vehicle."

Spinning, he cages me in with his arms. "Hi," he says, brushing a soft kiss on my cheek. "You look gorgeous." Max runs his fingers down the length of my flowy ponytail, and my heart beats so fast I think I might have some sort of arrhythmia.

We're leaning in, Sadie. Letting fun control our life.

"Alright, lover boy... you look great too. But I would put fifty bucks down on the fact that Dee Dee is spying around the corner of the garage right now. Can we maybe do this somewhere else?"

Max twists his head, scanning the space for my mother's prying eyes. He chuckles when unsurprisingly, she waves from the edge of the bushes like a weirdo. Hurriedly, Max places one hand on each side of my torso and lifts me into the truck. Swinging my legs in, I grab my bag and situate it by my feet, then buckle my seat belt while Max closes my door and jumps in like it's the easiest thing in the world.

"She's like Mabel 2.0." He shakes his head, reaching over to give my buckle a tug as if he's checking to make sure it's secure. "Never thought I'd see the day that she had met her match."

Sliding my sunglasses off my head and onto my face, I grin at him. "You have no idea."

Max puts the truck in reverse, exits the driveway, and turns toward the beach. Music strums in the background, and my heart skips a beat when he reaches out for my hand, holding it while gently stroking his thumb over my bandage.

"I didn't really think about the stitches. Is it okay to go to the beach today? We could do something else."

The thoughtfulness makes me feel warm and gooey inside. I've never been out with a man who so selflessly considers me—this should be bare minimum, but the bar is very low these days.

"Yeah, Vera put this second-skin stuff on it. I can get it wet and everything. I've just been keeping the bandage on as an extra layer of precaution, and because it's kinda gross to look at."

His dimple pops, but his eyes stay trained on the road.

"Good. I want to swim in the ocean with you. When was the last time you did that?"

It takes me a minute to think as I slide my phone from my pocket and open my calendar. "Well, the last time I was here during the summer was four years ago. But I don't remember coming to the beach."

"Jesus, Sade. Maybe your boss wasn't over-exaggerating. When's the last time you took a vacation?"

"Okay, let's not get judgmental. It's harder than you think to take time off. My job isn't on the same schedule as the team. I work year-round, planning and preparing during the off-season."

Max squeezes my hand. "I wasn't judging, just asking. And I'm kind of glad."

"What? Why?"

He pulls into a parking spot near the public beach access entrance. "Because it'll be more fun doing this with you. Like experiencing it for the first time."

I unbuckle, biting my tongue so I don't crack up.

"Hate to break it to ya, big guy. You don't have to work so hard to get me to like you." I scoot closer, feeling bold. "This backwards hat, and these big brawny arms do it for you."

Leaning in, I press a quick kiss on his lips. I've never been overly affectionate like this, but something about seizing the moment, and knowing this has a deadline, makes me feel like I can just go for it. Or maybe it's just easier with him.

Max wraps his hand around the back of my neck, pulling me close enough that our lips are almost touching. "You're making me feel like a piece of meat, Sade." He smiles against my mouth. "Keep it up, and we won't actually see the beach." He slides his lips up and presses a kiss to the center of my forehead.

Holy hell, I'm in over my head.

Max pulls the handle on his door, exiting the truck and skirting around it before I can make it back to my side.

"Ready? It's SOGO season."

Cocking my head to the side, I struggle to put together what the acronym means.

"Sun's out, guns out." Max flexes before wrapping his hands around my ribs and lifting me down. He's ridiculous in the best way.

"Remind me not to make your head bigger than it already is." I nudge him with my elbow when my feet are safely planted on the ground. "One teensy compliment, and I can already tell you're going to remind me all day."

Max laughs, grabbing my bag from the truck and sliding it onto his shoulder over the two beach chairs already slung on his arm. We walk side by side across a wooden plank pathway over a small sand dune. Sea oats line both sides of the path, intermingled with flowers that perfume the salty air. As the ocean comes into view, so do the waves lapping at the coast. There are large boulders intermixed with the cream-colored sand and a few patrons sprawled out on a rainbow of towels.

Max leads the way, heading left down the sand until he finds the perfect clearing. He drops my bag and the chairs, and I immediately grab two towels while he assembles our seats. It hits me that we seem to make a good team, with unspoken communication passing effortlessly between us.

Stepping to drape my red and white striped towel over the back of the chair, I do a double take. In the sand, about five feet behind my seat, are the words: **Quite The Pair, Indeed.** It's as if the words are a response to my own thoughts, as if somehow the universe knows what I'm thinking.

"Um, Max. Do you see that?" I point toward the letters, but as soon as he spins to look, a gust of wind kicks up the sand, erasing any sign of them.

"See what? The sand?"

I shake my head. "No, I could swear something was just written there. Like, you know how people will draw their names and stuff." I cross my arms. "It's fine, nevermind."

Max places his towel on his chair and flops down as he pats mine, pulling my seat closer to his. "What did it say?"

"Quite the pair, indeed."

"That's random as hell."

"I don't think it is." My cheeks flush, and I pull my tank top out away from my chest where it's starting to stick—probably from the heat, but also Max's proximity. "I had just thought about how we make a good team, then I turned around and it was there. Like an agreement to my internal monologue."

He chews on his bottom lip, staring at the waves crashing. "I wish I could say that's the most unbelievable thing I've heard, but it's not. After Olive's situation, I'm not sure much is out of the realm of possibility."

"What's my situation?" A sweet voice drifts out from behind us, and Max turns in his seat.

"Ollie?" His eyes widen, and I turn to follow his gaze. "What are you doing here?"

His sister-in-law giggles, then tosses down her beach bag. "Well, someone may have leaked that you two were coming here—"

"Mabel," Max says, with a slight beat of annoyance in his tone.

"Actually, no," a gorgeous brunette that I recognize as Ariella Marino says as she steps up beside Olive. "Hey Sadie, you probably don't remember me. I'm Ari."

"I know exactly who you are." I cross my arms. She's been leading Howie on for years. I don't know enough about her to dislike her, but I can't foresee us being besties any time soon. Howard deserves the world, and from what I know, she isn't giving it to him.

"Ice cold... I love you already," she coos before throwing a towel down beside my chair and getting comfortable.

"Who told you then?" Max demands.

His brother and Howie saunter up, schlepping a cooler and a couple of chairs. They're followed by two other women and a man with neatly trimmed blond hair that's carting a mini grill and some sort of net in a wagon.

"Aunt Dee Dee told me." Howie drops his side of the cooler and uses his foot to nudge Ariella out of the way so he can set up a chair.

Max looks at me, his eyes wide but apologetic, and all I can do is burst into a hearty laugh. Of course my mother would send a whole pack of people to our first official "hangout" to spy. Max follows my lead, leaning back in his chair while cracking up.

When I finally get it together, I manage to address the situation. "Okay, so let me get this straight. You're all working adults?" A chorus of yes's and nods rain down. "And you decided that coming to hang out with Max and me at the beach on a Wednesday was more important than going to said jobs?"

Again, they all nod or provide some form of agreement, and I remain baffled. I haven't called out of work, maybe ever—and they all just did it like it's no big deal. No wonder Max doesn't have a girlfriend. He's surrounded by the world's largest group of cockblockers.

He reaches out, squeezing my hand where it rests on my thigh. "Well, since you weirdos decided to come and make this a party, I guess I better make introductions."

Max runs through the list: there's Olive and Sam, Ariella and Howie, which I already know, obviously. Then he introduces his sisters Bridget and Nora, and Nora's boyfriend Thad. He winces a little when he says his name, and I make a mental note to ask him for more intel on that situation later.

The group scurries about, setting up a volleyball net, so many chairs, and the grill, which is promptly lit for burgers and hotdogs. It's not the day I thought I was going to have, but I find it amusing the way they are all so willing to meddle in Max's life, the way they're all so protective of him.

Twenty

Max

Sweet Oblivion

Diving for the ball that my brother shanked, sand flies in all directions as my body crashes to the ground.

"Max!" Bridget yells, wiping sand off her legs. "Keep it over there."

My eyes scan the group of ladies. They've moved their chairs into a semicircle, and Sadie is parked right in the middle of it. It's obvious they're grilling her. Her cheeks are rosy, her eyes turned down as she picks the hem of her shorts.

Pushing myself up, I slip casually around the cooler and approach my girl. Dropping to my knees in front of her, I subtly slide my palm up her thigh and lean in to whisper in her ear.

"You doing okay?"

Her breath hitches, and a shiver runs through her. She turns to me, her lips brushing my cheek. "I'm doing fine. You told them my secret."

My heart skips a beat. Obviously, Howie already knew, but I probably shouldn't have blabbed to my family, even if I was doing it with good intentions.

Leaning back, I push to stand and reach my hand out for her. "Sorry, ladies." I glance at the peanut gallery. "I'm going to steal her for a few minutes."

As I pull my shirt off and toss my hat toward her beach bag, Sadie follows my lead and steps out of her shorts. She effortlessly drags her tank top over her head and tosses her sunglasses onto her chair. My eyes trail from her painted toenails up her lean frame to a simple yet sexy black bikini. I swipe my hand down my face, trying to get my body to calm down as my heart thumps so loudly I can hear it in my ears.

Sadie is sleeper-hot—she keeps it on the down-low how downright breathtaking she is. I've always known. But seeing her here with my people, looking like this all while I know how brilliant and kind she is... It's taken a lot of self-control to make it through this day.

"Ready?" She links her fingers in mine, and we walk toward the edge of the water.

"I'm sorry." Glancing at the side of her face, I wait for some sort of reaction, but Sadie remains stoic. "They've been through this before, and we all just want to support you. But I should have asked for your permission first."

We push past the initially brisk temperature of the water, wading in silently until Sadie is almost neck-deep.

"It's okay that you told them. They're your people, and since you're involved, it seems fair that you would." She bounces up and down in the water, leaping each time a wave passes. "I'm actually sort of thankful I didn't have to do it, that I didn't have to watch their reactions."

That makes me chuckle thinking back to the coffee shop. "Ari's was the funniest. But I didn't share anything else, nothing about your work situation. I promise."

"Oh, I know!" Sadie narrows her eyes at me. "I've gotten the whole rundown about how I should keep in mind that you're leaving, as if I'm not. Your sisters are kind of terrifying. And Ari has made it widely known that she thinks I should... hmm, how did she put it?" Sadie places a finger on her temple and taps lightly. "Oh yeah, fuck you as many times as possible for all of womankind. And then report back."

I step toward her, wrapping my arms around her and spinning her in the water until her back is pressed tightly to my front. Brushing my lips over the shell of her ear, I whisper, "Is that so?"

Sadie laughs but pushes off of me playfully. "She's lost her mind if she thinks I'm—"

Pulling the hair tie out of her ponytail, she sinks under the water, leaving me hanging. I thought I was feeling a vibe between us. I mean, *she* kissed *me* earlier. But maybe she really just wants to have friendly fun without benefits?

When she resurfaces, her hair is slicked back away from her face, water rolls down her chest, and she's laughing. Sadie wraps her arms around my torso, and I hold her so close I can see the tiny droplets of water that dot her eyelashes. "Sorry, forgot to finish my sentence," she says coyly. "I'm not sharing any details with her."

Leaning in, I press a soft kiss to her lips, tugging the bottom one with my teeth slightly. "That was cold, Sade. I thought for a second I had misread the vibe."

She rolls her eyes, but laughs cheerily. "Nope, I'm embracing the vibe." Sadie pulls away from me and spins in the water. "Look at me, practically the definition of carefree."

I should have known she'd take this whole thing to another level. The woman is top-speed all the time. Give her a test, and she's studying for it even after she's memorized the book. Ask her to have fun, and I guess she's suddenly a clown.

"We should probably get back up there. It looks like most of them are packing up. And I still need to help you solve your next clue."

Sadie nods, moving toward the beach. Once we are clear of the water, we trek up the sand to our towels. My sisters and Thad waved their goodbyes while we were still knee-deep, but Howie, Sam, Olive, and Ari wait idly.

"Sadie, it was so nice to spend the day with you. Please let me know if you need anything." Olive pulls her into a tight hug, not seeming to care about getting wet, and Sadie shudders a little. She's affectionate with me, but I haven't seen her be that way with anyone else aside from her nieces.

Sam nods, echoing the sentiment, before slapping me on the shoulder and shooting me a skeptical look. He's always been our protector, so I'm not surprised that he's being cautious about this whole situation.

"Sade, I'll see you on Sunday for family dinner. Call me if anything comes up." Howie gives her a side hug, and she punches his arm lightly. I can tell from just a few hours that they have a special bond, that they used to be tight and probably still would be if she weren't so busy with the Flames.

Ariella smirks at me, nodding between the two of us and tossing me a thumbs up. If Sadie notices it, she doesn't acknowledge it. There's some tension there, I'd guess over the man with red hair.

Once everyone has left, Sadie and I pack up our belongings and begin our walk back to my truck.

"Did you have fun?"

She tightens her grip on the bag she refused to let me carry. "Yeah. You have a lot of people. It's nice." Her voice goes up an octave when she says it, like the words are uncomfortable.

"Do you have a lot of friends in Golden City?" I chance the question, knowing she's shared her lack of a social life. The answer is one I can probably guess, but I'd like to know for sure.

"Hmm, I have a roommate, Meg. And a couple of friends at work, but we don't really hang out outside of the arena." Sadie steps up next to my truck. "I don't think you understand how busy these jobs are. You aren't going to have a ton of free time either."

I'm sure that's true, but I can't imagine being in Washington without anyone. Making friends—people I can count on—is a priority for me. It's hard for me to reconcile why it isn't for her. But I also don't want to dig too deep, as that's not what this is.

"Maybe. I guess I'll find out," I say instead. "Do you have the puzzle book with you?"

"No, I left it at my mom's house."

I hit the key fob, unlocking the door, opening it, and hoisting Sadie inside. Once I'm tucked in next to her, we head toward her house.

"Can I ask you something?" Sadie peers out the window, like she's watching for something.

I grab her hand. "Of course. I'm an open book, Sade."

"What's the deal with Thad?" She immediately bursts into a giggle as his name leaves her lips. "Do we like him?"

"No, he's a complete douche." I bite my cheek, trying not to laugh just from the sounds rolling out of her.

"Thank God!" she shouts. "I was worried I was the only one who noticed. He was literally checking out every woman within a one hundred yard radius."

I hit the turn signal a little harder than necessary. Just the thought of that dude pisses me off. "Yeah, Nora... hasn't quite figured out what she deserves. It's really hard to watch, but Mabel basically threatened us so we wouldn't give her a hard time. Something about her needing to make mistakes."

Sadie nods. "Makes sense, but Thad... I honestly feel bad for her. Maybe not dating is for the best. Do you want to know a secret?"

"Obviously." I slide my thumb over the back of her hand. Her comment twists my stomach, but I force myself to remember what this is—temporary. "Are you good if we stop and let Benny out really quick before getting the book?"

Sadie beams at me. "Obviously." She throws my word right back at me. "I sort of like Ariella, even though I want to hate her."

A hearty laugh rolls out of me, and Sadie joins in.

"That wasn't much of a secret, Sade. You don't filter your face very well."

"I do too."

"No, you do not."

She crosses her arms over her chest, huffing. "Okay, fine, whatever. But why did she have to be funny and nice in her own way? I've hated her for years, and then she just worms her way right into my heart. It's rude."

Blowing out a breath, I pull into my driveway and put the truck in park. "Now you know why How is in love with her." I unbuckle my seatbelt, and Sadie does the same. "Believe me, I've tried to tell him to move on. Those two are super codependent, though. I think if anyone has a secret, it's her."

Sadie's eyes widen comically big. "What secret is she keeping from him?"

"That she loves him too." Shrugging, I jump out of the truck, rounding it to open her door. "You know, I sort of like how short you are."

"What? Why?"

"Because you can't fight me on being a gentleman. You have to let me help you out of the vehicle so you don't break an ankle."

"My knight in shining armor." Sadie mocks me with her hand over her heart as she sticks her tongue out at me. I help her down, kissing her cheek as I do.

"If she loves him, I wish she'd admit it already." Sadie walks ahead of me up my front porch steps. "He's too nice to get his heart broken." She says it like it's a matter of fact, and honestly, it is. We all love Howie, even Olive finds the whole thing frustrating.

Pushing my key in the knob, I open the front door, and Benny leaps from his bed, plowing into Sadie. She drops to the floor, cuddling him and peppering him with kisses. But when she excuses herself to the bathroom, I force my pup to use the restroom outside.

My back porch isn't large, just big enough to have two iron chairs and a small table between. When I step out with Benny, smack in the middle of the table is Sadie's book.

What the hell?

"Sade!" I holler through the screen door. "Can you come here? There's something—"

"You've got to be kidding me." She pushes out the door, spotting the book. "I literally locked it in my suitcase before I left. With an actual lock."

"Does it... hmm... do you usually have to lock it up?"

"No. The damn thing just follows me around. I've tried everything, and it'll just show up. I threw it in the trash can before I ran into you at the diner that first day, and you picked it up off the floor. It makes no sense."

"It's magic."

Benny does his business, and I let him back into the house. Sadie folds herself into one of the chairs, running her fingers over the title, and I sit opposite her.

"You know what's so weird about this?"

"Other than the fact that it follows you, the ink changes color, and hints apparently appear in random places?"

"Yeah. Other than that." Sadie works to untie the twine holding it closed.

"Nope. No idea."

Sadie sighs, flipping it open to pull out the letter. She holds it up. "It's from Beth. I've known her my whole life, and I never once speculated that she had powers? Was a witch?"

Holding up a finger, I dart inside and grab two Diet Cokes from my fridge. Returning, I motion for her to proceed, popping the tabs and handing her one. Sadie takes a small sip.

"Sometimes people only show us who they want us to see. Maybe it's not something she wanted you to know."

"But why now?"

Standing, I grab our drinks, placing one in the crook of my arm and reach my free hand out to her.

"Let's go inside." Sadie doesn't question it, but the truth is simple. I feel compelled to be close to her during this conversation, to touch her or hold her if I need to.

We settle on the couch, our drinks on the small sofa table that sits behind it. Bridget insisted I needed it, and I have to admit it comes in handy. Holding her injured hand, I draw small circles on her palm.

"Is it possible she's showing you now because she decided that the risk of not helping you is greater than telling you the truth?"

Sadie peers at me, her neck flushing red. "No, I don't know. That's another thing that doesn't add up. I've always been this way. I mean, even in school, I was so focused I didn't really have a life. You remember. And none of these clues make sense. The ones we've solved have nothing to do with my life."

She's getting frustrated. Her chest heaves rapidly, and she's twisting her hair with her fingers like she wants to pull it out.

"I remember you went to prom with Bradley Bushnell. Seemed like you had a life that night." My skin heats at the reminder. Xav was right. I had a serious crush on her. I was just too young and too dumb to do anything about it.

Sadie snorts. "Oh my God. Are you jealous right now?"

I shake my head from side to side, biting the inside of my cheek.

"Yes, you are. Someone call the Mage Hollow Messenger!" Sadie pretends to yell to the empty room. "Max O'Reilly, the prince of Mage, is jealous of a boy whose hands shook so badly on the walk in he could barely escort me."

I tickle her side. "Okay, laugh it up. I'm not jealous."

"Yes, you are." Sadie continues to fall apart, trying to wiggle out of my hold. But I pin her to the couch instead with one arm on each side of her face.

"Okay, fine. I'm a little jealous. But only because I had a tiny crush on you." I bury my face in her neck, holding my weight off her as much as possible.

"What!" Sadie laughs harder now, her shoulders shaking uncontrollably. "There... is... no... way."

Pulling back slightly, I trail a finger down the side of her cheek and brush my thumb under her bottom lip.

"Sade, I'm not sure if you know this, but you're kinda sexy as hell." I dip forward, brushing my lips across hers lightly. "You've got the whole brainiac thing going on, always so organized, not to mention this face, among other things."

She blushes, closing her eyes as she shakes her head back and forth. "Max, stop."

"No."

"Yes."

"The best friendships are built on open communication, Sade. I'm being honest. I'm like really into you." I roll my hips forward so she can feel how much I'm telling the truth.

She covers her face, mumbling through her hands. "I secretly wanted you to ask me out back then."

"Sorry, I didn't hear you? What did you say?"

"Max!"

"Move your hands and look me in the eye when you tell me all my hot-for-my-high-school-tutor fantasies were real."

She moves her hands, but instead of admitting it, she kisses me. Her soft lips move over mine, teasing and testing. When she pushes her hands into my hair, I wedge my arm between her and the couch, rolling us so she's on top of me.

Sadie runs her tongue along the seam of my mouth, and I open willingly. We're frantic, tongues dancing over each other, desperate for more. My hands drift down her back, grabbing her ass hard as she grinds her hips into me. When I run my fingers under her tank top, her breath hitches briefly, but she bites my bottom lip before soothing it with tiny flicks.

Sliding my hand up further, my fingers wrap around her rib cage, and my thumb grazes her peaked nipple. A small moan releases from her throat, and I buck my hips up. It all feels so good, so right that it's almost too perfect.

Pressing tiny kisses down her neck, I glance up at her. She's a mess, in a good way—her hair is wild from air drying, lips swollen from being thoroughly kissed.

"Can I?" I tug on the hem of her tank top, and she quickly nods. With both hands, I slide it up and over her head, tossing it to the floor. Running my fingers along the edges of her triangle bikini top, I lean forward, pressing my lips to the salty skin directly over her heart.

"More, Max," she demands as she reaches behind her head and unties the string.

The triangles fall to her stomach, revealing her handful-size breasts, with tight pink nipples that are begging for me.

"Fuck, Sade. You're stunning."

I wrap my hand in her hair, pulling her back to me for a searing kiss. After only a moment, I release her lips, sliding my tongue down her neck until I'm sucking one of the tight buds between my lips. Sadie's breaths are heavy, slow puffs of air interspersed with sounds of approval as I spend equal time on both nipples.

She's grinding into my cock, riding me like there aren't several layers of fabric between us. It's too much to take—the sight of her, how perfect she is with those breathy little moans. I don't want to stop. I need to see her like this—falling apart in my hands.

"Sade, I have to—"

"Don't you dare stop, Max." Her eyes dart to mine, they're glassy, dazed.

Following her lead, I continue my assault on her chest, biting lightly then blowing gentle puffs of air on the marks I'm making. Sadie's legs start to shake, but she doesn't stop rolling her hips. Her mouth pops open, jaw going slack like she's seconds from ripping apart at the seams. She's enchanting, divine, like nothing I've ever seen—and as much as I've tried to hold out, I fall into oblivion—her name on my lips.

"Max, did you just?" Sadie stiffens as her eyes widen, and her lips tip into a grin. "You know?"

I run a hand down my face. "Sure did. And I'm not even a little bit ashamed about it."

Sadie snorts before leaning in to kiss my forehead. "Looks like you owe me one."

Twenty-One

Sadie

The Mirror of Truth

Max literally came in his pants last night, and it was the single hottest thing I've ever seen. To have someone so into you, so in the moment that they simply can't hold back—I'm riding a high I might never get over.

And it's strange because for the entire afternoon I didn't stress about work. Not once did I wonder if Levi had returned the youth coaches' emails, or if he'd gotten suckered into committing to something for Cooper's team that'll be hard to pull off.

I woke up feeling a little mixed up, like my insides were revolting but happy at the same time. It's not guilt, just a mild buzzing that's made its way under my skin—a trepidation stemming from dipping my toe over the line.

Max

> Hey, so I may have given Ollie your number.

> Thanks?

Max

> No, it's a good thing. But could we maybe keep what happened last night out of the conversation?

A burst of laughter rolls through me as my phone pings with a new notification. If he doesn't know that I'm not an over-sharer by now, I'm not sure he ever will.

Olive

> Hey Sadie. Max gave me your number. This is Olive, btw.

> Hi.

Olive

> I was wondering if you'd want to get lunch with me. I think we might have more in common than you realize.

> Sure, I don't have much going on. Want to meet at The Wharf?

Olive

> Sounds perfect. See you at noon?

> (Thumbs up*)

She obviously doesn't know that Max told me about what she went through last year. And why would she? Max has made it clear it's not something that she'd want to advertise. But I feel a little awkward knowing a secret about her—a little deceptive.

Max

The silence is deafening.

Sorry, I was texting your sister-in-law. Your secrets are my secrets.

Max

Phew! They already had a whole thing going about my journal… I think my mom sent the girls' photos of it.

And you're saying Olive has these pictures?

Max

Hilarious.

I'll ask her to bring them to lunch.

Max

You guys are hanging out?

Max

I'm not sure "displays of affection" is the right description of what happened between us last night—it was more passion-filled than loving. But affectionate isn't a word I would associate with myself. And one I'm not sure has much of anything to do with my fate despite being the most recent answer to a clue. After Max cleaned himself up yesterday, we ordered takeout, put on a movie we didn't watch, and spent way too much time trying to solve it.

4. Down

Heated: Demonstrative

Sliding my arm across my bed, I flip the book open to the fourth puzzle. The letters are spelled out in boxes, the gold script sunken deeply into the page. Four down, four to go. A sense of accomplishment sinks into me. I'm halfway through, halfway to figuring out what this is all supposed to mean, yet I couldn't feel further away from deciphering it.

I've been doing crosswords for years and have stacks of finished puzzles in boxes that I'm saving for a rainy day—the one that will come when I have a house of my own and can frame my favorite ones. The thing that's throwing me is that they always have a theme. Sometimes it's broad like a day at the beach, but occasionally it's something specific like a crossword that covers a particular sport. This one, albeit oddly easy to solve with Max, doesn't follow a pattern that I can tell. It's arbitrary, random words that could be classified as character traits—but traits I don't necessarily possess.

Scanning the four I've solved: Altruistic, Helpful, Reliable, and Affectionate—I find myself wondering if this puzzle even has anything to do with me. I could define things that I have done to fit each category, but the caviling in my brain makes me think it has nothing to do with me at all. These could describe literally anyone who is a decent human being, and that brings me back to my original conclusion—this is busywork.

Checking the time on my phone, I leap from the bed, throw the blankets off me, and dart toward the shower. I can't answer the questions that linger about why she gave me this or how it's enchanted, but I can go to this lunch and find out more about the last time this happened.

The Wharf is a classic New England waterfront restaurant. It sits on the edge of the water with enormous concrete pylons dotting the edge of the patio's retaining wall. There are round, weathered tables with creamy wicker chairs, and navy umbrellas that drop into the center of each one. The view is incredible, with sailboats and yachts of all shapes and sizes lining the marina. The water laps at the seawall, creating its own euphony over the sound of the humming restaurant.

Wrapping my hand around a long wooden handle to step inside, the smell of buttery seafood, french fries, and salty air wafts over me. It smells like home, exactly as I remember it, and my stomach growls.

"How many?" A blonde host greets me. She's dressed in a signature blue t-shirt that features a humpback whale on the breast pocket.

Scanning the restaurant, I lean in, trying to get a view of the patio from inside. "I'm actually meeting someone. I'm not sure if she's here yet."

"Does she have the most incredible tattoo sleeve? Red hair?" The woman holding a menu in her hands asks.

"Yes."

"Follow me."

Stepping through a glass door onto the same patio I've spent countless afternoons hanging out on, I spot Olive immediately. She's at a table in the far back corner, one that's right on the edge of the water. Her hand raises, waving delicately.

"Hey. I hope it's okay that we sit outside. I've been at Black Kettle all morning and needed a little air."

I slip into the seat across from her, nodding. "Of course, this weather is heaven compared to what I'm used to."

"I thought you lived in Golden City? It's not the same?"

A laugh rolls out of me. "No, I do. But most of my time is spent inside a chilly arena. I work for the Flames."

"What does that mean?" Her eyes narrow as she places her menu on the table.

"The hockey team? How do you get engaged to an O'Reilly and not know about the Golden City Flames?"

Olive giggles, sipping the water that's in front of her. "Oh. Yeah, I don't really pay attention to sports. When they watch it, I usually just read instead." She flips her hand in the air. "It's not really my thing. But it makes a lot more sense why Max thinks you're the coolest person he's ever met."

Tucking a chunk of hair behind my ear, a small smile forms on my lips. "You want to know a secret?"

"I've been dying to. Tell me everything."

"I'm not really a sports girl either." Her mouth falls open, and her eyes bug out of her head. "I know. It's shocking."

Olive laughs, and it's sweet sounding, like she's one of those genuine people who don't just laugh with you because they think it's the right thing to do.

A server approaches, a young guy with a shirt that matches the host's. He has golden-brown skin, neatly trimmed hair, and a set of dimples that would make even the toughest critics swoon. The name badge he's sporting reads: Manuel.

"Hello, ladies." He reaches to top off Olive's water glass, then fills mine. "Have you been here before?"

We both nod, momentarily enraptured by his smile. He probably makes a million dollars in tips—it should come with a warning. He's perfect for Nora, and apparently I'm now a matchmaker.

"Yes, I have," Olive purrs, and I raise an eyebrow at her.

Smiling, I nod. "Yep, me too."

"Well, I'm happy to give you more time if you'd like, or I can take both your drink and food orders."

"Manuel? This might seem a bit forward, but do you have a special someone in your life?" Olive asks, her voice full of a southern charm I hadn't noticed before.

He chuckles, rubbing his chin awkwardly. "People usually call me Manny. And unfortunately, no. I recently moved here. I'm not really into married women though." His eyes dart to the rock on Olive's finger, and she blushes.

I feel like I'm watching a train wreck. She isn't asking for herself, at least I highly doubt it with how into Sam she seemed yesterday.

Olive places a hand on her chest. "Oh, no. Good gravy. I didn't mean me." His eyes dart in my direction. "Nope, not her either. I have a sister-in-law who is adorable. I'd love to set you up sometime... as friends, of course."

He beams. "Yeah, that'd be cool. I'll write my number down for her." Pulling a notepad out of his apron pocket, he scribbles on the sheet, then tears it off and hands it to Olive. "What would you ladies like to order?"

We agree on sharing a couple of appetizers instead of getting our own meals: steamed shrimp, hush puppies, and calamari. And for drinks, she orders a Pellegrino with lime, while I opt for one with fresh pineapple. Manny swaggers away—a little more pep in his step than when he approached, if I'm not mistaken.

"Not going to lie, I wasn't sure where you were going with that whole thing for a minute," I say, pulling my sunglasses on.

"He's perfect for Nora."

"I thought so too, just from an objectively everyone has to be better than Thad perspective."

She throws her head back. "Ugh, I know. Mabel won't let any of us say anything, but I literally want to shower after being around him just to wash the ick off."

We tumble into a fit of laughter—one that feels easy, like I've known her forever. Manny drops our drinks off, smiling at both of us.

Olive straightens as we gain control of ourselves. "I have a bone to pick with you."

Having just taken a sip of my drink, I nearly spit it out. "What did I do? I barely know you."

"You told me you were going to tell me a secret." She points her finger at me. "And I thought it was going to be about the magical puzzle book. Since you basically let Ariella do all the talking and assuming yesterday."

"She is good at assuming, isn't she?" I snip, watching Olive's eyebrows shoot to her hairline.

That may have been too far. I meant what I told Max. She grew on me yesterday. I just want my cousin to be happy, and it seems like she's not going to give him that.

Olive pats my hand across the table. "I know she's annoying you because of How. It bothers me too, but everyone has their own path. Would it be easier if I told you what happened to me last year?"

Well, I guess that resolves that. Max must have shared that he told me.

"Sure, I'd love to hear your take on it."

Olive recounts the whole thing from beginning to end, without sparing a single detail. I'm in awe of her. My situation, it's something I can avoid or refuse to look at. I can't imagine having my feelings in an ever-changing tattoo on my arm. I also didn't ask for this and am not quite convinced it's not all just a ruse. My mind could be playing tricks on me, the same way a magician does a sleight of hand. Maybe I've imagined things happening that aren't really there.

"And now it's just there permanently? Your love story?" I pluck a shrimp off the platter that Manny delivered mid-story and pop it into my mouth.

"Yep. But it's sort of beautiful, right?" She twists her arm, pointing to the swirling colors embedded in her skin.

"It's stunning. I have only one question." I sip my drink, washing down the bite I finished chewing. "Do you regret it? Asking for help like that, then being given something so life-changing? It had to be confusing."

"No." Olive picks her fingernails. "I did. I wanted nothing more than to be done with it, done with Irina. But in the end, the gift she gave me is the one that led me to Sam. I don't know if we would be where we are today if I hadn't learned the lessons I needed to learn."

Her answer is poetic yet again, vastly different from my experience. I have learned nothing from the clues—nothing of substance, anyway.

"That's beautiful." I scooch back from the table. "I'll be right back. I'm going to use the restroom." Standing, I walk toward the glass door that leads inside, but Olive slides up next to me.

"What? I have to go too." She shrugs, pulling open the door.

"And our table? We could have taken turns." I slip past her, headed for the back of the restaurant.

She laughs. "I reserved it for the afternoon. No one is stealing it."

I guess she expected this conversation to take a lot longer than it has. We push into the two-stall bathroom, each taking one. When I'm three-quarters through relieving myself, a voice rings out, one I don't recognize.

"Hello, Olivia. It's been a long time."

That's weird. I didn't hear her exit the stall. I shift forward, looking at the ground under the wall to my left. Her feet are still there—painted toenails, brown sandals. The room is painfully quiet, as if Olive froze in place.

"Stop it, Irina. You guys made up. You're not toying with her," Beth's voice rings out.

The first one cackles. "Ollie, dear. You know I'm just having a little fun. How's Samuel? I guess my wedding invitation got lost in the mail."

My heart lurches into my throat, and my hand freezes midway to the toilet paper holder. Am I going to get the chance to ask Beth what all this nonsense is about? I spring into action, finishing what I came here to do, and exit the stall. The bathroom is empty—there's not a soul in here.

"Olive?"

Silence.

"Olive?"

"Uh, yeah. I'm good. I'm here." There's another flush, and she emerges to stand at the sink beside me. We wash our hands without saying a word. Did I imagine all that? Or did she hear it too?

"Did you—"

"Yes," Olive answers before I can finish, then spins to grab a paper towel to dry her hands. "Sadie, look." Her body freezes, all except her hand. She's pointing at a key that's dangling from the doorknob. It's affixed to one of those vintage hotel keychains shaped like a diamond.

As we glance back at the mirror, it fogs over as if we've been running the hot water too long. Then, suddenly, words are revealed one letter at a time as if someone is drawing them with their finger.

Your future won't wait forever. This will help you understand.

Olive clutches my arm, digging her fingers into my skin. "I'm calling, Sam. Grab the key and let's go."

"Why do we need the key? It might not even be related..."

"You always take what they give you, Sadie." She smiles at me, but chews her lip nervously. "If I learned anything, it's that everything is a clue."

Twenty-Two

Max

Mary-Kate & Ashley

"Sadie? Are you here?"

Laughter rolls out from my brother's living room, washing over me but not quite settling my anxiety. Rushing, I slip out of my tennis shoes and slide down the oiled wood entryway in my socks like I'm Tom Cruise in *Risky Business*—except with pants on.

Gliding to a stop halfway between the living room and kitchen, I see my friends. Sadie is perched near Olive on the couch, Howie's slumped on the floor by the whitewashed stone fireplace, and Sam's relaxing in his stuffed leather chair.

The only one who turns to acknowledge my entrance is the one I'm hoping to see most. Sadie's holding her hands out in a slow clap, and when our eyes meet, I feel nothing but relief. I wasn't sure what I was walking into. While my brother's been down this road before, I didn't find out until it was nearly over.

All I was aware of coming here is the vague message I got from Howie saying that Sadie and Olive had been confronted by Irina and Beth—that they were in trouble, and we were going to do something about it. What? I have no idea.

"Hey Maxie," Olive coos from her seat.

I nod, entering the room to slide up next to Sadie. Swiping the back of my hand over her cheek, I take my time checking for any injuries.

"Um, Max? What are you doing?" she asks, with a single brow raised and an amused grin on her face.

"What happened?" I continue my perusal. "Are you hurt?"

She laughs, tilting her head backward to rest on the cushions. "No. She wasn't even there, not really anyway."

"I thought you said there was a confrontation?" I shoot daggers at Howie. It's not that I'm mad about leaving my workout at the rink. It's more that I almost had a heart attack trying to get here.

"There was," he spits back, crossing his arms over his chest. "A verbal one."

Sam and I look at each other, a silent conversation passing between us. He's not happy Olive's involved in this. He never wanted her to see Irina again after Ollie cracked her head open in the cemetery, and the last time she did was the night they broke up. His concern is completely valid.

"Okay, now that you're all here. Let us just tell you what happened. Then we can decide if action is needed." Olive stands, pacing as she continues.

My sister-in-law recounts the story, everything from some guy named Manny to a key and a message in a bathroom mirror. The whole time she's speaking, I attempt to gauge how Sadie is feeling, but she remains stoic as ever—unbothered.

"And then, we grabbed the key, paid Manny, and called Sam on the way here," Olive finishes.

My brother huffs. "Who is this Manny guy? And did you need to be so descriptive?" He glares at his fiancée with an almost imperceptible smirk, but all she does is laugh before crawling in his lap.

"He was cute, but no different from you talking to Brooke the bartender from Golden City," Olive playfully pats his chest.

Sadie perks up at the name. "Brooke Larkin?"

"Fuck if I know." Sam shrugs.

"Was she stunning, with shoulder-length brown hair, best friends with Levi Montgomery's fiancée?" Sadie prods.

Sam runs a hand through his hair. "Actually, yes."

Sadie sucks her teeth. "It's a good thing you haven't seen her, Olive. She's as gorgeous as Manny was hot."

"Oh, I have. I internet-stalked her." Olive giggles to herself. "Considered sending her a thank-you card for sending this one home alone, even."

"Wait a minute." I hold up a hand, taking a calming breath. "What did Manny have to do with this story? Other than the two of you wanting to get in his pants?" The words taste bitter coming out of my mouth. I know Sadie and I aren't even really a thing, but I don't want to think about her with someone else.

"Nothing, just wanted to see y'all's faces," Olive explains as Sadie stands to high-five her.

"It was pretty priceless. I think even Howard got jealous for a second," Sadie adds.

"So you just dragged us all here to fuck with us?" Howie mutters. "Uncle Lon is going to be so pissed at you, Sadie. I left in the middle of the rush."

Her shoulders push back, and her legs widen just slightly, as if she's preparing for an argument. My heart rate increases—Sadie, ready to throw down, sends a rush of excitement due south.

"No, How. I'm not saying this coulda been an email. I'm saying that one tiny part was included for our enjoyment. The rest of the story is true." She reaches into her pocket and pulls out a gold key that's affixed to a flat, diamond-shaped keychain. "See?"

"What does emailing have to do with this?" Sam asks.

Ignoring him and reaching out, I pull on her hand until she comes back to sit beside me. My palm rests on her thigh out of habit, or maybe for my comfort at this point. Sadie holds the key out to me, and the moment it hits my fingers, it shocks me.

"Jesus fuck!" I shout, dropping it. "The thing just gave me a zinger."

Sam shakes his head while the rest of the group is left both shocked and amused. Sadie bends forward, grabbing it from the floor.

"Do we have any idea what it goes to?" Sam asks. "Or is that what they emailed?"

Sadie looks at the key clutched in her hand. "It was a joke, Sam." Sadie deadpans. "And nope, just that it's supposed to help somehow."

Olive pries herself off my brother's lap, standing and walking toward the kitchen. "I'm going to get some stuff to help us think."

By stuff, she meant an Aperol Spritz for her and Sadie and a beer for each of the rest of us. She returns with a tray like a server flitting around her own house, and we inspect the key.

"Looks like any run-of-the-mill key you'd get from the hardware store." Howie finishes staring at it and tosses it to Sam.

My brother catches it, turning it over in his palm a few times. "Any thoughts on what JBI could mean?"

The keychain itself is fairly plain except for the inscription.

"Ooh, ooh, I know." Olive raises her hand like we're on some sort of trippy game show. "Josephine, Beth, Irina." A shiver rolls through her on the last one.

Sadie's eyebrows shoot to her hairline, and she gulps her drink.

"So, it would be safe to assume, given what happened..." Howard pushes his hair back with his hand. "That maybe this goes to something they've wanted you to find. We could try the house."

Olive groans, Sam tightens his grip on the beer bottle he's holding, and Sadie nods.

"Yes, let's do that. It's been restored, so we could just walk in like a couple of tourists and see what we find."

The Hollowell House was discovered this past fall after an old map of Mage Hollow was found in the city archives. We'd all known the house was creepy with its overgrown vines and decrepit roof, but the rumor was always that it had been abandoned by a judge's wife when he was found guilty of some murders in the sixties.

When the map was found a few weeks after the Hollow Hearts Festival, the town went crazy. Several times during restoration, it was broken into by teens looking for a good scare. And there was one group of women who claimed to be descendants of Irina who protested the work by chaining themselves to the trees out front. After months of work and drama, it opened for tours this spring.

Gravel crunches under the tires of my truck as we pull into the parking lot. The front lawn, now cleared of trees, is expansive enough to fit fifty vehicles. Today, there are only three—they all belong to us.

"This is kind of silly, right?" Sadie leans forward to glance out the front windshield. "This key could be completely random. Maybe it wasn't even part of the message." Her voice goes up, and her knee bounces.

"Sadie, it's probably related. But you've known Beth for years. It's not like she's going to harm you." My thumb grazes the back of her hand. "She said she's doing this to help you."

"No, you're right. I don't know why I'm nervous. I guess it's just that before the book thing seemed silly—like it was just a distraction." She takes a deep breath, releasing it slowly. "But hearing their voices in the bathroom, knowing they weren't actually there—"

"It's all real now?"

Her eyes dart to mine. "Exactly."

Howie, Olive, and Sam have exited their vehicles and are waiting by a lap rail fence built out of hemlock that lines the walkway to the door.

"Well, I made you a deal. We're supposed to have fun in exchange for solving this mystery..." I hold up a finger to my brother in the universal sign for *one second*. "Why don't we pretend we're trying to solve a mystery that has nothing to do with your future?"

"Like Mystery Inc.?" Sadie asks, smirking.

"Who?"

"You know, Shaggy, Scoob..."

Her eyes widen, and her lips purse as if she's trying to hold in a laugh, like she can't believe I didn't immediately know what she was referring to.

"Personally, I was thinking more like Mary-Kate and Ashley," I say, and Sadie bursts out laughing.

"Deal."

Hopping out of the truck, I help Sadie down, and we walk hand in hand toward the group.

"Took ya long enough." My brother checks the watch he isn't wearing.

"Sorry. I needed a little pep talk from Mary Kate," Sadie says, dropping my hand and stepping up next to Olive.

"What? I thought I was going to be Ashley." Stomping my foot, I stick my bottom lip out in a pout.

Howie chuffs. "And you guys think I'm the weird one."

Our group approaches the entrance, taking the two steps onto the freshly lacquered porch. Olive sighs, commenting under her breath about how different it looks from her last visit. Sam reaches for the door handle, but a bubbly blonde flings it open. From the overly welcoming smile and the branded t-shirt, it's clear she's an employee.

"Welcome to the Hollowell House. Are you here for a tour?" She scans our group, likely not expecting such a big one on a random summer day. I imagine it'll be much busier during fall, especially close to the Hollow Hearts Festival.

Olive extends her hand. "Hi, I'm Olivia Bowman. I work at Black Kettle Bindery." The girl shakes her hand. "We were hoping to have a look around... self-guided?"

"I'm Katie." Her gaze coasts across our group. "I'm not really supposed to let people do that. We usually walk you through and explain everything."

Sadie digs her elbow into my side, nodding her head toward the girl.

"Hi Katie." I glance at Sadie for reassurance, and she tips her chin so slightly no one else could've noticed. "Have I seen you around?"

Her cheeks blush, and her lashes flutter. "Oh, maybe? Do you hang out at the Iceplex?"

Sadie nudges my foot with hers. "Do I? I basically run the place, babe. I'm Max O'Reilly." I drape my arm over her shoulders, turning her so we can walk into the house. "I think I've seen you there. Don't you think we could work something out? A little favor for an old friend?"

"Max? As in Mad Max, star forward?" She chews her bottom lip.

"The very one. What do you say?" I trail my fingers down her arm, squeezing her hand gently. I know I'm flirting for a reason, but my stomach knots slightly. I've never had a problem with it before. It's harmless, really. But something about it feels wrong, different with Sadie standing only a few feet away.

"I, well, sure. I guess it couldn't hurt. Just promise to be quick. Ten minutes, then I'm coming to find you."

A small scoff comes from behind me, and Olive giggles. Spinning, I wave my arm for my group to proceed. Howie heads for the back of the house, Sam and Olive step toward what appears to be a kitchen with a small work table directly in the center, and Sadie skips toward the steps. Following closely behind, I have to take them two at a time to catch up to her.

She pushes into a wooden door that appears to be made from three boards nailed together by cross sections at the top and bottom. There's a wooden handle with a string latch, and it's stained a rich brown color.

"In a rush?" I ask, stepping in behind her.

Sadie rolls her eyes, crouching to look under the bed. "You didn't have to follow me."

"Oh, hmm. Was I supposed to stay with Katie?" Her head whips around at lightning speed, her lips pursed in a tight line. I can't help but smirk.

"Sure, that would be fine."

"Okay." My heart stutters, a small part of me—the needy part—hoping she'd rather I didn't hang out with the woman downstairs. Turning on the ball of my foot, I take a step toward the door.

"Max, wait."

"You jealous, Sade?"

Another eye roll. "No." She chews her lip.

"Sure about that?"

"Okay, fine. Maybe a little. But that's not important... I think I found something." She slides a small box out from under the bed. It's dusty, like it's been sitting here far longer than the restoration.

Dropping beside her, I squeeze her shoulder gently. "Try it."

Sadie fumbles with the key, pulling it from the pocket of her cross-body purse. She moves to insert it into a small hole at the center of the box, but before it touches the small iron lock, the latch flips open. My mouth drops open, and Sadie sucks in a deep breath.

"I didn't even put it in," she whispers.

"We seem to have that problem a lot these days."

A laugh bursts out of her, and I promptly make a shushing noise while flipping the lid open. Inside sits a single piece of parchment with a message.

Like a clue reveals your one true fate. A key unlocks a future—one you cannot escape. Your destiny is binding, a path so crystal clear when you stop minding.

Sadie grabs her phone and snaps a picture before closing the lid and sliding the box back into its place.

"What does it mean?"

Sadie shakes her head. "I have no idea. It makes it sound like this is metaphorical, like it doesn't actually unlock something physical."

"Any luck in here?" Howie pokes his head into the room just as we stand to move toward the door.

"Maybe." Sadie holds her phone out to him, and Howie reads the riddle. "It's not here. It can't be, right?"

Howie confirms with a nod of his head, and we head back downstairs to find Sam and Olive.

We may not have gotten exactly what we came for, but one thing is clear as we exit the house—Beth is playing a game with Sadie. She just doesn't realize that Sadie teamed up with a guy who plays every game to win.

Twenty-Three

Sadie

The Bubble Bursts

The sound of rain tinking off the roof makes it hard to sleep. For most people, that would be calming, and it would lull them to sleep as if they were counting sheep, one drop after the next. But for me, it's incessant—an unwelcome chorus to the rhyme already playing in my head on repeat.

The key is going to unlock a future. Not mine specifically, just a future that I won't be able to escape. What does that even mean? I've asked myself a thousand times since we left the house, a thousand times in the past thirty-six hours.

This whole thing started as a way to find my fate, supposedly. And now the first real development, the first time I feel like this has moved beyond just another item on my to-do list... it's not even my riddle to unravel. I'm practical, I play it safe, and this—it's infuriating.

I reach for a glass of water on my nightstand, and the alarm clock reads 5:46 am. It's too early to mosey to the kitchen to make coffee. But it's too late to fall back asleep and not waste the day away, so I lay here. Staring at the ceiling, hoping something other than Max starts to make sense.

But when did that happen?

When did my new friend start to be the only thing in my hectic life that made any sense? On paper, he doesn't—we are both leaving in a couple of weeks. The adventures (some planned and others not), the fun, the laughter we've shared... it will all be a distant memory soon. A time I look back on with reverence.

So why, when everything else has always taken top priority in my life, is it so easy to get lost in him? It's too easy to forget everything else exists when he's in the room. Max takes up space. Maybe too much space.

My phone vibrates on the bed beside me, the glow of the screen illuminating the room with a message.

Alex

Hey Sadie, just wanted to check in. Hope things are going well.

A scoff sneaks between my lips. Alex is kind, caring in a way that's not fake, but we aren't really friends. And she has to know after months of working closely together when her son was the spotlight player, that being away like this isn't easy for me.

Hey. Things are fine. What's wrong?

Alex

Nothing. Just making sure you're okay.

Alex... it's not even six in the morning.

My phone rings.

"Hello?"

"Okay, so I didn't want to alert anyone and start a shitstorm for Levi. But... I heard something." Her voice is hushed, and the faint sound of water running trickles in the background.

Sitting up in bed, I pop my earbuds in, grab my laptop, and power it on.

"I'm listening. What's going on?"

"Hold on." The phone goes silent except for a door clicking open, then closed. "Okay, sorry. I had to sneak out of the house so I wouldn't wake anyone up."

"Yeah?"

"Well, it could be nothing. It's probably a rumor, and..."

I push the earbuds in further because she's either beating around the bush or I'm not fully awake. "And?"

"And there's an expose. I heard one of the moms at Coop's practice gossiping about how they aren't sure it's a good idea for any of the boys to support an organization that's not keeping a full accounting of where the Gala money is going. She said there's an article coming out."

Laughter rips through my body. The notion is hilarious. It's so untrue it's not even believable.

"Sadie!" Alex huffs. "I'm serious."

I bite my cheek to contain myself. "Oh, I know. But it's not true. I file hundreds of documents every year with the IRS, not to mention the ones that are needed to keep the charitable arm designated as a 501(c)(3). Which mom was it?"

"I know, but Levi can't take another hit after last season's scandal. It almost broke him, Sadie. Why do you think you're on leave? He's worried about his people being okay, healthy, happy..." Alex's voice cracks as she trails off. "It was Jeremy's mom, Evelyn Green."

I type her name into my social media app, nodding as soon as her picture populates. "Yep, that's who I assumed. Do you still have access to my email?"

"Yeah, why?"

"She has a folder." I set my computer on the bed next to me. "Classic helicopter enabler if you ask me. Look through the folder, and if you're still concerned, I'll do some digging."

Alex hisses as the echo of her fingers clacking computer keys rattles through the phone.

"Is this bitch for real?"

"Yep." Burrowing down beneath my quilt, my stomach unknots. I was worried for half a second. But I know for a fact that Evelyn Green only cares about one thing—letting everyone know her son is the best. She was furious when Cooper was chosen as our first spotlight, and I've been ding-donged by her almost daily since. She'll say anything—*threaten* anything—to nab the honor for her son.

"Thanks, Sadie. I'll handle it."

"Of course. You know I could come back now, if you need me..." My heart thumps at the words, but for the first time in forever it's not with excitement. It's with hesitancy, like I'm ready but also not at all.

"No, we're good. I hope you're having fun, taking this leave seriously."

"It was worth a shot. But yeah, I am."

"Good. Talk to you soon."

"Bye, Alex."

The phone clicks off, and I strip the earbuds out. This is the thing I should be focusing on. I should be spending my free time making sure I can hit the ground running when I return.

A sense of relief hits me. While talking to her is a reminder that I've all but forgotten the rink for the last few days, it's also the first time that I haven't felt unsure about my status there. When I arrived in Mage Hollow, I didn't know if Levi would take me back. Now, after gaining a bit of perspective, I'm confident he will. Maybe *that's* the progress he was hoping to see.

I wish I could tell him, share the epiphany... but his fiancée just snuck out to chat with me. I refuse to be the one who wakes him. So instead, I text Max.

> **Guess what?**

Max

> **Is this a dream?**

> **What?**

Max

> **It's 6:16... AM!**

Whoops! I sort of forgot how early it was.

> **Sorry! Call me when you wake up. I have news.**

Tossing my phone aside, I lay back against the pillows. I'm still wide awake, but now it's not annoyance that plagues me... it's excitement.

"Remind me again why you drive a literal monster truck?" Max grins as he hoists me out of the passenger seat, setting me down gently.

My ankle-height Wellies squelch in the soggy grass, still overrun with water from the overnight showers, as he releases his hold on my waist. The sun hangs high in the sky, starting to reheat the air after the summer storm. But the breeze lingers, dropping a fine mist on everything it touches.

A shiver runs through me, and I clutch my cardigan.

"Cold?" Max asks while unclipping Benny from his vehicle harness, lifting him down, and double-checking his leash.

I shrug, looping my crossbody over my head. "Not really, it's just damp."

"I thought they'd cancel." Max shuts my door and tugs my hand toward a small white building sitting off in the distance. Windows cover almost every wall, like a greenhouse of sorts but with a standard asphalt shingle roof. And it's surrounded by the most beautiful flowers I've ever seen, rows upon rows of mounded zinnias in a rainbow of colors. It's a sight so serene I'm confident it'll be permanently inked into my memory.

"I'm shocked my sister still wanted to come," Max grunts.

He filled me in on the ride over. Apparently, Bridget recently started dating the eldest Zarichny daughter, Zuri. And since she teaches a bouquet-making class every Saturday morning in the summer, Bridget thought it would be nice to support her. As for how Max got roped into attending—he wouldn't say, but I'm also not complaining. I'm a sucker for a classroom setting, and I haven't visited this farm since I was a kid.

Benny bounds between us as we make our way to the building. There's a pea gravel pathway about twenty feet out from the building leading to a matching patio, and I'm grateful that both he and I are out of the mud. His short little legs were sinking with each leap, and I'm confident his belly is covered.

Only a few steps away from the entrance, I stop, unzipping my purse to pull out a small travel pouch of puppy wipes. Dipping down, I pet the sweetest boy on his head.

"Sade?" Max's voice washes over me. "Did you bring those just for Benny?"

Peering up at him through my lashes, I smile shyly. "Maybe?" I pull open the top of the blue package and remove one. "I hoped you were bringing him, but I also didn't want to carry him the whole time." I swipe the cloth over his belly, working to clean off the brown gush coating him.

"It felt like we'd be going backward if we didn't allow him to walk on the grass."

He looks like he wants to say something, but his eyes zip to my right instead. Following his line of sight, mine land on a pair of red hunter boots that are attached to a shivering Bridget.

"Please tell me he looks like that because you're taking care of his baby voluntarily and not because he asked you to," she coos, and I laugh.

"Just being practical." I raise my hands, shoving the dirty wipes into the pocket of my black denim overall shorts. Cleaning Benny required the entire package, so it looks like one of us is carrying him despite my thinking ahead, unless this is an indoor class.

"Mm-hmm." Bridget smirks. "Okay, so I don't really know what to expect. Just that Zuri said we would do a class inside first, then a tour." She fiddles with the hem of her knotted tank top.

"Don't forget the picnic." Max winks at his sister.

"I didn't know there was a picnic." I grab the leash from Max's hand, twisting it around my wrist a few times so Benny can't stray far enough to undo my work.

Bridget's cheeks flush, and she gnaws on her bottom lip. "Ugh! You're the worst, Max." She shoves her brother's shoulder. "Sadie, I sort of begged him to come and make this a double date after class. Things are new, and our mother keeps insisting that Zuri come to family dinner. I thought easing her in, one sibling at a time, might make us easier to digest. But it was all supposed to seem natural... spur of the moment."

"Like you eased me into it at the beach when seven people randomly had a Wednesday off?" I laugh. She groans, mumbling an apology under her breath. "It's fine. I'm not long-term, but Zuri could be."

Max's face twists at my statement, mimicking the way my heart felt saying the words. We can't be anything, but voicing it doesn't make it easier—I'm falling for him. In a perfect world, I think Max and I could make this work. He has everything I've ever looked for in an ideal man. But that's not reality when the timing isn't right.

He clutches my hand, pulling me closer to his side as the door to the little white cottage swings open, and out steps a tall, slender woman with hair as black as a raven's feathers.

"Welcome!" she calls to us and the group of guests that have congregated on the stone patio. "Come on in and find a seat. We will get started in about five minutes."

Bridget leads the way, greeting Zuri with a small peck on the cheek. It's adorable, heartwarming to watch the way they look at each other—like no one else exists because they are completely and hopelessly enamored. Squeezing Max's hand a little tighter, we slip past them and find a spot near the far back corner.

The space inside the cottage is set up exactly like a classroom. There is one long table at the front, with large white buckets overflowing with flowers in a line down the center. And there's about ten smaller rectangular tables made of whitewashed oak in two equal rows, with matching stools for the guests to sit at.

"So, a picnic? What did you make?" I elbow Max gently while rubbing my other hand over Benny's head. Max is cradling him in his arms like a baby.

He kisses the puppy's head. "I bought stuff as cooking isn't really my strong suit. But I think you'll like it."

Max is sweet, and he continues to surprise me. On one hand, he can be such an overzealous flirt, but on the other, he is kind—caring enough to help his sister out on a Saturday when he could be sleeping in. I lean in, pressing my lips to his cheek. He leans his head toward me, resting it on the crown of mine while I burrow into his shoulder. I'm sure we look like a picture-perfect couple, and for a second, I close my eyes, allowing myself to pretend we are.

"What did you want to tell me this morning?" he whispers as people continue to shuffle in and find their seats.

"Oh, I talked to Alex this morning—Coach Montgomery's fiancée." I shift back to an upright position. "I was worried that maybe he wouldn't bring me back after all this... but it sounds like my job is secure." Picking at the strings on the hem of my shorts, I avoid his eyes.

"Of course he is. He'd be crazy not to." Max tips my chin up with his index finger. "You're amazing at what you do. You'll be helping those kids again and burying yourself in work before you know it."

And the bubble I built around us this morning bursts.

Max is right. The clock is winding down, and I still have so much to figure out. I don't have time to fantasize about what this could be between us, not with puzzles to solve and riddles to unwind.

Twenty-Four

Max

Shadow Daddy

"Alright, everyone. Welcome to Zarichny's Zinnia's. We are thrilled to have you all with us this morning." Zuri captures the attention of the room, taking her seat on a stool at the front table while Bridget slides onto the seat next to me. "I'm going to start by explaining the fresh flowers we have and how to build a perfect bouquet for any occasion, then we'll do a tour."

The room erupts with applause, particularly from what looks to be a bachelorette party up front that may have overindulged on mimosas this morning. This isn't really my scene, but they seem enthused.

"We should have ridden on their party bus to get here," Bridget whispers, making Sadie giggle.

Zuri holds up a green flower with a long stem and bunches of leaves hanging off it. "This is a Queen Lime. It's the only variety of Zinnia that comes in this shade, and it's perfect for filling in your bouquets as it creates depth amongst the brighter colored Benary's Giants." Zuri waves her arm toward the buckets filled with purple, pink, crimson, and yellow flowers.

She continues telling the group about how the stems are grown, proper harvest techniques, and what a balanced arrangement looks like. I'm sure it's valuable information to have. Heck, I'd consider giving the whole gardening thing a whirl if I planned to stay here. But right now, the only thing on my mind is the woman seated next to me.

Sadie said she was worried they wouldn't allow her to come back, and that gives me pause. We've talked about this work thing before, about what happened. But today feels different, like she finally fully admitted that she was actually scared. Why would she assume anyone would consider losing her? I've never seen her in action at work, but I know without a doubt she's brilliant at what she does. Sadie remembered wipes to clean off my dog for God's sake—she's three steps ahead at all times, which would be valuable to any boss.

People shuffle around the tables, making a neat line toward the front to grab flowers. Sadie and Bridget move to stand.

"I'll just wait here." I nod toward a sleeping Benny, cozy in my arms. "Just grab me some of the pink ones."

Sadie smirks but nods in acknowledgment before leaving me at the table alone. Watching her walk to the front with my sister feels right. This is where I'm supposed to be, not chasing a fragment of my old dream. But there's the rub. My life recently has amounted to nothing more than glorified settling. I wanted to play in the NHL and worked for it since I could barely tie my shoes. Now, I'll be sharpening skates and handing sticks to the players that actually get to. I've spent most of my life looking at the love my parents shared, aspiring to find it. And now I'm with a woman who checks all the boxes, but the timing is wrong. It feels unfair, but... what in life isn't?

My role here isn't to fall for the girl—I know I don't get her in the end. But reminding my heart not to latch onto all the little things that make her so uniquely magnificent is a tall order. Especially when the whole guise of this arrangement is to have fun. It's like being on one of those dating shows where everything seems perfect because real life doesn't exist in our little summer bubble—I just need to remember that.

"I grabbed you a bunch of pink, but I threw a few green ones in there in case you wanted to create depth." Sadie sets what looks to be fifty flowers on the table in front of me. "It was a fight with the ladies up there, but when they saw you sitting with Benny they caved."

"I don't think it was the dog that did it, as much as I hate admitting that," my sister chimes in, already arranging a bouquet next to me.

Sadie huffs, makes eye contact with a tall blonde staring in our direction, then plants one on me. Her lips are commanding, like she's asserting her ownership, and I can't help but sink into it. The fact that she so openly displays affection, that she stakes her claim, is beyond attractive. Sadie wraps her hands in my hair, stroking her thumb along my cheek. We break apart only when Bridget coughs dramatically.

"Seriously? Get a room, would ya?"

A laugh bubbles in my chest. "Sorry, Bridg. I can't help it that the ladies love me."

That earns me a hit to the shoulder from the only woman in the room for whom I hope that's true. But I wink at her, and she slips into the chair beside me, wrapping her arm around mine to pet Benny.

After some time has passed, the bouquets are finished, and the room is cleaned up, Zuri leads the group of us outside for the tour. Because of the muddy terrain, most of the guests duck out early—including the bachelorette party who announce their next stop, Union Tavern—which allows for Zuri to pass off the tour to one of her sisters and for us to get a private experience on the way to our picnic.

Sliding onto the back of a teal-painted golf cart, Sadie, Benny, and I settle in while Bridget and Zuri sit up front.

"How long have you owned this place?" I ask Zuri.

"I'm fourth generation. There wasn't much of a choice growing up, we were raised to be flower farmers." My sister glances at me from the front, a look that tells me I shouldn't announce how bad Bridget is at keeping plants alive. "I love it. Getting to be in nature, seeing the literal fruits of your labor. I wouldn't want to do anything else."

Sadie pinches my thigh, and I yelp in response.

"What was that for?"

"Fix your face," she whispers.

I stick my tongue out at her instead.

We ride in silence for a few minutes, streaks of color passing us by as the cart carries us over a small hill and into a clearing. There aren't any flowers planted in this spot, making it the perfect place to spread out, but it overlooks what Zuri refers to as "The Valley". Neat rows of flowers line the field, sorted by color, making a pristine rainbow.

"It's beautiful. Oh my gosh, Max, look." Sadie points to the flowers, her eyes lighting up in delight.

I drop a kiss on her forehead before placing Benny on the ground and moving to spread out a blanket I packed. The sun dried some of the dew from the grass while we were inside, but our butts still might end up wet. Bridget pulls out our sandwiches, some chips, and a baggie of food for Benny.

"Wait, Max, did you bring drinks?" My sister digs in the picnic basket, searching for the water I know I put in there.

"Yeah. I even threw in two extras. Did you check under the spare blanket?"

"It's empty. There's nothing in here." Bridget narrows her eyes at me, obviously annoyed, so I pop up and look myself.

"I swear I packed them. I left the bag out in front of the building. You don't think someone would have taken it?"

Bridget places a hand on her hip. "Who would steal our water?"

"The leggy blonde—"

"The Bachelorette—"

Sadie and Zuri speak at the same time, tumbling into laughter.

"It's okay, Bridg. Let's just run back to the house real quick to grab some," Zuri says.

I shrug. "Yeah, you go. Sadie and I will stay here and save the spot."

We don't really need to save it, as it's not like anyone is flocking here to take it. But I wouldn't mind a moment alone, and I'm sure my sister needs a little one-on-one time with her girl as well. They hastily agree, zooming away as we remain on the side of the hill.

"I have so many thoughts." Sadie slides down onto the blanket, and I take the seat next to her. "What an interesting job."

I slide my hand into hers, intertwining our fingers. "I guess. It's pretty cool though, having something guaranteed. Bridget will never last out here... she's killed every plant she's ever been given." Benny slips between us, curling up in Sadie's lap. "Speaking of jobs though, why'd you think Levi wasn't going to take you back?"

"That's loaded." She blows a raspberry. "I guess I've never had anyone outside of my family and Beth that really cared if I stuck around. My dad abandoned us when the burden of his family became too great. I think a part of me assumed that since I had a panic attack, since I'd sort of become the burden, that he'd think it was easier to replace me."

My heart breaks for her. No one should have to wonder if they are enough, if one singular trait is enough to categorize them as unworthy, unlovable.

Scooping Benny from her lap, I settle him on the blanket and pull Sadie in between my legs so her back is leaning against my chest. Resting my chin on her head, I stroke my hands up and down her arms as tenderly as I can.

"We promised to be honest, right?" I ask, waiting for her nod. "We haven't known each other that long, especially if you don't count the tutoring days. But I know one thing as firmly as I know my own name. You are worthy of every dream you have, Sade, of everything you could ever want. Anyone who would even consider replacing you is an idiot."

"Why? Everyone is replaceable, Max, especially at work."

"Not you." I kiss her neck. "You're a unicorn, a breath of fresh air, a rare work of art that's so beautiful to look at it almost hurts. There isn't a single other person on this planet who comes remotely close to being you. And the fact that I get to spend time with you, that you'd even consider being in my life, or working for Levi... that's a gift that neither of us could ever repay."

"So are you—a cocky, funny-ass unicorn, but a unicorn, no less." Sadie turns in my arms, kissing me.

I'd call her on the deflection, but her tongue traces the seam of my lips, and I get lost in the moment, lost in exploring her. Running my fingertips along the side of her overalls, Sadie twists until she's straddling me. My hands assist, sliding to her ass to pull her closer.

Sadie toys with the button on my shorts, beginning to slip it through the hole—and Benny barks. It's not his quiet puppy dream-grumble, instead, it's as loud as I've ever heard him. I pull back as we both turn to find what's got him riled up.

Perched not over ten feet from the end of our blanket is a ground-hog in a t-shirt?

"Do you see—"

"Does that say what I think it says?" Sadie asks, her mouth hanging open in disbelief.

Benny continues barking, and the damn thing just stares at us. Lifting Sadie off my lap, I move to stand. But before I'm all the way up, Benny leaps off the blanket and chases the damn rodent down the hill.

"Benny, wait!" Sadie shouts, springing up to chase after them into the rows of flowers.

I run straight while they take a loop, hoping to head them off. It's like a comedy show—Benny following the groundhog under each mound of zinnias while Sadie is leaping over them. They make zigzag after zigzag, weaving so much that Sadie looks like she's playing some weird game of hopscotch. I stop, considering which direction would give me the best chance to catch them—but the next thing I know, Sadie's boots are over her head, and a scream rips through the air.

Rushing toward the scene, I'm relieved to find her laughing. Sadie is sprawled out, flat on her back in the mud between two rows of pink and orange flowers. Benny is at her side, nudging her leg, while the groundhog looks on from fifty yards away with judgment on his face.

"Hey, are you okay?" She laughs harder, clutching her stomach with one hand and her cheek with the other. "How's the mud?"

"It's great, like being at a high-end spa." She grins, sitting up. "Can you believe that just happened?"

"What? The high-speed chase, or the wild animal wearing a shirt that says *Shadow Daddy?*" I glance toward the chunky rodent—he's still watching us with a smug expression. Sadie continues to laugh hysterically while tears streak down her face, and Benny gives up curling into the mud beside her. "You need me to help you up?"

"Yeah...that...would...be...great," she wheezes.

Extending my hand, I link our fingers and pull. But my feet slide in the slippery goop, and the next thing I know I'm lying right on top of her with the ground squelching around us.

Water splashes the grass in my backyard as I rinse suds off of a very soapy—but finally mud-free—Benny.

"Two words, Max." Sadie holds up her fingers while I continue spraying my pup. "Shadow Daddy."

We've been laughing about the groundhog in a t-shirt for the last hour, and I don't expect it to stop soon. It was the craziest thing I've ever seen. When Zuri and Bridget returned, they explained that Zuri's youngest sister had recently adopted him after the family spent a year being plagued by the rodent. Apparently, he is friendly but also quite a shit-stirrer.

"I think he's rinsed. Do you want me to take you home? Or... we could clean up here." After the last few hours, I hope she opts to stay. I'd like to spend more time with her, but I don't want her to feel pressured one way or another.

Sadie saunters toward me, a sheepish grin gracing her lips. "I'd like to stay." She runs a finger through the mud on my cheek, trailing it down my bare chest. Removing my shirt to wash Benny seemed practical—now it feels like an unintentional thirst trap that's thankfully working for me.

"Let's go." I put my hand on her lower back, guiding her to the door.

We kick off our shoes, and Sadie waves her arm for me to lead the way. The tension between us is thick—neither of us saying a word. Each step feels weighted, as if we are about to check a box that can't be unchecked, ring a bell that can't be unrung.

Pushing into my bedroom, I grab a change of clothes for each of us from my cherry wood dresser.

"I think these will fit if you tie the string extra tight." My voice shakes as nerves race down my spine. I'm not even sure why I'm nervous. This isn't my first rodeo.

Sadie steps into the attached bathroom, reaching into the shower to turn on the spray, and I stand on the threshold, my hands gripping the top of the door frame.

"Are you go—"

"We don't have—"

She grins, walking back toward me and wrapping her arms around my waist.

"Max... honesty time." Sadie kisses my chest softly. "What's wrong?"

Looking into her eyes, I realize the answer is simple—nothing. Everything is right, exactly as it should be. And missing out on this because I'm afraid the fallout of leaving is going to hurt would be like missing out on touching the stars.

Bending down, I kiss her softly. "Nothing, I'm just really thankful for this summer with you."

"Feeling is mutual." She runs her hand over my abs, and a shiver runs through her. "Now get in here, shadow daddy. The water's warm."

Twenty-Five

Sadie

The Flower Girl

Max O'Reilly is the single most attractive man on the planet. His bulging biceps are accentuated by the way he's gripping the door frame above his head and dotted with sporadic tattoos. He has stacks of muscles on his stomach and thighs so thick they practically beg to be set free from pants. The second he removed his shirt outside, I nearly had a heart attack from the view.

He seems hotter, different from at the beach, but maybe that's because we're alone. Or because I've felt what he's keeping hidden below his belt. Call it objectification, but I feel like I might pass away on the spot if I don't get to see all of him, experience what it's like to be with him fully. And he's sweet. I can tell he's nervous, holding back so that I can lead. Except I don't want to—I want to be ravished, I want to be consumed by him. I want to forget momentarily about everything else going on.

Sliding the straps of my overalls down my shoulders, I spin to face the shower. Shimmying out of my clothing and reaching behind my back to unfasten my bra, I suck in a deep breath when his fingers brush mine.

"Let me," he says, his voice thick and gravelly.

I nod slowly, closing my eyes as his hands work to push my bra down my mud-covered arms. I spin, searching his hooded eyes.

"God, you're beautiful." Max slides each of his palms into my hair, pushing it away from my face. "I've never seen anyone so perfect."

Heat flashes up my chest, and I'm sure my cheeks are bright crimson. But there's no time to focus on why it's so hard to accept his compliments as Max leans forward, pressing a searing kiss to my lips.

It's punishing at first, filled with frustration. But as quickly as it starts, it changes to something different. Max sucks my bottom lip between his teeth, biting gently before licking soothing flicks along the same spot. And I reach up, tugging the hair at his nape, while I dip my tongue in for a taste. We're teasing, exploring each other thoroughly, and I've never been more captivated.

Max's hands slide down my ass, lifting me until I'm wrapped around his lower half. He steps into the shower anyway, not caring that he's still wearing briefs and I hadn't removed my panties.

The warm water coasts across my skin as he holds me under the spray. Each droplet pelts my overheated skin like tiny shards of glass, splitting me open. Max flicks his tongue against mine, biting my lip harder as he pulls back, and it steals my breath.

"I have to clean you up before I make a mess of you." Desire is etched on his face, and his pupils are blown.

A whoosh of air releases from my chest as I nod my agreement, followed by a buzzing anticipation when Max reaches for the shampoo. I'm consumed by the surrounding sounds—the water raining down on me, the flick of the bottle opening, the way the shampoo slides in Max's hands as he rubs them together.

He motions for me to turn around as his hands sink into my hair. He scratches my scalp lightly, then applies a pressure that feels so good I moan.

"Fuck, Sade." He wraps a soapy hand around me, spreading his fingers across my abdomen as he turns me back around, then slides a hand under my chin, tilting my head into the spray to rinse. "Are you going to let me taste you? Please let me taste you."

"Yes." I couldn't deny him if I tried. I ache with need, and my center is impossibly slick.

Max lathers a loofah with body wash, running the soapy and scratchy puff over every inch of my body. I feel like I'm on fire, each stroke or caress purposely driving me mad. When he reaches the black lace panties I'm still wearing, he drops to his knees and pulls them down with his teeth.

Holy hell!

Max on his knees in front of me might be the best view in the world. Better than any field of flowers, better than the Eiffel Tower in spring, better than any ocean in any corner of the world—not that I've experienced most of those things.

He lifts my right leg, tossing it over his shoulder as he continues to wash off the mud. He takes his time, working the soap into my skin with his free hand before setting it back down and switching to the other leg.

"You didn't wash my..." Max rights my leg, making sure I'm stable as my voice trails off as my mind swirls with questions about how someone could be so thorough, yet miss an entire section.

"Say it."

"What?"

"I didn't wash what, Sade? What did I miss?"

"Max... you know." I wave my hand in front of my vagina.

"Tell me. Use words." His voice is commanding, and I know he's not going to let me off the hook.

"My pussy. You skipped it," I relent.

"And wash away the flavor of you... how much you need me. I don't fucking think so." He flashes me a devilish grin. "I'm going to feast on you, savor every single drop until you're begging me for mercy."

My mouth drops open to protest, but Max tosses my leg over his shoulder once again and sucks on my clit, exchanging anything I could have said with pure bliss. He works me over, switching between long licks and suction. He nibbles and hums until my legs are shaking, and I'm worried I won't be able to support my body weight. But Max wraps a hand around my ass and pulls me closer to him.

My hips move on their own, grinding into his face in search of more. Tremors race through me, and I bite my cheek to stifle a moan.

Max halts, pulling away from me, and narrowing his eyes.

"What are you doing?" An exasperated breath rushes out of me. "Why'd you stop?"

"You're hiding. You're not letting me hear how much you love riding my face, Sade." He nips at my inner thigh, then soothes it with a flick of his tongue. "I might only get to do this a few times—the entire neighborhood needs to know who this pussy belongs to, even if it's temporary."

Rolling my eyes, I nod my head, and Max smacks my clit. A cry rips from my chest. "Fuck, Max." The sting of it quickly turns to pleasure, and while this is a first for me, I think I'd like it to happen again.

"That's better," he says, blowing a puff of air on my sensitive bud before diving back in.

I've never had someone so devoted to tasting me the way Max is. I'm relishing every twist of his tongue, every time he plunges two of his rough fingers inside of me. Stars blink in my vision, and when Max thrusts his tongue inside me, I explode into a thousand pieces like stardust floating across the night sky.

"Oh my God, Max!"

He continues to soak up every drop of my orgasm with slow, languid licks. And when I've finally come down, he stands before me, pressing small kisses to my neck and cheeks.

"You're exquisite, Sade." Another kiss just below my ear. "Like the purest honey. I'm afraid I might become addicted."

My cheeks heat at his adoration, but it's my turn to repay the favor. Grabbing the loofah that's been abandoned on a hook near the shelf with an assortment of products, I lather it up and begin washing him off.

"Take off your underwear," I command, running the body wash over his abs.

Max slowly pushes his boxer briefs off. His cock springs to life between us, and my eyes widen in disbelief. It's impressively long, thick, and a tad angry-looking from all the waiting. Pre-cum beads at the end, and I crouch down, running my tongue over the slit.

He hisses, slamming his hand against the tiled shower wall. "Fuck, Sade."

Abandoning the loofa to the floor, I reach behind me to rinse the soap from my hands and drop to my knees. Wrapping my hands around him, I lick the crown like an ice cream cone, and Max's stomach tightens.

"It's been a while since I've done this, so tell me if it's not working." Chancing a glance at him, his face is pained.

"I came in my pants from making out with you. I'm pretty sure just holding it would do the trick."

That pulls a smile from me—a memory I'll never forget.

"Stick out your tongue. This will be quick. But if it's too much, pinch my leg." Nodding at his command, I open wide.

Max pushes between my lips, hitting the back of my throat in one fluid motion. Gagging a little, I reach around him with one hand and palm his ass for stability while working the base of his shaft with the other.

He thrusts in again, and this time I hollow my cheeks before swallowing the tip. Max curses, but picks up his pace, pounding into my mouth like he couldn't stop if he wanted to. I cup his balls, rolling them in my hand as I moan around his length. He digs his hands into my hair, guiding my head in rhythm with his hips.

"I'm going to cum, do you want me to pull out?" His breathing is ragged, as if he's holding on for dear life.

Shaking my head no, he continues working himself over with my mouth until warm jets of cum hit my throat, and his pace slows. I swallow all he offers, cleaning up every drop the same way he did for me.

"Remember when we promised not to fall in love?" Max says, with a goofy yet sated grin on his face. "You're making it really hard for me to keep that promise, Sade."

It's been a couple of days since I've seen Max, since we hooked up in the shower. He's had lessons to teach at the rink, a scrimmage to coach, and work to help with at his mom's. And I've stayed busy planning for when I go back to work. I've made spreadsheets, spent an exorbitant amount of time researching how other organizations are expanding their programs, and I narrowed the locations for this year's gala down to the final three. All of this, of course, is off the books, but it felt good to accomplish something.

On Saturday, we finished cleaning ourselves up, promptly ordered pizza, and curled up on the couch with Benny to watch a movie. We talked about everything from my dad leaving to what his biggest fears are about moving. But mostly, we discussed our dreams—how his have shifted since he can't play, and how mine seem to be expanding with this whole learning to have fun again thing.

I realized Max is the kind of guy any girl would dream of ending up with. He's handsome as hell, good with his tongue, but most important-ly… I'm not sure there's a human alive that's kinder than Max. He has this way of listening that most people don't possess. It's like he actually tries to understand instead of listening simply to respond. It's not rushed, and there's no urging me to get on with the story—he's patient, empathetic. He's impossible not to love—at least in some sense of the word—like a golden retriever that's content with nothing more than spreading joy.

Stepping out of my car, a gentleman in a blue blazer and creamy-col-ored chinos approaches.

"Valet?"

"Uh, I guess." I hand him my keys, shoving the ticket he gives me into my wristlet.

Max invited me to a family dinner. He said it was a special occasion and to wear a dress, but other than that he didn't give instructions. My mom encouraged me to go, and I considered skipping it because it feels like something a girlfriend would do. But the truth is, I miss him.

So, here I stand in front of a sprawling mansion. One that looks like it was built with the single goal of having a magnificent view from every room. It's painted a deep blue color, with open-air wraparound patios on both levels. Windows stretch from floor to ceiling, covering most of the walls, and there are so many rounded arches I can't help wondering how long it took to build.

Striding onto a cement pathway, I follow a group of guests who appear to have stepped directly out of the country club. The women are wearing colorful dresses made of silk and chiffon, paired with floppy hats that probably cost a fortune. The men are in three-piece suits. Glancing at my emerald sundress, I feel grossly underdressed.

What kind of family dinner is this?

I've joked with Mal about the O'Reilly's being Mage Hollow royalty, but this makes me feel like maybe they actually are on another level of wealthy.

Reaching the first-floor entry, a large wooden door stands open, with windows cut out in four equal rectangles. Large topiaries with white and blush flowers dot each side. The group in front of me shuffles in, and I follow, captivated by a double-sided marble staircase that sits just inside.

"Welcome," another man greets me. "Are you here for the bride or the groom?"

Shit! Did I just accidentally crash a wedding?

"Oh, um..." I quickly pull my cell from my bag, scanning Max's text for the address. How embarrassing is it that I showed up at a wedding and actually thought for a second that I was in the right place? "I don't think I'm supposed to be here. Is this Lakeview Manor?" I stammer.

He narrows his eyes at me, and the thick grey handlebar mustache adorning his upper lip curves down in disapproval. "Your name, Ms.?"

"Sadie... Wells."

Mr. Serious pulls a walkie-talkie from his back pocket and presses the button on the side as he speaks. "I have a Sadie Wells here. Is she on the guest list?"

The walkie-talkie crackles, static rolling into the open foyer like a signal to the group of lords and ladies standing near. The women shoot me a disapproving look while the men ignore it altogether.

Mabel's voice breaks through the static, the first familiar thing I've heard since arriving. "Yes, she should be seated in the front row next to Thadeous."

"Follow me." The man shoves his communication device into his pants and starts toward the back of the house. "How does one not know they are invited to a wedding?" he asks judgementally.

"Well, have you met Max?" I stare at my shoes, following each step he takes. "He told me it was a family dinner," I explain.

The man chuckles, shaking his head as he pushes through a door that looks identical to the one at the front entrance. "That sounds about right, actually. Can you find your seat from here?" He steps to the side, waving his arm at the sprawling backyard that overlooks the coast.

White chairs are set up on two equal sides—at least a hundred on each. The view is breathtaking, with waves crashing on the cliff's edge, the blue of the water melting into the horizon line. A large wooden trellis sits at the end of the aisle, and it looks hand-carved with greenery draped along the top and full white flowers intermixed like stars dotting the night sky. To the right side, long white wood tables are set up with more giant blush-colored flower arrangements running the length of them. There are candles scattered everywhere, as if someone just threw them wherever they wanted, but with purpose.

"Ma'am? Did you hear me?" The man huffs, crossing his arms.

"Yes, sorry. Front row, next to Thad—"

The asshole himself turns at the same time I answer, waving to me like a lunatic from the front. Smiling softly, I grip a white handrail that lines the steps and make my way to the front. Slipping into the seat next to Thad, my mind races. I'm not prepared to be at a wedding.

"Sadie, I didn't know you were coming." Thad elbows me, and my skin crawls. Something about him creeps me out, like a bad finance bro that can't take a hint.

"Neither did I," I mumble, looking over my shoulder as the chairs begin to fill with guests.

The group that walked in with me takes their seats on the bride's side of the aisle, effectively blocking the view of anyone who sits behind them with their hats.

Taking stock of the situation again, my blood boils with annoyance. Why wouldn't he tell me I was coming to a wedding? My dress is fine—a sundress works for a summer wedding—but compared to the tuxes and high-end gowns surrounding me, I look unprepared.

Music rolls out over the space, a symphonic blend that's almost soothing, and Sam walks down the aisle, taking his place at the front. My heart thumps, and emotion sticks in my throat. I don't know Olive well, but I love what I do know about her. She's funny and kind. I feel honored to be here to witness her day, even if I had no idea what I was walking into.

The wedding party begins its march down the aisle, with a few faces I've never seen and a few I have. Howie looks dapper, his hair slicked back and his deep navy tux fitted exactly right. Ariella is on his arm in a stunning pale pink satin dress. Her hair is pulled back from her face, and her makeup looks almost airbrushed on. My heart rate increases, and my palms sweat. I'm not an insecure person, but anyone would feel frumpy in this situation.

The music changes, shifting to something lighter as the parents take their seats. Max hasn't made his appearance yet—he has to be in the wedding, right? Presumably, the best man.

A wave of laughter drifts through the air, starting at the back of the seats. Sam makes direct eye contact with me, a rueful look on his face as it's clear he's fighting his own laughter. Turning in my seat, I glance down the aisle to see what the fuss is about.

And there's Max.

A small baby cradled in one arm, her dress draped over him, with a basket full of flowers on the same wrist. He's reaching in and grabbing handfuls to toss as he makes his way down. There's a crown of flowers atop his head, some white and some pink, with a cascading ribbon that whips in the slight breeze—he's the fucking flower girl, and I can't hold in my laughter.

Each step he takes brings a wave of petals coasting through the air until he reaches the end of the aisle. He steps to the right, making his way to the end of our row where he hands the baby to a beautiful woman with brown skin and piercing green eyes. She smiles at the baby, cuddling it close to her chest. Max drops the basket at her feet, then steps toward me, removing the flower crown and dropping it onto my head as he crouches down. He presses a kiss to my cheek, then whispers in my ear.

"Surprise, Sade. You look stunning."

Twenty-Six

Max

Dancing at Dark

"How many pictures do we have to take?" I grumble to Howie.

"We need the groomsmen. Line up over here, please, and smile. We're almost done." Olive's mother commands us, snapping her fingers toward the group.

The photographer, a fierce-looking woman dressed in all black, smiles at our group half-heartedly as we make our way toward the water—if I had to guess, she's as annoyed at Anne Bowman as the rest of us. She snaps a few pictures, directing us to make a funny face before the last one.

We've been at this for a solid forty-five minutes, and my palms are itching to get to Sadie. She looked out of this world when I saw her, the green dress accentuating the golden flecks in her eyes. They were narrowed at me for most of the ceremony—my surprise apparently didn't have the desired effect.

"You're free to go. Sam and I will take a few more before we come to eat dinner," Olive coos, grabbing my brother's hand and dragging him toward the wedding arch while her mom looks on with something similar to icy approval.

The staff has cleared most of the seating, leaving the lawn clear for the dance floor to be set up. But I'm not sticking around to watch. Howie and Ari lead the way, marching across the grass toward a large white tent with tables underneath it. The walls have been rolled down, probably so the guests didn't have to watch the production that was us taking a million and one photos.

Stepping inside, music rolls through the space, something classical—maybe Beethoven. I'm sure Olive's mom picked it since the vibe screams trust fund.

"We're over here," Ari says, pulling Howie's hand toward a table near the front.

Approaching, only a few of the seats are occupied, and Sadie's isn't one of them. Glancing around, I search the tables for a green dress. Only stopping when my eyes snag on the bright emerald near the bar. Swerving right, I slow my pace when her melodic laugh reaches me across the makeshift room.

It's soothing, like a warm hug—one I've been longing for all day.

"Put her drink on my tab, Walter," I say, slinking up beside her.

The bartender is a family friend who's been working weddings for at least thirty years that I know of. Always flirting his way into his next fling, like an older George Clooney slinging drinks.

"Max... I'm pretty sure it's free." Sadie turns her body toward mine, rolling her eyes.

"Nah, Walter's just been giving you freebies in an attempt to steal my date." I wink at the man in question.

"Wait, really?" Sadie reaches into her purse, pulling out a couple of bills. "I've been up here twice, let me—"

A chuckle roars from my chest, and Walter follows suit.

"I'm kidding. Does this look like the type of wedding that has a cash bar?"

Sadie smacks my chest.

"No." She shoves the money into Walter's tip jar. "But... to be fair, I didn't even know I was coming to a wedding, so anything's possible, right?"

Grinning, I wrap my fingers around her arm gently and pull her toward me. "Fair. Your expression was so worth it, though."

Sadie scoffs before grabbing her glass of wine and my lager from the wooden bar. She steps toward our table, taking her seat just as our meals are set down—steak for me, salmon for her.

"You should've told me." She grabs her napkin and drapes it across her lap. "I look like I'm going to a backyard barbecue, not *this* wedding." Her eyes widen as she scans the reception.

Taking a sip of my beer, I reach below the table, grab the leg of her chair, and pull it closer to mine before settling my hand on her upper thigh.

"You look amazing. So good it took my breath away when I saw you seated in the front row." Leaning in, I press a kiss to her cheek. "Could've passed out and dropped the rings if I hadn't looked away."

"Max..."

"Don't Max me. I'm serious, even wearing a paper sack, you'd still be the only woman in this room that I see. The only woman in any room, actually."

Sadie turns to me, pressing a quick kiss to my lips. "Okay, Casanova. You win."

She stabs a fingerling potato with her fork, but pauses halfway to her mouth. "How did you know to order me fish?"

Chewing my bite of steak before answering, I hold up a finger. "Well, you liked the oysters so much I assumed it was the safe choice. Was I wrong? We can trade."

She smiles at me while simultaneously cutting into the fish in question. "It's one of my favorites, just shocked you put that together."

"I notice things, Sade." I smirk at her, relishing the way she's digging into her plate like she hasn't had a meal in years. I eat a lot, so I need someone who can match my energy with food.

Someone who won't judge me for ordering double meat everywhere I go.

We eat in amicable silence, talking to family and friends as they approach the table. Sam and Olive make their grand entrance, and the mood shifts as dinner wraps up. I'm looking forward to dancing, but there's a special spot that I had set up just for Sadie—a final surprise for the evening she wasn't expecting.

"Hey," I whisper in her ear. "Sneak out the back of the tent. I'll follow in just a second."

"What? Why?" Her expression shifts, clearly confused.

Grinning, I nod toward the spot where the walls meet, a section that will be easy to slip out of. "Trust me."

Sadie nods, sliding off her chair and heading toward the exit. I lean toward Sam, filling him in on where I'm headed. He smirks at me, but shoo's me away. He probably thinks I'm headed for a quickie, but that couldn't be further from the truth.

When I sneak between the walls of the tent, Sadie is on the other side pacing. Wrapping my arms around her waist from behind, I inhale her peach scent.

"I'm not sure it's good form to crash a wedding, then sneak off for a quickie."

Jesus, does everyone think I'm that obvious?

"While I wouldn't turn it down, you're oh for two." I nip her earlobe, and Sadie squeaks. "You didn't crash... you were on the guest list. And I have a surprise for you—one that doesn't involve my cock... unless you want it to."

Stepping in front of her, she rolls her eyes again. And I loop my arms behind her knees, hoisting her against my chest to head toward her surprise. She yelps, but sinks into my hold after a second of squirming.

"You don't have to carry me."

"I want to."

"Why?"

I shrug. "Your legs are two feet long, we'll get there quicker."

"Wow. What a gentleman!" Her sass is just one of the things I'm coming to love about her.

Running across the grass, I get us to the brick pathway in less than a minute. It's tucked between trees, purposely hidden like a secret garden. Setting Sadie down, I wrap my hands over her eyes.

"Okay, you have to walk for this part because I don't want you to see it before it's time."

I planned the whole thing with Burt, the groundskeeper. He's supposed to turn on the lights at exactly seven. Checking my watch, I see we have two minutes.

Leading Sadie down the pathway, we enter the opening to a small cobblestone patio with candles lit on the ground sporadically.

"I need another minute. If I uncover your face, do you promise to keep your eyes closed?"

"Yes."

Running my hands up her arms, I lean in and kiss her. It's soft, sweet, but Sadie leans into me and I can't resist deepening the kiss. Tangling my hand in the hair at her nape, I angle her head to the right as I run my tongue against the seam of her mouth. She opens for me, and I savor her taste, nibbling on her bottom lip.

We break apart as the twinkle lights turn on, but Sadie keeps her eyes closed. I should tell her to open them, but I steal the moment, drinking her in. Freckles dot the bridge of her nose, and I trace them with my finger. Her lips are swollen, pink from the kiss we shared, and I steal a peck. Sadie's long chocolate hair cascades in effortless waves down her back, and the swell of her breasts rises and falls with each breath she takes. I feel like I'm looking at a painting, a picture of perfection. I'm pulled to her in a way that's illogical, like a moth to a flame, not afraid even though I know I'm going to be burned.

"You're enchanting." Kissing her cheek, I reach around her middle, spinning her in my arms so her back is pressed to my front. "Open your eyes, Sade."

She gasps as she takes in the scene before her. Twinkling lights hang from the trees like tiny fireworks dripping from each branch. Candles of varying shapes and sizes dot the ground, illuminating the stone beneath our feet.

"This is... I've never seen... oh my God." Sadie spins, wrapping her arms around me. "You did this... for me?"

Smiling, I squeeze her back. "To be honest, there's not much I wouldn't do for you, Sade. This was nothing compared to the lengths I'd go to see that look on your face."

Music drifts into the space, a slow beat that I know is Sam and Olive's first dance. It whispers through the trees, just loud enough to hear over the sound of my heart beating in my chest.

"You're the best man I've ever met." Sadie peers up at me from under her lashes. "Thank you, Max. Not just for this, but for everything."

I'm overwhelmed with the need to stay in this bubble, to dance with the girl and pretend she's mine forever. I've hinted to her that I'm falling for her, but I haven't told her outright. And I know I can't. That wouldn't be fair—to either of us. But if circumstances were different, I'd hold on and hope she would never let go.

"May I have this dance before we go back?"

"Of course, Max." Sadie slides her hands around my neck and into the hair at the base of my head. "I'm not sure I ever want to dance with anyone else." A single tear streaks down her face, and my heart triples in size.

She's not an overly emotional woman. I'd describe her as pragmatic most of the time. A tear of any kind is unusual. I've watched her talk about her dad abandoning them, her stitches being placed, and a lot of other things that would make me cry—but she always remains stoic. This display is confirmation that she's just as torn by our predicament as I am.

"Me too, Sade. Me too."

We sway to the sound of the music, leaning into each other with each slow turn. It might be the most romantic moment of my life, a moment that could only exist in a movie. But that's what she inspires in me—a need to move heaven and earth to make her happy.

As the song ends, another rolls through the trees just as beautiful as the last, but a little faster. I spin Sadie, making her giggle when I dip her back for a film-worthy kiss. She closes her eyes as she's bent backward and smiles. It takes up her entire face, a look of pure, unadulterated bliss. But when I lift her back to standing—small pieces of paper in every color rain down on us.

Blue, green, pink, orange, yellow, white... They are everywhere, whipping in the light summer breeze. They weren't part of the plan, and my mind races with questions.

Did Burt go rogue? Is this more magic?

"How did you—"

Shaking my head, I release her, bending to grab one from the ground. "I didn't."

Sadie snatches it from my hand, unfolding the two-by-two parchment, and reading it aloud.

"The answer to most questions can be found in the silence that sits between laughter." She looks at me, then back at the paper. "Do you think this was Beth?"

"It has to be. What's the next clue in your book?"

Sadie digs in her purse, and I don't fail to notice how she shoves the tiny scrap of paper into her bag for safekeeping. She removes her phone and opens the photo app, turning it toward me.

6. Down

To grant indulgence

"What the hell does that mean?" I ask, looking at another one of the papers. I've unfolded a few, and they all say the same thing.

"Humor... I think." Sadie zooms in on the picture she took. "It has five letters. I'll have to try it when I get home."

My heart leaps into my throat as the book and a pencil appear suddenly over her left shoulder. I know I'm not dreaming as I blink a few times and it remains.

"Or... you could try it now." I grasp Sadie's shoulders, turning her around so she can see it—floating in front of the tree, suspended weightlessly in mid-air.

She sucks her teeth, releasing a hissing breath.

"I guess now's as good a time as any." She smiles softly, grabbing it and opening the book.

Sadie scribbles in the letters. As the lead-colored letters melt into gold, Sadie slumps against me like she's relieved or defeated—possibly both. But I can tell from her expression she doesn't want to discuss the wild thing happening to her.

"Let's go back to the party." I tuck the book under my arm and guide her toward the path.

Sadie stops, turning to press a kiss on my cheek before grabbing the book and placing it on the ground.

"Just leave it here. It'll follow me home, anyway."

Twenty-Seven

Sadie

Battle of Balloons

"Aunt Sadie, will you put that stuff on my face?" Lily asks, pointing at the black under my eyes.

My sister rolls her eyes as she's never been a fan of Mage Hollow's annual water balloon bonanza—she says it promotes more violence than it teaches about history. But that's like Mal to be overly opinionated about something that is fun.

As kids, we didn't take part until high school. And even then, I rarely went because I always had something more important to do. But when I came back from college one summer, Howard convinced me to go, and I found it incredibly cathartic to hurl water-filled sacks at our neighbors, young and old. Since then, if I'm in town when it happens (only twice), I've made it a point to have the whole family attend the event. And this year, it feels like a no-brainer, like we could all use a moment of joy.

Swiping my now torched eyeliner under Lily's eyes, there's a knock at the door.

"Sadie, I think your special friend is here," my mom coos.

Tiny feet pound against the hardwood floor as Magnolia and Poppy race to open the door for Max. My body erupts in goosebumps just knowing he's here. It's only been twelve hours since I saw him, but I find myself wanting to be near him.

"Hey Sade." He steps into the dining room, a girl in each of his arms, and my heart beats faster. Leave it to Max to look unfairly attractive in camo shorts, a black t-shirt with the sleeves cut off, and a backward baseball hat. "You in charge of battle makeup?"

He nods toward my niece's face, and I accidentally swipe the black material down her cheek. So much for not being obvious about how much he affects me.

Grabbing a makeup remover cloth, I clean Lily's face, ensuring she has two perfect rectangles under her eyes. Max watches with rapt attention as the girls wiggle in his arms.

"Aunt Adie, me nest," Poppy yells.

"No, it's my turn, Poppy. I called it," Magnolia whines.

"Hey, Max." My sister saunters into the room, reaching to grab Poppy from his arm. "Girls, Aunt Sadie will get to both of you. Please be patient."

Max sets Magnolia on her feet, then pulls out a chair next to me. "If you have another one of those, I could help." He nods toward the pencil in my hand, smirking in that delicious way that makes his dimples pop.

Rummaging through my makeup bag, I pull out a liquid version and place it in his awaiting palm. He looks at it, turning it over in his hand as if it's the most foreign thing he's ever seen. But the girls break my appraisal of Max, pushing each other as they scramble to line up in front of him.

I guess my rating of favorite just took a nosedive.

Max chuckles as Poppy—the sneaky little thing—wins out and Magnolia huffs, moving onto the chair Lily just vacated. Quickly, I draw the lines on Mag's rosy little cheeks, having minimal to clean up. But when I look at Poppy, a wave of giggles rolls out of me.

Max is struggling. Liquid eyeliner rolls down both her cheeks like some sort of misshapen lightning bolt.

"Need some help?" I ask, biting the inside of my cheek.

He shakes his head, then leans forward to whisper in Poppy's ear. She giggles, her cheeks turning pink as she nods her head in response to whatever he told her.

"We were going for battle-worn, you know, like she was working so hard it already melted," he explains as my niece hops off the chair and squeals in delight at the sight of herself in the mirror. "Will you do mine exactly like hers, so we can match?"

Covering my mouth with the back of my hand, I stifle the squeak that's begging to break free. His matching with my niece, his attempt at making her feel special compared to the others—it's too much for my heart to take. Poppy adores him, and I think I might be falling in love with him too.

"Sure, Casanova." I motion for him to move onto the chair in front of me. "Just be careful not to break her heart, or I might have to kill you."

Max grins, winking at me. "I'll do my best..." He leans forward, brushing a stray tendril of hair from my face as his lips coast across the shell of my ear. "But I think her aunt might be the one responsible for breaking her heart when she finds out I'm here for you."

My cheeks heat from the proximity, and the words coming out of his mouth. This man—although adorably sweet—is deadly with his tongue, in more ways than one.

"We'll cross that bridge when we get there." I touch his shoulder, pushing so that he's sitting upright, and get to work on his makeup. "Have you done this before?"

"The Balloon Bonanza?"

"Yeah." Swiping the liquid stick under his eyes, I do my best to make it look sloppy. "Does your family usually take part?"

He smirks, assisting my attempt at copying Poppy's face without even trying. "Only every year since the time we could walk. Mabel is like a sniper. I'd watch out for her today."

Somehow, I'm not in the slightest bit surprised to hear that. Mabel O'Reilly is one of a kind—she's definitely the type to take you out when you don't see it coming.

"And will the ladies in the enormous hats be out there today?" They were perfectly nice, cutting up the dance floor last night without a care in the world. But something tells me that getting soaked in Mage Square wasn't on their itinerary.

Max chuckles, smiling so big that his eyebrows nearly touch his hairline. "Nah, Ollie said they wouldn't be into it. They will relax at the manor today, then tomorrow I think they rented some sort of yacht for the fireworks."

"That sounds about right, though it would've been fun to watch them out there." I finish up his face, turning to throw all the supplies back in my black makeup bag. "Are you going on the yacht?"

He shakes his head. "No, I was actually hoping you'd—"

"Sadie Marie... are you ready to go? We're going to be late if you don't stop flirting and get a move on," Dee Dee sings from the front door, cutting off Max's question.

"Yeah, Mom. We're coming." Max stands from his chair, extending a hand to me as I do the same. "She just had to get that dig in," I grumble under my breath.

Slipping into my sneakers by the front door, I tie my tennis shoes quickly as Max helps Sebastian load two huge buckets filled with water balloons into the back of Max's truck—every family has to bring twenty balloons for each participant. But before we load into the vehicles to drive uptown, Max calls everyone for a meeting in the front yard.

Kneeling down so he's eye level with the little girls, he gives us a pep talk.

"Okay, little ladies, there are going to be a lot of people where we're going. I need you to promise me you'll stay close to one of the adults at all times." Seb lifts his chin in approval. "Water balloons are going to be flying, so make sure you tell us if you don't want to get wet so we can keep you guarded."

"I'm going to throw so many!" Mag's shouts.

"I'll throw more than you do, Magnolia. You're still little," Lily chimes in.

"I stay with Max," Poppy leans toward him, placing her tiny hand on his knee.

Max grins up at me, a mischievous look that says, *I told you so* from our previous discussion.

"Okay, as for the adults, I've never lost this competition. But my family will gun for us since I switched teams this year. Target my mom because she's slippery and will get you when you're not looking. Remember, the rules state that once you've been hit three times, you exit the playing field. If you're out, tell someone in our group so we can cover the little girls." My heart beats rapidly in awe of how much care he's putting into making sure my nieces remain safe, and we know the rules. It's a glimpse into how I assume he is as a coach—thorough and unwavering in his conviction. "There's a spot near the far left corner that has three barricades set up. If we can hide behind those, we should be good to go."

My mother claps, bouncing up and down like he just gave us a super inspiring speech. My sister looks down at him with adoration, probably thankful for his thoughtfulness, and Seb slaps him on the back.

"Okay, everyone, load up." I grab Max's hand, pulling him back to standing. "We'll meet you in the lot behind Union. Lonnie gave us permission to park there."

My family piles into my sister's van while Max hoists me into his front seat. Once inside, he tugs on my belt, making sure it's secure, and backs out of the driveway.

"That was sweet." I toy with the edge of my black biker shorts.

Max flips on his turn signal, eyes trained on the road to avoid pedestrians. Some people walk to the event—we would if we didn't have to carry so many balloons.

"I want them to have fun, but it would be easy to lose a kid up there." He shrugs. "Just want to make sure it ends up a good memory and no little girls run into the street chasing balloons."

Groaning at the callback to my mishap with Poppy, I stare out the window. He wasn't kidding about the size of the event. I think it's nearly tripled since the last time I participated based on the crowd forming.

We pull into the lot, finding an open spot at the end. Mal and the rest of my family park next to us, piling out of the van before I can unbuckle my seatbelt. Reaching for the red button, Max leans over, stopping my movement when he presses his lips to mine. His kiss is claiming, chaste but urgent.

"Sorry, I've been holding that back for the last hour."

Rolling my lips in, I fight a smile. "You don't have to apologize. You can do that whenever you want."

"Good to know."

He leaps from the truck, helping me down before grabbing one of our buckets to carry around the corner and into the square. Mal, Mom, the girls, and I follow closely behind, with Seb bringing up the rear.

Once positioned on the sidewalk in front of Union, Max points out the spot we are aiming for. It doesn't matter that it's far from our balloon buckets since a few people from the town council arranged them around the perimeter of the sidewalk so there's equal opportunity for everyone.

The O'Reilly clan, all but Sam and Olive, approach and dole out hugs to my family.

"Sadie, good to see you this morning." Mabel sweeps me into her arms. "You looked absolutely radiant last night."

I chance a look at Max, and he winks at me mid-conversation with his dad.

"Thank you. Everything was so beautiful." I fiddle with my cropped tank top strap. "I'm surprised you are all out here this morning. Clean-up must have been late."

Max and I stayed to help with some of the smaller stuff, but his parents insisted we leave around midnight.

Mabel waves her hand through the air. "It was no big deal. I wouldn't miss this event. I have too much fun throwing balloons at Beatrice Bushnell. That woman can be a menace." She giggles at her confession, glancing around to see who's within earshot when a loud whistle blows.

Ariella Marino's father, Tony, stands on a tall platform near the end of the roped-off course with a megaphone.

"Welcome, neighbors and friends, to the Mage Hollow Balloon Bonanza. We do this event every year in remembrance of the battle that took place not too far from here, in which we gained our independence as a nation. Please remember that if you get hit three times, exit the playing area and watch the remaining contenders compete for the honor of being named victor. Watch out for the little kids, and most importantly, have fun."

Max steps closer to me, eyeing Sebastian and nodding his head toward the corner we discussed. Another loud whistle blares across the square, and people take off running in all directions, some in the road and some in the patch of grass that lies in the center of the square. Max scoops the two littlest girls, while Seb grabs Lily, and we sprint to the barricade. Mal and Mom trail behind, both heaving for air by the time our pack of eight clears the edge of the inflatable boxes that will serve as our haven.

Balloons of all colors whip through the air, splashing as they land on people's bodies. The girls giggle uncontrollably, laughing at the hysterical reactions of grown adults yelping and squealing. I'm glad that Mal got a babysitter for Marigold—it would have been impossible to keep her from getting hit.

"Should we make a break for one of the buckets to load up?" I ask to anyone listening.

"Mal and I will go," Seb says. "And then you and Max can once we get back."

They leap around the corner, heading toward a green barrel that's full of balloons. But within a few feet of the bucket, Mallory takes a balloon to the face and two to the chest from none other than Patrick O'Reilly. My sister doubles over in laughter as she dips below the yellow rope that seals off the course.

Mom and Lily make a break for it in the opposite direction, reaching an orange tub and grabbing two balloons each. They fling them through the air, smacking Bridget and Zuri once each, and missing with the other two. Bridget pays them back with an assist from Nora to take them both out of the game. Down to five.

"Hiding back here? That doesn't seem like your style," a husky voice rolls out from behind me, and I spin to see Howie and Ari standing in our corner with a balloon in each of their hands.

"Don't even think about it, Howard. I'm unarmed."

My cousin laughs but pops a balloon on each of the girls' heads instead. Poppy and Magnolia squeal in delight as Ari drops to a crouch beside them.

"Do you think we should pay him back for that?" she whispers to my nieces, and their heads bob up and down in approval.

Ari lobs both balloons at Howard's chest, and the girls clap when they burst open. But I don't miss the twinkle in his eyes or the breath she sucks in when his shirt sticks to his chest muscles. She's an idiot for not dating my cousin—he's a catch.

Max, whom I hadn't even noticed leaving, returns with a shirt full of balloons. There's a strip of skin exposed on his stomach, revealing his abs and the line of brown hair I know heads directly south. I stare at it far too long for it to be innocent before he bends down to my ear.

"Stop eye-fucking me and throw these, would ya."

Shaking my shoulders, I grab a couple of balloons and spin to finish my cousin off. But instead of hitting Howie, one of my tosses slaps Ari in the chest. She tumbles into laughter as Max nails her on the cheek and Howie in the shoulder.

"I'm out," my cousin says, as Mabel sneaks up and finishes Ari and the little girls.

"Who's left?" Max's mom asks, a smirk that matches her son's painted on her face.

Turning, I see Seb sulking under the rope. "I think it's just Max and me."

She grins again, but instead of pelting us with balloons, she drops the remaining ones in her apron to the ground and saunters away.

"What the hell is happening?" Max asks, dipping down to grab the balloons she abandoned. "My mom never quits."

Peering over the edge of our barricade, it looks like we are down to only four remaining contestants, including ourselves.

Tony's megaphone sends a shrill noise over the course. "And then there were four. Please come out from behind your barriers to the center of the course. We will move to a sudden-death round where each contestant gets a single throw until we are down to a winner."

Max and I walk to the middle, carefully placing the balloons at our feet. Standing across from us are Thad and Nora. *This will be fun... that guy deserves a direct hit.*

Tony directs Nora to go first, and she takes aim at me but misses slightly to the left. Thad takes his shot, but it soars over Max's head, and his face drops. Bending down, I grab a purple balloon and toss it lightly into the air, catching it with my hand. When Thad looks to the left of the course, winking at a blonde that's entirely too close to the rope, I nail him right in the side of the face.

I can hear Max laughing beside me, but I see Nora's expression falter slightly when she watches him walk over to the girl. My stomach knots for her—she deserves so-much better.

"This is just a game, but that isn't," Max says to his sister. "I'm going to take you out, but you need to go ditch his ass." Nora nods, a smile filled with relief blossoming on her face as the water balloon he threw hits her on the arm.

She marches toward Thad, purpose in every step as she gets closer. My heart hammers for her, and I hope she dumps him and never looks back.

"Alright, everyone, we are down to the final two. This is it, Max and Sadie. Please grab a single water balloon and face each other. On the count of three, you will release them, and whoever hits first is the winner."

I shuffle across from Max, a bright blue balloon in my hand compared to his green one. "Don't you dare consider letting me win to be nice, Casanova," I warn him.

"Wouldn't dream of it, Sade."

The crowd begins the countdown... three...

"Will you go on my boat with me tomorrow?" he rushes out.

Max has a boat? Two... *When did he get a boat?*

One...

A balloon smacks me in the chest, and water splashes down my arms, running across my hand as it still holds the balloon.

"You distracted me!" I shout as Max wraps his arms around my waist and spins me in the middle of Mage Square. I reach above his head and pop the balloon over his hair.

"All's fair in love and war, Sade." He laughs as water trickles down his face, and I kiss him as we continue to spin.

Twenty-Eight

Max

We're Boat People

"I can't believe Mom let you win." My brother sips his coffee across from me, raising his eyebrow.

"It was weird... she just gave up." I fiddle with the menu, opening and closing it. "Do you think she knew Thad was going to be a douche and flirt with that girl? Was she setting me up to help Nora?"

Sam chuckles, shrugging. "I don't fuckin know, but someone needs to. First it was Charlie, then Brad, Chad, and Thad..."

"Our sister has a problem with men whose names end in ad." Taking a small sip of my coffee, I try not to laugh at her terrible choices.

Sam runs a hand down his face. "No, she has a problem with trying to replace her 'Patrick'."

"Is that like Olive is your Mabel? You really think that guy was her forever?" I ask.

"Yeah... unfortunately, I do."

Sam's shoulders slump, and his face twists with sympathy for our sister as Jo, one of the owners at 1793, steps up to our table to take our order.

"What can I get for you today?"

Sam orders, handing her the menu without making eye contact. I think he's uncomfortable coming here after everything we've learned—can't say I blame him, but their breakfast remains the best in town.

"I'll have pancakes, bacon, sausage, two eggs, and a side of hash browns." Closing my menu, I extend it to her as she scribbles on a notepad. "Oh, and can I ask you a question?"

"I suppose." Jo's eyes flick between Sam and me—almost as if she knows we're involved in her sister's antics but doesn't think we're brave enough to confront the situation.

"Where's Beth?"

"Vacation." Her response is sure, steady. But I don't buy it.

"Nah, tell me where she really is. Is she hiding out with Irina? I know they're both wi—"

"Max!" Sam scolds, shooting daggers at me.

Josephine's face twists in consternation, but she waves me over and slides into the booth next to me. "I'd appreciate it greatly if you could keep your voices down." She closes her eyes briefly and inhales through her nose. "We have never harmed anyone."

Sam snorts at that, shaking his head in disbelief.

"You disagree?" She challenges him.

"Yeah. My wife had to go to the hospital because of your sister... I wouldn't exactly call Irina a saint."

Jo grabs my coffee cup, swirling it slightly in her hands—the black liquid turns creamy before my eyes as she takes a small sip and my mouth gapes. For a person who refuses to confirm my suspicions, she's not trying very hard to hide her powers.

"Olive chased her, and she slipped trying to grab my sister." She flips her hand absentmindedly in the air. "An unforeseen mishap."

Sam grumbles something under his breath before excusing himself to the restroom. While I wish he'd stay, it's probably for the best that he doesn't.

"What about Sadie? Why is Beth forcing her to do this stupid puzzle? It doesn't even mean anything."

Josephine grabs the salt shaker, sprinkles a hefty amount on a small coffee saucer, then snaps her fingers. Watching the salt, I'm not sure what I expect to happen... but it looks the same to me.

A small laugh rolls out of Jo—probably at my expense. "Did you think I was going to show you something special, Maxwell O'Reilly?"

Why is she using my full name? How does she even know it in the first place?

"I, uh, I'm not sure how to answer that, honestly." She makes a tutting noise with her tongue, as if I should have known better, or at the very least, given her a more truthful response.

"Maybe try to be honest. You are the one who came to my diner and questioned me." Jo sips *my* coffee, clearly not giving a single fuck about stealing it. "Why do you care so much anyway?"

That one is easy to answer, but I hesitate, not knowing how much I should share. "I care about her. Sadie is one of a kind, and I don't want to see her get hurt."

"I've known her longer than you have, Maxwell." Jo places her hand on top of mine, and a shutter rolls through me. My heart rate increases, thumping so loudly I can hear it. "Sadie belongs to us. She's family. We would never harm her... we only ever aim to help."

She slides out of the booth, my coffee still in her hand.

"That doesn't answer the question," I blurt out.

Jo spins on her heel, leaning over our table to whisper to me. "Sprinkle some pepper on that plate, and you'll find everything you need to know."

With that, she scurries away, punching in our order on a computer screen before refilling some coffees for guests seated at the bar. I watch her mill about performing normal tasks as Sam slinks back into his seat, eyeing me suspiciously.

"Couldn't help yourself, huh?"

I grab the pepper shaker, lightly tapping the base in my palm as I consider testing what Jo suggested. "Nope." Turning it upside down, I sprinkle a fair amount on top of the salt, deciding to go for it.

"What are you—"

The salt and pepper crackle on the plate, bouncing around as if each individual fleck is dancing.

"What is happening?" Sam asks, leaning in to get a closer look.

"I don't know. She poured the salt and told me to add the pepper to find out what I *need* to know." I pull the saucer closer, staring into the vibrating particles. But just as I'm about to chalk it all up to some odd chemical reaction, both the salt and pepper move to the outer edges of the plate. And sitting smack in the middle... is a Golden City Flames logo.

I blink rapidly, convinced I must be imagining it. But Sam pulls out his phone and takes a picture. He stares at his screen, and his jaw drops open.

"What?" I reach across the table to grab it, and my hand knocks into a coffee mug, spilling hot liquid all over the table and my lap. "Shit... that's hot."

My brother spins the device so it's facing me. But there isn't a picture of what we both just saw. Instead, it's one of only my hands wrapped around the very cup of coffee that I just spilled.

Sam and I exchange a look, having an entire unspoken conversation. We need to get the hell out of here, and fast—before anything else bizarre can happen.

Jo rounds the end of the diner's counter with our plates in hand, but Sam stands and I follow, throwing a few twenties on the table. We don't walk to leave, rather, we sprint and don't look back until we're tucked safely into the cab of his truck.

"Are you going to tell her?" he asks, turning the ignition and barreling out of the lot.

"Should I? She might be mad that I confronted Jo."

Sam taps his fingers on the top of the steering wheel. "Not that... although you have to explain in case she hears about it. I meant that you're in love with her."

"I'm not in—"

"Yes, you are." He pulls to a stop sign, turning to look at me. "She's your Mabel. We all know it."

My brother's words hit me like a lightning bolt. I've known I'm falling for Sadie. That's not a question. But having Sam confirm it, having him acknowledge that she's my once in a lifetime, makes my heart hurt. How—if that's true—am I ever going to let her go? How am I going to move half a world away?

Walking down the weathered dock at the marina, the boats in their slips bob in the water all around us. Some are gigantic yachts, while others are small skippers meant for fishing. Sadie takes it all in, her gaze lingering on some of the bigger boats like she can't believe they even exist.

"Is it that one?" Sadie points to a sleek black Benetti that costs more money than I could make in a lifetime.

"Yep." I step toward the ramp that leads to the state-of-the-art boat, and her eyes widen comically. "I can totally afford this on private lessons and the volunteer work I do at the rink."

Sadie laughs, pulling my arm so that I'm forced to step back beside her. "Okay, I can see that was a dumb question. I think I'm a little mixed up after the wedding that was fit for the Duchess of Sussex."

"Who?"

"Nevermind... which boat is yours?"

We mosey a little further until my sailboat comes into view. It's mid-size, painted a rich navy with amber-stained wood.

"Here she is." I spread my arms out wide, motioning toward the boat. "Got her when Pap passed away. He taught me to sail when I was little, and I loved spending the summers on the water with him."

"Max..." Sadie trails off as she takes it in. "This is beautiful. And so meaningful. Thank you for sharing it with me."

Pulling her into my arms, I kiss her forehead. "I usually spend the holiday watching fireworks alone. It never felt right to bring someone with me after we lost him four years ago. But I want you to see it. They're magical when you're lying on the deck watching the bursts of color float across the sky."

Sadie squeezes my arm and raises onto her tiptoes to kiss my cheek. There's always been a height difference between us, but it's more significant in flip-flops than in the heels she typically wears. "How did you name it?"

My eyes shift to the golden script adorning the stern. To me, she's always been *The Josephine*—I never really asked why.

"I didn't," I start. "My grandfather never discussed the name, only told us it was named after our great-great-great-grandmother."

A whirring breath releases from Sadie's lips. "Oh, thank God. I was worried for a second that this was another trick. That Beth was going to interfere in our day somehow."

We step up onto the ramp, slipping onto the back of the boat with ease. As I do my pre-checks, my mind wanders to what she said. I've never put together the matching names with Josephine from 1793, but after this morning, it seems the woman is a prominent figure in my life—at least today.

Securing the ropes and working to make sure the anchor is pulled up, I watch as Sadie looks around the small interior cabin before making her way to the bow of my boat. She looks right here, like she belongs. With each steady step she takes, each time she runs her hand along the safety bar that runs the length of the vessel, she seems sure of herself, not afraid of this new adventure.

Sadie finishes her self-led tour, taking a seat in the cockpit next to me as I pull the lines out of their cleats and off their winches—making sure there aren't any bindings in them. I attach the sails, both main and jib, and turn on the motor after detaching the dock lines to guide us out of the marina.

"You know I saw her today..."

"Who?"

"Josephine." I use the wooden wheel to steer us out into open water, positioning us toward the wind to hoist the sails. "At the diner with Sam. We, uh, talked."

"About pancakes?" Sadie nibbles her bottom lip as she runs her fingers up the main sheet. "She's not really a talker."

"No, I asked her about her sisters." My gut churns with doubt—I was probably crossing a line. "I confronted her."

Sadie snorts, and deep, belly-rolling laughter escapes her while I sit, mesmerized.

"You didn't," she manages in between breaths.

The boat leans, and the wind picks up in the sails and propels us forward as ocean spray mists us lightly.

"I wouldn't say I had any revelations from the discussion. She's very cryptic." I run a hand through my hair—the wind is whipping it wildly. "She performed some magic tricks for me, though."

"There's literally no way that's true. I've known her my whole life, and never once did she give me any sign that she was a witch."

"Neither did Beth, but here we are."

Sadie crosses her arms over the white tank top she's wearing. "Well, then... what did she do?"

Reaching out, I pull her into my lap and put her hand on top of mine to help me steer. Her peach scent surrounds me, and I nuzzle her neck briefly. "She stole my coffee and somehow made creamer appear in it with a single swoosh of her hand—"

"Did you drink it?"

"No." That makes me chuckle. I'm a risk-taker, but I'm not insane. "She did, though. And then she poured salt on a plate and told me to add pepper so the things I needed to know would be revealed."

Sadie hums, clearly intrigued. "And what was the big surprise?"

My heart sinks. When Sam dropped me at home to change and prepare for this date, the only conclusion I could make is that the Flames logo means Sadie is leaving soon. I knew it was coming, but I think it'll be quicker than we expected. While we've both been aware that she has a little less than two weeks left on her leave, something in my soul knows it's probably more like days.

"The logo for the Flames, and subsequently, a hot ass cup of coffee spilled on my lap." I tickle her side, choosing not to share my suspicion and ruin the day. "I guess she just felt like taunting me with the one dream I'll never achieve."

"I'm sorry, Max."

Sadie has nothing to apologize for. She didn't ask for any of this, and I tell her as much. We continue sailing, basking in the warm breeze as it coasts across us. The saltwater splashes the side of the boat in a rhythmic beat. I've never felt as at peace as when I'm out here—away from any sign of worry or disappointment.

Approaching the area where boats park for the fireworks show, the water becomes crowded. There's everything from yachts to small schooners and speedboats, all angling for the best view. I steer us toward the far left side, toward an uninhabited island that sits back just enough to still enjoy the view but not get stuck in traffic when the show is finished.

Sadie has moved from my lap and is now sitting opposite me.

"Okay, so we are going to be running soon, with the wind at our backs. When that happens, this thing"—I tap the boom that sits under the mainsail—"is going to swing toward you. I will tell you when it's coming, but you should either duck or come over to my side before it happens."

Sadie nods, eyeing the large pole that runs parallel to the boat. "I'll duck."

I adjust the sails, and when I'm ready, I grab the wheel to turn the boat. "Okay, it's happening. Make sure you duck."

"I changed my mind—"

Sadie stands at the exact moment the boom swings hard in her direction. The metal pole slams into her chest, and the last thing I hear is the sound of her scream before her body plummets into the ocean.

Twenty-Nine

Sadie

The Last Breath I Take

Cold—my body feels so cold.

Dark—why is everything so dark?

Dead—am I dead?

My body sinks, the weight of something heavy sitting on my chest, but all I can think about is the people I love. My mom, my sister, the girls, Beth... what are they going to think when they find out I died? Will they be mad, or will one of them stand up at my wake and talk about the fact that at least I went out doing something fun? That my last moments were spent with the warm breeze of the Atlantic Ocean whipping through my hair—that they happened with Max?

Max.

He will never recover from this. The man spends the majority of his time attempting to be happy, to show the world that he's the guy who's always down for a good time. But I've seen him, the real him. The emotional, tenderhearted man who isn't afraid to speak his mind or show me how he feels. The one who cared enough to give up his free time to make sure I had the best couple of weeks of my life.

Max isn't like every other man out there, and he's certainly not a typical hockey bro. Of course, he's full of himself, funny, and the life of any party—but he's also selfless, thoughtful, and painfully romantic. He rescues little girls from the middle of the street, wipes ice cream off faces, plans insanely gorgeous surprises with candles and fairy lights, and loves his family so much that he's willing to smell like fresh lobster for the better part of three days.

I've known for a little while that I was falling for him. I think it happened when we first kissed—how cliché. At that moment, something shifted. It was like coming home for the first time in my life, like everything from that second onward would be different. He didn't just alter my state of being. Like an artist, he took brightly colored oil pastels and painted a new picture of my once bleak reality. I should have told him when there was still time—should have made it clear how much he's changed my life. If this is the last breath I ever take, I'll regret not thanking him.

"Sadie."

The sound of my name is like a whisper, so faintly hidden amongst the whirring and whooshing of the surrounding water.

"Sadie."

There it is again, a tad louder. Is this how it happens—how the undertaker calls me home? Where's the ship? Shouldn't there be one to ferry my soul wherever it's supposed to go?

A strong hand grips my bicep, tugging me through the chilly water until my head surfaces. Bright light blinds me, and I clamp my eyes shut.

"Sadie!" Max's gravelly voice overwhelms me. "Are you okay?" His calloused hand rakes down my face as water continues to slosh around us.

Prying open my eyes, I search his face as I cough up more water than should be humanly possible. "Am I dead?" I choke out.

Laughter that's threaded with relief booms out of him at the same time I realize he's treading water, his arm wrapped around me trying to hold me up. My legs move, working with him to support my body weight.

"Come on, we have to swim to the stern. I dropped the ladder."

He pulls me by my hand, leading us to the back edge of the boat. I clamber up the ladder, shivering so hard my teeth clank against themselves. It's summer, but the water out this far from the coast is freezing, or maybe it's just adrenaline. When Max joins me on the back of the boat, he pulls a couple of towels out of a bin I hadn't noticed, along with a plush, red blanket, and wraps them around me.

"Shhh, you're okay." He swipes my face, wiping away tears I hadn't even noticed were falling. "I'm so glad you're okay."

"I love you!" I blurt out, immediately covering my mouth with my hand. I didn't mean to say that. I hadn't planned to. It was supposed to go to the grave with me—the watery one I was just headed for.

Max rears back, and I cover my face, expecting him to be mad or maybe disappointed. Instead, he peels my hands away from my eyes, cradling my cheeks. "I love you, too. I didn't want to, and I know it's selfish. But I do."

My heart explodes like a butterfly wrenching itself from its cocoon.

Wrapping my hands around his neck, I kiss him. Pressing every ounce of my body into his, I tug at his back, pulling him closer. Our lips tangle, teeth clanking together as we furiously explore each other—like it could be the last time we ever do. His tongue plunges into my mouth, and I bite his bottom lip the way he's done to me so many times before.

Max leans back, breaking the kiss. "Sade... as much as I want nothing more than to continue this." He motions between us. "I have to move us somewhere safer, somewhere that you won't end up back in that water." His gaze is pleading, like he can't stand the thought of me falling in again.

Nodding my head reluctantly, I let him help me to a safe spot near the cabin door. There's a cushioned seat he settles me on as he pulls the blanket tighter around me and steps back toward the knobby wheel he steers with.

As Max maneuvers the boat, my heart hammers in my chest. I shouldn't have said it, shouldn't have told him I love him. He probably thinks this is one of those impassioned near-death experiences—and it is. But the sentiment is genuine. I thought I'd been in love before, but nothing has ever compared to the way I feel about Max, the way I think of him every second of every day. And my heart breaks all over again—because we can't be together.

Timing is a funny thing that way. When it's on your side, it's glorious. But when it isn't, there's no greater thief of joy. If things were different, if I didn't have a fate to find, a job to win back, a future so predetermined and thoughtfully planned that only a true act of cosmic design could derail it, then I could have Max. And if he didn't have to move thousands of miles away—he could have me.

"I can see the gears spinning in your head all the way from over here." Max glances in my direction, steering us closer to a small island I hadn't noticed. Trees line the edge on all sides, rocky cliffs hanging like they could fall into the ocean at any second. It isn't until we get a little closer that I notice a small dock leading to a path.

"I'm fine," I answer him, still scanning the space in front of the boat.

Max scoffs. "We said honesty, Sade. You promised."

He guides our vessel up to the dock, reaching out to tie some rope to the pylons before dropping the anchor.

"Do you need that?" I point toward where he just tossed the large metal shape over the edge. "I thought when you tied off a boat that was good enough."

"Just putting it in as a safety precaution." He smiles at me, and I feel it from the top of my head all the way to my toes. "In case any bigger boats come by. I'm not sure how stable this dock is, and I don't want another overboard situation."

"Am I the heiress in this situation? Or is it like the new one?"

He rolls his eyes but can't contain the laugh that escapes him. "I think maybe you are the rich one. It couldn't be me... I barely have a job."

"Stop, yes, you do. Coach Nash is going to be so lucky to have you." The weight of my words passes between us. There's that timing problem rearing its ugly head again as the butterfly that was flapping in my chest just minutes ago slowly dies.

"Can we just pretend for tonight?" Max begs, his lips pulled in and a hint of sheen in his eyes.

"Pretend?"

"That I'm not leaving. Hell, that neither of us are running off to our jobs in a matter of days." He lifts me from the seat I'm in, opening the cabin door with his free hand. "Can we pretend that the words we said not ten minutes ago are enough?"

"I would love that." Pressing a soft kiss to the bicep draped over my shoulder, I duck my head through the door and step into the sleeping quarters.

I'm not lying, I would love to pretend nothing else exists outside of our bubble—and I'll do my best to fake it until I make it. But we both know this isn't a solution. Instead, it's a temporary salve that will lessen the sting for a little while, only for it to come back twice as hard in the morning.

The cabin isn't a large space with only about two feet at the end of the bed. But it's cozy, and the blue patchwork comforter looks to be not just well-worn but soft in a way you know will be comforting.

I slip my still soaking wet jean shorts off and toss them out the cabin door. They land with a thud on the deck, followed by my tank top. Max strips, ditching everything including his boxers—leaving me breathless.

"See something you like?" Max smirks, running his hand through his hair so it's slicked out of his face.

"Mm-hmm." I slip my lace thong down my legs, kicking it off with my feet before ditching my bra.

Max pulls the comforter back, motioning for me to lie down, but I shake my head and point my finger to the spot he just uncovered. The book is sitting in the center of the pillows, and it's open to the next clue.

"For someone who says they want to help you, Beth really knows how to kill the moment," Max jokes, climbing up to it and lifting it from its spot as he scans the clue. "This one's easy. It's protective." He tosses me the book, followed by a pencil.

I read the clue aloud. "Three across... a human behavior that is comparable to sunscreen." Grabbing the pencil, I scribble in the answer and watch the letters melt to gold. "You're getting better at those, or Beth gave an easy one so we could get onto the good stuff."

Max rolls his eyes. "Yeah, maybe toss it aside now?"

Following his command, I drop it to the floor and dip a finger through the wetness that has pooled between my legs, holding it up. The lighting in the cabin is dim, but it illuminates the room enough for Max to see it glistening.

"You said you loved me..." I purse my lips, fighting a smile. "I think maybe you should prove that... even if it's just for tonight."

It's official—I'm a masochist. With the way he's looking at me, the way he so easily saved my life and confessed his feelings... I couldn't deny him this moment any more than I could deny it for myself.

Max scratches the back of his neck lightly. "Is that so?" Nodding, I finally give in to the smile—allowing myself to grin. "What are you proposing?"

Cocking a hip out, I hold my finger up and motion for him to come to me. "Crawl over here and find out."

Max leaps forward, reaching me in only a few quick movements. He pulls me on top of him, grabbing my hand, sucking the finger that was inside me a second ago into his mouth.

"Mmm..." He swirls his tongue around the tip. "You know, I think I'm getting hungry."

Pressing myself up with my hands, I move to scoot off of him. "Oh, uh, yeah we can eat instead."

He chuckles, pulling me so that I'm straddling his chest. "I meant you. I'm ready for my meal." Max pushes on my ass, hoisting me forward so that I'm hovering over his face. And when he sinks his tongue inside of me, I see stars.

He circles my clit slowly, like he's savoring every pass of his tongue. And then he suctions his mouth onto my already sensitive bud while plunging two fingers inside of me.

"You taste so sweet, Sade." He whispers, the warm breath fanning over my pussy. "Ride my face, baby."

My hips move in slow circles as Max brings me to the brink. But when my thighs start to shake, he pulls back, grinning up at me.

"What are you doing?" I brace my hands on the small piece of wood that serves as a headboard, lifting off of him slightly.

"Taking my time... there's no rush."

His hands grip my hips harder, pulling me back down again as he flattens his tongue and presses punishing flicks to my clit.

"Fuck, Max!"

He chuckles but continues switching between light circles that are so good but frustratingly not enough, and a full-on devouring. Every time I get close, he stops, and I feel like my skin is on fire. Every nerve cell in my body is buzzing.

"I need more, Max." I pull back, sliding down his chest until I'm hovering above his abdomen. I lean down and kiss him, our tongues tangling in a passion-filled moment. "Please, fuck me."

"Let me grab a condom." He pats my leg gently, waiting for me to move.

"Okay." I slip beside him, grabbing his hand as he moves to get up. "I'm on the pill. I mean... if you want to, we can, but I'm okay if we don't."

Something about there being a barrier between us feels too reminiscent of our situation. I should keep that wall up, keep the distance between us—but the reckless side of me doesn't want to.

"Are you sure?" He stares at me over his shoulder, judging my answer by my expression. "I'm clean. I haven't been with anyone in a while, never without one... and I've been tested."

"I'm positive. I haven't either... without one and not since my last exam. Everything was good." I lean forward, pulling him back to me.

He climbs on top of me, holding himself up so I'm not smushed as he peppers my face and neck with quick little kisses. Max swipes his nose over mine, back and forth.

"I need you to know that I was telling the truth." Another kiss, this one on my forehead. "I'm in love with you, Sade. And I know that's not ideal considering our situation... none of this is. But I need you to understand that no matter what happens—this thing between us is real."

My heart thumps rapidly, and tears prick the backs of my eyes. I bite my cheek, hoping the physical pain will help me keep it together. "It's real for me too, Max. I love you, even if it's the shortest love story in history—it's our story."

With that, Max lines himself up at my entrance and pushes into me in the sweetest, most deliciously painful way. His cock is so big it feels like too much to take, like he's consuming every inch of my body.

But isn't that what love is? All-encompassing, a connection so powerful you can't see where one person ends and the other begins.

Thirty

Max

When Sparks Fly

"Are you okay?" I ask, watching her face twist in discomfort.

"Yeah," she says breathlessly. "I just... it's huge, Max."

"Don't hold back, Sade." I smirk down at her. "Tell me more about how big my cock is, how it feels buried deep in this pussy."

"Move, Max." She glares at me, but there's a hint of amusement dancing at the corners of her lips. "Stop gloating and fuck me."

Pulling out slowly, I ease back until just the tip sits inside her. When she nods, I slide back in with a bit more force than the first time, just as she requested. And it takes everything in me not to immediately blow my load. She's not only the woman I love, but her pussy is drenched, gripping me like a greedy fist.

"More, Max." She bites her bottom lip, sucking it between her teeth. "For the love of God."

Thrusting faster, I pound into her as we find our rhythm. Her hips lift each time mine move forward, as if she's meeting me halfway. She feels like heaven, like she was designed just for me—my twin flame, a perfect match.

"Fuck, baby. You feel so good."

Dipping forward, I suck one of her tight pink buds into my mouth as I work her other breast with my hand. A soft, breathy sound escapes her—a sound I could listen to forever.

Each stroke inside her is better than the one before it, and when my balls tighten, I pull out quickly, willing myself to make it last longer with a hard squeeze from my hand at the base of my shaft. Sadie whines from her spot on the bed as she reaches to pull me back to her.

"I just need a second..."

"Okay, Casanova." Her face lights up, and she wraps her hand around my cock. "I guess I can give you a second... or two."

I almost think she's going to slip me back inside her, but she rubs my head over her clit like it's her own personal vibrator. Her legs shake each time it passes over her most sensitive spot, and I inch forward, applying more pressure.

"Max, God... your dick feels so good." She continues sliding it back and forth across her clit. "Please fuck me again, I'm so close."

Leaning in, I capture her mouth. Our tongues tangle, with the taste of her still present on my lips. We're drowning in each other, plunging off the deep end so quickly it can't be stopped.

Pulling back, I roll onto the bed beside her and grip the headboard with my arms stretched above me.

"What are you—"

"Ride me." I smirk. "You loved using my dick as your wand just a second ago. Let's see you do it again."

Sadie rolls her eyes and laughs, but climbs on top of me, one leg on each side of my hips. She leans forward, pressing a soft kiss on my cheek, then slowly runs her tongue down my neck and across my chest. Her descent continues until it's not her pussy closing around my cock—it's her mouth.

She swallows me in one fluid motion, tears pricking her eyes as I hit the back of her throat. But she doesn't stop, instead, she bobs up and down on a mission to drive me mad. Each flick of her tongue along the rim, each time she takes me so deep I have to will myself not to lose it—she's playing with me—and it's a game I don't intend to lose.

Releasing my grip on the wood above my head, I reach out and wrap her long chocolate hair around my fist. "Do you want me to take control?" I pull just hard enough to lift her eyes to mine. "Are you trying to make me lose my mind?"

She nods slowly, still sucking on the head of my cock like it's the best thing she's ever tasted.

Moving swiftly, I lift her off of me, repositioning her so her face is resting on the pillows and her ass is in the air. Without giving her notice, I bring my hand down on her ass with a loud crack. She yelps, but doesn't pull away. In fact, she pushes her perfectly round globes toward me.

Taking the hint, I do the same to the other cheek. Bending this time to lick the spot that's quickly turning a bright shade of red.

"Touch yourself, Sade." Positioning my tip at her entrance, I push in slightly. "This isn't going to last long for me, and I refuse to come first. Get there, baby."

Sadie runs her hand down her torso, beginning to make small circles over her center. And I thrust deep inside her, pounding in and out as fast as I can. Her thighs shake, and her pussy clenches around me as she screams.

"Max! Shit, Max! Holy..."

I pump in and out a few more times while she rides the wave of her orgasm, and when I can't take it any longer... I explode inside her like a bomb detonating, blowing every previous experience so far out of my mind it's like no one else has ever existed.

Sadie slumps onto the bed as I ease out of her, yawning, and I fold myself around her. She snuggles against me, turning in my arms so we're staring directly at each other. I run the backs of my fingers down her cheek, captivated by the woman in front of me, not just by her beauty, but by her as a whole.

"You're everything, you know that?" Pressing tiny kisses to her cheeks and forehead, I whisper.

Sadie wraps her leg over mine, inching ever closer. "I'm mad," she mumbles.

"Why?"

"Because we wasted so much time." She flops onto her back and runs a hand down her face. "What if it was supposed to be us all along? What if we wasted all these years when we could have been together?"

Scooping my arm beneath her, I roll her toward me—my chest pressed against the milky skin on her back. "You mean in high school?"

"Yeah..."

A low laugh bubbles in my chest. "Nah. Sade, I wouldn't have known what to do with you back then. I would've messed it up."

She releases a slow breath that I can feel ghosting over the hand I have pressed to her chest. "Timing," she says faintly, as if she's exasperated by the word. "It's never right when I want it to be."

I kiss her neck. "My dad told me once that it's not the number of days we get with someone, but the quality of them that counts." Biting my cheek, I stuff down the emotion that wants to burst out of me. "I think... we've had some really spectacular days. And we aren't out of them yet. Maybe we just look at this time with gratitude instead of sadness."

She twists her neck, and I meet her halfway to kiss her. It's filled with emotion, like a silent acceptance that even though we only have at most a little over a week—we are going to make every second count.

A loud boom sounds above us, followed by the faint sizzle of a firework floating down from the sky. Sadie shoots up straight, grabbing the blanket and leaving me uncovered.

"Come on, Max." She slides off the bed, wrapping the comforter around her. "We're missing the show."

Following her lead, I snag the red blanket that she used earlier and wrap it around my waist, then I grab the pillows. Sadie steps onto the deck, carefully walking to the front of the boat. When I'm sure she's steady and in a place where she won't repeat her earlier reenactment of *Overboard*, I toss the pillows toward her.

She lays them out on the bow, motioning for my blanket. "Throw me that so I can spread it out."

I'm glad there isn't another boat even remotely close to us—I'd be giving them quite the show. Handing her the blanket, she lays it down, then folds herself onto it, waving her arm for me to do the same. Sadie drapes the comforter over top of us, and we snuggle into the pillows, one of my arms wrapped under her neck and my other hand sprawled across her stomach.

Brilliant shades of gold, blue, green, and red erupt in the sky—some that look like starbursts, others that fall like the vines of a willow tree floating in the breeze. Each time another one ignites, I'm captivated, not by the light show in the sky, but by the way it illuminates the girl beside me. Her eyes twinkle with delight, her smile is so breathtaking it hurts, and the way she seems so relaxed... my heart tumbles for her all over again.

"Water Patrol. Permission to come aboard."

I scrub my eyes, my back aching and my skin dewy as I startle awake.

"Water Patrol. We're coming aboard." A loud voice booms again, followed by the sound of heavy boots thudding against the deck.

"That's not funny, Max." Sadie stirs beside me, rolling over as my brain finally registers what the hell is happening. I sit up hastily, glancing at the woman beside me—now fully exposed from the waist up. Grabbing the comforter, I pull it up as quickly as I can and shout toward the stern of my boat.

"Stop!" I stretch upward, spotting the boat tethered to mine with a big orange light at the top. "I'm not dressed, but everything is fine."

A deep voice beckons back to me. "Son, I'm going to need to speak with you. I need to see your boating license."

The man sounds pissed off—at the very least annoyed—about this situation. *Try the one being naked in broad daylight.* "I'll be right there, but I need to get some clothes on. Any chance you'd mind turning around?" The cockpit is blocking the view, but if he comes any further than two-feet onto the boat, he's going to see everything.

"Max?" he questions.

"Yeah?"

"Jesus Christ. Okay, I'm turning around." Apparently he recognizes my voice, but I still have no idea who he is.

I stand up, making my way around the edge of the boat and into the cabin quickly. Tugging a spare pair of sweats from a small drawer inside, I pull them on, grab my wallet, and climb back out to greet my wake-up call.

The man spins and... you've got to be fucking kidding me. It's Thomas, Brady's dad. The one I practically got into an argument with a few weeks ago over the fate of his child's hockey career. He's dressed in black pants, a green t-shirt with the water patrol logo, and boots.

"What a strange turn of events finding you here," he drawls with a smirk on his face.

"Not really." I widen my stance, reminding him that even though this is his turf, I'm not the guy that backs down from a fight. "I've been coming out to this dock for years."

"That so?"

Nodding, I cross my arms and grind my teeth together.

"Max, is everything oh..." Sadie's honeyed voice rings out, and when I glance over my shoulder, I see her standing near the edge of the cockpit where the white rises to make room for the cabin door. Thankfully, she has the comforter wrapped around her.

"We're good, Sade. Why don't you just sit down up there while I take care of this?"

She nods, returning to her spot, but when I turn my stare back on Thomas, he has a stupid-ass smirk on his face.

"Honestly, this just keeps getting better and better." He chuckles, running a hand along his jaw. "I shouldn't have to tell you this, but you can't sleep out here overnight. It's private property."

My shoulders dip. I've never slept out here before, and I honestly didn't intend to last night, but it just sort of happened.

"Thomas, look, man, I apologize. I didn't realize anyone owned it. My Pap used to bring me here all the time." I step toward him. "Won't happen again."

He stares at me like he's contemplating what to do, but then his partner calls out to him. "We've got a reported BUI. We need to go, Tommy."

He nods his head and turns to leave, but stops. "Max, this is a warning. Don't let it happen again." He moves to step from my boat back onto his and unties the ropes connecting us. "I bet Brady will play a lot in today's scrimmage. Wouldn't want anyone to find out about your sleepover." With that, the asshole steers away, taking his smug expression with him.

"Sade... you can come over here now," I holler. "They're gone."

She shimmies around the edge of the boat, carefully watching each step as she makes her way directly into my arms. Sadie pushes up onto her tiptoes and gives me a kiss.

"Morning," she whispers, smiling up at me.

"It is... How did we fall asleep?"

She laughs quietly. "Between the slow lulling waves lapping at the side of the boat, the warm body next to me, and the mind-blowing sex... I honestly don't know."

"Okay, smart-ass. Mind-blowing? Let's talk about that some more."

Sadie smacks my chest playfully. "I'd rather hear about that guy... is his son on your team or something?"

Rolling my eyes, I huff while grabbing my phone. Glancing at the time, I realize I'm due at the rink in a little less than two hours, and I still need to get us back to land. Thankfully, I left Benny with my parents, so if I can make it to the marina in forty-five minutes, I can swing by Sadie's for her to change and still have time to grab my gear.

"He is, and let's just say we don't have the best history. I love his kid, but the dad's an asshole." Sadie nods in understanding. "Will you come to my game? To see me in action?"

"Of course, Max. I wouldn't miss it for the world."

"We both might miss it if we don't get a move on. Then Thomas will tell everyone I'm a man-whore out here on my boat with a naked mystery woman." I swat her ass lightly. "There's a change of clothes in the small drawer to the left. Get dressed, and I'll get everything ready out here."

Sadie smirks, tucking her hair behind her ears before she ducks inside the cabin. Moving to prep the sails, I only turn back when she calls my name.

"Max..." She pops her head out of the cabin, tossing me a wink. "If he calls you a man-whore, I'll just tell all the rink moms how mind-blowing you are."

Thirty-One

Sadie

A Short & Sweet Goodbye

The last two hours have been a whirlwind—honestly, the last month has been too. When Max said we needed to get moving, he meant it. I've never seen a sailboat gliding across the sea so fast, and when we tore into the marina... he didn't even take the time to clean everything up properly, saying that he'd take care of it later.

My guess is that he doesn't want to risk arriving after Thomas, and that makes the whole thing funnier. We weren't doing anything wrong—minus the whole public indecency and hanging out on private property thing. On second thought, maybe it's good that we got here first.

It's been years since I stepped foot in the Mage Hollow Iceplex, but not much has changed. The same blue carpet lines the floors, there's still a snack shack to the left of the door, and the actual rink is separated by a tall glass wall with four doors for entry to the seating area.

Max had coach things to do when we arrived, so he dropped me at one of the small round tables near the fried food and soft drinks. Pulling a gooey cheese stick from my mouth, I'm happy as can be.

Last night was incredible and painful—the juxtaposition of emotions warring inside me like Benny when he plays with his Kong and shakes it side to side without abandon. On one side, I'm in love... the happiest I've ever been, and I'm not even worried about balancing it all because for the first time I know I can. On the other, I'm waiting for an anvil to drop—hyper aware that the rug could be pulled out from under my feet at any second.

Slurping my soft drink, I stand from my seat and toss the remaining three cheese sticks in the trash nearest the restroom. The game should be starting soon, though it's technically a pre-season scrimmage, I don't want to miss it. Not only do I get to watch Max in action, but it's also a good opportunity to scout a new spotlight player for this year's program.

Heading through the bathroom door, I slink into the stall to relieve the pressure on my bladder before entering the chilly arena. The door opens and closes while I'm mid-pee, and a faintly familiar perfume drifts into the space. I don't spend a lot of time with Alex, but it hits me the way nostalgia usually does. It's the same thing that happens when you walk into an old, musty room and are suddenly transported to another memory—mine being a failed attempt on skates at the roller rink.

Finishing up, I exit the stall and move to a long stainless steel basin sink to wash my hands. Lathering the soap, I take my time looking at the reflection staring back at me. I wouldn't say I look all that different—a little sun-kissed, maybe—but there's a sparkle in my eyes that wasn't there before. When I arrived in Mage Hollow, I was hanging on by a thread. And I had one singular focus—get back to work. Now, while that's still very high on my priority list—so high it's inevitable—I don't feel consumed by it.

"Sadie?" Alex's voice rings out from behind me.

Looking past my reflection, our eyes meet, and I feel a little less creepy for thinking the stranger next to me smelled like her.

"Alex? What are you doing here?" I step to the side, grabbing a paper towel from the roll to dry my hands.

She steps up to the sink and begins washing hers. "Coop has a scrimmage." She smiles when she says his name, the look that a good mother gets thinking about their child. "Levi is going to be so happy to see you."

"I somehow doubt that." I throw the soggy paper I'm holding into the trash. "Is everything okay?"

Alex's gaze focuses on her hands, and my heart races. Something is obviously wrong... but what?

"You should come sit with us. What are you doing here anyway? Scouting kids?" She raises an eyebrow in challenge, and I hold my hands up.

"Not entirely."

"Okay?"

Tucking a chunk of hair behind my ear, I sigh far too dramatically. "There's a guy... we're-having-a-summer-fling," I rush out.

"Nooo..." Alex bounces excitedly. "Wow, I like it... is he a single dad? One of the coaches? Tell me everything!"

A laugh bubbles out of me, and I try to conceal it with my hand. "Sadie!" Alex squeals. "I think that's the first time I've ever heard you laugh. This guy is good for you, and Mage Hollow is so close to GC... it could totally be more than just a fling."

My face must twist at her words, because she covers her mouth with her palm as if she's trying to stuff them back in.

"He lives here... but he's taking a job as equipment manager in Washington."

"Badgers or Titans?"

"Titans." Alex pulls me into a hug, wrapping me up tight. "It's all going to work out. You know... maybe we cou—"

"No." I grab the door handle and hold it open for Alex. "Mixing work and pleasure never ends well."

She scoffs, bumping her hip into mine as she exits. "For obvious reasons, I'll pretend you didn't just say that to me." Alex winks, sashaying through the lobby toward the one and only Levi Montgomery.

Following a few steps behind her, I consider what she said. It's true that I could ask Levi to consider Max, but would he even want me to do that? He loves hockey and wanted to play professionally—settling for a makeshift job we create feels like a step below the position he has. And what if it doesn't work out? We've said we love each other, but it's easy to get swept up in things when you're not working eighty-hour weeks.

"Sadie freaking Wells!" Levi booms as he sees me approaching. "What are you doing here? I was planning to swing by your mom's with a coffee when we finished up with the scrimmage."

Why would he come to my childhood home?

"Hi, Coach Montgomery." Fiddling with the hem on my sweatshirt, I glance around at the crowd staring at us. "Alex said Coop is playing, how exciting."

"Would it kill you to call me Levi? I'll settle for Monte even... just ditch the coach," he grumbles, and I laugh.

He turns to Alex, draping an arm over her shoulders. "Is she laughing?"

"That's what I said! It's nice, huh?" Alex smiles at me, and it doubles in size when big, brawny arms wrap around my middle.

"Hey, Sade." Max releases his hold on me when he realizes who I'm talking to. Stepping to my side, he extends his hand. "Coach Montgomery, it's an honor to meet you. I'm Max O'Reilly."

Levi shakes his hand, narrowing his eyes at Max. "Why do I know that name?"

Max's cheeks turn bright red, and he runs a hand through his hair. "Well, it could be the fifty scouting tapes I'm sure my mother sent you over the years, or from Coach Nash."

Levi snaps his fingers, pointing one at Max. "That's it. Nash said he hired a new EM... a guy who coulda played but took one too many hits up here." He points to his head.

"That'd be me." Max sighs, reaching down to tangle his fingers with mine. "Moving out to Washington next week, but I'll always be a Flames fan."

Max's watch buzzes, and he leans toward me, pressing a kiss to my cheek. "I've gotta get out there." He walks away, but stops when he's close to the glass double doors. "Yo, Monte... is your kid playing today?" he calls out.

"Yep! Name's Bennett... he'll give your guys a run for their money."

Max nods and disappears through the door.

"Do you want to go find a seat? Sounds like it's starting." I wait expectantly.

"Yeah, let's go."

Cooper has scored twice and is working toward a hat trick. He's skating much smoother than most of these kids, but a couple on Max's team seem to keep up. Alex has been on the edge of her seat the entire game, yelling loudly and banging on the glass in front of us. I, on the other hand, haven't been able to take my eyes off Max.

Even from the other side of the rink, I can tell how much he enjoys coaching. It's obvious in the way he talks to each player when they come off the ice, in the way he pays such careful attention to how they feel. He was born for this sport, and my heart swells with pride for him.

It's hard knowing that our time together is ending, but it would be so selfish of me to ask him not to pursue his dreams—or to settle for something that doesn't have a career path leading to the title coach.

"Sadie, I need you to come back to work," Levi says, under his breath so that only I can hear.

Turning to make sure I heard him correctly, I notice a worried look settled into his brows.

"Okay. When are you thinking?"

"Today."

My eyes widen, and my mouth opens and closes a couple of times.

"What's wrong?" There has to be a reason, and while I'm happy to know I'm needed, I thought I'd have a little notice. A couple of days at least.

He runs a hand through his hair. "Remember when Alex called you?" I nod, thinking about that morning. "Well... the mom"—he tips his chin to the very one that's blown up my email for months—"she didn't make veiled threats. She talked to a reporter who's trying to run with a story about gala profits being mishandled."

"What!" I say louder than I should, and several heads turn in our direction.

"Sadie... shh." He faces forward, watching Cooper sink the puck in the net at the final buzzer. We stand and clap, but Levi continues through gritted teeth. "I know it's all bullshit, but you know these numbers better than anyone. I can't comb through it all fast enough, and I need this shit squashed before the media grabs hold of it."

My mind races, and a lump forms in my throat. I know there's nothing to hide, but the idea that someone would question my work, my ethics—it's infuriating. A string snaps inside of me, and I know I have to go back.

Searching the ice, I spot Max talking to Cooper's coach. As much as I don't want it to be this way—it's time for a short and sweet goodbye.

"I'll gather my stuff from my mom's and get on the road." I turn toward Levi. "Should I meet you at the arena?"

His eyes are full of pity as he tips his chin toward Max. "I'm sorry that's ending this way. But I'm proud of you for living, for taking my advice."

Squeezing his arm, I straighten my spine and bite my cheek so I don't cry. "Thanks. I'll call you when I'm close."

Moving out of the bleachers, each step feels harder than the last. Max isn't expecting this. We had plans to grab stuff to grill at his house. We were going to take Benny to the dog park. As I round the corner, closing in on where I know I'll find him... I will myself to make it quick. Not just for his sake—but for mine too.

"Hey, great game, huh?" Max says, wrapping me in his arms. "Wait, what's wrong?"

"Is there somewhere we can talk?" My lips tremble as the question comes out.

"Uh, yeah." Max pulls my arm toward a hallway I hadn't noticed, not stopping until we're stepping inside a utility closet. "What's going on, Sade?"

Breathing deeply, I recount the entire story for him, from the initial conversation with Alex to the emails that have flooded my box and the story now at risk of causing a big ass untruthful mess.

"—and I'm the only one who knows those numbers backward and forward. This is years worth of work, a program I helped build," I finish, pushing my tongue to the roof of my mouth and begging my body not to cry.

Max runs his hands up and down my arms. "What do you need from me? How can I help?"

My lip quivers as I fight the reaction my heart wants to give. "I need to leave." I wrap my arms around him tightly. "Tonight."

Max hugs me back, infusing the embrace with everything we're both feeling. "Okay." He slides his hand between us, tipping my chin up with his thumb and forefinger. "This month has been the best one of my entire life. I love you, but we both knew this had a deadline." He stares into my eyes, searching my soul. "I would never hold you back from doing what you need to do. If there's anyone alive who understands chasing something just to have it ripped away—it's me. Just make me one promise."

This man is so good, he can't even bring himself to be selfish, or mad, or any of the thousands of other emotions that are raging inside of me. He's just understanding—supportive even—and the dam inside of me breaks. Tears streak down my face, blurring my vision as my chest heaves.

"What's the promise?" I choke out.

Max grips my face, one hand on each cheek, as he wipes my tears. "Promise me you won't lose balance. That you'll remember you deserve happiness outside of work, and that you need multiple legs on your stool."

He kisses me. It's chaste and simple, but infused with a thousand things neither of us will voice out loud. It's goodbye. It's an 'I love you'. It's an 'I'd sacrifice anything for you to reach your dreams'. And I'm not sure I'll ever recover from it.

"I promise." Stroking a hand down his face, I press a kiss to his cheek. "Give the Titans hell, Max. I'm so proud of you, and thank you... for everything."

With that, I slip past him and beeline through the rink. Heartbroken isn't a feeling I'm used to, but maybe the work will distract me. Or maybe the bitter cold arena will freeze the cracks inside me, filling them with ice so deep that I'll be numb forever.

Thirty-Two

Max

The Last Minute Knock

"Do you really want to take this shitty old mattress?" Sam bellows down the hall from my bedroom.

"It's the only one I have!" I shout back at him, slumping onto the floor as Benny leaps onto me and licks my cheek.

My whole family is here helping me load the moving truck. I'm leaving tomorrow morning after one final sleepover at Mom's, and my stuff has to be out by three so the landlord can collect the keys. I don't have time to wallow, but it's all I seem able to do.

When Sadie walked away a week ago—leaving me alone in a small utility closet with nothing but a broken heart—I sat there and licked my wounds. Even though I've changed locations, the feeling hasn't left me.

We knew it was coming. Hell, we were practically watching the train barrel down the tracks toward us. I just couldn't have expected how I'd feel without her. How empty and lonely it would be when I know she isn't going to pop up around the corner at any moment.

I'm relieved for her—happy even—and that itself is hard to reconcile. This wasn't a breakup, not in the typical sense. We didn't have a fight, so there's nothing for me to overanalyze or stew about. It was simply a goodbye... a parting of ways that was mutually agreed upon.

So, why does it hurt so much?

Neither Sadie nor I would have asked the other person to stay. It wouldn't have been fair or even rational with the short duration of our arrangement. But a part of me knows that if she had, I probably would've agreed. And that's a problem—one I can only solve with distance and perspective.

"You doing okay in here?" Olive asks, bouncing into the guest room and flopping on the floor beside me. "I know it's hard starting over, but it'll all work out." She squeezes my hand lightly.

"Yeah, fine." Moving Benny aside, I slide onto my knees and continue stuffing sheets into a box. "I just hate packing. Do you think it would be weird if I showed up with a small duffel full of clothes instead?"

She follows me, picking up a blue pinstriped set of sheets and shoving them in the box. "That would be very weird. You're not a grifter. They're expecting someone professional...prepared, some would say."

"Hilarious." I shove the flaps of the box closed and pull the packing tape over to secure it. "Hand me that marker, would ya?" Pointing to a large Sharpie on the other side of the room, I smooth the tape down with my hands.

"Maxie-pad. What else needs to be done?" Bridget sticks her head in the doorway, her whole body hidden behind the wall as if I'm going to throw something at her—the thought occurred to me, since she won't stop using that stupid nickname.

"We're finished in here," Olive answers, tossing me the marker, then double-checking that the closet is bare. "I think the only room left is the kitchen."

"That stuff is mostly Ma's," I add in, scribbling **sheets** on the top of the sealed box. "We should just load it in the laundry baskets and take it back when we go to dinner."

Olive scoffs, and Bridget rolls her eyes.

"You can't move without a single pot or pan, Max." Sam enters the room, scooping his wife up into his arms. "There's this thing... It's called eating. You still need to do it sometimes." My smart-ass brother has to come in here and be logical, but I just haven't had an appetite in six days.

Maybe I'm doing worse than I thought.

"Speaking of food, could we get some?" Nora skips into the room that's quickly becoming crowded, pulling Bridget in with her.

"We're eating in two hours, Nor," Bridget mumbles. "I'm not getting blamed if we show up to the feast Mom's making and everyone's full."

"What about happy hour, then? A few light cocktails... maybe some of those fried green tomatoes you love, Maxie..." Nora is trying to tempt me, to get me to eat something for the first time in days, and as much as I'd love to say no—my stomach rumbles audibly.

"Fine. You guys get started in the kitchen. It shouldn't take long. I just want to do one more walkthrough before handing these over to Pete." Reaching into my pocket, I pull out the keys and jingle them in the air.

As the three women closest to me—outside of Mabel—scurry down to finish the final room, I slip down the hall and into my bedroom. Sam doesn't follow me, probably sensing I need five minutes alone. I tug the closet doors open, scanning the space top to bottom, but everything is empty, and it hits me that my whole life could be boxed and stuffed into a U-Haul in less than two hours.

I'm not sure what that says about me, but it feels like it represents that, as of today, I've got a whole lot of nothing. Benny whines at my feet, so

I bend down and scoop him into my arms. He nuzzles his smushed-up face into my neck, and I stroke his back.

"I miss her, Ben." Stepping into the bathroom, I dip to check the cabinets. "I thought it would be easier, but moving and not knowing if I'll ever see her again feels like there's a hole in my chest." Benny whimpers, licking my face. "I know she meant a lot to you, too. I mean, you learned to love the grass because of Sadie... that's a special bond if I've ever known one."

"Max!" Olive's voice rings out from the bottom of the stairs. "We're ready when you are."

"Coming!"

They did that quicker than I expected, but the only real things in there were a coffeemaker, a toaster oven, one set of dishes, and a single pot and pan. Sighing deeply, I carry Benny down the hall and the steps.

"Can you explain to us how you survived with almost no kitchen supplies?" Nora smirks at me, her arms crossed as she taps her foot lightly on the floor. "How many meals did Mom prepare for you on a weekly basis exactly?"

"So many... eat your heart out, Nor. I'm the favorite."

"Oh, good." Bridget punches me in the arm. "Looks like the first round is on you then." She links hands with Nora, and the two of them skip a little too happily out my front door.

Sam locks up the back door, checking each of the rooms downstairs carefully for items we may have missed. And I sign the move-out paper-work, dropping the keys onto the counter as I was instructed. Stepping out onto the front porch for the last time feels both sad and hopeful. I'm forever changed from the last few weeks with Sadie, but maybe that's a sign that I'm more ready for this change than I think.

"Ma, we're here!" Bridget yells as we pile in the front door.

Nora shushes her, Olive snorts, and my brother—ever the stoic one—rolls his eyes. We had a few drinks at Union before coming over for the O'Reilly version of a going-away party. I'm facing a set of numb ass-cheeks and a cross-country drive at a top-speed of fifty-five miles per hour, but at least I'll have a full belly.

"We're out here!" Mabel calls to us from the back patio.

Shuffling down the hall, I'm suddenly hyper-aware of my surroundings. Things that I haven't noticed in years suddenly seem to stand out, like the small dent in the wall right next to the backdoor from the time Sam and I tried to recreate a scene from *Jackass*, or the way the house always vaguely smells like warm cookies even when Mom isn't baking.

Stepping onto the patio, we pile into the wicker seating, and Mom curses under her breath.

"Who let those three get drunk?" she asks Sam and me with a pointed stare. "I had a whole toast planned, but now the peanut gallery is going to have to use water instead of champagne."

Sam rolls his eyes, pointing a finger at me where he thinks I can't see it.

"Don't look at me." I hold my hands up. "This is Ariella's fault. She showed up and made a big deal of it being the group's last hurrah."

"That girl—"

"Is my best friend in the entire world!" Olive finishes the statement my mom was making.

"I was going to say... that girl is something else." Mabel pats my sister-in-law's arm. "Nothing negative, Ollie. But she needs to stop toying with Howard's heart."

"I know!" Olive points at my mom, shouting her agreement. I'm finding she only has one volume when the alcohol hits her veins, and it's not quiet. "She's going to lose him, eventually."

"Mabel, hunny, is it time to eat?" my dad asks, glancing at the mess his children have become. The three girls are half falling out of their chairs, Sam is struggling to maintain a straight face, and I'm just thankful that I'm having some fun on my last night in town.

Mom stands, heading inside, and the rest of us follow. We had a few appetizers, but not enough to fill our bellies—mine personally is ready to chow like a beast that's been awakened after hibernation.

Settling around the table, Mom brings in dish after dish of my personal favorites. There's Irish stew, soda bread, cabbage with bacon, colcannon mash, a variety of cheeses on a board, and bread pudding. It smells delicious, and my mouth waters as soon as the feast is spread on the table. We dig in like a pack of wild hyenas, piling our plates so full that they almost need sideboards.

"So, Max. What's the plan?" Dad asks from his spot at the end of the table.

"Fo wha?" I reply, a forkful of potatoes in my mouth.

"Are you planning to stop along the way?" Dad narrows his eyes at my lack of manners. "Should I look up a hotel and make a reservation?"

Taking a sip of the filled water glass in front of my plate, I shake my head. "No, to the reservation. The team travel coordinator mapped out my trip and scheduled stops for me. I should make it to Chicago tomorrow, then it's across the Dakotas the next day."

He nods, satisfied with my answer.

"Do they have a place set up for you to stay when you get there?" Mom chimes in, her eyes noticeably misty.

"Ma..." I plaster the biggest smile I can muster on my face. "I'm going to be fine. They put me up at a swanky hotel for the first two weeks. I'll have time to find a place before they give me the boot. I'm not a grifter, right, Ollie?"

My sister-in-law nods enthusiastically as I throw her words from earlier back at her. And Sam smiles, tipping his chin in my direction.

"You're right. I know you're going to be fine." Mom stands from the table, stepping toward the kitchen. "I'm grabbing the champagne. Are you girls sober eno—"

She trails off when a knock sounds at the door and switches directions, moving to open it. The room falls so quiet you could hear a pin drop. We aren't expecting anyone, but maybe Howie or Xavier stopped by for one last goodbye?

But then, I hear six words I never expected.

"Sadie? What are you doing here?"

Thirty-Three

Sadie

The Key to Everything

12 Hours Earlier

The alarm clock blares beside me, and I roll over with a groan. It's been six days since I left Mage Hollow—144 hours since I walked away from Max, barreled into my mother's house, packed my shit, and raced off.

This week has been nothing short of hellacious for so many reasons, but coupling the disappointment on my mom's face when I said I couldn't stay for dinner with the absolute devastation knowing that I may never see Max again has been a lot. To say I'm struggling would be a gross understatement. I'm drowning, completely submerged in paperwork that's all wrapped up in a bow that screams *pathetic*.

And don't get me started on Beth's book.

As I turn to slap my alarm for what feels like the twelfth time this morning, I find it perched exactly where it is every morning—spread open to the next clue with a pencil floating mid-air above it on my dresser.

Tossing the covers off, I rub my eyes, trying to pull myself out of my stupor. Levi, Alex, and I were at the arena until well past midnight, putting the final documents together for the lawyers. As suspected, I was able to find both physical and digital proof of every payment received and every donation made. The reporter—and the too big for her britches mom—will be able to stick their exposé where the sun doesn't shine around noon.

The only thing left to do is sit down with Mr. Bennedito, the Flames' in-house counsel, then it's business as usual. In other words, I'll be sorting through the thousands of emails waiting to be answered from prospective spotlight players and gala vendors.

Shuffling to the kitchen, I roll my eyes at the mess I'm pretty sure I noticed last night but chose to ignore. Mae was cooking again, which means there's a pile of dishes so high I'll be lucky to fit the coffeepot under the faucet for a quick rinse.

"Hey." The offending chef waltzes into the kitchen in a neon orange bathrobe and pink bunny slippers. "Sorry about the mess. I'll clean it when I wake up."

Glancing at the time on the microwave clock, my mind twists in confusion.

"It's 7:00... in the morning."

"And?" Mae looks as confused as I feel.

"Are you sleepwalking?" I do my best to push the coffeepot under the faucet, only bumping a few plates as I do.

"No? Is that something I normally do?"

Spinning, I place the semi-clean pot onto the hot plate and dump just enough grounds to fuel me through another long day into the mesh holder at the top. Pressing the on button, I lean against the counter.

"I don't think so? But it's not nighttime, so... nevermind."

Having this discussion with her isn't worth the energy. Now that I'm pretty sure things are good to go with the whole debacle at work,

I plan to drink a cup of coffee, attempt to finish the puzzle book so it'll stop taunting me, and ready myself for the day. Whatever Mae does has nothing to do with me.

When the drip stops, I pour a cup of black coffee and make my way back into the solace of my room. Mae stared at me confused for a few minutes before falling onto the couch and promptly beginning to snore. I'm starting to think I might need a new roommate or, better yet, no roommate at all.

A pang sinks into my stomach—Max would've been the perfect person to live with. I could've had Benny snuggles—and Max snuggles—any time I wanted. I miss him so much it hurts, but I think I've been too busy this week to really realize just how much.

Grabbing the book and pencil from my dresser as I pass, I set my coffee on my nightstand and slip back under the covers. As I thumb through the last two clues, a guilty feeling gnaws at me. The entire premise of this book was to do it with someone, to do it with him. I scan the next clue:

2. Down

An agreement between friends.

The answer is crystal clear—understanding. Probably because it's a word I've turned over in my mind several times over the last week. Max was understanding, my family not so much. They were happy that I had my job back but sad that I had to run out. Howie texted me a few times, mad at first that I left without a goodbye, then sad for me with an undercurrent of pity that feels like more than I can stomach right now.

My phone buzzes on the bed beside me, Mal's name illuminating the screen.

"Hey," I answer.

"She's alive!" my sister shouts loudly, and I rip the phone from my ear, smashing the speaker button.

"Jesus... if I wasn't that would've woken me from the tomb."

She giggles. "Oh, sorry, I just wanted Mom to know you actually answered." I can hear a door open and close in the background as the faint sound of the girls playing drifts away. "How are you? What's going on?"

I gave my mom a brief play-by-play as I stuffed my belongings into my suitcase and ran out the door to head back to Golden City, but other than that, our conversations have been limited.

"I'm surviving. The stuff with work should be done today."

"And Max?"

I release a slow breath. "He's moving... tomorrow, I think." My voice cracks on the last word.

"Sade, have you considered that maybe you're supposed to be together?"

"Mallory, don't." Of course, I've thought about it. My entire drive to Golden City was spent with tears running down my face, and I haven't slept well in almost a week. But it's not possible.

"I'm just saying, sometimes instead of doing what your brain tells you, maybe you need to listen to your heart." She sucks in a breath noisily. "Maybe that was what Beth was trying to tell you."

I stare at the book lying on my lap, and memories from the past month hit me. Every page of this thing is directly linked to him—every memory tied to our time together. In the end, it may have just been busywork—a distraction from my problems—but it brought me closer to him.

"In a perfect world, you'd probably be right." I close the book on my lap, running my hand over it thoughtfully before tossing it aside. "But he deserves this opportunity. I can't take it away from him."

"Then go with him! Get your head out of your ass, Sadie. I've never seen you happier, more alive than when you were with him."

Tears streak down my face at her words. There's only one problem with what she's suggesting.

"He didn't ask me to."

6 Hours Earlier

"Thanks for coming back." Levi holds the door to the conference room open for me, and I step around him into the hallway. "We never would have found everything you did."

Nodding, I smile softly at him and Alex. "Of course, I love my job. I'm grateful I was able to help."

"How did he take it?" Alex asks, sympathy etched into her expression.

"Uh..." I blow out a heavy breath, then bite the inside of my cheek to stave off any chance of getting emotional. "It was fine. We both knew what it was."

"Are you sure? I saw the way he looked at y—"

"I'm sure." My face heats and a lump forms in my throat. "I'm just going to take a walk. I'll be in my office if you need anything."

I turn and leave, walking away from them as quickly as I can without it being obvious that I'm running off to cry alone. Winding around the arena, I slink into one of the suites. It's dark but secluded enough that no one will find me here.

There are a couple of stuffed leather chairs, and I curl into one of them, bringing my knees to my chest. Looking down at the glossy ice, I feel small compared to what we do here. Insignificant.

How long has it been this way?

Maybe this is how I've always felt—maybe this is the reason I've worked so hard to get where I'm at, why I've sacrificed everything. I've always thought that if I could just make a name for myself—if I could be successful—then everything else would fall into place. But that's not true. None of it matters when you're alone. *That's* what Levi wanted me to learn.

I'm not sure what makes me move, but the realization that this wasn't all for nothing sparks something inside me. There's a lot that has happened, some things I can't take back or change. But for the first time in days, I feel the fog beginning to lift.

Exiting the suite, I turn in the direction of my office. I've walked the halls here millions of times, and I'm pretty sure I could find it blindfolded and three sheets to the wind at this point. But, for some reason, I spend my time really soaking it all in, from the pictures on the walls to the fresh coat of paint that must've been done recently. I pass the coaches' offices, the locker rooms, and the shooting bay. The social media director's office is up ahead, followed by mine and Alex's directly across. Light seeps out from under her door—they are either just as bad as I am at work-life balance or she forgot to turn it off.

Shaking my head, I approach the door and raise my fist to knock. But my eye catches on the handle of the door next to hers.

What the fuck?

Dangling from the round silver knob—jammed into the lock—is *the* keychain. I glance both ways down the hall, checking my surroundings before bending down to look at it. The keychain is the same flat diamond shape, and when I turn it over, it's got the same inscription: JBI.

I take a step back, moving until my spine crashes into the wall behind me. My breathing is ragged, and my heart races. Slinking to the floor, I press the palms of my hands into my eye sockets.

You're making this up. You've had very little sleep, and this is just a mirage.

Taking a deep breath, I blow it out slowly, attempting to calm myself down. Uncovering my eyes, I stare at the door as if that will somehow tell me what the fuck is going on. But when I do, my vision catches on a small silver nameplate fastened to the wall. It looks just like mine and all the others.

Springing up, I take two steps back toward the door and read it: Johan Berg-Isaksson.

Who the hell is that?

The lights seem to be off, but I knock on the door anyway. If we hired someone new and they're here, I should introduce myself. Maybe that'll make it less awkward when the cameras reveal the complete meltdown I just had in the hallway—the one that will look like I'm either a creep or I've actually lost my mind.

No answer.

I knock again—still no response. Turning away, I step toward my office, but a faint voice rings out—one I'd recognize anywhere.

"Go in, Sadie." Beth's voice ghosts over me as softly as a whisper.

Grabbing the doorknob, I turn the key and push inside, closing the door behind me as quietly as possible. There's not much in the way of furniture, just a single desk with a rolling chair on one side and a small cushioned one on the other. Taking another step into the room, the lights flicker on with the motion sensors. And lying in the middle of the empty desk is a note, the book, and a golden gift box with a huge white bow.

Slipping into the wheeled chair, I unfold the note and read it.

My dearest Sadie,

I was hoping we would eventually get here. You put up quite the resistance in the beginning, my girl. Yes, I saw you throw my book into the trash can—you owe me a glass of wine the next time I see you.

At this point, I'm not sure if you've figured out the theme of the puzzle, but I know you've found your fate. The thing I learned when I played this same game many, many years ago is that as much as we can fight it—the heart always wins out over the head in the end.

I hope you will listen to it.

Don't be afraid to take a chance. It'll all work out as it's meant to, I promise.

I've left you a small gift—a token of my love for you. While I never had a daughter, Sadie, you are the closest thing to it. Inside you will find all the answers you've been seeking, but you must solve the final clue to release the glue.

Here's a hint.

He calls himself Mr. Altruistic because he'll never put himself first. If you need a helping hand—he's actually reliable—it's not a curse. He may be affectionate, but humor is the key. He'll protect you from danger and is always understanding. But most of all, he's patient—when you look for him, you'll find his home vacant.

—B.

Max. It's always been about Max. Grabbing the book, I scan each clue again, piecing together the hint with the clues. She knew from the beginning. It was never about my job, or keeping me busy. Beth wanted me to be happy, to find true love—the kind that is undeniably right for me.

Hastily, I grab the gift box, the note, and the book as I scramble to the door. A picture falls out as I push into my office, so I throw the items on a chair to grab it.

"Knock knock," Levi's voice sounds from behind me, making me jump. "Hey, is that Max?" He points to the photo in my hand, and I look at it for the first time—it's me in his arms, spinning at the balloon bonanza after he'd won. We look so happy, so in love that I hardly recognize myself.

She was there watching.

"Uh, yep." I tuck it against my chest, directly over my heart.

"Any chance he hasn't left for Seattle yet?" Levi walks into my office and leans his arm on one of the bookshelves that line the left wall. "Johan backed out. I need an equipment manager... like yesterday."

"I'm sorry, what?" I stammer, not believing the odds.

"He said something about Americans not being able to cook meatballs properly." Levi runs a hand through his hair, clearly annoyed. "Probably wouldn't have been a good fit. But Max..." He points at the photo I'm clutching. "He seemed like a great guy and a hell of a coach with the way he talked to those kids. I need someone who's looking for long-term, with potential for advancement on the coaching track."

"Yeah." I can barely catch my breath, but I nod my head. "I'll ask him right away."

Levi turns to walk out but stops. "Oh, and Sadie. Tell him I'll double whatever Nash was going to pay as long as he doesn't break your heart." He winks at me, then leaves.

Holy shit! Is this actually happening?

Reaching into my desk drawer, I grab my laptop bag and stuff the things Beth left for me inside, then pull out my keys.

I have to get to Mage Hollow—I have to get to Max.

Present Time

After running home to grab a few things, showering to make myself look a little less haggard, and calling both Howie and Mal—I finally jumped in my car and hit the road. I've gone over what I'm going to say a million times in my head as I sped toward Mage Hollow. But none of it feels exactly right. I know Max gets me, but there's a part of me that's worried maybe this isn't what he wants.

I took his acceptance of my leaving as a sign of understanding, but what if he was just letting me down easy—relieved that I was the one who had to go? What if asking him to work directly across the hall from me for the long haul is too much pressure?

I pace the front yard of his parents' house for the third time, darting behind a row of bushes twice when I thought someone might've seen me.

"Get it together, Sadie," Beth's voice whispers in my ear—or at least it feels like it. She's not actually here. "He's waiting."

"I know! Okay! I'm going," I whisper back like a lunatic on the front lawn talking to myself.

I take three deep breaths as my feet climb the steps, propelling me forward until I'm standing at the door. I can hear voices inside, and it sounds like his entire family is laughing at something someone said. After waiting a few more seconds, the noise inside calms, and I raise my hand—knocking twice.

Stepping back from the door, I don't have to wait long before Mabel opens it.

"Sadie? What are you doing here?"

"I was hoping to talk to Ma—"

My words are cut off by the man himself as he wraps me in a tight hug and lifts me off my feet. Max peppers my forehead and cheeks with kisses.

"I didn't know *when* or *if* I'd ever see you again," he says, releasing me. I'm sure my face is filled with shock—that wasn't the greeting I was expecting. "Sorry, that was a little much."

"No..." I sputter, failing to form words. "Can we talk?"

Max tips his chin at his mother, and she closes the door, giving us privacy. He wraps his hand around mine, linking our fingers. "Sure. Here? Or should we walk?"

"The car, maybe?" I dart my eyes to the large bay window in front of the O'Reilly's home, noting at least four pairs of eyes glued to the spot were standing.

Max follows my gaze. "Yeah, a drive would probably be good."

Moving to my vehicle, we duck inside. I turn the ignition and back out of the driveway. I don't go far just a few houses down, before I park on the street. Just being near him makes me want to spill everything, but I know this needs to come out just right.

Turning slightly in my seat, I reach for his hand. "Let me start by saying that all the things I'm about to tell you are going to feel like a lot." Max smiles at me, and any anxiety I'd been feeling melts away. "I know that we have only been hanging out for a short time, but I meant what I said on the boat. I love you, Max. And I've realiz—"

"I love you, too." He leans over the center console and kisses me. "Sorry, continue."

A laugh escapes me. "As I was saying, I've realized that no matter how hard I work or what accolades I collect... none of it matters if I don't have someone to share it with. You made me see that my life could be so much more than it is—that I could have love, happiness, *and* a career." He nods along, still grinning at me. "The past week has been a nightmare. Between work stuff and missing you, I've never felt more alone. And I thought that was the way it had to be, that it wouldn't be fair to want this... until today."

"What changed?" he asks, squeezing my palm. "Actually, wait. Before you tell me, I love you too. Obviously, I already told you that. And I have been the same... barely getting through the days without you. I don't care what it takes. I'd sacrifice everything just for the chance to date you, Sadie Wells—for the chance to see where this goes."

I bite my cheek hard, trying not to laugh at the irony of the situation. We both felt the same way, but the minute we stopped communicating was the minute we were both miserable. I don't think we could have had a conversation to avoid this—it had to happen—but it just goes to show that if we're honest about how we feel, nothing is impossible.

"Do you want to work for the Flames?"

"I always have, but that's not an option."

"It is." I reach out, running my hand down his cheek. "Levi told me to tell you he will double whatever Nash offered you. There's only two tiny catches..."

His eyes widen, and he cocks his head to the side. "I, what? I don't understand."

"Johan, the equipment manager Levi hired, backed out. The job is yours if you want it, but the office is directly across the hall from mine. Oh, and you're not allowed to break my heart—according to Levi." I hold my hands up in surrender.

"Yes."

"That's it? No other questions?"

He shakes his head. "No other questions. I have always wanted to be there, but seeing you across the hall is a bonus. And I couldn't break your heart if I tried... I care about you too much to ever cause you pain intentionally."

Folding myself over the console between us, I kiss him hard. It's chaste at first, but Max deepens the kiss, angling my head slightly and licking into my mouth. We savor each other, exploring like we're coming home for the first time in forever. A soft moan escapes me, and Max bites my bottom lip, pulling slightly. I'm lost in him, but for the first time I feel seen.

"Wait, I almost forgot," I say, breaking the moment. "I think I solved the puzzle, and that fucking key Olive and I found... you'll never believe where it led me."

Max smiles in a way I know he reserves just for me—and maybe Poppy. "Tell me everything."

I recount the day I've had, sparing no details.

"— so now I know the whole thing was made for me to find you. Every clue, every adventure... it was all about you, Max."

"Well, what are you waiting for? Let's open our present then."

Grabbing the book from my bag, I scribble in the last two words and watch as they melt into gold script. As I go to close the book, it vanishes as if I had never been holding it at all. Max and I look at each other, clearly both confused. But I reach into my bag and pull out the gift box. The white bow has been replaced with a small ribbon made of twine—almost identical to the knot that held the puzzle book closed. And when we untie it together, a book sits inside.

"Would it be funny or infuriating if this had more clues in it?" Max asks with an eyebrow raised and a dimple on display.

"Infuriating."

"Definitely hilarious."

We speak at the same time, and I roll my eyes. I'd probably laugh, but I'm ready to move on from the magic—to live a life where I'm not searching for the next answer because I already have everything I need—because I have him.

I unclasp a small gold push lock that sits at the center and secures a purple strap that matches the jade leather binding, gasping when I open the first page. It's our story. Each piece of parchment is complete with the clue and answer we found, with a picture of the adventure we had that helped to solve it.

"It's our story, Max."

"Nah, Sade. It's our fate found in clues."

Epilogue

3 Months Later

Sadie

"Are you ready to go?"

Max pokes his head into my office, smirking at me with his perfect pouty lips and coiffed hair still styled back out of his face. The suit he's wearing fits his impossibly sculpted body like it was painted on, and the slight flush to his cheeks from standing by the ice is endearing as hell. I can't help the smile that tips my lips up, or the way my heart still skips a beat seeing him—even if it happens every day.

When Max agreed to take the job working for the Flames instead of booking it to Washington, I was excited but also a little nervous about putting so much togetherness into our relationship so soon. Yet, since that day I've never once questioned if being with him was the right move.

For the first time in... well, ever... I have my person—my best friend—beside me, at home and at work. And honestly, it hasn't made things harder. It's made them fun.

Spinning in my chair, I close my laptop and grab my bag to stuff it inside. "Yep." I can feel my face shifting into a frown with the same question that's been lingering on my mind for the last two weeks hitting replay. "Did you try asking him again?"

Max steps fully into the room, a regretful expression lingering on his face. "Yeah." He runs a hand through his hair. "He said to tell Sam and Ollie he's team boy, and he's sorry that he couldn't make it."

I slip my toes into my flats, stand, and round my desk, practically slumping into Max's awaiting arms. He wraps them around me, bringing his hands to my shoulders and kneading lightly.

A rush of relief zips through me as tension seeps from my body. "I know he's hurt..."

Max nods and finishes my sentence. "But we can't let him abandon his people just to avoid her."

"Exactly." I press up on my toes to give him a quick kiss. "He has to face the music, eventually. Time off doesn't last forever."

Max bends down, kissing me more thoroughly this time, and when we break apart, we both laugh. I'm not sure why—maybe because this is all so effortless. It's so simple. Or maybe because we're the lucky ones who aren't staring down the barrel of a misguided attempt at putting space between something clearly meant to be.

"Sade... I have a tiny confession to make." Max's face morphs from one of bliss to another suspiciously close to naughty.

"Is Howie in your trunk?"

"What? Jesus." He runs a hand along the back of his neck, scratching lightly as he shakes his head. "You have to stop assuming I'm into breaking the law. First drugs, now kidnapping."

I shift the bag on my shoulder and wink at him. "You did say I had a murderous vibe. Is it out of the realm of possibility for me to think that maybe I started to wear off on you?"

That makes him chuckle as he guides me out of my office, flicking off the light and closing the door behind us. "I guess not. But no, I did not kidnap Howard. I called my mother for help."

My feet stall out, stopping any further movement down the hallway. "Max... we said we wouldn't let her meddle." My eyes widen to the point of watering. "I love Mabel, cherish her even. But we both know she's like a hound on the hunt when she smells gossip in the air." He runs his hand down my arm in soothing strokes, guilt wrinkling his brows. "I promised Howie. No meddling from anyone. Ollie promised, too."

"I know, Sade. But this is nuts. He can't stay with us forever. It's cramping our—"

"Hey, you two heading out?" Levi swaggers down the hall toward us, probably going to grab Alex from her office. "Great job today, Max. Thanks for falling for him, Sadie. We'd be lost without him."

I smile at Levi, and Max's cheeks turn an obnoxious shade of red. I can't tell if it's from the compliment or the fact that he was about to tell me how having a houseguest has forced us to be more creative with our sex life. I'd wager it's the latter since Levi has made a habit of thanking me nearly every day in some form or fashion.

"You're welcome. And yeah... back to Mage Hollow but just for the weekend. If you need anything, please call me."

Levi nods. "I won't. Have fun." With that, he continues past us, and we pick up the pace toward the parking lot.

My mind spins, a rush of racing thoughts thanks to my ADHD medication wearing off and Max's confession. Mabel can't force Howie to make an appearance at a gender reveal party anymore than I can convince him that maybe Ariella moving on is for the best—that someone more willing to give him what he needs is bound to come along. But that doesn't mean she won't try. Between watching the girl he loves go on dates and our uncle Lonnie deciding he's going to retire after Thanksgiving, my cousin needs a break. His whole life is one big question mark—I get it, as I was there not so long ago myself.

We walk silently out of the arena and toward Max's truck. He opens the door, hoisting me in per usual, then hops in the driver's seat.

"Sade, she's not going to do anything crazy."

His attempt at reassuring me falls flat. I know she always means well. But the last time she got involved, we ended up with half the town of Mage Hollow standing in our apartment. The group of them gave us advice about everything from where to put the end table lamps to Beatrice Bushnell listing the reasons we shouldn't be sharing the master in our tiny two-bedroom. The woman doesn't even drive, yet she found a way to get thirty miles down the road to Golden City, climb four sets of stairs, and root through nine boxes all in the name of shaming us for *living in sin*. That has Mabel written all over it.

"All I'm saying is... if she does, you're taking the fall for it." I sink into my seat and roll my head so I can stare at the utter work of perfection he is.

"I wouldn't have it any other way, Sade." Max leans to the side, eyes still trained on the road as he kisses me briefly. "I love you."

"I love you too, Max."

Max

"Benny..." Sadie grumbles from beside me, her words trailing off as she pulls a pillow over her head and points her finger at the beagle in question. With sleepy eyes, I watch as Benny leaps on top of her, licking at her arms and nuzzling his head under the pillow to get to her face.

My dog—who became *our* dog the first day he met her at the dog park—could give a rat's ass about me at this point. It's Sadie who he goes to for his morning walk, every time he wants his bowl refilled, and for all the puppy snuggles.

"I can feel you smiling over there." She removes the pillow, propping herself further up on the pillows while glaring at me. "If your aunt *Lenora* hadn't insisted on opening that last bottle of wine, I'd willingly take you out, sweet baby." She strokes Benny's head and kisses his nose. "But it's your dad's turn since he failed to tell me his sister's government name *and* allowed me to drink a third glass of red."

The glare is back, pointed at me, but this time with a hint of amusement in it.

I hold up my hands in surrender. "Literally no one calls her that. She's been Nora in this family forever. There's only ever been one guy..."

"One guy, what?"

"One guy who called her..." *Fuck, what did he call her?*

I wrack my mind—fucking memory loss. Was it Nori? No, that doesn't feel right. It was something with the *Le*.

"I'm on the edge of my seat here. What did he call her, and why is this relevant?" She rolls her eyes and flips her hair over her shoulder.

Reaching over, I scoop Sadie into my arms, tickling her as I blow a raspberry on her bare chest. "Give me a second. It's relevant because it's her name."

The door to my childhood bedroom bursts open, followed by a shriek, then laughter. "Jesus, get a room, you two. My head hurts too much for boobs at seven in the morning, which is precisely the time I was instructed to come in here." Nora throws something and quickly leaves the room as an envelope lands on the bed.

Sadie and I exchange looks but quickly fall into laughter. She picks up the envelope, turning it over in her hand. "How are we getting mail here?"

"Lenny! He called her Lenny. My mom hated it, but she liked the guy anyway."

Sadie doesn't respond to my outburst. Instead, she slips her finger under the flap of the envelope and opens it. My heart beats wildly in anticipation of her surprise. We might be in town for my brother's party, but that doesn't mean I don't have a few tricks up my sleeve.

Sadie gasps as she unfolds the piece of paper she pulled out.

"Tell me you did this, and it's not just my being in Mage that makes puzzles appear."

Instead of answering, I shrug, then bend down to press a kiss to her forehead.

"Max... seriously."

I slip out of the bed, giving her a view of my bare backside before stepping into the attached bathroom and turning on the shower.

"We can talk about it in here if you'd like!" I holler above the sound of the spray tinkling off the tiled floor as I step inside.

"Two questions..." Sadie pops her head around the shower curtain. "Did you actually tell your mom about Howard?"

Her eyes trail the length of my body while I lather soap over my torso. She is just as addicted to me as I am to her, and I love it.

"Yeah. But mostly because I know how worried you are about him." I tug her hand, pulling her into the shower with me. "That was only one question."

Water cascades down her face, dotting her eyelashes and lips with tiny droplets that look like diamonds sparkling in the warm lighting over our heads. I bend to kiss her, peppering each spot that's shimmering with my lips.

Sadie lets out a small whimper. "Did you make that puzzle because you were nervous I'd say no later, or because you know I don't like surprises?"

She grips my biceps, almost as if she's nervous for the answer, and it makes me smile. I'm completely enamored with every single thing about her, including her unique ability to over-analyze every detail.

"Honestly?"

"Always."

"Both." I grip her hips as I stabilize myself—and my nerves. "There's no doubt in my mind that you're it for me. From the moment I met you, all the way back in high school, I've been completely captivated by you. I know four months is not a long time. Hell, it's probably not long enough for most people to even put a label on things..." I clear the emotion from my throat. "But the way I see it... you've had a piece of my heart for over a decade. I'm hopelessly in love with you—"

"I love you so much, Max."

Her interruption, while great to hear, also settles the nerves in my stomach before I continue, "I know you better than anyone, and I didn't want you to feel obligated to say yes in a room full of people. But also, I wanted you to know that this is more than just a title. It's a promise."

Sadie nods her head, a single tear streaking down her cheek as she acknowledges the commitment she's making. "I know. And my answer is one to you too."

I scoop her up, kissing her hard as I walk her backward, only stopping when her spine is pressed to the tile wall.

"What do you say, Sade? Will you be a member of baby O'Reilly's Cool Aunt's Club? Group? Whatever the fuck it's called."

"On one condition." Sadie laughs as she runs her hands through my wet hair, pushing it out of my face.

"Name it."

"When you actually make me her aunt—officially, not just because I'm your, well whatever I am—make the puzzle harder to solve. I got that in like two seconds."

We never officially had the conversation about what we are, but she feels like so much more than a girlfriend—she feels like my whole heart, my soul, walking around outside of my body.

"You're my...*everything*. And deal."

A deep rumble of laughter bursts from my chest as I tickle my girl. I may never be as smart as she is—or as good at solving puzzles. But the privilege doesn't come with being the one who fixes every problem. It's the honor of watching her unravel each clue. The gift of walking alongside her, ready and willing to lend a hand or lift her up when she needs it. Because she's the star of the show—the main character in the only story I've ever wanted to read.

Acknowledgements

On the road again... I've been working on the—just kidding. I'm not going to make you sit through my recitation of the classic song. But I will say that this is going to read similarly to the thanks I've written in all of my previously published works because the people helping to make this happen haven't changed... much.

First and foremost, Cory—I bet you didn't think we'd be onto the fourth book in just a little over a year. But when have I ever been anything short of a chaotic turn of events? Thanks for loving me through it all, for cheering for me, and mostly for closing the kitchen cabinet doors when I inevitably forget. You've been loving me for twenty years, and while I mostly feel undeserving of that... I'm so incredibly grateful.

L&G—there were a couple of times this year that I almost threw in the towel. And on a few of those occasions, I had basically decided I was done. But each time I looked at your sweet faces or made an out-of-pocket comment about how you should chase your dreams even if mine weren't quite what I had cooked them up to be... you lovingly said, "Mom, don't you dare quit" or "Mom, this is what you were born to do". This book exists solely because YOU refused to let me quit. I'll love you forever (I'm your mom; it's my job), but I'm inspired by your steadfast commitment to supporting me. You're the coolest kids I know, and I'm so proud of the men you are becoming.

Sarah—another one bites the dust. We did it, AGAIN. I love you for (and despite) telling me to scrap the first twelve chapters of this book to start over. And I love you for talking me through how to lean into the fun, let go of the drama, and just write the damn book. I couldn't (read: wouldn't want to) do any of this without you.

Cee—what a ride we're on, my friend. Every time I think the rollercoaster is about to stop, or that it's time to get off the ride... you sweep in with some idea that gets the wheels turning all over again. There's not another living person in this world that I'd want to do this journey with. From the constant laughter, reminding you how funny I am, and literally reading each other's minds—you've become one of my life's greatest gifts. Thank you for being unapologetically you, for knowing how to show up without being asked, and for letting me borrow Sadie for a while.

Amber—where in the world would I be without you? Oh, that's right... crying in a quiet corner of the internet with crappy posts and edits that look like my eight-year-old made them. You've not only taken my feed on socials from something amateur hour would un-abashedly roast to something drool worthy—you've answered every unhinged voice message, every request for a sanity check, and every single random question without hesitation. Some may call you my assistant, but to me you're the unicorn I desperately needed to find, the prize at the end of the rainbow, the be-all and end-all to keeping this train on the tracks.

To the swath of people who read this book in a wholly unfinished state and didn't laugh me out the door (Annie, Jessie, Stef, Dani, Nikki, Jules, Angela, Maggie, & Mal)... THANK YOU! I trust you all implicitly, and I wouldn't put something in the world that didn't have your stamp of approval.

To my family—you keep showing up to read these, and I can't say what that means. From the book events you sit at for hours to the purchases and general fangirling... you're the ones that have taught me to be unwavering in my commitment to my dreams. I love you.

To A & M—my life partners, my best friends, and my soul sisters. Thanks for still believing in me, for describing how to shuck an oyster and the proper steering equipment for boats. Thanks for hyping me up on long car rides to book signings, and for simply asking... *when can I buy it* each time I tell you about something new I'm working on. It's hard to believe a couple of men in leather vests brought us together when it feels like you both are woven into the very fabric of who I am.

Finally, to the readers—you show up more than anyone, and I'm here to say, I SEE YOU. Thanks for loving these characters, for finding a home away from home in Mage Hollow, and for screaming about it to all your friends. We have one more to go! I'll see you in late fall when we once again enter the witchy world... bring your hot cocoa and snow boots.

Until next time,
KC

Also by Kelli Cooke

If you enjoyed A Fate Found In Clues, check out these other titles by
Kelli.

A Heart On A Sleeve (Book 1: Mage Hollow Magic):

https://a.co/d/0emDLixl

Coincidentally Kismet (Standalone):

https://a.co/d/0gLDd8wh

About the Author

Corporate Girl turned Author, Kelli Cooke writes vibrant, funny, and authentic love stories. As a hopeless romantic, Kelli strives to bring a creative twist on what love looks like in real life, infused with the kind of comedy that will keep you laughing long after finishing her books. While comedy is the star, she also focuses on threading in raw emotion and hopes to impact hearts for years to come.

When she's not writing, she can be found chasing around her two kids or binge-watching a show with her husband. Kelli never expected to become an author, but has embraced harnessing her creative ability and adores sharing her vibrant tales with her readers.

https://kellicooke.com/